STRAVAGANZA
City of Stars

STRAVAGANZA
City of Stars

Mary Hoffman

BLOOMSBURY

First published in Great Britain in 2003 by Bloomsbury Publishing Plc
38 Soho Square, London, W1D 3HB

Text copyright © Mary Hoffman 2003
Chapter head illustrations copyright © Peter Bailey 2003
The moral rights of the author and illustrator have been asserted

A CIP catalogue record of this book is available from the British Library
ISBN 0 7475 6123 0

Export paperback ISBN 0 7475 6946 0

Typeset by Dorchester Typesetting Group Limited
Printed in Great Britain by Clays Ltd, St Ives plc

10 9 8 7 6 5 4 3 2 1

All papers used by Bloomsbury Publishing are natural, recyclable products made
from wood grown in sustainable, well-managed forests. The manufacturing
processes conform to the environmental regulations of the country of origin.

For Bexy – star of the city

Acknowledgements

With thanks to my Italian consultants, Edgardo Zaghini from the Young Book Trust and Carla Poesio of Florence. Thank you also to Graziella Rossi for her help and kindness in the Seventeenth of the Ram, Roberto Filiani for his regular Palio e-mails, Reuben Wright for his company in the Campo in July, Frances Hardinge and Saint Galgano for an unexpected walk in the woods and the black dragonfly and to Eileen Walker for extra resources on the August race. Alan Dundes's and Alessandro Falassi's *La Terra in Piazza* was an invaluable reference book. And thanks to Professore Luigi Bernabei of Santa Chiara and Giuliana and Giorgio Citterio of Podere Vignali for providing the perfect settings in which to create sixteenth-century Remora.

'There have been treaties and alliances made, which may render it impossible for the best horse to win. For this is no common race. It is warfare. And, if the victory cannot be obtained by speed and strength, it must either be purchased or stolen.'
William Heywood, *Palio and Ponte*, 1904

' ... A sound of bronze
falls from the tower: the parade moves on ...
The present fades
and the finish line is there: beyond the pennant-
forest, over the pealing
in the unleashed air, out of the sight
of man ... '
Eugenio Montale, *Palio*, 1939 (translated by
Jonathan Galassi, 1998)

'Nella vastità della casa mi aggiravo come in un bosco incantato. Bosco senza draghi nascosti, pieno di liete meraviglie.'
Giuseppe Tomasi di Lampedusa,
Ricordi d'infanzia, 1955

('In the huge expanse of the palace I wandered as if in an enchanted forest. A forest without hidden dragons, full of happy marvels.')

Contents

Prologue: *The Flying Horse*

Cesare had hardly left the stables for days. His favourite mare, Starlight, was heavy with foal and until she gave birth, his place was with her. He even slept in the straw in the empty stall beside hers, with the result that his brown hair was turning blond with strawdust and his clothes itched and prickled.

Now, after bolting his dinner before running back to the stables, he hiccupped as he groomed the grey mare, whistling softly to her between his teeth. Starlight's mane was silver in the twilight and, as he brushed it, she huffed at him through her nostrils. She stirred restlessly in her stall.

Nothing mattered but Starlight. Cesare's family lived near the Ram stables and his father, Paolo, was the Horsemaster for the Twelfth of the Ram. Paolo had given him the responsibility of looking after Starlight and Cesare was determined not to let him down.

'Not long, now, my beauty,' he whispered and she whickered back at him, seeming to nod her white head in the darkening stables. The other horses were unsettled too. They were all part-Arab and highly strung; the Ram was interested only in racing animals. In a stall on the other side, Arcangelo the young chestnut gelding shifted about in his sleep and twitched his ears as if dreaming of victory.

Cesare settled down to sleep in the straw and his dreams were of victory too. He dreamed of the same thing, by day and by night – to ride the Ram's horse in the Race of the Stars and to win.

A small grey cat twined round the stable door and made her delicate way across to where Cesare was sleeping. Slowly, carefully, she insinuated herself into the crook of his arm and began to purr.

Just before midnight the sounds in the stable changed. Starlight was restless. At the same time Cesare woke up and was aware of his father's presence. It was unnerving the way Paolo did that. He always knew where he was needed and when. He had brought a torch with him which he thrust into a bracket set high up in the wall so that sparks wouldn't set the straw on fire. Cesare sprang lightly to his feet, dislodging the disgruntled cat, who went to wash in the doorway.

By the flickering light of the torch, father and son attended quietly to the mare, whose time had come. It was an easy delivery, not her first. But as the foal slipped out into Cesare's hands, he recoiled as if it had been burning hot.

'What is it?' whispered Paolo. The whole stable seemed to be holding its breath. 'I don't know,' Cesare whispered back. 'Can't you feel it? Something's different about this one. When I caught it I felt a shock – like a bolt of lightning in the sky.'

Starlight turned her beautiful head to lick her new foal. The filly was not just dark with the wetness of her birth, but black, black as the night outside, where the bells of the city's churches were sounding midnight. She staggered to her feet, her mouth blindly rooting for her mother's milk like any other newborn.

The stable door, left ajar by Paolo, moved in a sudden gust of wind. A shaft of moonlight fell across the stall. Cesare gasped. By the silver light of the moon and the golden glow of the torch, the foal that had just been brought into life was a creature of myth and magic.

The little long-legged filly, pulling at her mother's teat, was rapidly drying in the warm night air. Her coat was a glossy black and she was clearly going to be a first-rate racehorse. But that was not all. As she tried her new muscles, gaining confidence in her spindly legs, she flexed her shoulders and spread out two small damp black wings about the size of a young swan's.

'Dia!' said Paolo on a sharp intake of breath. 'It has happened. Here, in the Ram, the winged horse has been born to us.'

Even the grey cat came over for a closer look. And Cesare was suddenly aware that every horse in the stable, even Arcangelo, was awake and looking at the new foal. A wild feeling overtook him. He didn't know whether to whoop for joy or burst into tears. He only knew that something magnificent had happened and that from now on his life would never be the same again.

Chapter 1

Families

The winged horse was covered in a layer of fine dust. It was in a corner of the crowded window of a little antique shop, where Georgia had been to look at it every day on the way home from school since it had first appeared. That was a month ago and she had saved up nearly enough money to pay the price on the little white label tied round its neck.

Saving had taken a while because most of her pocket money went on lessons at the riding school, which she could afford only once every two weeks.

'Why does she have to have such an expensive hobby?' her stepfather Ralph had grumbled to her mother, when they first kitted her out with hard-hat and jodhpurs. 'Why can't she be interested in the sort of things other girls like?'

'And you think those are cheap?' Georgia's mother had mocked, in a rare moment of taking her daughter's side. 'Just be glad she doesn't want new clothes every week or make-up and mobile phones and hair dye. Besides, she pays for the lessons herself.'

That had been two years ago, when Ralph had first married Maura and brought his son Russell to live with them. But at the thought of Russell, Georgia's mouth went dry and she felt her palms sweating. Quick, concentrate on the winged horse.

If you could really find a horse with wings in nature, it would be so easy to take off into the sky on its back and ride away for ever. Georgia closed her eyes and imagined the movement of a horse beneath her, the moments of changing up from walking to trotting, trotting to a canter, cantering to galloping and then, yes, why not one more shift? Like feeling fifth gear on a motorway, there would be one more smooth transition and then the beating wings would lift horse and rider away from solid ground and up where no one could reach them.

A rapping on the glass made her eyes fly open. A face with grey hair and glasses was looking at her through the window and making beckoning gestures. Georgia recognised the antique shop's owner – Mr Goldsmith, if his name was the same as the faded letters over the shop window. He beckoned again and she pushed the door open.

Paolo knew that the black filly had to be moved from the city as soon as possible. If news got out of the miraculous birth, she would be at risk from kidnappers. It was a fantastic piece of luck that this had happened to their ward of the city, the Twelfth of the Ram, and a good omen for this summer's Race of the Stars, but Paolo was adamant that it should be kept secret.

'We can't race her,' he told Cesare. 'We'd never be allowed to get away with such an advantage.'

'But we wouldn't be able to race her this summer anyway,' said Cesare. 'She'll be too young.'

'Don't be so sure of that,' Paolo replied. 'These winged ones are said not to be like other horses. They grow at a different rate.'

Father and son kept guard all night, rubbing down foal and mare with straw and giving them clean bedding and fresh water. It was true that the black filly seemed strong and mature within a few hours of her birth, but horses were like that anyway. It was one of the many things Cesare liked about them, the way that their babies got up and got on with life. Not like his little sisters and brothers, who needed so much of his mother's attention and took such ages to turn into proper people.

He much preferred being in the stables with his father, with the warm smell of horses, to staying in their crowded house which always seemed to be full of washing and bubbling pots of baby semolina. Besides, this was the only place where he could get Paolo to talk, to tell him about miracles like the winged horse.

'Every hundred years or so,' said Paolo. 'That's how often it happens in Remora. It's the first one I've seen – and it came about in our Twelfth.' Paolo was jubilant. 'It's the best thing that's happened to the Ram in my lifetime.'

'But *how* does it happen?' asked Cesare. 'I mean, we know the sire. You had Starlight covered by that stallion from Santa Fina – what's his name? Alessandro. There's nothing special about him, is there? A great horse, of course, and he won the Stellata in '68, but just a horse – no wings.'

'It doesn't work like that,' said Paolo slowly, looking at Cesare thoughtfully and weighing his words carefully. 'There's no way you can determine the arrival of a winged one by using a stud book. It happens when times are unstable – as indeed they are now – and it is a good omen for the Twelfth where the foal is born. But it doesn't guarantee success. And it carries its own dangers with it.'

They decided to move the mare and her filly the next night. It would be safe to take her to Santa Fina in the dark. Alessandro's owner, Roderigo, was someone they could trust and the filly could be kept hidden while she grew. If word of her presence got out, the Ram's rivals, particularly the Twelfths of the Twins and the Lady, would move heaven and earth to capture her and rob the Ram of their good luck omen. It would be safe enough to reveal her once this year's race was over.

'What shall we call her?' asked Cesare.

'Merla,' said his father decisively. 'Blackbird. May she ever fly true.'

The inside of Mr Goldsmith's shop was the untidiest,

most interesting place Georgia had ever seen. It was a complete jumble of furniture, ornaments, clothes, weapons, books, jewellery and cutlery, all mixed up together. The untidiness intensified in the area behind the cash-desk, where a brass umbrella-stand held two swords, a blunderbuss, a green silk parasol and a pair of crutches. Mr Goldsmith's chair was wedged between tottering heaps of sheet music and scuffed leather-bound books. He peered at Georgia from within his fortress.

'You've obviously taken a fancy to something in my window,' he said. 'I've seen you looking in most days at about this time. So, what's the problem? Not enough cash? Come on lad, spit it out!'

Georgia felt a blush beginning. She was always having this problem. It was her very short hair, plus the fact that she was flat as a pancake in front. It was embarrassing enough in her class where all the other girls were impressively endowed. She had taken to slouching forward and wearing baggy jumpers. And lately she had used the tomboy image as an excuse – as if she didn't *want* to look feminine. Hence the haircut. And the silver ring in her right eyebrow.

Mr Goldsmith was looking at her quizzically.

'It's the horse,' said Georgia. 'The winged one.'

'Ah,' he nodded. 'My little Etruscan beauty. A copy, of course. Probably from a museum shop in Italy.'

'Don't you know?' Georgia was surprised.

'Not for sure,' said Mr Goldsmith. 'Stuff finds its way here by all sorts of routes. I think that was from an old lady's house in Waverley Road. There was only a great-niece, who was in a hurry to sell up and get the money. She brought in boxes of knick-knacks.

None of the furniture, unfortunately. Got a dealer on to that. Still, there was a very nice pair of silver candlesticks that brought in a fair profit.'

Georgia remembered the candlesticks. She had seen them in the window the day the winged horse had appeared. She never went straight home from school – she always dawdled, looking in shop windows and taking long detours. She never wanted to be at home alone with Russell before her mother got in from work.

'It's lovely,' she said quickly, to divert her thoughts. 'It looks old.'

'You're not a chap at all, are you?' said Mr Goldsmith suddenly. It was his turn to blush. 'Sorry. I can't keep up with you young people's fashions.'

'It's OK,' said Georgia. 'I should have said straightaway. My name's Georgia O'Grady. I go to Barnsbury Comprehensive in Waverley Road. I think I know the house you mean.'

'And I'm Mortimer Goldsmith,' said the old man, offering her his hand to shake. 'Well, now that we've been properly introduced, let's get that horse out of the window.'

He reached in and dropped the black horse into Georgia's palm. It was warm from the sun shining through the window, as if it were alive. She took a tissue from her jeans pocket and gently wiped the dust off. Mr Goldsmith was looking at her.

'How much have you got?' he asked quietly and, when Georgia mentioned a sum two pounds short of the amount on the ticket, he took the horse from her and began to wrap it in cotton wool.

'That'll do,' he said. And from that moment

Georgia felt she had found a friend.

By the time she got back, Russell was already at home, playing metal CDs very loudly in his room, so Georgia was able to sneak up to hers without being noticed. She locked the door as soon as she got inside and gave a sigh of relief. This was always the trickiest time of the day. Whenever Russell was there, it was always touch and go whether she'd make it to the sanctuary of her room before he realised she was back and started on her.

Mondays were all right, because he played football after school and on Tuesdays Georgia had a maths tutor. Fridays she went for violin lessons, but that still left Wednesdays and Thursdays with two hours between school and the return of their respective parents in which to avoid Russell.

He was two years older than her and two years above her at Barnsbury. From the moment they had first met, they had loathed one another. 'If you think I'm going to let your poxy mother get her claws into my dad, you're dead wrong,' he had hissed at her behind the grown-ups' backs.

But he hadn't been able to stop Ralph marrying Maura and he hadn't had a say in the matter when both the parents sold their flats and bought a house together. It hadn't helped that both Georgia and Russell were virtually only children. Russell had a very much older sister, Liz, who had gone with his mother when she left him and Ralph. And ever since then he had assumed that it would be him and his dad against the world.

Now it was just him against Georgia. Russell tolerated Maura because she put his dad into a generally better mood than he had been in on his own. But he resented her for breaking up their twosome and, since he couldn't get away with being nasty to her, he took it all out on Georgia.

Georgia would have loved a proper older brother. She had had a little one once, but he died when he was only a few days old. Not long after that her own dad had left. Georgia had been very young at the time and didn't really remember either of them. She just had a vague memory of her mother always in floods of tears. And then one day, Maura had dried her eyes and said, 'That's that, then. We are just going to have to cope on our own.'

And they had, until Ralph came along. Georgia didn't mind him so much. He loved Maura and he could be quite funny when he was in a good mood. But he worried a lot about money. And he brought Russell with him.

Georgia unwrapped the winged horse and put it on her chest of drawers. Then she went to her computer and logged on. 'Etruscan', she typed into the search engine, 'Etruscan+horse+flying.'

987 matching entries, her computer told her, but Georgia was an old hand at Internet research and looked at only the first hundred. The best sites included an American one showing a beautiful little gilt bronze ornament, which had been offered at auction three years ago but not sold. It was only just over three inches long and similar to the one that Georgia had just bought, but its reserve price was between $2,000 and $3,000 – rather more than she had paid.

Another good site told her about a bronze vase

from Monteleone, wherever that was, which had a chariot pulled by winged horses. There was no illustration unfortunately, but Georgia felt she could imagine it.

In the Twelfth of the Twins, Riccardo the Horsemaster was expecting an illustrious guest: Niccolò, Duke of Giglia and head of the powerful di Chimici family. He was staying with his younger brother Ferdinando, who was Pope and also Prince of Remora. Although Remora was the official centre of the di Chimici's growing Republic, it was to the north, in Giglia, that the real power lay, with the Duke and his heirs.

Niccolò, great-grandson of the founder of the di Chimici dynasty, had five living children, four of them sons, and was the most ambitious man in all Talia. Under his direction the di Chimici family had spread their network through all the major cities in the north of the country and now held power in most of them. Only the tiresome city-state of Bellezza off the north-east coast had held out against any alliance with him or his family. And Niccolò had a plan about that too.

But here in Remora, his position was secure. As he walked the few hundred yards from the Papal palace to the stables of the Twelfth of the Twins, he had to stop a dozen times to exchange pleasantries with wealthy merchants or accept the homage of poorer citizens who wanted to kiss his hand. Niccolò arrived at the stables in a very good mood.

Riccardo, the Horsemaster of the Twins, was bursting with pride. The Pope had visited the day before and now here was the Duke of Giglia, reputed to be the richest man in Talia, coming to inspect the horses. He saved the best animal till last.

'And this, your Grace, is the one we shall run in the Stellata.'

Niccolò looked at the highly-strung bay, who flared his nostrils and bucked slightly in his stall. He stroked the horse's nose with his gloved hand and spoke soothingly to him, then turned to the Horsemaster.

'What's the competition this year?'

'Well, your Grace, you know how secretive everyone is about their horses in the city,' Riccardo began a little nervously.

Niccolò di Chimici fixed him with a cold stare. 'But you are paid not just to tend horses but to find out such secrets, are you not?' he said.

'Yes, your Grace,' muttered the Horsemaster. 'And things will be easier now I have a new groom. He came specifically recommended by your Grace's nephew, the ambassador to Bellezza. Signor Rinaldo tells me this man has done him some great service and is renowned for his ability to sniff out secrets.'

Niccolò smiled. He had heard something of the service done by this man in Bellezza. If it was the same man, he had rid the city of its fiercest opponent to the di Chimici family. And though the Duke's nephew Rinaldo had failed to replace her with a puppet Duchessa, surely the city's new ruler – a mere chit of a girl – would be much easier to influence?

'Does he know anything about horses?' was all he said to the Horsemaster.

*

Gaetano di Chimici was restless. He was staying in his uncle's Papal palace while his father visited the city and he didn't know what he was doing here. He would have much rather been in Giglia continuing his studies at the University. And he had a growing feeling that his father had some plan he was not sharing with him.

Gaetano sighed. It was hard being part of the most important family in Talia. His father was at the centre of so many plots, always scheming how to get richer and more powerful. But Gaetano wasn't really interested in any of them. He wanted to be left to his books and to his friends who, like him, were interested in painting and sculpture and music; not caught up in schemes for financing petty wars between city factions or forging alliances with other mercantile and princely families.

It might have been different if he had been one of the older sons, but there was no one younger than him, except Falco, and poor Falco didn't really count, much as Gaetano and all the family loved him. Fabrizio the eldest brother would inherit the Dukedom of Giglia. Carlo would be Prince of Remora, since Uncle Ferdinando as Pope had no children. Beatrice would doubtless be married off to one of the cousins – Alfonso perhaps, so that she could be Duchessa of Volana now that Uncle Fabrizio had died.

What did that leave for him? He thought at one time that his father's plans might have him marrying one of his cousins – Alfonso's sister Caterina, maybe. As a child, Gaetano had been very close to another cousin, Francesca, whose father was Prince of Bellona, but he had heard a rumour lately that she had been married off to some old man in Bellezza as part of one of the family's dynastic schemes.

Gaetano shook his head. What a family! And now he was anxious that his father's new plan might involve the church. Uncle Ferdinando would not live for ever and Niccolò must have decided who would succeed Ferdinando as Pope. Carlo had made it clear that he had no intention of going into the church – and that left Gaetano.

'Well, I won't do it,' he resolved. 'The church should be a vocation, not a political appointment. Why can't I just be left to my studies?'

But he knew the answer to that. All the di Chimici had to work for the success of the dynasty; even the women had to be prepared to marry where the head of the family decided they would. Their opinions and preferences didn't come into it. And it was no different for the sons. Receive this Princedom, marry this Princess, take an embassy to this city, be ordained – it was all the same.

Gaetano wondered if he could be the first di Chimici in five generations to say no.

'Families,' thought Georgia. 'Why isn't there another way of living together?' Dinner at their house was always fraught and Georgia couldn't see why her mother bothered. But Maura, who was a social worker, was completely opposed to people snacking and grazing or eating on their laps in front of the TV.

'It's the one time of the day we can sit down

together as a family,' she insisted, 'and catch up with one another's lives.'

There were two things wrong with that idea, thought Georgia. Firstly, they were not a family and never would be. Even if she ever came to see Ralph as a father, she would never accept Russell as her brother. And secondly Maura was a lousy cook. Ralph was no better, and often the all-important family meal was heated up supermarket pizza or fish and chips from down the road.

None of that made any difference to Maura. Off went the TV and radio, Georgia and Russell had to set the table with knives and forks even for food intended to be eaten with fingers, and the four of them sat down for twenty minutes of excruciating politeness and indigestion.

Conversation consisted of questions from the adults and replies from the teenagers. Georgia and Russell never spoke directly to one another at dinner. In fact, Georgia realised, they never spoke to one another when their parents were around at all.

On their own – a situation which she avoided as much as she could – Russell was much more communicative. He was that kind of bully. Sometimes Georgia wished he were less clever and more of a thug. If he had ever hit her, it would have been in some ways easier. If she'd had bruises on her body to show her mother, he would never have got away with it.

But his was the harassment of hate, which left no visible marks, but made her shrivel inside. He got hold of her deepest fears and insecurities and dragged them out into the light, turning the harsh spotlight of his sarcasm on them.

'Dog' was his mildest epithet for her. He analysed in detail her unattractiveness, her lack of femininity, her obsession with horses. 'We all know what that's about, don't we? Absolutely classic – a substitute for sex – all that muscular power between your legs. All horsey women are spinsters and dogs – just like you.'

On and on the poison would spew out of his mouth and Georgia had no defence. Of course she had told her mother, several times, and had even spoken to Ralph about it once. But they insisted that she was exaggerating, that she must expect some teasing from an older brother, that she was too sensitive. And afterwards Russell would be worse, taunting her with her weakness in running to her mother for protection.

Georgia would withdraw further into herself, hiding her vulnerability, hunching her shoulders further and speaking only in monosyllables, unable to understand why she inspired so much hatred in someone she hadn't chosen to share her life with. After all, she had just as much reason – or as little – to hate him.

The day that the flying horse came into her life ended badly. Although she had escaped spending time with Russell after school, she was horrified to discover at dinner (Sainsbury's shepherd's pie with frozen peas) that Maura and Ralph were going out to the cinema. This happened about once a month and, since the sort of films they liked were art house movies, often shot in black and white, they had given up asking Georgia and Russell if they wanted to join them. And at fifteen and seventeen there was no question of a sitter to keep them company.

Georgia made for her room before the adults were

out of the front door. She was soon immersed in biology homework. But eventually her own biology betrayed her; she had to go to the loo.

Russell was on the landing. He lounged casually in front of the bathroom door, large and menacing. It crossed Georgia's mind that it wouldn't be beyond him to bar her access till she wet herself. That would give him wonderful new ammunition to ridicule her with. She was already mentally calculating a dash into Maura and Ralph's tiny en-suite, when he moved his bulk away from the door and she made it just in time.

When she came out of the bathroom, he was still there and he followed her into her bedroom; she wasn't quite quick enough to lock him out. Now she was stuck with him there in her room until he chose to leave – one of her worst nightmare scenarios. He said nothing for a while and suddenly she saw her room through Russell's eyes. It wasn't like the room of other fifteen-year-old girls. There were no posters of popstars or TV heroes or even a good-looking continental footballer.

The only poster in fact was a tatty old one of Everest Milton at the Horse of the Year Show, which Maura had taken Georgia to when she was seven. There was a framed print of a black horse and a white one galloping beside a river in full flood. Georgia knew it wasn't a very good painting but she loved it anyway. The flying horse stood on her chest of drawers.

'You are seriously retarded, you know,' said Russell conversationally, almost pleasantly. 'Girls of your age grow out of the horse thing, you know. Except those saddoes at the stables. And they're all dykes.'

Georgia couldn't help herself. 'You've never been to the stables – you don't know anything about the people there!'

It was always a mistake to defy Russell. He laughed unpleasantly.

'I bet I do. I bet that's why you like going there. They've probably started hitting on you. And you're probably glad. After all, no bloke would ever look at you. Unless he was drunk and on a bet.'

He was wandering round her room, picking up her things and putting them down carelessly. Georgia inched round till she had her back to the chest of drawers, shielding the winged horse from his gaze. She was going to have to hide it; it was too precious to let Russell get hold of it.

'Actually, that's not a bad idea,' he was carrying on. 'Why don't you put up the money to get one of my friends hammered? And for a bet, to give you one? It'd be better than riding.'

Georgia clenched her hands. A wild rage was building inside her and she wanted to hurl herself at Russell and pound him with her fists, even though she knew she would just look ridiculous against his bulk.

Just then, the phone rang and Russell went off to answer it. She heard the casual supercool tone he adopted when talking to his friends. Georgia leapt to her door to lock it. Her hands were shaking. There was no way she would go back out to clean her teeth tonight; she would just go to bed and risk the plaque.

Cesare took his lunch out to the stable, relieving Paolo

from guard duty. He stroked Merla's nose and spoke soothingly to her mother. 'Don't worry,' he said. 'We'll soon have you safe. No one will take your foal.'

He propped his back against a post and stretched his legs out in the straw. The grey cat emerged from nowhere and pushed her way on to his lap, purring and thrusting her wedge-shaped head into the hand holding his bread and cheese.

Georgia lay on her back in the dark, tears seeping out of the corners of her eyes and trickling down into her ears. She was clutching the flying horse. She had never been as unhappy as this. Even when her baby brother had died and her dad had disappeared and her mum had cried all the time, Georgia had not been miserable herself. She had been a kid then and more concerned about whether there would be cake at tea-time and what to call the new doll Mum had given her when Ben was born.

But now her life was a nightmare. She had few friends at school; most of the girls she had known at primary school seemed to have moved on in their lives. There was only one new girl, Alice, who seemed as if she might turn into a real friend. Russell was right in a way – Georgia was retarded, socially. She didn't get asked to parties and she knew that the in-crowd in her class went to pubs and clubs at the weekends – places she would never have got into. Even with make-up and a short skirt and heels and a top that showed her belly button. In the dark, Georgia managed a small smile at the thought.

And life at home had turned into one stratagem after the other to avoid Russell. But now keeping out of his way wasn't enough. He was actively seeking her out, never happy unless he was tormenting her. She simply couldn't carry on like this. If Mum wouldn't help her, she would have to run away.

Georgia fell asleep with the model of the flying horse in her hand, wishing she could find a place where horses had wings and she could fly away from her troubles for ever.

Cesare was dozing. It was the cat who woke him up. She suddenly tensed on his lap, sitting bolt upright, her fur sticking out in all directions and a growl rumbling in her throat.

He saw straightaway what had alarmed her. A boy, cowering in the corner, his eyes wide and terrified. Cesare leapt to his feet, amazed. He hadn't really believed that one of the Ram's enemies would send someone to kidnap Merla – least of all a skinny boy like a scared rabbit. But maybe he was just a spy?

Cesare stepped forwards and raised his fists.

'What do you want?' he asked roughly. 'You've got no business here – be off with you!'

Georgia understood nothing, except that she was in a stable. It was only the warmth and the familiar comforting smell of horses that was stopping her from screaming. She had no idea how she had got there or who the angry brown-haired boy was. He seemed to be deliberately blocking her view of something behind him. Something in his stance reminded her of herself shielding her ornament from Russell. Slowly she unclenched her hand that was holding the winged horse.

The boy gasped. And as he moved forward to get a better look, she saw behind him a miraculous creature that could have been the model for the horse in her hand. A beautiful coal-black foal with two small feathery wings folded at its shoulders.

Chapter 2

A New Stravagante

The two figures in the stable were frozen in time, each staring wide-eyed at a flying horse. Cesare relaxed a little. This strange boy, who didn't seem much of a threat, was obviously completely surprised by the sight of the black filly. But why then did he hold a model of her?

'Where did you get that?' he asked.

'Where am I?' asked Georgia at the same time.

It was such an odd question that Cesare forgot his own. He took a closer look at the boy. He was very odd indeed. His clothes for a start were made of some fine material such as only a rich merchant would wear in Remora, but they were baggy and shapeless without any grace of design or ornament, like something stitched together by the humblest of peasants. Yet he wore precious silver in his ears, like a young prince, and on his brow – something Cesare had never seen in Talia. It was all a riddle. Especially his not knowing where he was.

'How did you come here, if you don't know where you are?' asked Cesare.

Georgia shook her head. 'I don't know,' she said. 'One minute I was in my bed in London, the next I was here in this stable. But it's not part of the stables I go to. I don't know any of these horses. Especially that one. But she's a real wonder, isn't she?'

Cesare recognised a fellow-enthusiast. He let Georgia move closer to the little filly. Surely, this strange boy who loved horses wouldn't harm her?

'And yet you carry her image,' he said. 'It is surely too much of a coincidence that you should arrive in the Twelfth of the Ram within hours of her being born, if you didn't know she was here.'

'But I didn't,' said Georgia. 'How could I? I mean, horses with wings aren't real. They just don't happen.'

'They do in Remora,' said Cesare proudly. He couldn't help himself. 'Only once a century or so – and this time the honour falls to the Ram.'

'I'm sorry,' said Georgia. 'I don't know what you mean by the Ram.'

'Aren't you from Remora?' asked Cesare.

'No,' said Georgia, 'I told you. I live in London, in Islington.'

Then, as the boy still looked blank, she added, 'In England. You know – Europe, the earth, solar system, the universe,' the way she used to write it in her schoolbooks.

'Anglia?' said the boy. 'But you are in Talia now. In

Remora, its most important city. How could you have come here without knowing it?'

He looked closely at the boy to see if he was lying. Then he noticed his swollen eyes and the dirty tracks of tears down his face and felt ashamed. Something had made this lad desperately unhappy. He was only a year or so younger than Cesare but the Talian boy couldn't ever remember being so unhappy that he had cried like that.

'Is there something wrong?' he asked awkwardly. 'Has someone been hurting you?'

And then it all came flooding back to Georgia. Russell's bullying, her feeling of being trapped in her room, her longing to escape to a world where horses could fly. Maybe she was back in the time and place where the Etruscans lived? What was that called – Etruria? But the boy had said Remora, in Talia, and she hadn't heard of either of those places. She closed her eyes wearily. Perhaps when she opened them again he would have disappeared, along with the miraculous filly and the whole stable?

What happened instead was that a big, grey-haired man, so similar in appearance to the boy that he must be his father, came into the stable and looked at her in amazement.

'Who's this, Cesare?' he asked abruptly, but not unkindly.

'I don't know,' said Cesare truthfully. 'He was suddenly just – here.'

'I'm Georgia O'Grady,' she said, realising that Cesare had no idea she was a girl.

'Giorgio Gredi,' said the man, and Georgia realised that she had again been mistaken for a boy. But there was no chance to put it right now.

'I am Paolo Montalbano, Horsemaster of the Twelfth of the Ram,' said the man formally. 'And you seem to have met my son, Cesare. Now please tell us what you are doing here.'

*

In another stable in the city less than a mile away, a new groom was being introduced to his charges.

'And this,' said Riccardo, 'is Benvenuto, our choice for the Stellata.'

The new groom cast an appraising eye over the bay. He scratched the horse between the ears. He was enjoying being back among animals; it had been unnatural in Bellezza with nothing to ride. In fact he was glad to turn his back on the whole poncy, trumped-up city, with its elaborate life-style and its crazy worship of its woman ruler.

Enrico was off women; give him horses any day. His one serious relationship had led to disaster: his fiancée had disappeared in mysterious circumstances, run off with another man, as he now suspected. But her father had given him half the dowry anyway, and his old employer, Rinaldo di Chimici, had paid him handsomely for services rendered in Bellezza. Enrico didn't really need this job in Remora.

But spying was in his blood. And he was coming closer to the beating heart of the di Chimici family. His new employer was the Pope, Rinaldo's uncle, member of the senior branch of the family. And Enrico's job, nominally to work in the stables of the Twins, was really to ensure that their horse won the

Stellata, by whatever means necessary.

'*Siamo a cavallo*,' he said softly to Benvenuto. 'It's in the bag,' and the horse whickered back.

*

It was about halfway through Georgia's story that the Montalbani, father and son, realised their intruder was a girl. 'But why do you dress as a boy?' asked Paolo.

Georgia looked down at what she had on – grey tracksuit bottoms and a baggy T-shirt – her usual nightwear. She shrugged.

'This is the sort of thing boys and girls both wear where I come from,' she said.

'Girls wear pantaloons?' said Cesare, disbelievingly. 'And they cut their hair like that?'

'Not all,' admitted Georgia, running her hand across her spiky head. 'But they do all wear pant ... I mean trousers. Jeans, usually, during the daytime, leggings or tracky bottoms at night.'

Then she had a thought. 'It's not night-time here, is it?'

For answer, Paolo threw open the stable door and the bright sunlight flooded in. The cat strolled over to the doorway and started washing her ears in the sunshine. Cesare gasped. Georgia saw that he and his father were both staring at her open-mouthed, amazed by her all over again.

'What?' she asked, feeling very self-conscious.

Cesare pointed behind her. 'You haven't got a shadow,' he said.

After his courtesy visit to the Twins' stable, Niccolò di Chimici crossed the city to the Twelfth of the Lady. His route took him into the no man's land of the Strada delle Stelle, which ran from the Gate of the Sun in the north of the city to the Gate of the Moon in the south. It was a broad thoroughfare, wide enough for two horse-drawn carriages to pass one another. At the halfway point, the centre of the almost circular city, lay the Campo delle Stelle, the spacious round Piazza, divided into fourteen sections, where the annual Race of the Stars was run.

Niccolò paused on the edge of it, surveying the bustling life of the Campo. In the dead centre was the fountain with its circular stone parapet which provided the best view of the race. Rising up out of the fountain, surrounded by its spouting fish and its marble nymphs with overflowing water-pots, was a tall slender column, little more than a pole, surmounted by the figure of the wild lioness suckling Remus, founder of the city, and his twin brother Romulus, who had wandered further south and set up the rival city of Romula.

The houses around the Campo and the grand Palazzo Papale where Niccolò's brother Ferdinando lived all had elegant balconies overlooking the racetrack. In a few weeks' time every balcony would be draped with the colours of the Twelfth they supported – white and rose for the Twins on the Papal balcony, green and purple for the Lady, red and yellow for the Ram ... Niccolò ground his teeth at the thought of the Ram.

'Some refreshment for your Grace?' said a bold stallholder, coming up to the Duke with a tankard of iced lemon sherbet.

It was a timely interruption and Niccolò drank deeply, tossing the man silver far in excess of the cost of the sherbert. Then he paused to wonder if he should have been so reckless. He didn't normally eat or drink anything outside his family's palaces, where he had tasters to check for poison; he was getting careless in his old age. But today he was lucky – it was just a drink of lemons.

Niccolò crossed the Campo and plunged into one of the narrow passages on the other side that led to the main street of the Twelfth of the Lady.

'Careless again,' he muttered, looking over his shoulder. But no assassin was following him and the Duke proceeded along the Via della Donna to the main Piazza of the Twelfth, passing many statues of the Lady, who in some places looked like an Eastern goddess, in others like the gentle mother of the baby born to be the world's king. The discrepancy didn't bother Niccolò. He was a Talian through and through and used to believing in two religions simultaneously, or at least paying lip-service to them.

He felt more at home in the Twelfth of the Lady than anywhere else in Remora. Its allegiance was given to Giglia, just as every Twelfth owed allegiance to one of the city-states that made up the country. So it was a little slice of the City of Flowers here in the City of Stars. Niccolò would have his money on the Lady's horse, even though his brother's household would of course cheer for the Twins'. That Benvenuto of theirs was a good-looking animal; it was time he visited the Lady's stable to see what his own people would be running.

*

Paolo was trickling the remains of Cesare's lunchtime ale into Georgia's mouth. She had gone very white and sat down suddenly in the straw when she saw that she cast no shadow.

'What does it mean?' she asked now. 'Does it mean I am not really here?'

'In a way,' said Paolo seriously. 'It means you are a Stravagante.'

This meant nothing to Georgia, but she saw Cesare making what looked like the sign of the cross, as if he had been told she was a witch or devil.

'What shall we do?' he asked. 'We can't hand her over to the authorities.'

'Certainly not,' said Paolo calmly. 'We shall merely get in touch with another Stravagante.'

'How will we do that?' asked Cesare, clearly very worried. 'Aren't they dangerous and powerful magicians in places like Bellona?'

'Not necessarily,' said his father, smiling. 'For example, I am one myself.'

Now it was Cesare's turn to sit down suddenly.

Georgia didn't know what a Stravagante was, nor how she and this broad-shouldered man could both be one, especially since he clearly did have a shadow. But she could see that Paolo's information had been a terrible shock to Cesare.

'Come,' said Paolo. 'It's time that you knew. I had been thinking of telling you for some time. Two of my brethren will be visiting here in the city in the next day or two and they will advise us what to do about young Georgia. In the meantime, we must find her some clothes that will make her less conspicuous.' He turned to Georgia. 'But because of your hair, I'm afraid you must wear boy's gear. And you'd better continue to be Giorgio while you're here.'

'That's all right,' said Georgia hastily. She dreaded to think what girls wore in this ancient-seeming place she had somehow fallen into – wimples perhaps, definitely corsets.

Cesare went off at his father's bidding to find her some spare clothes and Georgia went to take a closer look at the winged filly. She showed Paolo the model.

'It's uncanny, isn't it?' she said. 'It must have something to do with why I'm here.'

'It does,' said Paolo. 'It's a talisman. All Stravaganti have them. They're the key to travel between our worlds. But if I were you I'd keep it hidden. Particularly here in Remora. The city is a stronghold of the di Chimici and they are very interested in stravagation.'

'I'm sorry,' said Georgia. 'You must think I'm very ignorant. But can you go back a bit? I don't know what stravagating is or why you think it has anything to do with my being here, or who these kimmy people are. And how long will I be here, by the way? My mother is going to go mad if I'm not there in the morning.' She stopped. 'Or would it *be* morning there?'

Paolo shook his head. 'I don't have answers to all your questions,' he said. 'But I'll tell you what I know and what I suspect. The Stravaganti are a brotherhood of scientists, scattered throughout the city-states of Talia. I am the only one in Remora. It is a dangerous calling, so I mask my involvement in it by also being a Horsemaster. Even my family don't know that I am a Stravagante – at least they didn't till I told Cesare just now.'

'He looked horrified,' said Georgia. 'Why is it dangerous to be one?'

'The first Stravagante came to our world from yours by accident,' said Paolo. 'He was the founder of our brotherhood. He came from what you call England and we call Anglia. He was a natural philosopher, an alchemist as they were also known, and he found his way here as the result of an explosion in his laboratory – an alchemical accident.'

'What was his name?' asked Georgia, making a mental note to look him up on the Internet.

'William Dethridge,' said Paolo. 'At least that was his name then. He first came to Talia twenty-five years ago, when the grip of the Chimici was beginning to tighten on the whole country. Ever since then, he has been training Talians to use talismans he brought from his world to travel to it themselves. More importantly, they have taken other talismans from Talia to your England, to enable new travellers to make the journey from your world to ours.'

'Talismans?' said Georgia. 'You mean like my winged horse? It came from Talia?'

'Yes,' said Paolo. 'I took it myself.'

It was Georgia's turn to shake her head. Though with her it was more like a dog shaking water out of his ears so that he can understand what his master is saying to him.

'You've been to England?' she said disbelievingly. 'To my world? When? And how? Mr Goldsmith sold me the horse in his antique shop. He said it came from an old lady's house in Waverley Road.'

'A few months ago,' said Paolo, 'matters were coming to a head between the di Chimici and the Stravaganti.' He ran his hands worriedly through his dark grey hair. 'There is so much to explain to you, that you must understand. A new arrival like yourself is like a new-born lamb among wolves, especially since you've been brought straight to one of the di Chimici's centres of power.'

'You keep saying that name,' said Georgia. 'Who are they and why are they a threat to the Stravaganti?'

'They are a powerful family,' said Paolo, 'the most powerful in Talia. Members of the di Chimici clan are Dukes and Princes in most of the city-states in northern Talia. In those places where they don't hold power, they have alliances with city-rulers. Here in Remora, which was the capital of the great Reman Empire, the Pope, who is also our Prince, is the second son of the current generation of di Chimici. They are fabulously wealthy and their ambition is without limits. They want to rule all Talia. They've been pretty successful in the north, with one exception, and they are turning their attention to Romula and Cittanuova in the south. Once all the twelve city-states have joined their Republic, you can be sure that the Republic will become a Kingdom. And you can guess which dynasty will supply its first king.'

He looked at Georgia expectantly. She answered slowly.

'The di Chimici? I'm sorry, but I really don't see

what any of that has to do with me. I don't know anything about politics and yours seem so different from ours. I mean, what century are you living in?'

In Georgia's world this would have been an insult not requiring an answer, but now she really wanted to know.

'The cinquecento,' said Paolo. 'The sixteenth century. I know that you come from more than four hundred years later. Remember, I have visited not only your world but your time.'

'That's another thing,' said Georgia, frowning. 'This Talia of yours seems to be some version of our Italy, going by all your names, but I can understand what you're saying and I've never had an Italian lesson in my life.'

'Stravaganti can always understand the language of the country they travel to,' said Paolo. 'Though so far the gateway has been only between your England and our Talia.'

'Then why is it hundreds of years ago here?' asked Georgia. 'I mean, for me? Sorry, there's still so much I don't understand. You said I was brought here, but why? I'm just a kid, younger than Cesare by the looks of him. What can I do to help the Stravaganti against a rich and powerful family? I can't even handle one member of my own.'

At that moment, Cesare came rushing in with an armful of clothes.

'Sorry it took so long,' he gasped. 'There was a visitor in the house. I've persuaded him to take some wine with Teresa, but we've got to get Georgia out of the way. And not just Georgia. He wants to see the horses.'

'Who?' asked Georgia and Paolo at the same time.

'Duke Niccolò,' said Cesare. 'Niccolò di Chimici is in our kitchen. And he'll be here any minute!'

Chapter 3

A City Divided

Duke Niccolò had been impressed by the Lady's racing mare Zarina. She was a spirited brown three-year-old, ready to do her all in the Stellata. But something had been nagging at the back of his mind about the Twelfth of the Ram and he had decided on a whim to visit their stables too.

Just as the Lady was associated with Giglia and the Twins with Remora itself, so the Ram was the Twelfth which owed allegiance to Bellezza and he was particularly keen that their horse should come nowhere in the race. Not that he would allow any such feelings to show, of course. It was an honour for these humble stable people to be visited by the great Duke of Giglia and he was courtesy itself, as behoved an aristocrat among his inferiors.

And they did seem sensible of the honour, the Horsemaster and his son. They were quite flustered at his presence in their stable and eager to show him their star horse – the idiots. If they'd had any sense they would have told him they were racing some other animal! He was certainly a handsome brute, this Arcangelo of theirs.

'Splendid, splendid!' he said heartily, every inch the gracious patron. 'The Lady will be hard-pressed to beat him, though we have a good horse too.'

'Well, your Grace,' said Paolo politely, 'it's early days yet. Much can happen before race day and indeed on the day itself.'

'Very true,' said the Duke. He was tired now and keen to get back to the comforts of the Papal palace. But on his way out of the stable he stopped to look at the grey mare with her black foal. It had a blanket over it.

'What's the matter with the little one?' he asked.

'A slight fever, your Grace,' said Paolo. 'We are just being careful, because she was born only last night.'

Niccolò nodded. 'Best to be on the safe side,' he said and waved his hand vaguely as he left the stable, stooping slightly as his head almost grazed the top of the door. Paolo went with him to see him off the premises. As soon as the two men had gone, a massive sneeze from above his head sent Cesare up the ladder and into the hayloft in a trice.

Georgia had seen the whole encounter through a gap in the floorboards.

'Good job you didn't sneeze when the Duke was here,' said Cesare, and they both started to giggle, feeling silly with relief that the visitor hadn't seen either Georgia or the little filly. At least, he *had* seen the foal but hadn't known what he was looking at.

Paolo's grizzled head appeared through the trapdoor. 'All clear,' he said. 'But that was close. The sooner we get Merla up to Santa Fina the better.'

'We're taking her and Starlight out of the city,' Cesare explained to Georgia. 'My father thinks it will be safer. The other Twelfths would be jealous if they knew what had happened here in the Ram and might try to kidnap her.'

Georgia had pulled on the boy's clothes while Duke Niccolò was in the stable. She and Cesare were much of a size. Either he was short for his age or Talian boys were not as big as their twenty-first century equivalents. Paolo looked at Georgia critically. 'You look more like a Remoran now,' he said. 'Though people might still wonder at your silver jewellery with your stable-boy's clothes.'

'Well, I'm not a Remoran,' said Georgia. 'And I still don't understand anything about your city and this race that seems so important. And you haven't finished telling me about the Stravaganti.'

'Time enough for that later,' said Paolo. 'But you do need to find your way round the city. If your stravagation is like the last one from your world, you'll need to be back off home at nightfall. That still gives you a few hours. I think Cesare should take you out for a tour around Remora. He can tell you all about the Stellata.'

*

In the Papal palace the Pope carefully removed his

silver brocade cope. He was now in his rose silk soutane, cutting an impressive figure, even though he was not as tall as the Duke, his brother. Ferdinando was less ambitious than Niccolò too. He liked the good life, his fine wines and exquisitely prepared food, his soft bed and his library of rare manuscripts. He didn't mind not having a wife and family. The fires of passion had flared only briefly in his youth and he would rather have a glass of Bellezzan red and a debate with his cardinals on theology than the chore of keeping a woman happy.

The only women he knew now were his sisters-in-law and his nieces; the di Chimici were a predominantly male family. The only thing that bothered Ferdinando about this state of affairs was the succession. His second nephew Carlo would be Prince of Remora, but who would be Pope after him? It was unthinkable that such a role should now pass to someone outside the family. He had hoped that the visit from his third nephew Gaetano presaged an interest in the church, but so far the boy had seemed sulky and ill at ease in the palace.

It made Ferdinando uncomfortable. For most of the time he was able to ignore the fact that he was a figurehead, a puppet manipulated by his cleverer and more ruthless older brother. Of course it had been Niccolò's idea that Ferdinando should enter the church and his money that had ensured Ferdinando's rapid rise to Cardinal and eventually Pope. It made him squirm to remember how conveniently the old Pope, Augustus II, had died. But he had been an old man; Ferdinando quickly turned his thoughts away from his predecessor.

To be Prince of the country's major city and head of its church ensured comfort, luxury even, and respect, at least on the surface. When he walked down the street, people fell to their knees as he passed. But he couldn't always forget that he wasn't like the Popes of the past when the Reman Empire was at its height. And the clear gaze of young Gaetano had brought it back to him.

'Dinner is served, Your Holiness,' his serving-man announced.

Ferdinando manoeuvred his considerable bulk out of his chair and made his way in to the meal. His eyes glittered at the sight of his silver dishes and goblets, the table ablaze with as many candles as the high altar in Remora's Duomo. There were only himself, Niccolò and Gaetano to sit down at the snowy cloth, but there were at least a dozen servants to attend to their every need.

After a brief Grace, intoned in Talic, the ancient tongue of Remora and all Talia, the three men set to. Ferdinando ate slowly with relish, savouring each carefully prepared dish. Niccolò ate little and drank a lot. Gaetano devoured everything put in front of him as fast as was compatible with good manners, as if he had put in a hard day's labour in the fields instead of mooching about the palace missing his friends and his books.

'How have you passed your day, Brother?' enquired Ferdinando.

'Most profitably,' answered Niccolò. 'I have seen your fine Benvenuto, visited my Zarina, and then paid a call on the Ram.'

Ferdinando raised his eyebrows. 'And what are

they running this year?'

'A fine chestnut gelding called Arcangelo,' said Niccolò. 'A good-boned, high-spirited horse. I'd say they had a good chance.'

Gaetano made a noise like a snort, then pretended his wine had gone down the wrong way.

'You should have come with me, Gaetano,' said his father smoothly. 'You might have enjoyed yourself.'

It was true that Gaetano loved horses; he was one of the best riders in the family. Perhaps it was the wine, but he felt his annoyance with his father and with Remora dissolving. 'Perhaps I should,' he replied pleasantly. 'Is it your intention to visit all the stables? I should like to come with you tomorrow.'

'Yes, perhaps I will,' said Niccolò, who had had no such intention an instant ago. 'It can do no harm to see the competition, and we don't want the other Twelfths to feel neglected, do we?'

*

As they walked through the streets of Remora, Georgia's jaw dropped. It was one thing to be told by Paolo that they were in the sixteenth century, quite another to be in a city with cobbled streets, no cars, and houses so close together that washing lines were strung across the street between them and cats leapt from one rooftop to another.

Everywhere in what Georgia was learning to recognise as the Twelfth of the Ram, there were signs and symbols of that animal. At every crossroad there was a statue of the beast with its curled horns, some of the houses were draped with red and yellow banners displaying a prancing ram with a silver crown, and every few yards or so there were little iron rings under the shape of a ram's forepart with its front legs raised.

'What are they?' asked Georgia, pointing to one.

'Hitching posts for horses,' said Cesare. 'And look up!'

Georgia raised her eyes and there, thirty feet off the ground, saw more of the rings.

'For flying horses,' whispered Cesare. 'All the Twelfths have them, just in case.'

He led her into a small square. On the north side was a large impressive church and in the middle a fountain. The sun shone brightly down on the water, turning the fountain into a glittering fan. The water came spurting up through the mouth of a giant ram, whose horns were made of silver. More silver glinted on the tridents of the tritons surrounding the basin.

'That's the Fonte d'Argento, the silver fountain,' explained Cesare. 'The Ram is allied to the silversmiths' guild and they decorated it for us. Every Twelfth is linked with one of the city guilds. The Lady's one is Painters, the Twins' is Bankers.' He laughed. 'It could be the other way round. The di Chimici are bankers and Giglia, the Lady's city, is their headquarters. Still, they are famous for their patronage of the arts too, so painters is fair enough.'

'You've lost me,' said Georgia. 'I thought the Lady was another section of *this* city. How can it belong to another one?'

They sat down on the stone fountain-seat and Cesare explained patiently. 'Each Twelfth of Remora owes allegiance to one of Talia's city-states. Only the

Twelfth of the Twins supports Remora itself. The Lady looks to Giglia and the Ram to Bellezza.'

'What are the names of the other Twelfths?' asked Georgia. 'I've only heard you mention those three.'

'The Bull, the Crab, the Lioness, the Scales, the Scorpion, the Archer, the Goat, the Water-carrier and the Fishes,' recited Cesare, counting them off on his fingers.

Georgia thought for a bit. Then, 'I get it!' she said triumphantly. 'It's the zodiac, isn't it? Astrology? But wait a minute. Why Lioness? It's just a lion where I come from – Leo.'

'Only a lioness could have suckled the twins,' said Cesare matter-of-factly. 'You know – Romulus and Remus.'

'It was a wolf in my world,' said Georgia. 'But why isn't that Twelfth allied to Remora too?'

'That one is for Romula,' said Cesare.

Georgia shook her head. It would take ages to get this lot sorted out.

'Come to the Campo,' said Cesare, getting up. 'It will be easier to explain there.'

They walked through a narrow alley and out into the most dazzling place Georgia had ever seen. Stepping out into the Campo was like being set free from prison, like being born after a long labour. It made Georgia want to shout out loud.

The space was a circle, but a huge one, open to the bright sunshine, with houses and grand buildings all around. There was an elaborate fountain in the centre, with a slender pillar rising from it. And the space itself, floored in a sort of herring-bone pattern of bricks, was divided up into equal sections divided by straight lines. It looked like an orange cut in half horizontally. Each segment had a star sign in the centre of it.

'You see,' said Cesare. 'Twelve sections – one for each Twelfth. And the way into each Twelfth of the city leads from its segment. We are standing on the Ram's portion.'

Georgia counted. 'But there are fourteen sections, not twelve,' she objected.

'The extra ones both lead to the Strada delle Stelle,' explained Cesare. 'It's a kind of neutral territory running between the Gate of the Sun and the Gate of the Moon. You see the signs of Sun and Moon in those segments. Anyone can walk along that street at any time.'

'And you can't on the other roads?' said Georgia disbelievingly.

'Well, it depends on your Twelfth,' said Cesare. 'The Ram is allied with the Lioness and the Archer, but in enmity with the Fishes. The Fishes is the Twelfth next to us on the south-west, so it is particularly dangerous for one of us to stray there.'

'How would they know?' asked Georgia.

'By the colours,' said Cesare simply, pointing to the neckcloth he was wearing. It was the same red and yellow that Georgia had seen on one of the banners in the streets of the Ram. She realised that she was wearing one too, another badge of loyalty. She shook her head. It was like street gangs in Los Angeles.

'Can't you be independent?' she asked. 'I mean, not belong to any Twelfth?'

'Not belong to a Twelfth?' said Cesare incredulously. It reminded Georgia of the way Russell said 'does not compute' about anything he didn't understand.

'Everyone in Remora is born into a Twelfth,' Cesare tried again. 'Even if a baby comes unexpectedly while the woman is visiting in another part of the city, she will have travelled with a sack of earth from her Twelfth so that it can be spread under the bed and the child can be born on its own native soil.'

Up until now, Georgia had imagined the city as being like a collection of fanatical football club supporters, but now she began to see that it was something far deeper.

'OK,' she said. 'You have two close allies and one enemy. What about the other eight?'

'Oh, it is safe enough to walk in those Twelfths,' said Cesare. 'Would you like to visit one?'

They strolled across the Campo, which was full of stalls selling food and drink and banners and flags in a whole rainbow of colours. Georgia picked out the red and yellow ones of the Ram. She began noticing that every passer-by wore a neckcloth or some other coloured token. Some more grandly-dressed people sported satin ribbons instead.

Blue and purple, green and yellow, red and black, Cesare pointed them out and assigned them without thinking: Scorpion, Goat, Lioness. And then they passed a group of young men wearing pink and blue ribbons. Immediately they started to point and jeer at Cesare and Georgia.

'Quick,' hissed Cesare. 'Fishes!' He dragged her into an alley on the far side of the Campo from where they had entered it. 'This is Archer territory; they won't follow us in here.'

The Fish boys went clattering up a neighbouring alley. 'They've gone into Scorpion,' said Cesare listening. 'That's one of their allies, of course.'

'Of course,' said Georgia sarcastically.

Cesare gave her a serious look. 'This is not a game,' he said. 'You need to learn these rules, if you want to be safe in Remora.'

Georgia noticed that the Twelfth of the Archer was arranged very much like that of the Ram. There were the same statues everywhere – though these were of a centaur with bow and arrows – the same square in front of a church, with its fountain in the centre. This one was called the Fonte Dolorosa, according to Cesare. He nodded to a couple of boys who passed wearing red and purple colours and they waved back. 'Archers,' he whispered.

'Dolorosa,' said Georgia, rolling the syllables on her tongue. 'That sounds so sad. Why?'

Cesare shrugged. 'I don't know. The church is San Sebastiano; maybe it's sad because of the arrows.'

'Hang on,' said Georgia. 'You have these churches in all the Twelfths, and saints and things, but everything is arranged according to the signs of the zodiac. Isn't that a problem? I mean in my world, the church is anti-astrology – it's a bit too much like mumbo-jumbo. Mind you, the non-believers – which is most people – think the church is mumbo-jumbo too.'

She could see that Cesare had no idea what she was talking about. So she dropped it and asked, 'Which guild is the Archer associated with?'

'Horsemen,' said Cesare happily. 'We are fortunate in our allies, aren't we?'

'Does every Twelfth have a stable?' asked Georgia. She suddenly felt as if she could really belong in this city.

'Of course,' said Cesare. 'Every Twelfth has its stable and its Horsemaster. They are responsible for the horse ridden in the Stellata.'

'That's the race your dad was talking about, isn't it?' asked Georgia.

'Yes, the Race of the Stars,' said Cesare. 'We are running Arcangelo this year.'

'The big chestnut?' said Georgia. 'He's gorgeous. I wouldn't mind riding him myself. Who will be the jockey?'

'I will be, I hope,' said Cesare modestly, but Georgia could tell he was bursting with pride.

'The race is run in the Campo,' he went on, 'the Campo delle Stelle.'

'What, that circular one we just crossed?' said Georgia. 'But it's so small! I mean it's huge for a Piazza but not for a race-track. How long does the race take?'

Cesare looked offended. 'At least a minute and a half,' he said.

Georgia could tell from his face that she wasn't supposed to laugh. Cesare wasn't joking. This race, which was such a big deal in this extraordinary city, would be over in less time than it took to write a text message. But if she was going to come here again, she had to learn to respect its customs. And she realised she did want to come back. Very much.

As if he had read her mind, Cesare looked up at the sky. 'It'll be dark in an hour,' he said. 'We'd better get back to the Ram.'

Georgia sat up in bed with a jolt. She was sweating and her mother was hammering on the door.

'Georgia, hurry up, you'll be late for school,' yelled Maura. 'I wish you wouldn't lock your door.'

'What's happened?' thought Georgia groggily. It was taking her a while to adjust to being back in her proper life. The prospect of a day in Barnsbury Comp. seemed suddenly unbearably dreary.

She had lain down on a rough mattress in Paolo's hayloft and fallen asleep with the model of the winged horse in her hand. The last thing she remembered was Paolo and Cesare preparing to take Merla to her refuge in Santa Fina, wherever that was.

'I must remember to ask,' she muttered, heading for the shower. And then she realised she was still holding the little Etruscan horse. She thrust it quickly into the pocket of her sweatpants. She didn't want Russell to see it.

Whatever it all meant and wherever the horse city of Remora might really be, that little winged horse was the key to the way back to it.

Chapter 4

A Ghost

A horse-drawn carriage pulled to a stop outside the Horsemaster's house in the Twelfth of the Ram. Two passengers descended, one stiffly, moving his joints with caution. The other, much younger, jumped down with a lithe step and offered his arm for the older man to lean on. There was an obvious affection between the two. Father and son, an observer might have said, but they looked very different. The boy was slender with a profusion of curly black hair, allowed to grow long in the Talian fashion and tied back loosely with a purple ribbon. His clothes indicated wealth but not extravagance.

The older man was broad and vigorous looking, in spite of his stiffness. His hair was white and he had a distinguished look; he might have been a professor at a university, yet he had the calloused hands of one who does practical work.

The two of them now stood on the cobbles of Remora in the early morning air, looking round them in evident curiosity.

'Anothire citee, Lucian,' said the older man. 'And a fyne one too. Yet whatte wolde they saye if they knewe from how farre we hadde really travelled?'

The young man had no time to answer before the door of the house opened and a large, grizzled man stood before them.

'Maestro!' he said, his eyes lighting up. 'Well met! I'm glad to see you. And your son, too.'

The two men hugged like brothers and the Horsemaster then took the younger man into his burly arms.

'You must meet my Cesare – you're much of an age. Come in, come in, both of you. Teresa will give you a hearty breakfast.'

Georgia passed most of the day in a daze. She didn't even notice when Russell called her Dopey at breakfast. For the first time in years she had something to think about which took her attention away from him.

She had known, even when she was there, that the star city would seem like a dream when she returned to her own world. But she knew it hadn't been a dream. She might not have had a shadow there, but she had been perfectly solid, had drunk some ale and eaten some bread and olives before settling down to sleep in the hayloft. She had thought it would take her ages to drift off, especially since she knew that Cesare and Paolo were going to move the winged horse and her mother during the night.

She would have loved to stay and be part of that adventure, but Paolo had explained that, if she remained in Talia at night, her body would be found unconscious in her bed in the morning in her own world.

'Your parents would be frightened,' he had said. 'They would think you were sick. You must go back and you will, as soon as you fall asleep – as long as you are holding your talisman.'

And he had been right. Whether it was the ale or having lived two days one on top of the other, Georgia soon fell into a deep sleep.

She found it very difficult waking up in her own room. Everything seemed loud and harsh – the radio blaring out the news and weather, even the toaster and kettle carrying out their morning duties and Maura checking if everyone had what they needed for the day. When Ralph's mobile rang, Georgia nearly jumped out of her chair.

But in spite of the noise and bustle, her world also suddenly seemed thin – a meaningless jumble of events and busyness without purpose and focus. Georgia realised that the formal design and the many rules of Remora, as well as its obsession with horses, made her feel oddly at home in a way she no longer seemed to be in her own world.

'Ridiculous,' she thought. 'I've spent one afternoon there and I don't know if I'll ever be able to get back.' And yet she couldn't stop thinking about it – the

Twelfths, the Campo delle Stelle, the winged horse, Cesare. It was like being in love, but not with a person, with a whole place. This struck her with a sudden force. She had liked Cesare and he was a nice-looking boy two years older than her. Theoretically, she should have had an enormous crush on him, mad though that would have been – like falling for a young man in a Renaissance painting – but she hadn't.

It had just been so good to spend time with a boy who didn't hate her. She realised with a shock that it must be like that to have a proper brother. And for the first time she dared to think that the problems with Russell were his, not hers.

She spent the lunch-break in the library, using the school computer to look up *'Talia'*, *'Remora'*, *'di Chimici'* and *'Stellata'*. There was nothing under any of them, though she tried several spellings. She gave up on the computer and tried a dictionary of Greek and Roman mythology, which told her that Romulus and Remus had been the twin sons of Rhea Silvia and the god Mars.

Their birth was a shameful secret and their great uncle had thrown them in a river and stolen their grandfather's kingdom. After being fed by the she-wolf – the one bit of the story that Georgia already knew – they had been brought up by shepherds and, when grown up, had recovered their rights and decided to build a city. They couldn't agree on a site and so each twin had started his own. When Romulus had built a boundary-wall of a few inches high, Remus had jumped over it in scorn and his brother had killed him in a rage.

There was a lot more about Romulus, including the

interesting fact that no one knew what had happened to his body after his death and so he had been made a god. But what really caught Georgia's eye was a small footnote that said the twins had argued about whether to call their city Roma or Remora. Georgia sat back in astonishment. So in Talia the fight had gone the other way and Remus had founded the city she had visited and it had gone on to take the place in Talia's history that Rome had in Italy's.

That means Romulus *didn't* kill Remus in Talia, she thought.

After school, she called in at Mr Goldsmith's shop. He was delighted to see her. 'Back so soon?' he said. 'I hope you don't want to return the horse?'

'No, far from it,' said Georgia, who had transferred it to her jeans' pocket. 'I love it. I wanted to ask you more about it, in fact.'

'Ask away,' said Mr Goldsmith. 'But first let me make us a cup of tea.'

'OK,' said Georgia, 'though I can't stay long – I've got a violin lesson.'

Gaetano and his father were making their tour of the stables in Remora. Wherever they went, the Remorans, although startled, were honoured by the visit. Stable after stable showed off their racing horses – the greys and the chestnuts, the browns and the bays, the roans and piebalds.

They left their visit to the Scales till last. This was tricky. The Lady and the Scales were adversaries. It had already been a little awkward in the Twelfth of the Bull, because although Niccolò and his son were lords of Giglia, the Lady's city, they were hand in glove with Remora and the Twins were the Bull's sworn enemy. These enmities and alliances were ancient in Remora; they went back centuries.

The Scales' Horsemaster, Giacomo, greeted Duke Niccolò and the young princeling cordially enough. After all, though the Lady was their foe, the Twins were one of the Scales' allies, whose own guild, strangely enough, was that of the chemists – the chimici.

Still, it irked Giacomo to see the green and purple ribbons in his stable and it took all his reserves of politeness to keep the anger out of his voice. 'This is our mount for the Stellata, your Grace,' he said, as neutrally as he could. 'Il Corvo.' Gaetano felt an immediate sympathy with the black horse. He was proud and highly strung like all the best Reman horses, but he was also beautiful, with strong clean lines. Gaetano would have loved to ride him.

That of course was out of the question and the Duke brought their visit to the stable of the Scales to an end as soon as he decently could.

'That's that, then,' he said to his son. 'Duty done. Now I've visited them all. What did you think of that one?'

'A real beauty,' said Gaetano. 'A pity it won't win.'

Niccolò gave him a quizzical look. 'Prophecy now, is it? "There is no winner till the race is run" – isn't that one of Remora's most ancient sayings?'

'Yes,' said Gaetano, 'and that might have been true when it was first said. When the Stellata was run fair and above board – before it was all rigged in favour of our family.'

They had come back out into the Campo and automatically crossed the cobbles back to the Lady's segment. Even the Duke of Giglia wouldn't want to stand on enemy territory a minute longer than was necessary.

Niccolò frowned. This was not the sort of conversation he wanted to have in broad daylight, especially so close to the Twelfth of the Scales.

'Let's go somewhere neutral,' he said, and steered Gaetano down the Strada delle Stelle. They walked on the Goat's side of the street, down into a little square near the Porta della Luna where there was a sleepy little inn.

'I'm not so well known down here,' said Niccolò, 'so we can have a quiet talk in peace.'

The inn-keeper brought a greenish wine for both of them and a large plate of sugary cakes, which only Gaetano paid any attention to.

'There's obviously something on your mind,' said Niccolò, eyeing his son as he contemplated the cakes. 'Do you want to tell me what it is?'

'It's this city,' said Gaetano evasively, through a mouthful of crumbly pastry. 'It's so false. Everything divided up so neatly and everything run according to the rules. And yet when it comes to its precious race, all the rules are broken. It's the Twelfth that can afford the biggest bribes that wins.'

The Duke looked round cautiously. Even in neutral territory, there were things best said in a low voice if they had to be said at all.

'You know how much this city believes in omens and portents,' he said quietly. 'If the winner isn't the

Lady or Twins, they take it as a sign that our power is waning.'

'It could be the Bull or the Scorpion or the Goat, come to that,' said Gaetano. 'Our family rules all their cities. Or even the Scales, since Bellona's one of ours too.'

Niccolò sighed. It was of course maddening that Remora housed these ancient feudal loyalties within itself. But the tradition of each Twelfth owing allegiance to one of the twelve city-states went back centuries, much further than the di Chimici family; it couldn't be changed overnight. Of course, all its citizens were Remorans and when outside the city they had nothing but fierce loyalty to it. Two Remorans in a foreign city would sit and drink together even if they were from rival Twelfths.

But within the city itself a sort of madness reigned all year round, from one Stellata to the next. It was especially so in the weeks surrounding the race itself, and the streets were more dangerous the closer they were to the Campo, which was also the racetrack. Out by the city gates, all fourteen of them, people were fairly relaxed and that's where the stables were. But the segmented pattern of the circular city meant that each Twelfth narrowed to a deadly daggerpoint aimed at the heart of the Campo. It was suicide to stray outside the boundary of your Twelfth on the day of the Stellata.

It had been a Pope who decided to remodel the city after the zodiac, in an attempt to curry favour with a population much more interested in astrology than in the church. It had taken decades to re-name all the streets and squares and develop the crests and mottoes and banners of each Twelfth, and by then the misguided Pope was long dead. But the Remorans had taken to the new system like ducks to water. The city had anciently been divided roughly into twelve and the city loyalties long established. All that the next Pope, Benedict, had to do was build the broad neutral boulevard and the famous Campo – the citizens took care of the rest.

So perhaps another Pope could modify the city again? Niccolò mused on his brother sitting in his comfortable palace fronting on to the Twins' segment in the Campo delle Stelle. He could, over time, issue pronouncements banning the excessive displays of loyalty to any city but Remora itself. Niccolò found himself looking into the eyes of his son over an empty cake plate. A twitch of annoyance passed over his aristocratic features. Perhaps the church would have been the right career for this insatiable son of his? He could have rivalled Ferdinando in paunch, given time.

But Duke Niccolò was good at concealing his emotions. 'I'm sorry,' he said out loud. 'I was thinking about what you said.'

'But the real trouble is I don't know why you have brought me here,' mumbled Gaetano truculently. 'Isn't it time you told me what you have in mind?'

'Certainly,' said Niccolò. 'How would you like to marry the young Duchessa of Bellezza?'

'I don't know that much about the Etruscans,' said Mortimer Goldsmith, over an elegant cup of Earl Grey. 'They're more the speciality of archaeologists and anthropologists. I go in for more recent history – Chippendale and Sèvres are more my line. More tea?'

'No thanks,' said Georgia, who thought it smelt like aftershave and tasted like washing-up water. 'But they were some sort of early Italians, weren't they?'

'Oh yes, that's certain. Though I believe very little else is. There's no literature you know – just a few inscriptions.'

'And models of flying horses,' added Georgia.

'Yes, and a few urns and things. There's one in the BM if my memory serves,' he said. 'Or is it the V and A? I've definitely seen one somewhere.'

Georgia had spent many Sundays in the places he was talking about. 'The British Museum?' she asked, to be sure, 'or the one in South Kensington?'

'I'm pretty sure it's the British Museum,' said Mr Goldsmith finally. 'Figures from a bronze urn – something like sixth century BC. Those horses weren't winged though – just part of some barbaric race where the riders rode bareback.'

Georgia made a mental note to go to the British Museum and check – and to ask Paolo if the Stellata was run bareback.

'I'm sorry, I have to go,' she said getting up. 'Thanks for the tea. It was nice talking to you.'

'My pleasure,' said Mr Goldsmith, making a formal little bow. 'I'll get some Darjeeling in for next time,' he added, noticing her almost full cup. 'And some chocolate biscuits. I don't often have young people to entertain.'

Georgia had to run all the way to her music lesson, her violin and music case banging against her leg. She didn't make a very good stab at her piece, because it was so hard to concentrate. She couldn't wait to get home.

'I can't believe it,' said Luciano. 'Another Stravagante? So soon? We must tell Rodolfo. Dottore, do you still have the hand mirror?'

'In dede,' said Dethridge. 'It is inne mye satchele. Bot let signor Paolo telle us more.'

'It is my son who spent more time with her – for it is a young woman this time,' said Paolo.

They were in the comfortable sitting room of Paolo and Teresa's house in the west of the city, near the Gate of the Ram. The visitors had made a hearty breakfast indeed, of fresh baked rolls and fig jam and great bowls of milky coffee. The little children were playing in the yard under Teresa's supervision as she fed the hens and collected eggs for a lunchtime frittata.

Cesare and Luciano, after the stiff politeness of their first greetings, were beginning to relax with each other. And now that Luciano knew Cesare had met someone else from his world, all constraint was gone. It made him feel very strange. It was true that Talia was his world now but he couldn't just forget that he had been a twenty-first-century boy, and the idea that he might meet someone from his own time was excitingly disturbing. Even Doctor Dethridge, Luciano's foster-father, who had left that same world, albeit from a time many centuries before, was affected by the news.

'Is she coming back?' asked Luciano.

'I'm sure she will if she can,' said Cesare. 'She was so interested in the flying horse.'

That of course raised more questions than it answered and the horsemen of the Ram had to explain everything about the black filly, the visit of Duke Niccolò and their night-time expedition to Santa Fina to hide Merla and her mother.

'It lyketh me noghte thatte such a felawe is in the citee,' said Doctor Dethridge. 'The Duke is up to noe goode, I trowe.'

'He is officially visiting his brother the Pope,' said Paolo. 'But taking the opportunity to check on horses in his rivals' stables at the same time.'

'It's all just a show, though, isn't it?' asked Luciano. 'Rodolfo told us that the race is rigged every year for one of di Chimici's favourites to win.'

'That's what usually happens,' admitted Paolo. 'But we don't usually have a winged horse born in the city. I'm hoping that means victory for the Ram.'

*

'The Duchessa of Bellezza?' said Gaetano stupidly; he was too surprised to stop himself. 'What for?'

His father sighed. 'It will take a lot to make a diplomat of you,' he said. 'To make you Duke of course, and bring Bellezza into the fold.'

'Into the family, you mean,' said Gaetano, playing for time. But he didn't hate the idea. Surely as Duke of Bellezza he would have ample time for his books and his music? 'What is she like?' he asked.

'Very pretty,' said Niccolò dryly, 'and I should think about as easy to handle as Zarina.'

It took Gaetano a moment or two to remember that Zarina was the Lady's spirited grey mare.

Supper was fish and chips, followed by ice cream. It was usually Georgia's favourite because there wasn't anything Maura or Ralph could do to ruin it. Only tonight she just wasn't hungry. She wanted to rush through her homework and get an early night. Even Russell wasn't making much impression on her.

'Homework on a Friday night?' was all he could manage to hiss at her. 'You're turning into a real geek as well as a freak.'

She didn't remind him that it was her Saturday for riding tomorrow. She just wanted to keep her head down and not draw attention to herself. But the evening dragged on interminably. Maths, English, French, then bed. And once in bed no chance of sleep. She had the winged horse in her tracksuit pocket and a clear vision of the hayloft in Remora in her mind, but sleep refused to come. Perhaps it was because she was so eager to get there. Or it might have been something to do with Russell's metal music blaring out in the room next door.

'Please,' she wished as hard as she could. 'Let me be in the City of Stars.'

Luciano was pacing excitedly up and down the room. 'I bet it has something to do with Arianna's visit here,' he said. 'I don't know how much you know about my stravagation, but Rodolfo thought I was brought to Bellezza to save the last Duchessa. Perhaps this girl from my world is needed because of a plot against Arianna? You know that's why we are here, because she has been invited to the Stellata?'

'Yes, wee are supposed to lerne al thatte we canne about the citee,' nodded Dethridge, 'and its wayes and maneres during this race of such grete importe.'

'And I bet the Duke is up to something too,' added Luciano. 'It's too much of a coincidence that he's here at the same time as us.'

There was a light tap at the door. Paolo went to open it while Luciano continued his pacing.

'I really don't think it's safe for her to come here,' he was saying. 'Everything we know about the city makes it seem a hotbed of villainy – I mean, it's the centre of the di Chimici's world, isn't it?'

His pacing had brought him opposite the door. His jaw fell open when he saw the slight short-haired figure with the silver eyebrow ring.

And the effect on Georgia was no less dramatic. She recognised the black-haired boy. She had been staring at his photograph only a few hours ago at her violin teacher's house.

'I promised you two more Stravaganti, didn't I, Georgia?' said Paolo smiling.

'Lucien!' said Georgia – and vanished.

Chapter 5

The Shadow of Doubt

Georgia woke suddenly in her bed in London, her heart racing, but it wasn't morning. The house was quiet and dark. She was in a whirl of confusion. Dreaming of a city with flying horses was one thing – even if it turned out not to be a dream and the city was real. But coming face to face with someone from her own world, someone she knew to be dead – that was something else again.

She lay in the darkness, holding the flying horse in a tight grip, waiting for her heart to slow and her thoughts to settle. Half of her wanted to go back to Remora immediately, but the other half was still terrified. It had definitely been Lucien that she had seen in Paolo's house. There was no way she could have mistaken him, even in his sixteenth-century

Talian clothes. Georgia was an expert where Lucien Mulholland was concerned.

He had been in the year above her when she joined Barnsbury Comprehensive, and she had seen him once or twice at his mother's when she went to violin lessons after school. But it had been only in Year 10 that she had begun to feel differently about him. Russell was quite wrong about her; she *was* interested in boys – at least in one boy. But Georgia was shy as well as unhappy and her butch image had been developed to protect her feelings.

If Lucien had been aware of those feelings, he had never shown it. They both played in the school orchestra and the irony of being second fiddle to Lucien wasn't lost on her. But once Georgia had joined the orchestra, it not only gave her more chance of seeing him, it meant that when they met at his house, he would actually talk to her. Gradually she had realised that he was shy too. He didn't have girlfriends; that was one blessing at least.

But just when she was hoping that they could be friends and that perhaps one day he might return her feelings, he had become ill. Lying there in the dark, Georgia re-lived last year's agony of discovering that Lucien was seriously ill, that he had to be off school for weeks having chemotherapy, that he had lost his beautiful hair. His mother stopped teaching and Georgia was cut off from all news of him, except what she could glean from the school gossip machine.

There had been a few weeks last summer when she had believed that he was getting better, that he would return to school in the autumn term cured. Georgia had even seen him again when she had resumed violin lessons. He seemed older somehow and a little remote, but not unfriendly, just preoccupied. She had made up her mind to tell him how much she liked him, but then terrible news had filtered through and put an end to all her plans: Lucien was in hospital, he was in a coma, he was dead.

She had gone to the funeral like a zombie, not believing that the only boy she had ever liked could be lost to her for ever. Only seeing his grieving parents and hearing his best friend Tom's voice cracking as he read a poem, convinced her that Lucien had really gone.

And now there he was again in Talia, looking gorgeous and as healthy as when he sat in front of her in orchestra and she watched his hair curl over the collar of his shirt. What could it possibly mean? She now began to wonder if Talia was a fantasy world which her unconscious had created for her to escape to. Horses, flying ones even, and now the resurrection of a boy she had had a huge crush on – it was all too symbolic for words.

But what was she to do? Seeing Lucien was going to be painful – a quick glimpse had convinced her of that – but how could she give up going to Talia? Georgia looked down at the little black horse in her hand. It had to mean something, the way it had come into her life. There must be something she was meant to do in Talia or she wouldn't have stravagated there. Was that what Lucien had done? Why was he there, and did it have anything to do with why he had died?

Georgia felt seriously frightened. In her short experience of Remora, she had been like a member of the audience at a play, watching the story unfold. But seeing Lucien there had felt like being dragged up on the stage and made to participate in the action. From now on, if she went back to Talia, she knew she would have an active role in whatever drama was being played out there. And now she realised that it was dangerous.

In Paolo's house chaos reigned. Luciano had turned deathly white, Cesare was clearly terrified and both Paolo and Dethridge were completely at a loss. 'Do you know her?' asked Paolo, and Luciano had just had time to say he did, when Georgia was back.

Luciano was the only one who understood what had happened. He led Georgia to a chair and asked Paolo to bring her a drink. Georgia sat in silence gulping some rough red wine, letting herself be looked after, enjoying the sensation of having Lucien's attention focused properly on her for the first time.

She was feeling a bit woozy now and didn't really understand why she had re-entered the same scene she had left so precipitately. It had taken hours to get back to sleep – which was what Paolo had explained that she had to do to stravagate back to Talia. She must go to sleep holding the talisman and thinking of Remora. It had been much easier earlier in the night, before her fright over seeing Lucien.

Back in Talia it was as if someone had pressed a 'Pause' button and the scene had been frozen at the point where she had left it.

'If you stravagate twice during the same period of time,' Luciano was saying, 'the same day or the same night, you end up back in Talia only moments after leaving it.'

'But why did she leave us at all?' asked Cesare, looking warily at Georgia as if she were a ghost.

'I think she must have fainted when she saw me,' said Luciano. 'And she must have been holding her talisman. If you lose consciousness in Talia, while you have the talisman, even if you aren't thinking of home, you will end up in our world. It's a sort of default setting.'

He was speaking directly to Georgia now, who nodded; it made a sort of sense.

'Georgia comes from the same part of our world as I did,' continued Luciano. 'We went to the same school. She knew I was dead. I expect you thought you had seen a ghost,' he said, looking straight at her.

Georgia nodded again, incapable of saying anything yet.

'Can I see your talisman?' Luciano asked gently.

She uncurled the fingers of her right hand. The wings had cut into her fingers leaving red marks; she had been clinging on to it so hard. She let Luciano take the little horse and examine it.

'It's just like our Merla,' said Cesare.

'Is she safe?' asked Georgia. 'Did you get her away?'

'Yes,' answered Paolo. 'She and Starlight are in Santa Fina. We trust that the di Chimici won't find her there. Though there is still a risk. Unfortunately, they have a summer palace in Santa Fina too, but they won't use it while they're visiting the city. And we can trust Roderigo.'

'Could I go and see her?' asked Georgia.

'I'm sure you can,' said Paolo. 'It's not far. You could be there and back in hours.'

Luciano gave her back the little model.

'Keep it safe,' he said. 'The di Chimici would be as interested in your winged horse as in the real one.'

'And in the mayde hirselfe, I trowe, if mayde she bee,' said Dethridge. He had been looking at Georgia's stable-boy's clothes in some puzzlement.

'She is a boy in Talia,' said Paolo, 'even though a girl where she comes from.'

'Ah,' said Dethridge. 'It is a disguise. I understonde. We use such a devyse in monye of the playes in our citee playhouses.'

'Why does he talk like that?' Georgia whispered to Luciano.

He smiled. 'You hear it too? It's because he comes from our world, from England in Elizabethan times – four-and-a-half centuries ago. Let me present to you Doctor William Dethridge, founder of the Stravaganti. Though here in Talia his name is Guglielmo Crinamorte and he is a great man in Bellezza.'

Dethridge bowed.

'My name here seems to be Giorgio,' said Georgia.

'I have been re-named too,' said Luciano. 'I'm Luciano now, Luciano Crinamorte. Dottore Crinamorte and his wife Leonora are my foster parents.' Quickly he looked away from Georgia.

But she had noticed something else.

'There's something I don't understand,' she said. 'I'm a Stravagante from another world, or so Paolo tells me and he could tell that because I don't have a shadow. But you and Doctor Dethridge both clearly have shadows and yet you come from the same world as me, even if he is from centuries ago. Will someone please explain it all?'

*

Rinaldo di Chimici was profoundly glad to be back in Remora. His sojourn in Bellezza had been uncomfortable and at times frightening and he was not a brave man. He had hated the city with its smelly canals and the unreasonable cheerfulness of its citizens. And its unnatural absence of horses. Above all he had hated its Duchessa, so clever and beautiful and so much more experienced at diplomacy than him that she made him feel like a callow boy.

Still, he had got his own back on her with a vengeance. The formidable Duchessa of Bellezza was no more and, even though he had not succeeded in replacing her with one of his family, the daughter who had taken her place was only a girl, and surely no match for his uncle, Duke Niccolò?

Rinaldo made his way down to the stables of the Twins. He wasn't sure what direction his career would take him in next, but in the meantime, there was nothing he wanted more than a fast ride on a fresh horse.

Since his father's death two years ago, when his older brother Alfonso had become Duke of Volana, Rinaldo had been at a loose end. There was no other title for him to inherit and no obvious work for him to do, so he had drifted to Remora and settled in one of the many rooms of his uncle Ferdinando's palace, until Duke Niccolò had sent him to Bellezza as his ambassador.

Rinaldo now felt as at home in the Twelfth of the Twins as he ever had in the rather gloomy family castle in Volana many miles to the north-east. He had stopped off there on the way back from Bellezza, to visit Alfonso and their younger sister Caterina, but it no longer felt as if he belonged there. His brother had been preoccupied with the idea of getting married, wondering whether the Duke had someone in mind for him. Rinaldo was supposed to find that out.

He wondered whether to suggest their cousin Francesca, his failed candidate for Duchessa of Bellezza. The di Chimici were quite keen on inter-marriage, so Niccolò might look kindly on the idea. One of Rinaldo's current missions in Remora was to get Uncle Ferdinando to dissolve Francesca's first marriage, which Rinaldo had rather hastily arranged to a much older Bellezzan Councillor, in order to qualify her for election to the city's rulership.

'Good morning, Excellency,' said the Twins' Horsemaster. 'I have a mount saddled and ready for you – Bacio, the bay mare.'

'Superb!' said Rinaldo, looking affectionately at the mare. She was his favourite horse in the Twins' stables, not a race-winner like Benvenuto, but a smooth ride and a beautiful animal.

'In good shape, isn't she?' observed a familiar voice from the shadows, and Rinaldo jumped at the sound.

He flinched when he saw the speaker. Enrico had been picked up in Bellezza like a bad smell that the young ambassador could not shake off. The city had not been a place that either of them wanted to stay in after the Duchessa had been assassinated. The di

Chimici and anyone associated with them were highly suspect after the explosion, even though there had been no evidence to link them with the crime.

Rinaldo had not been able to deny Enrico a job in Remora and had recommended him to both his uncles: to the Pope as an experienced horseman and to Duke Niccolò as an unscrupulous spy. But the very sight of the man unnerved him. He had carried out an act of cold-blooded murder, more than one probably, and even though the most recent such act had been on Rinaldo's orders, he looked on the assassin with fascinated horror, knowing that he would just as easily slit his own master's throat, if paid enough.

'Ah, how are they treating you here?' he asked Enrico nervously, anxious to get away from him and out of the city for his ride in the hills.

'Very well,' said Enrico. 'It's good to be back among horses. They're more reliable than humans, if you know what I mean.'

Rinaldo thought he did. This scruffy spy had a grudge; his good-looking fiancée had disappeared and the man had got it into his head that his old employer knew something about it. Rinaldo had met the girl only once and knew nothing at all of her fate, which had in fact been very different from what Enrico suspected. The ambassador had no time for young women himself, beautiful or otherwise. They were quite alien to him, apart from his sister and cousins. And the last thing he wanted was for Enrico to harbour any malice against him. He could do Rinaldo a lot of harm, and not just physically.

'Excellent, excellent!' he now said vaguely. 'Let me know if there's anything you need.' And he led

Bacio out into the yard, with Enrico's mournful brown eyes following him.

*

'Where shall I begin?' asked Luciano. He, Cesare and Georgia had left Paolo and Doctor Dethridge closeted together, and taken the road west out of the city walls through the Gate of the Ram. They had been sent off with instructions to spend the day continuing Georgia's education about Remora and sharing information.

'Well, how did you get here, for a start?' asked Georgia. They were sitting on the small wall of a farm just outside the city.

'Today I arrived by carriage,' said Luciano, smiling. 'But I suspect that's not what you want to know. I came from Bellezza. That was the city I first stravagated to last May.' His smile faded. 'That is where I live now – it is my home.'

The three young people remained silent for a while. Cesare was rather in awe of this elegant young man, who was a year younger than him and yet had known such wonders. Luciano was a Stravagante and Cesare still wasn't sure what that meant. Cesare had been told that Luciano was apprentice to Signor Rodolfo, the most distinguished Stravagante in Talia and that he lived in Bellezza with Doctor Crinamorte, who had founded the brotherhood. And now he had turned out to be not only a visitor from another world, but a friend of Cesare's own personal Stravagante, the mysterious girl with a boy's hair and no shadow.

'There is nowhere in our world like Bellezza,' Luciano eventually continued. 'It looks like Venice,

85

except that everything gold in Venice is silver in Bellezza. They don't value gold here, you know; it's silver that is the most precious metal. Bellezza is a city visited by people from all over this world – not just Talians – because of its incredible beauty. And as soon as I arrived in it, I felt really well again. My hair had grown back and I was strong, just as I was before the cancer came.' He stopped and took a deep breath, then plunged back into his story.

'I can't tell you everything in one day. I have spent months as apprentice to Rodolfo – he's wonderful, the cleverest, most magical person – and he taught me about being a Stravagante. He had been expecting me, because he took my talisman to our world.'

'What was your talisman?' asked Georgia curiously.

An expression of pain passed over his face. She could see that this new Luciano was not quite as she remembered Lucien. He looked older and as if scarred by experience. He said he hadn't been ill in Talia and yet he looked as someone might who has had a serious illness and recovered from it in body but not yet in mind.

'It was a notebook from Bellezza,' said Luciano. 'But I can't use it any more.' He stood and paced up and down in front of the wall. 'As you see, I have a shadow now. I am still a Stravagante, but from this world to yours. I have made that journey only a few times and it is very difficult for me.'

'Is that because of, you know, what happened in our world with your illness?' asked Georgia, feeling stupid and tactless even as she said it, but she had to know.

'Yes,' said Luciano. 'As you know, in your world,

which is no longer mine, I died.'

Cesare looked at him with awe; he had heard Luciano say he was dead in his old world but he still couldn't believe it.

'Is that what happened to Doctor Dethridge too?' asked Georgia quickly, to disperse the tension.

'In a way,' said Luciano. 'He stravagated to Bellona, his city in Talia, to escape a death sentence in England. And then later, he found he had a shadow here and realised he must have died in his old life.'

'Why did you think the Dottore talked funny?' Cesare asked Georgia. 'He sounds quite normal to me.'

'He sounds old-fashioned to us,' said Georgia.

Georgia looked to Luciano for explanation, but he just shrugged. 'But do we sound normal to you?' he asked Cesare. 'Because we don't speak Italian or Talian and yet we can understand and make ourselves understood here.'

Georgia tried another tack. 'What did you do in Bellezza,' she asked, 'besides learning about stravagation?'

'First I was chosen by the Duchessa to be a mandolier – that's like a gondolier in Venice,' he said, 'but then Rodolfo got me out of that and I made fireworks. I visited the islands, dived in the canal, fought with an assassin, was given lots of silver, had a warrant out for my arrest, got drunk, was kidnapped, helped get a new Duchessa elected, danced with her at Carnival . . .'

His expression had changed again and Georgia felt a tightening round her heart.

'How old is the new Duchessa?' she asked.

'About my age,' said Luciano. 'A month or two older.' His tone was super casual; Georgia recognised it. It was the same tone in which she had asked Vicky Mulholland how Lucien was when she went for violin lessons.

'How exciting!' said Cesare. 'You've had so many more adventures than me. And I'm nearly a year older than you. I've done nothing except ride horses and help my father in the Twelfth. And you've met the Duchessa of Bellezza – both of them. It makes my life here seem very dull.'

'I have a feeling it's not going to stay dull,' said Luciano grimly. 'You can't be the son of a Stravagante in one of the main cities of the di Chimici clan and not be in danger.'

'I didn't know he was a Stravagante till yesterday,' said Cesare. 'And I still don't know what it means.'

'You and me both,' said Georgia. 'And I'm supposed to *be* one!'

'It's a traveller between worlds,' said Luciano. 'At least, one between Georgia's world and ours.' He turned to Cesare, deliberately identifying himself with him rather than with Georgia. 'The travel can be in either direction, but the talisman – the device that helps the Stravagante make the journey – comes from the world that is not the Stravagante's own.'

'But you said you've been back to the other world, since – you know,' said Georgia. 'Have you got a talisman from there now?'

'Yes,' said Luciano, but he didn't elaborate.

'Why do you think you two were chosen?' asked Cesare, rather shyly. 'You must be very special in some way.'

Luciano and Georgia snorted in unison.

'Not at all, in my case,' said Luciano.

'Nor me,' said Georgia.

'Unless . . .' said Luciano and then stopped, confused.

'What?' said Georgia.

'I've had plenty of time to think about this,' he went on reluctantly. 'I have wondered whether my talisman found me because I would have been doomed in my own world anyway. I mean, although I got stranded here because the di Chimici kidnapped me and I couldn't stravagate back because I didn't have the talisman, I think I would have died in my world anyway. The cancer had come back, you know.'

Georgia nodded.

'So I wonder if it was somehow connected – if it was because I was already dying. And now, I wonder ... I hate to ask, but are you quite well in your own world?'

Chapter 6

The Youngest Son

'Are you sure you're not sickening for something?' asked Maura, when Georgia gave her fourth huge yawn at breakfast.

'No, really, Mum, I'm fine – honestly,' she said. 'I just didn't get much sleep last night.'

This was true enough. Lucien had warned her about that. 'I was always exhausted back home when I was stravagating every night,' he had said. 'But at least I had the excuse of being ill.'

She thought she had been able to reassure him – and herself – on that point. She was pretty sure she didn't have a serious illness.

'Perhaps you should give the riding a miss today?' said Russell, feigning brotherly concern. Georgia shot him a poisonous look.

'Perhaps you shouldn't play your "music" so late at night,' she rejoined. 'It kept me awake.'

'Now, now, don't squabble, you two,' said Ralph. He hated any kind of disagreement at mealtimes.

Georgia was already wearing her jodhpurs and riding boots. Sometimes, when she was very lucky, Ralph or Maura would give her a lift to the stables, but it was a long way out and took up the whole morning, since they had to wait for her. So most weeks, like today, she had to take the tube out to practically the end of the line, carrying her hard-hat and crop.

Since these were difficult accessories to disguise, some wag or other was bound to ask, 'Where's the horse?' on the journey and laugh uproariously at his wit. Today she barely noticed but kept score out of habit. 'Only three,' she muttered as she took the bus from the station to the stables. 'I must be losing my touch.'

The familiar smell of the stables made her think immediately of Remora, where horses were treated almost like gods, even when they didn't have wings. She had spent most of last night – or the day before if you thought in Talian terms – talking to Lucien and Cesare about the di Chimici, Bellezza, stravagation and Talian magic. Now she couldn't wait to go back and find out more about the horse race that seemed to dominate the city. And to see Lucien again.

Lucien had ended their conversation by suggesting that she shouldn't stravagate every night or she would be too tired. Then he had warned her that the gateway from her world was notoriously unstable. He and Dethridge and the mysterious Rodolfo, who was obviously a big hero to Lucien, were working on ways of stabilising it, but even if she missed out a week, she might find that only a day had passed in Talia.

But could she bear to miss even one chance of seeing him? Common sense told her that she had as much hope of getting together with Lucien as if he really had died. After all he had, as far as her world was concerned. And even if she stravagated to Talia and stayed there permanently – which was certainly not on her agenda – she didn't think he would ever be more than a friend. Remembering how he had looked when he talked about the young Duchessa of Bellezza made Georgia feel desperately sad all over again.

The Duchessa was called Arianna, apparently, and there had been a secret about her birth – she was actually the daughter of the previous Duchessa and Rodolfo. Lucien had been Arianna's friend long before she knew of her parentage and was just a simple girl from one of the islands in the Bellezzan lagoon. But then her mother had been assassinated and the truth had come out.

'Georgia!' called a voice, jolting her out of her reverie. 'Are you going to ride today or just stand in the yard all morning?'

It was Jean, who ran the stables and was one of Georgia's favourite people.

'Sorry – I was miles away,' said Georgia, truthfully.

Falco di Chimici was alone, apart from the servants. He had the whole palace to roam in. The di Chimici summer palace at Santa Fina, about ten miles from

Remora, was the most lavish of all the homes of the Dukes of Giglia. It had been built by the second Duke, Alfonso, Falco's grandfather, who had been too busy making money to get married until he was sixty-five.

Despite his age he had gone on to sire four sons, the oldest, Niccolò, when he was sixty-seven and the youngest, Jacopo, now Prince of Bellona, ten years later. Duke Alfonso had died at the age of eighty-seven, more than twenty years before Falco had been born, leaving Niccolò to take over as Duke when he was only twenty. Alfonso's wife, Renata, had been much younger than him and Falco could just remember her, a tiny, white-haired figure, hobbling about the palazzo with a stick, very bright-eyed and interested and very proud of her splendid sons and grandsons.

Even me, thought Falco, as he limped slowly and painfully from room to room, using two wooden sticks. But that was an uncharacteristic thought; Falco didn't approve of self-pity.

He had been the adored youngest child of a wealthy and influential family and the best-looking son of his branch of it. His father, Duke Niccolò, had held him in his arms minutes after his birth and schemed of new princedoms to win or buy so that this beautiful child should bear a worthy title.

Falco had three older brothers who were all gifted in different ways. Fabrizio and Carlo were both handsome and clever, Fabrizio well suited to be their father's heir since he was interested in politics and diplomacy and spent many hours of each day closeted with the Duke. Carlo had more of a business brain, like the family's founder. Even when he was a little boy, building castles out of wooden bricks, he wanted to charge his brothers to use them for their toy soldiers.

The brother that Falco loved best was Gaetano, the closest to him in age, and he wasn't handsome at all. In fact, he was quite ugly, with a big nose and a wide crooked mouth. He was supposed to look like their grandfather Alfonso, who had built the great palace at Santa Fina. But Gaetano was the cleverest of all the brothers, and the most interested in the libraries at Santa Fina and at their uncle's Papal palace.

He was also the most fun to be with. Gaetano could ride and fence and make up the most wonderful games. The happiest hours of Falco's childhood had been spent with Gaetano at Santa Fina, acting out his invented romances of knights and ghosts and hidden treasure and family secrets of madmen and concealed wills and maps. Their older sister Beatrice could sometimes be persuaded to play the forlorn maidens or warrior queens which Gaetano's invention required, but often Falco himself, with his delicate features and huge dark eyes, had to submit to being wrapped in scraps of muslin or brocade to take the female roles.

His favourite romances, though, had been the ones involving swordfights. He and his brother had started with toy wooden weapons but graduated to bated foils when Falco was ten. They had fought their way up and down all the staircases of the palace from the grand sweep of the main marble one to the mysterious branched wooden stairs of the servants' quarters. They had duelled under the heavy chandeliers of the ballroom, reflected a hundred times in its mirrored walls. They had feinted and parried even in the palace kitchens, overturning pans and startling the maids. Although Gaetano was four years older than his little brother, they were well matched in skill and always collapsed out of breath and laughing at the same point.

It had been glorious. But it had all come to an end two years ago, when Gaetano turned fifteen. He was going to go to the university in Giglia and the boys' tutor, Ignazio, would be left with only one pupil. They would still have had their long summer holidays to continue their fencing and play-acting, if it hadn't been for Falco's accident.

He was thinking about it now, as he made his painful way up one of the staircases he had scaled so lightly in the past. He reached the great arched loggia overlooking the main entrance to the palace and rested, breathing heavily, on the parapet, surveying the countryside.

You couldn't see the stables from here and he was glad. He hadn't ridden since the accident, hadn't wanted to, didn't even know if it was physically possible. He couldn't face the indignity of being hauled awkwardly on to the backs of beasts he would once have sprung lightly up on unaided. Falco had his pride.

Gaetano had been given a new horse for his fifteenth birthday – a nervous highly-bred grey gelding, called Caino. Falco begged to ride the animal and his brother had, unusually, denied him. 'He's too big for you, Falconcino,' Gaetano had said. 'Wait till you are older.'

The grown-ups had laughed and Falco had seethed.

He had never been denied any treat on the grounds that he was too small or too young. And Gaetano of all his family should have known how strong and capable he was. Hadn't he that morning pressed his older brother to yield as they fenced round the twenty-foot-long table in the great banqueting hall?

He waited till after the grand birthday meal, held at that same table. Everyone ate and drank too much except Falco, who was too angry. After the table had been cleared, the guests all drifted off to different rooms on the cool upper floors of the palace for a siesta. Even Gaetano went to doze over his manuscripts in the library.

Falco went out to the stables and saddled up Caino. It had been madness. The grooms were all at their own meal, the horses were sleepy in the early afternoon heat and the grey did not know this boy who was leading him out of the stables. Still, he let himself be mounted, flattening his ears back only a little, and seemed reassured by the rider's sensitive hands.

But Caino did not want to be out in the blazing sun and soon turned tetchy. He minced sideways to avoid stones on the road that he didn't like the look of, slowed to a funereal pace and then, when Falco dug his heels in, accelerated into a gallop from a standing start and careered across the fields at full stretch. Falco was scared. He knew that Gaetano would be furious with him if he over-stretched his new mount. Strangely, he had no fears for himself.

Caino saw a high wall in his way and bunched up his hindquarters to clear it. He almost did. But a bird flew up and startled him at the crucial moment and he fell back, crushing his rider.

Only half an hour passed before a stable boy noticed that the grey was missing. The head groom alerted Niccolò, who rose irritably from his nap. 'Stupid of the boy to take him out in this heat,' he grumbled. 'But I suppose he couldn't wait to try his present.'

'No, your Grace,' said the groom. 'Your manservant tells me that master Gaetano is in the library.'

It took hours to find them. By then the horse was dead, his eyes rolled back and his beautiful head flecked with blood and foam. His neck was broken. It took five men to lift his body off the boy. One of them was the desperate Duke, who insisted on carrying the limp body of his youngest son back to the palazzo in his arms. He seemed to be scarcely breathing.

A runner had been dispatched to the doctor in Santa Fina and he found the boy in a dreadful state. For three days Falco hovered between life and death. He could remember it – a sensation of floating high above his weeping family, like the cherubs painted on the high ceiling of his bedroom. Like them, he had no feelings; he was made of light and warmth and ideas. And then, on the fourth day, his spirit had returned to his broken body and he began his new life of pain.

His broken ribs and his cuts and bruises healed with time, though he would always bear a scar on his cheek. But his right leg was shattered and all the doctor's skill with splints and bandages couldn't restore his lightness of movement and his easy gait. It had taken him two years to walk as well as he did now with his sticks, and each step still cost him effort and pain. He leaned now on the parapet with his chin resting on his thin hand, remembering how anguished his parents had been. His mother had died of a fever a year ago, giving Falco a new pain to carry. His father still loved him, he knew that. But it was a love he could never fully accept; the boy felt so ashamed of his now ruined body.

Gaetano had been so racked with guilt that he could still scarcely bear to look at his brother. He couldn't help feeling that the accident would never have happened if he hadn't refused Falco's request. Falco didn't blame him; no one did. Falco knew that he had no one to blame but himself. He couldn't forgive himself for the death of the beautiful horse and he felt that his own injuries were deserved. Sometimes he told himself that the loss of Gaetano's easy companionship was one more punishment that he had to bear, but it was hard.

'I wonder where Gaetano is now?' he thought.

And as if by magic, a horseman suddenly appeared on the dusty road from Remora. Falco knew straightaway that it was Gaetano – no one else sat a horse like that. In the old days, he would have run down to the entrance to fling his arms round his brother. Now he couldn't, even if he wanted to. He stayed where he was, wondering what brought his brother here in such haste.

Georgia felt much better for her ride. She was no longer tired but exhilarated. She was young, fit and healthy and she was going to see Lucien again tonight; she could spend all Sunday in bed if necessary. Even

Russell's sneering face waiting for her at home couldn't affect her good mood.

As soon as she got back, she ran herself a very hot bath, with jojoba-scented bubbles. She could hear Russell grumbling away outside the bathroom door, but it was one of Maura's unbreakable rules that Georgia should have a hot soak after riding. She lay in the water till it grew cold, topping it up from the hot tap and daydreaming about Remora.

With a jolt, she realised she was drifting off to sleep. She hastily got out of the bath and towelled herself vigorously. She slipped her dressing-gown on top of her underwear and dropped the jodhpurs into the clothes hamper, extracting the winged horse from the pocket first. It was protected by bubble-wrap. Awkward as it had been to have it there during the ride, she would not let it out of her possession. Not with Russell on the loose.

Gaetano took the marble stairs two at a time. The servant at the door had told him where Falco was. He didn't hesitate. He ran to Falco and took him in his arms as he hadn't done for two years.

'Brother,' he gasped. 'I had to see you. Father wants me to get married!'

Falco was touched. This was like the old days, when the two brothers had confided everything to one another. He returned Gaetano's embrace affectionately, looking into his troubled face.

'Who is she?' he asked. 'You don't seem very happy about it.'

'Oh, as for that, I don't care,' said Gaetano, rather more bitterly than his words suggested. 'I never expected to have much say in the matter. But I had begun to think Father wanted me to enter the church.'

'And are you disappointed?' asked Falco, surprised.

'No, no,' said Gaetano, impatiently pacing the loggia. 'You don't understand. It's not just about me. It seems that Father has now decided that *you* are to be the next Pope in the family!'

Falco was stunned. His quick mind understood it all, even as his brother's had. He was no longer the beautiful youngest son, fit to bear a crown or marry into any of Talia's princely families. No woman could be expected to look at him. So he could be relegated to the church, whose priests did not marry. He would grow old, having known no female touch but that of his mother and sister. And by the time Uncle Ferdinando died, Falco would be an eligible cardinal. The election would be rigged and he would be Pope.

Falco loved his father, but he had no illusions about him. Niccolò would fix everything and, if he died before Ferdinando, he would have made sure that his successor Fabrizio would carry out his plan. Falco felt that his whole future was mapped out for him at the age of thirteen. There was a tiny part of his brain that didn't even mind. He could become a great scholar-priest, write treatises on philosophy, become an expert on fine wines. He could see it all. But he was only a boy, even if a very clever one, and he hadn't quite accepted that his active life was over.

Gaetano looked stricken. 'I can't let this happen to you. We have to think of another way. The person I'm supposed to marry is the new Duchessa of Bellezza.

She's only a girl – younger than me. Father showed me her portrait; she's very beautiful.'

'They always are in paintings, aren't they?' said Falco. 'Remember the story of the Princess Rosa Miranda?'

Gaetano smiled his great twisted smile. The story of the princess had been one of his best inventions. It had carried them through one whole summer, a long complicated tale of lovers betrayed and family feuds, with many exciting swordfights. It wrung Gaetano's heart to remember that time, when Falco had been equally happy springing from stair to stair as the Baron of Moresco or wrapped in an old blue velvet curtain pretending to be the beautiful princess.

'Listen,' said Gaetano. 'This Duchessa. Her father and regent is Rodolfo Rossi. He's a powerful magician. Father told me he's a Stravagante.'

Falco's eyes grew even huger. 'What's that?'

Gaetano hesitated. 'I don't know exactly. But I do know that Father and the others are really impressed by them. They know all sorts of secrets. There seems to be enmity between them and our family though. Father would never just ask for their help.'

'About what?' asked Falco.

'About you,' said Gaetano. 'If I go through with this and marry the girl, I'm going to ask her father to help you. I'm sure he has skills that can make you better. Then you wouldn't have to be Pope. You could do whatever you want.'

Falco's eyes filled with tears. Not because he thought the Stravagante of Bellezza could cure him. He didn't believe that for a moment. But because Gaetano was his friend again.

This time Georgia was expected in the stables of the Ram. A horse had been saddled for her. Cesare smiled at her. 'We're going to visit Merla,' he said. 'Shall I give you a leg up?'

'Riding by day and by night,' thought Georgia, nodding. 'I'll have muscles like Schwarzenegger!'

'Where's Luciano?' she asked, as Cesare mounted his own horse.

'He's going to meet us there,' he said.

The two of them walked their horses up the cobbled street to the Gate of the Ram and through it. They trotted alongside the city wall, passing the Gate of the Bull and that of the Twins, till they reached the broad road that led north from the Gate of the Sun. They quickened their pace as they passed the Twelfth of the Twins, but a shadow on horseback slipped out of the Twins' gate behind them and followed their path. Not right behind them of course; he let several carts and travellers pass between them. Enrico was much too skilled a spy to let himself be seen.

Chapter 7

A Harp Plays in Santa Fina

Santa Fina was a revelation to Georgia. She had thought that Remora, with its narrow cobbled streets and sudden sun-filled piazzas, was the most amazing place she had ever seen. But Santa Fina seemed to consist entirely of churches and towers.

The main church, on what Cesare told her was the market square, was built like a fortress, with a broad flight of steps up to the front door. The steps were never empty; priests, pilgrims and tourists were constantly going to or coming from the church. Georgia could tell that this little hill-town was older than the present city of Remora. 'Mediaeval' was the word that came into her mind, yet it didn't seem as ancient as that term suggested. 'It must be because I'm in the sixteenth century here,' she thought. 'So the

Middle Ages aren't so far back.'

'What are you thinking?' asked Cesare, as they stood in the market square, with the daily life of Santa Fina teeming around them.

'It's like a film set,' said Georgia. 'I can't believe it's real.'

'I don't know what that means,' said Cesare, a small knot forming on his brow. 'But I know what you mean about it not seeming real. People often feel that way about Santa Fina.'

They turned off up a side street and walked their horses through a maze of little alleys, finally emerging outside the town to the west, where there was a large complex of stables, much bigger and grander than the ones in the Twelfth of the Ram. Luciano was waiting for them in the yard. He looked a bit embarrassed.

'I came by carriage,' he said. 'I can't ride.'

He looked up at Georgia in admiration and she felt her colour begin to rise.

'It's easy,' she said quickly. 'I could teach you.'

Luciano backed away a little, looking alarmed. 'I don't think so,' he said. 'I don't really like horses. They scare me.'

Cesare laughed. Here at last was something he could do that the handsome young Stravagante could not. He jumped lightly down from his horse and led Georgia into the stables where he was quite at home. Roderigo, the Horsemaster of Santa Fina, was a large jolly man who welcomed the young people heartily and showed them where they could stable their horses. As soon as the animals were installed and given food and water, Roderigo took Cesare and Georgia and Luciano round to the back of his premises. It was clear that he thought all three of them were young men, and he was much amused by Luciano's lack of experience with horses.

'We have one here that wouldn't frighten you, hey Cesare?' he said, clapping Luciano on the shoulder. 'Give her a few more weeks and she could carry you anywhere. You wouldn't need to worry about clearing walls or fences. Then you could progress to a more ordinary mount. A young man like you needs a horse. How else are you to ride behind the carriage of your lady-love? Or fetch her treasures from distant cities?'

'I live in Bellezza,' said Luciano. 'We don't have horses there.'

'Oh, that explains everything,' said Roderigo. 'To come to Remora from the City of Masks is a bit like going to sea for a farm boy. It just takes a while for you to find your new legs. We'll get you up and riding before we send you back.'

They passed a farmhouse, where Roderigo obviously lived, and went round behind it to what looked like an old barn. One of Roderigo's grooms sat outside on a bale of hay, whittling at a piece of wood with his knife.

'All right, Diego?' said Roderigo as they passed inside.

'Yes, all quiet,' said the groom. He was clearly guarding something and, like all guards, was bored by his duty.

It was dark and dusty inside the barn. A horse whinnied from the shadows at the back. Georgia went towards it. As her eyes became adjusted to the gloom she could just make out a beautiful pale grey mare.

'Hello, Starlight,' said Cesare affectionately, and the

mare tossed her head in recognition.

'She's gorgeous,' said Georgia, who had not really taken much notice of the mother the night she saw the winged foal. Even Luciano could see this was a fine animal.

'But wait till you see her foal,' said Roderigo proudly. 'Come on, girl. You can trust us.'

It seemed to Georgia as if the mare hesitated a little, looking carefully at her and Luciano, as if checking they were friends. But she obviously felt at home with Cesare and Roderigo. She moved aside a little and Georgia gasped. Both she and Luciano knew what they had come to see, but the sight was still stupefying, even though for Georgia it was for the second time. Luciano could not believe his own eyes and stood spellbound.

The black filly was perfectly made, with the blurred outline of a young animal still growing. But there on her back lay folded a pair of glossy black wings, something known only in legend. Even Cesare was impressed all over again.

'How she's grown!' he exclaimed. 'Father was right. He said these winged ones grow faster than ordinary horses.'

The wings had grown in perfect proportion. Their feathers were less downy than they had been at birth and, as they watched her, Merla lifted and stretched them as naturally as she arched her neck. It was an awesome sight.

'How long before she can fly?' asked Cesare.

'Soon now,' said Roderigo. 'But we can only take her out at night. We can't risk her being seen.'

'I'm taking you out,' said Gaetano. 'You have been shut up in the palazzo for too long.'

'But how?' asked Falco. 'I can't ride.'

He limped away a few steps so that his brother shouldn't see his expression.

'You can sit in front of me,' said Gaetano gently. 'Surely you wouldn't mind that? We could go down into town and I could buy us some granita.'

Falco suddenly felt an urge to see something outside the great palace. His hopes, as crushed as his body had been by the accident, were reviving, in spite of himself. Perhaps one day he would lead a nearly normal life again? At least he could make a start by going out with his big brother.

'All right,' he said, and was rewarded by one of Gaetano's huge crooked smiles.

*

Enrico let his horse saunter along the side streets of Santa Fina. He had seen where the young men from the Ram had turned off and he had no doubt that it would be easy enough to track them down. His restless brain was only half involved with today's task. His work for the Pope involved spying on the Twins' rivals and he had decided to start with the Ram, but he wasn't expecting any quick result.

Enrico was thorough. After the Rams, who were the Twins' enemy because of the rivalry between the cities of Remora and Bellezza, he would investigate the Twelfth of the Bull, who were traditional adversaries of the Twins. And then he would see what he could find out in the stables of the Scales, who were traditionally at daggers drawn with the Lady. And of course he would keep his eyes open in the Twelfth of the Lady itself. He might be in the pay of Pope and Duke, but there were always possibilities of further employment when you were a spy and Enrico was quite accustomed to serving several masters.

He was in his element in Remora. Like his old master, Rinaldo, he had disliked being in a city without horses. And he resented the place that had taken away his fiancée. But there was more to it than that. He liked the way that this whole city revolved around ancient antagonisms and alliances. And he appreciated the skill involved in rigging the great annual race. That was the sort of thing Enrico himself was good at.

He found himself outside the town and looking at a large stableyard. 'Interesting,' thought Enrico. 'I think my horse needs a rest.'

*

Georgia and the two boys left the stables in a daze. They were going to explore the town and come back for the horses later. Georgia was silent, thinking about what she had seen, and found herself back in the square with the huge church before she knew it.

Now she could see that Luciano was as intrigued by Santa Fina as she had been. His carriage from Remora had skirted the town, not being able to negotiate the narrow streets, and so he had missed the extraordinary square. Even though he was a Talian now, he couldn't help seeing Santa Fina through twenty-first-century eyes. Having Georgia with him intensified it. He was now seeing Talia from the viewpoint of a new Stravagante, just as he had nearly a year ago.

'What do you think?' asked Georgia.

'It reminds me of Montemurato,' said Luciano. 'The place where I first met Doctor Dethridge. That has lots of towers too, though those are round the edge. He was working in a stable there.'

There was so much that Georgia didn't know about Lucien's new life. She wanted to ask him about every aspect of it, but she felt shy in front of Cesare.

'You should see inside the church,' said Cesare now. 'It's famous for its paintings.'

The three young people climbed the steep steps up to the undecorated façade of the church. They passed out of the brilliant sunshine into a darkness as deep as that of Roderigo's barn. But this darkness was cold, not warm and friendly with the smell of horses. The smell here was of incense and the church was dimly lit at the altar end with large candles.

Once their eyes had adjusted, they could see that the walls were covered with paintings. Georgia could make out scenes from the life of Christ. But suddenly she spotted a side chapel with other subjects on the wall – Leda and the Swan, Andromeda and the sea-serpent – and there was Pegasus, flying through the painted clouds. She pointed him out to Cesare and Luciano.

On the floor was a circular marble inlay that was a bit like the Campo delle Stelle. It showed all the signs of the zodiac round the edge and was divided up like the great Piazza, except that it didn't show the Sun and Moon segments. It would have been quite out of place in a church in England, thought Georgia, but it seemed natural in Santa Fina.

They were all very quiet in the church, a bit overawed by the atmosphere. But they eventually came out into some cool cloisters, surrounding a grassy square with a fountain in the middle. And from beyond the cloisters, Georgia could distinctly hear the sound of a harp.

*

The journey wasn't as bad as Falco had feared. He let Gaetano lift him in his strong arms and place him in front of the saddle, where he clung on to the horse's mane. His right leg dangled uselessly, but his left knee came up and instinctively pressed against the horse's flank. Falco buried his face in the coarse hair of the mane and inhaled; it was good to be on horseback again. Gaetano was soon up behind him, passing his arms around Falco's waist to hold the reins. He had bound his brother's sticks behind the saddle.

And so they travelled, slowly, into the town of Santa Fina. It was filled with life: stallholders called out their wares in the market square, customers haggled loudly, dogs barked, birds wheeled round the many towers, the sound of chanting came from the big church.

They made their way round the edge of the square and out through an arch on the other side. They were heading for a place that had been a favourite haunt of theirs in years gone by, a tiny shop behind the church, where a woman known as La Mandragola made exquisite granita. Gaetano dismounted and tied his horse to an iron ring in the wall. Then he helped Falco slide off the horse's neck and propped him up until his sticks were restored to him.

As they sat on chairs outside the ice shop, spooning up the cold crystals of frozen apricot and melon, the notes of a harp tumbled and splashed through the warm still air. 'I must be in heaven,' Falco said to his brother. 'I can hear angels.'

*

Enrico soon made himself at home in Roderigo's stables. His eyes darted everywhere. He had easily identified the mounts of his quarries and spotted the two carriage horses with the Bellezzan rosettes on their harnesses hanging up in the stall. His easy ways and familiarity with horses ensured that the grooms were friendly to him. But it was when one of them left and another appeared from round the back of the farmhouse that Enrico's sixth sense kicked in.

'That looks like a change of watch,' he thought, even as he exchanged banter with two other grooms, and he went out of his way to be cordial to the newcomer, whose name was Diego.

'You look as if you've had a hard morning,' he said eventually. 'Let me buy you a drink.'

*

In a little square behind the church cloisters a young man sat playing a harp. He had straight black hair falling below his shoulders and an expression of intense concentration. He played without reference to any written notes and a small crowd had gathered around him, drawn by the purity of the melody. A young woman stood at his shoulder and, as soon as the last cascade of notes had reverberated to an end and the applause began, she moved briskly among the listeners, holding an old green velvet hat, which soon grew heavy with silver.

Three young men on the edge of the crowd, all wearing the red and yellow colours of the Reman Ram, dug into their pockets. On the other side of the square, two others, more richly dressed, who had only just arrived, asked the woman if the harpist would play again. The younger of those two had a twisted leg and leaned heavily on two sticks.

She went and bent over the young man, who sat with his eyes closed, oblivious of the people gathered around him.

'Aurelio,' she whispered. 'Will you play some more? There is an injured boy who wants to hear you.'

The young man nodded, opened his eyes and put his hands back on the strings. Everyone in the square fell silent, even the two men drinking outside a bar in the far corner.

Aurelio paused a moment and then played an even more beautiful piece of music. All the listeners in the square were entranced. For Cesare it stirred visions of riding Arcangelo to victory, carrying the banner of the Stellata to the cheers of his Twelfth. For Luciano the music brought back memories of his mother and long evenings of his childhood. For Georgia, it told hauntingly of unrequited love and lost idylls.

For Gaetano, it conjured up a vision of female beauty – an amalgam of the cousin Francesca he remembered and the Bellezzan Duchessa he imagined. For Falco, it was as if he really had been transported to a higher existence. It was a day he would remember for the rest of his life. His brother had returned to him, he had ridden a horse again, tasted anew La Mandragola's granita and now he was listening to the sounds of heaven. After two years his life had begun again.

Even Enrico was not unmoved. 'It reminds me of my Giuliana,' he whispered to Diego, wiping his eyes with his sleeve. 'Lost to me for ever.' Even Diego felt sentimental. He had no girlfriend, but if he had, he would have been thinking of her now.

The spell lasted a full minute after Aurelio had stopped playing. This time the hat was even more full of coins. Gaetano spoke to the young woman, who brought him over to the harpist, now sitting very still with his arms hanging at his sides. The majority of the crowd, seeing that there was to be no more music, started to drift away.

But the three of the Ram stayed as if mesmerised.

'That was sublime,' said Gaetano. 'I hope you'll come and play for my uncle.' He took a seal-ring from his finger and gave it to the silent musician. 'Present this at the Papal palace in Remora at any time and I shall have you and your companion treated like royalty.'

Cesare clutched Luciano's arm. 'di Chimici,' he hissed. The spell was broken.

'Or if you prefer, come to the Duke's palace in Giglia in the summer,' Gaetano was saying. 'He is my father and he could make your reputation.'

'Perhaps you would like to come to Bellezza instead,' said Luciano, stepping forward. Georgia was surprised. He was now no longer the dreamy-eyed boy she knew, but a wealthy courtier, prepared to go head to head with one of the sinister di Chimici.

'The Duchessa would love to hear your music, I know,' Luciano continued. 'I am apprenticed to her Regent and father, Senator Rossi, and I am sure that he would approve of my invitation.'

The harpist got to his feet and the young woman took the ring from him. He was very tall.

'I thank you both,' he said to Gaetano and Luciano. 'But I play for no one but myself. I do not care about reputation or money.'

Cesare looked pointedly at the velvet hat, but the glance was lost on Aurelio. As he turned his face indiscriminately towards them, they understood that his dark blue eyes were unseeing. He put out his hand to the young woman, who prepared to lead him from the square. She had intercepted Cesare's glance and now put her finger to her lips.

Georgia understood in an instant that Aurelio did not know about the collection and that the young woman – his sister? his girlfriend? – did not want him to know.

'Don't go,' said Gaetano. 'I didn't mean to offend you. Will you come back with us to our palazzo to take some refreshment, at least?'

Aurelio was silent, but turned his head to the young woman as if waiting to see what she thought.

'There are places nearer at hand for refreshment,' said Luciano firmly. 'I should be honoured if you would be my guests.' He didn't know why he was so drawn to this musician but he wasn't going to stand by and see him carried off by the di Chimici.

Luciano and Gaetano stood glaring at each other beside the blind musician and his helper. Falco had come hobbling over to them. With Georgia and Cesare, the young people now made quite a knot in the middle of the square.

'I should be glad of food and drink, Raffaella,' said Aurelio.

Raffaella had transferred the silver and the di Chimici seal-ring to a purse at her waist and now put the hat in Aurelio's hand.

'Then let one of these kind gentlemen buy it for you,' she said.

'I should be happier if they both did so,' said Aurelio. 'When two contenders are balked of the same prize, they may become friends.' He crushed the velvet hat on to his black hair, oblivious of the effect his words had created.

'Now there's something you see only when a Pope dies,' said Enrico to his new friend. 'Once in a blue moon.'

'What?' asked Diego.

'Three Rams and two of the Lady going off together,' said Enrico. 'Though to be honest, they don't look very happy about it!'

'That'll be the music,' said Diego. 'But the Ram and the Lady aren't adversaries are they?'

Enrico snorted. 'It's obvious you don't live down in the city! Fish and Scales may be their official enemies but Bellezza and the Lady don't mix and that lot are Bellezza. The curly-haired fellow I've seen in the city myself – a great favourite of the new Duchessa he is.'

'Well,' said Diego, not to be outdone, 'the Lady's men are di Chimici – sons of the great Duke himself!'

He was rewarded by a start from Enrico.

'Really?' he said quickly, recovering himself. 'What a coincidence! I'm working for the Duke myself. Which of the young princes are they?'

'These two aren't real princes, or likely to be,' said Diego. 'At least, not ones with Princedoms. Theirs are courtesy titles only. Gaetano is a scholar at the university in Giglia and poor little Falco – well, who knows what he'll be now? Two years ago and he could have been anything.'

'Is that the kid with the sticks?' asked Enrico. 'What happened to him? Listen, why don't I order some more drinks?'

One of Enrico's great skills as a spy was knowing when to stop trailing his quarry and settle down to collect information he could use later.

If he could have seen the party in the tavern by the town museum, he would have been sure that he had made the right decision. No one was saying anything. Luciano and Gaetano had vied with each other to order food and drink for the group and now there was silence while they waited for it to be brought. Aurelio sat calmly in their midst, his harp now wrapped up in a sack and propped against a wall. He was apparently unaware of the tensions around him.

'I should like to know who my hosts are,' he said. 'Not their positions in society,' he added. 'Just the names.'

Gaetano felt foolish. 'Of course,' he said. 'I am Gaetano di Chimici and here is also my younger brother Falco.'

Aurelio turned his face towards where the boy was sitting.

'You are the injured one,' he said quietly.

'And I am Luciano Crinamorte,' broke in Luciano. 'I am with my friends Cesare and Giorgio.' He stumbled a bit over Giorgio's name but managed to say it in the boy's way.

'I am Aurelio Vivoide,' said the musician, 'and this is Raffaella. We are Manoush.'

Everyone looked blank. But Aurelio did not expand. He seemed content to sit and wait for his meal. Then Gaetano seemed to make a decision. He turned to Luciano and said, 'Did I hear you say you worked for Senator Rossi? Is it true he's a Stravagante?'

Georgia couldn't help herself; she was tired of being ignored.

'You don't have to go all the way to Bellezza to find one,' she said. 'I'm a Stravagante myself.'

Chapter 8

The Manoush

'Georgia!' cried Luciano, forgetting she was supposed to be a boy, he was so horrified by her careless revelation.

'That word should not be used lightly,' said Aurelio. 'Or spoken at all except in private, between trusted friends. You don't know me. If what you say is true, I could be a great danger to you. And so could these young men.'

It was true. Georgia knew she had been more than careless. Who knew what danger she might have brought to Luciano and his friends? She was quite miserable. But help came from an unexpected quarter.

'Don't be too hard on him,' said Gaetano, who obviously hadn't noticed Luciano's slip. 'I know that my family have some sort of a feud with the ... with those you named. But I'm not interested in that. My father hasn't told me anything about it – I'm not important enough for politics. The only reason I want to meet a ... a you-know-what, is to see if they can do anything for my brother.'

It crossed Luciano's mind that Gaetano might be OK, even though he was a di Chimici. He believed what the young noble had just said; he was obviously very fond of his younger brother. And Falco was an attractive boy, intelligent looking and clearly very unhappy. Luciano understood the downside of living in the sixteenth century. Even a family as wealthy as the di Chimici couldn't heal a darling son if he had been hurt as badly as Falco seemed to have been. And Luciano knew how it felt to be incurable.

At that moment serving-men came out with laden trays. Everyone was hungry and there was no more discussion, except for what was needed in sharing a meal. And, strangely enough, by the time their appetites had been satisfied, the animosity seemed to have evaporated. But Georgia was still uneasy about her gaffe.

'Tell us about the Manoush,' she said to Aurelio. 'You're quite right; I don't know anything about you. There's lots I don't know about Talia.'

'We are not Talian, for a start,' said Aurelio.

Raffaella nodded. She looked quite a lot like the harpist. She was tall, with the same long black hair, except that hers was elaborately braided and intertwined with coloured ribbons. They both wore long, flowing clothes, patched but embroidered with silks that had once been bright. Raffaella's even had little mirrors stitched round the hem and on the sleeves. They were slightly darker skinned than Cesare and the di Chimici and their floating scarves and embroidered over-tunics gave them an exotic air. Georgia hadn't noticed at first because all Talians seemed exotic to her, but there was something different about Aurelio and Raffaella.

'We come from the East,' said the woman. 'But we have no country. We are wanderers from place to place. In that we are similar to those we have agreed not to name.'

'Are there many of you?' asked Falco.

'Many,' said Aurelio. 'As many as there are grains of sand on the shore.'

'But there are not so many of us in Talia,' added Raffaella. 'We are on our way to the City of Stars. There will be more of us coming over the next weeks.'

'It is a place of pilgrimage for us,' said Aurelio. 'It celebrates the life of our goddess, even though it doesn't know that is what it does.'

'I know who you are now!' exclaimed Cesare. 'Zinti, we call you, the travelling people. You come for the Stellata – I've seen you there.'

'We are not interested in your horse race,' said Aurelio, though he didn't say it rudely. 'It just happens to coincide with our older festival. Yours is not the only city to celebrate the day, but some of us prefer it to other cities. It feels right to us.'

He turned his face in Georgia's direction. 'You need not worry. We do not concern ourselves in the politics of Talia or any other country. Having no land of our own, we are not interested in disputes over who rules patches of earth – even those with great cities built on them. But as wanderers, we are interested in other travellers, from wherever and whichever time they come. We meet many people on our journeys and we strive to learn from them. The last place we were in, Raffaella and I were befriended by one of the same order that Signor Gaetano was mentioning. That city was Bellona and the man was wise and learned.'

'Exactly,' said Gaetano. 'That's what I've heard. But I was brought up to believe that they are powerful and dangerous and that they hold the key to some important mystery that could help Talia but that they refuse to use it for the common good.'

Luciano made as if to interrupt, but Gaetano gestured to him to wait.

'I know, I know. I no longer believe that to be true.' He turned to Falco. 'It pains me to say it, but I think that Father put that idea about so that he could get hold of whatever secret it is. And I don't think that he plans to use it to help the people of Talia.'

There was silence around the table. Luciano's opinion of the young di Chimici had gone up. He could imagine how difficult it was for Gaetano to admit his suspicions. Falco was struggling with his own feelings; he loved his father but he knew how dominating Niccolò could be. Had he not just heard that his own fate was to be arranged by the Duke without any reference to Falco's own wishes?

Cesare's emotions were also complicated. It was hard being both Remoran and a Ram; all such citizens had the problem of divided loyalties. Being traditionally connected with Bellezza, the Rams distrusted the di Chimici. But this was the first time he had ever encountered any of them. Stable boys, even the sons of honoured Horsemasters, did not normally socialise with the children of Dukes.

Georgia felt thoroughly out of her depth. She barely knew who the di Chimici were or why they were at odds with the Stravaganti. And she couldn't decide what to make of the mysterious Manoush. Aurelio said they didn't take sides, but could that be possible? Everyone in Remora seemed so sure where they belonged and where their loyalties lay.

'Believe me,' Gaetano continued, 'I am not trying to find out anything that will help my family with any plot. The only thing I want to know is – will Senator Rossi's secret help my brother?'

Luciano's mind went back to his first meeting with Rodolfo on his roof garden in Bellezza. 'The di Chimici want to help only the di Chimici,' the Stravagante had said. They had been talking about the ruling family of northern Talia wanting to use the art of stravagation to learn the secrets of modern medicine and modern warfare. Then it had seemed so much more sinister than it did now that he heard this earnest young man wanting a cure for his brother.

'I can't talk about Rodolfo's secrets,' said Luciano. 'You can't expect me to. But he is one of the cleverest and most powerful people I know, and he will be here in a few weeks. I'm sure you know that the Duchessa has been invited to the Stellata – she and her Regent will soon be here. My foster-father and I came from Bellezza to visit the Twelfth of the Ram, to make sure that they would be safe in the city of Remora. You will forgive me for reminding you that the Duchessa's mother was assassinated in her own city, so we have to be very careful of her coming to somewhere ruled by ... by her adversaries.'

Gaetano restrained himself; he needed this arrogant young Bellezzan's help. 'I'm sure her Grace will be as safe here as anywhere in Talia,' he said stiffly. 'And we are not her adversaries. We have no knowledge of her mother's assassination and were as shocked by it as the rest of the country. Indeed, my father is sending me to escort her here and I can assure you that I shall pay every attention to her security and comfort.'

This was news to Luciano, and he wasn't sure that he liked it. He believed Gaetano when he said that he knew nothing about the assassination, but he wondered how this ugly but likeable young man would react if he knew that the Duchessa had not been killed at all, that she was in fact living comfortably in Padavia, keeping an eye on her daughter, and her city, from a safe distance.

But all he said was, 'Then you will meet my master yourself. You can talk to him about your brother directly.'

Gaetano was not so easily satisfied. He looked at Georgia. 'What about you?' he said. 'If you are what you say you are, and not just boasting, perhaps there is something you can tell us?'

*

In a courtyard of a comfortable house on the outskirts of Padavia sat a well-dressed and striking middle-aged woman. Her green satin dress was cut full in the Bellezzan style and her hair was elaborately coiffed. She fingered a string of rubies round her neck as she waited for her visitor.

A tall red-haired manservant showed another woman out into the courtyard garden. She was a little older than the first and much plumper, but also looked prosperous. The two women embraced like old friends, although they had known each other little more than a year.

'Silvia!' said the visitor. 'You look as lovely and as young as ever.'

The other woman laughed. 'That was always my speciality, if you remember. But I have to achieve it on my own here. Guido, tell Susanna to bring refreshment out here please.'

They sat at a stone table under a vine. The flower-filled courtyard was quiet, with an air of sanctuary. Both women were aware of it. They had lived through dangerous and exciting times in Bellezza and now Silvia was safe. But was she a survivor or an exile? Her visitor voiced the thought.

'Doesn't it ever get dull for you here?'

'What can you possibly mean, Leonora?' said Silvia, mockingly. 'I have my embroidery and my good works and a vegetable garden to oversee. I'm even thinking of buying an olive farm – didn't Rodolfo tell you? I am always busy.'

Her friend was saved from answering by the arrival of the maid Susanna, with a tray of iced lemonade and cakes. The manservant, Guido, followed and remained positioned near the gate. It was obvious that he never left his mistress's side for long.

The two women were quite comfortable talking in front of the servants. Susanna had served her mistress for many years and as for Guido, though he had first encountered Silvia with the intention of killing her, he was now her devoted slave. She had used her own money to care for his sick father even though Guido had been employed to assassinate her. The old man had died a month ago, peacefully in his sleep, but he had not lacked for doctors or comfort in the last year of his life.

'What news from the city?' asked Silvia. 'How does the new Duchessa do?'

'She is a credit to you both,' said Leonora. 'And to me, though I am only an honorary aunt to her.'

Silvia nodded, satisfied. 'And your husband, the good Doctor?'

'He is well, as far as I know. But off on his travels at the moment, with Luciano. What a dear boy that is!'

'And what a comfort to you to have a child to love, so late in your days,' said Silvia. She spoke from the heart, her own child having been lost to her for more than fifteen years and only lately restored.

'I know we cannot replace his real parents,' said Leonora quietly. 'And he grieves for them so much. But we love him. I do hope he will be safe in Remora,' she added anxiously.

'I'm sure he will,' said Silvia. 'And he will make sure all is safe for Arianna too. Do you intend to join them for the race?'

'No, I . . .' Leonora stopped, seeing the sparkle in her friend's eye. 'Silvia! You can't be thinking of ... It's much too dangerous.'

'Why?' asked Silvia. 'There will be four Stravaganti there to protect me – not to mention Guido.'

'But the city will be swarming with di Chimici,' protested Leonora. 'You are bound to be recognised!'

'I don't see why,' said Silvia, getting to her feet and

walking restlessly up and down the terrace. 'No one ever recognises me without my mask. You know how often I have been in Bellezza in the last few months. And if they don't know me there, how much less will they in Remora?'

'The ambassador would, I'm sure,' said Leonora. 'And the Duke.'

'Then I must just keep out of the way of the Duke and the ambassador, mustn't I?' was all that Silvia would say.

*

In a room at the top of a tall palazzo overlooking the canal a man dressed in black was looking into a mirror. But not from vanity. It was not his own lined face and silvered black hair that he saw gazing back at him. It was the much older face and whiter hair of his old friend and master, William Dethridge.

'Gretynges, Maister Rudolphe!' said Dethridge. 'I am righte gladde to know that yore lookinge-glasse workes well here in Remora.'

'I have not been here the last two days,' said Rodolfo. 'It is a relief to know that you are safe. And the boy?'

'Lykewyse,' said the Elizabethan. 'Bot I have mor to telle.'

Rodolfo settled down in his chair to listen.

'The newe Stravayger has arrived,' said Dethridge. 'And yt is a mayde.'

'A girl?' asked Rodolfo. 'And she has come to Signor Paolo?'

'Aye. Thrice now. She is this daye with his sonne,

Cesare, in the toune of Saint Fyne. Master Lucian has gone with them.'

'Is she safe? Does she understand the dangers? What is her name?'

'Shee is as saufe as can bee in this nest of vipers,' said Dethridge, lowering his voice. 'Young Caesar and Lucian are teching hir whatte they canne about the perils. Hire name is George, or sum sich. The boy knows hir from before.'

'And what does Paolo say about the city?' asked Rodolfo. 'Does he think Arianna should accept the invitation to the race?'

'Hee says it wolde be a slighte for hir not to come – that the Chimici wolde use it as an excuse to move againste hire.'

'What is your thought?' asked Rodolfo.

'Wee have notte hadde much tyme for oure investigaytiounes as yet,' said Dethridge. 'Give us a little longire and then I will avise ye.'

'All right,' said Rodolfo. 'But I must soon send word to the Duke. I wish I were there in Remora with you. I should like to meet the girl.'

'Shee lookyth mor lyke unto a ladde, I sholde tell ye,' added Dethridge. 'A ladde who loves horsis.'

*

The party in Santa Fina was reluctant to split up. Gaetano wanted the Manoush to come back to his uncle's palace, Luciano wanted to take them back to Paolo's and Falco wanted to leave the empty summer palace and follow his brother and the strangers to the city.

'We do not sleep in houses, thank you,' said Aurelio. 'Manoush sleep under the sky. But if you will go with us to collect our bedrolls, we shall travel with you to the city. It is our destination too. And if we can camp in one of your courtyards, whether of the Ram or the Pope, that will suffice us.'

Georgia wondered if Raffaella was quite as keen on all this 'the Manoush do not do' so and so business as her companion. She remembered how the tall girl had silently pocketed all the money from Aurelio's recital and thought that she was probably the more practical of the two. Luciano and Gaetano were now involved in fierce negotiation about who should go where and by what means.

Georgia yawned. It was hard to believe that her other self was asleep in her bed in the world she had come from. Thank goodness she always kept her door locked. Maura hated it but Ralph had said, 'She's a teenager. Can't you remember what that was like?' and had arranged to have the lock put in.

In the end they all agreed to meet at Roderigo's stables in an hour. Gaetano would take Falco back to the palace to collect some clothing and tell the servants he was going to visit his uncle at the Papal palace. He would bring his brother to the stables where he would be transferred into Luciano's carriage, to make the journey into the city more comfortable for him. Gaetano would ride ahead to Remora to settle things with his uncle.

The Manoush would also travel with Luciano, much to Georgia's surprise. She thought that anything involving comfort might be something they 'didn't do' but Aurelio had accepted the offer easily. It appeared that anything which assisted travel was allowed, although they usually journeyed on foot.

*

The longer that Arianna was Duchessa, the more her respect for her mother increased. It was hard work. First there was the tedium of having to be dressed by servants and changing clothes several times a day. When she had been an ordinary girl living on the lagoon island of Torrone, she had not changed dresses as often in a month as she now had to do every day.

Now she had to submit to complicated underwear, with more laces and fastenings than she had ever seen, and even more complicated hairdressing, involving pins and often flowers or jewels. As the day wore on, the dresses, the hairstyles and the masks became more elaborate and luxurious. The masks in particular were irksome to Arianna, but since she was now sixteen, she would have had to wear them even if she had not been Duchessa of a great city.

The freedom of movement she had enjoyed as an island girl was gone for ever. As a result, she grew into the role. Her stride was shortened by the stiff petticoat and heavy dresses and there was no question of slouching in her tightly laced corsets. So the young Duchessa gained a reputation for grace and dignity as well as beauty, which would have greatly surprised those who had known her in her hoyden days.

While she was growing accustomed to the restriction of movement, Arianna also had to learn diplomacy and a lot more about politics, domestic and foreign, than she had ever wanted to know. Rodolfo was a demanding teacher. No matter that he was a fond father, whose life had changed with the recent knowledge that he had a daughter. He was also Regent of Bellezza and it was his solemn responsibility to make sure that Arianna was up to the job she had undertaken.

It was also part of the deal. Arianna had agreed to stand for election as Duchessa after a lot of thought and discussion with her first family. She had thought that she knew what she was in for. But many times over the last few months she wondered if she would have agreed if she had fully appreciated what being Duchessa would mean.

She understood her mother a lot better now. She could imagine how she might have grown weary of the endless presiding over Council and Senate meetings, listening to individual petitioners at her monthly People's audience. How she might have wished to escape from her many public appearances by using a substitute. But this was one thing Arianna had resolved never to do.

Two months ago she had gone through her first Marriage with the Sea, allowing herself to be lowered into the filthy water of the canal, till it lapped at her thighs and the people all cried out 'Sposati!' – 'They are married!' The celebrations had gone on all night. Bellezza was well and truly out of mourning for its last Duchessa and completely enchanted by the new one, who had just ensured the city's prosperity for another year. And all the time Arianna was thinking about the Marriage of the year before, which she had watched from her brothers' fishing boat.

Then, she had plotted to become one of the city's

mandoliers and had spent the night crouching on the loggia of the great silver basilica of the Maddalena. This year, she had appeared on that same loggia, standing between the two pairs of bronze rams, waving to her people down in the Piazza, before returning to her palazzo next door for a fine wedding feast.

Last year Arianna had found Luciano standing in that Piazza, looking dazed and lost. This year he had sat at her side, dressed in velvet and silver. Last year she had thought her parents were a simple museum curator and a comfortable housewife. This time she knew they were the previous Duchessa and the present Regent, sitting on her other side, guiding her through the formalities of the occasion.

Today she had visited a school for orphan girls, received petitions from citizens with problems ranging from a dispute over a consignment of flour to a marriage contract between cousins, she had dined with a visiting prince from eastern Europa and received an embassy from Anglia on the subject of a trade agreement. She had also held a meeting with the admiral of Bellezza's fleet, who suspected that aggression was building up in the countries bordering the lagoon's eastern shores.

It was now time to be undressed by her women and allowed to sink into her comfortable bed. Her personal maid, Barbara, was brushing her hair when there was a knock on the door. It was Rodolfo.

'I'm sorry to trouble you, my dear, but we have not had a moment to talk all day. Are you too tired to stay up a little longer?'

'Of course not,' said Arianna, dismissing her maid.

It was always a relief to be on her own with her father and away from the cares of state.

He sat on one of the little tapestry-covered chairs which had belonged to Arianna's mother Silvia, the last Duchessa. Rodolfo used to visit her in her chamber by means of a secret passage from his own palazzo, which was next door to hers. Now that route was even more of a secret, but not closed up. It could be useful again in an emergency. Both he and Arianna were always aware that Silvia had supposedly been assassinated, and the fact that she was alive and well and living in Padavia was neither here nor there. A woman had died in that explosion, and danger surrounded any Duchessa.

'I have two pieces of news,' said Rodolfo, as Arianna continued to brush her hair herself.

'Good,' she said. 'Is one about Luciano?'

'It is indeed,' said her father, smiling. 'Doctor Dethridge contacted me today by means of my mirrors. They are both safely arrived in Remora and already having adventures.'

'Adventures?' said Arianna longingly. Then her face clouded. 'But they aren't in any danger, are they?'

'No more so than any of us would be in a stronghold of the di Chimici,' said Rodolfo. 'And that brings me to my other piece of news, which I think you will be less happy to hear. I received an embassy today from Duke Niccolò.'

'Oh, about the Stellata, I suppose,' said Arianna. They had stalled on replying to the Pope's invitation to watch the race, until Luciano and Dethridge had checked on the safety of accepting.

'Not this time, my dear,' said Rodolfo. 'The purpose

of this embassy was to seek your hand in marriage with the Duke's son. Apparently Gaetano di Chimici would like to marry you.'

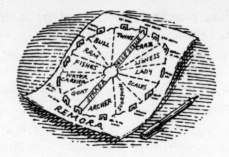

Chapter 9

Written in the Stars

They had spent a long time in Santa Fina, and by the time they got to Remora it would be getting late. Georgia knew she must go home in less than an hour. She and Cesare were to ride with Gaetano, even though they saw Luciano was not too happy about it. He knew what the di Chimici were capable of and, although he was beginning to like the two brothers, he thought it was too early to trust them. They didn't yet know that he and Dethridge and the Horsemaster were Stravaganti too, but Gaetano was unlikely to forget Georgia's outburst and would certainly pump her for information.

Before the party broke up at the stables, Luciano took Cesare aside.

'Be careful,' he said. 'And if he brings the

conversation around to the Stravaganti again, don't let Georgia give anything else away.'

Cesare nodded. He was not about to put his father in danger.

'I know the di Chimici,' he said. 'Trust me.'

The three riders made good time along the road to Remora. Each was at home on horseback and enjoyed the physical sensation of the exercise. There was no opportunity to talk until they slowed outside the Gate of the Sun, waiting their turn to enter the city through its busy portal. Gaetano manoeuvred his horse next to Georgia's.

'I should like to visit you tomorrow. You are staying in the Twelfth of the Ram?'

Georgia had learned her lesson and turned to Cesare as if to ask his advice. He shrugged. The young noble would be coming to see the Manoush anyway – that had already been arranged. And Georgia could decide not to be there. But she couldn't avoid him for ever, not if she wanted to keep coming to the city. And it would seem as if that was what she was meant to do.

'Yes,' she said, after a pause. 'You can find me and Luciano at the Horsemaster's house. But I don't think I can do anything to help you.'

'Believe me,' said Gaetano, leaning closer so that Cesare couldn't overhear. 'I'm not interested in the secrets of your brotherhood. I want to help my brother. That is all.'

*

'He's very ugly, isn't he?' said Arianna much more

calmly than she felt. She was looking at the miniature of Gaetano di Chimici which had been brought from Remora by the envoy. 'And he must be even worse than he looks here,' she added. 'The court painter must have tried to make the best of him.'

Rodolfo looked at her. 'We are not seriously entertaining this proposal,' he said.

'But what are we going to do about it?' asked Arianna. 'We can't just ignore it and we can't offend them by a flat refusal.'

'Now you are thinking like a Duchessa,' said Rodolfo, smiling. 'It is a tight corner, but we will get out of it. They are sending him here, to escort you to the Stellata.'

Arianna's eyes widened.

'They want you to have the opportunity to get to know one another,' said Rodolfo, 'and you must take it.'

*

Duke Niccolò was pleased to see his youngest son and happy to see the two brothers back in accord. His two older boys and his daughter were in Giglia and Niccolò loved his children. He was feeling particularly pleased with Gaetano, who had raised no objections to the marriage scheme with Bellezza, and now he had brought him his heart's darling. Niccolò had hoped that Falco would come with him to the Papal palace when they left Giglia but, perhaps because of the awkwardness with Gaetano or perhaps because of his love for its great lonely expanses, the younger boy had insisted on being left at Santa Fina.

Of course, Niccolò could have overridden Falco's wishes; he was only a boy. But ever since the accident, the Duke had been so eaten up by grief that he could not deny the boy anything that might give him pleasure. And now here he was, by choice, reconciled to his brother and smiling. Niccolò felt as if a long winter was drawing to an end, even though the spring could bring no real hope of an improvement to Falco's condition.

'You must hear Aurelio, Father,' Gaetano was saying. 'I tried to persuade him to come here, but he said he doesn't play for money. I'm sure he will play though, and you must hear it. It will make you feel as if you are in heaven.'

'Yes, Father, do try to hear it,' said Falco, his delicate face flushed with pleasure at the memory. 'He does play like an angel.'

'Sorry boys,' said Niccolò, dragging his attention back to what they were saying. 'Tell me again who this musician is.'

'He's called Aurelio,' said Falco patiently. 'And he and his sister are Manoush. They won't come here because they don't sleep in buildings. But we can visit them in the Ram.'

The Ram! Everything seemed to lead Niccolò's thoughts in that direction. He had a nagging feeling that he had missed something important on his last visit there. He would have to get Ferdinando's spy to dig further. And it made him uneasy to hear the Ram linked to the Zinti. Niccolò did not like the tribe. They did not conform to the di Chimici philosophy of growth and acquisition. There had to be something wrong with people who disprized possessions and did not own land.

Out loud he said, 'That is because all Zinti must be conceived under the stars. Even their unmarried women will not sleep indoors, in case a chance encounter leads to the beginning of a child. Foolish in the extreme, since it is more likely to lead to rape than if they stayed safe inside a house.'

Falco looked shocked, and Niccolò wondered if this would be a good time to bring up his plans for his youngest son. Better for him to accept a life of celibacy before he had experienced the force of desire.

Georgia spent most of Sunday in bed.

'Told you she was sickening for something,' said Russell, adding, 'or just *is* something sickening,' under his breath.

'There's no need to fuss,' Georgia told her mother. 'I'm fine. I just had a bad night. I'll take my school-books to bed and get ahead with my coursework.'

But, though she was propped up on a heap of cushions and pillows and surrounded by books and files, she spent a lot of the morning trying to sketch out a plan of Remora. She drew a rough circle on her lined pad and bisected it top to bottom. 'Strada delle Stelle,' she wrote, 'Road of the Stars.' She put in the Gate of the Sun at the north and that of the Moon in the south and drew a little circle halfway down the great thoroughfare to represent the Campo she had crossed with Cesare.

She drew lines across the bigger circle until it was segmented into twelve. She knew where the Twelfths of the Ram and the Twins were and roughly where they had escaped from the Fishes into the Twelfth of the Archer. But filling in the other sections was harder.

She muttered an old rhyme that she remembered from childhood:

The Ram, the Bull, the heavenly Twins
And next to the Crab the Lion shines
The Virgin and the Scales.
The Scorpion, Archer and He-Goat,
The Man who carries the Watering-pot,
The Fish with the glittering tails.

The only difference between Talian signs of the zodiac and the ones Georgia knew was that the Reman lion was a lioness and Remorans always referred to Virgo as 'the Lady'. When she had filled it all in, it was clear that Remora was arranged like an astrological map of the year, with the Twelfth of the Ram at the centre left, in the west of the city.

'Good, I should be able to remember that,' thought Georgia. Paolo had told her that she mustn't bring anything to Talia with her except the talisman and the clothes she wore at the time of stravagation. She had always found herself dressed in her Talian boy's clothes on her arrival, but they were on top of her night things, just as she had put them on the first time.

She wouldn't be able to take her map with her, but it made her feel better to have drawn it. On a fresh sheet of paper she wrote down what she knew about each of the Twelfths, but there were huge gaps. She knew more about the Ram than any of the others.

'Their adversary is Fishes,' she wrote, 'and their allies are the Archer and the Lioness.'

Suddenly she understood why. Georgia didn't believe in astrology, but she read her horoscope in the paper every day, like the rest of her family, and she remembered Maura once telling her that each sign of the zodiac was linked to Earth, Fire, Water or Air – three signs for each element.

'We're both Air signs,' she had told Georgia. 'Gemini for you and Libra for me.'

'Oh no,' said Georgia now. 'I'm Gemini – the Twins! I belong with the di Chimici!'

But a moment's thought showed her this must be wrong. However passionate the Remorans felt about belonging to their Twelfths, they couldn't arrange for their children all to be born under their matching signs.

Still, she was right about the pattern of alliances. As soon as she had remembered that Aries, Leo and Sagittarius were Fire signs, it made sense that the Lioness and Archer were allied with the Ram. Just a quarter of an hour's work produced allies for all the other Twelfths. Adversaries were harder, but she remembered what Cesare had said about the Twins and the Lady.

'Your adversary is the opposite to you, like Fire and Water,' she murmured, 'so Earth and Air must be the other opposites. And your adversary seems to be the nearest opposite to you in the city – Ram and Fishes, Bull and Twins, Crab and Lioness.'

'Can't you shut up while you work?' yelled Russell, thumping her door as he went past.

'Adversaries!' hissed Georgia. It was what she and Russell were, no doubt about that. The Twelfths of

Remora had a history going back hundreds of years, but Georgia and Russell had packed enough hatred and opposition into the last four to make up for centuries.

'But who are my allies?' thought Georgia, and a vision of Mortimer Goldsmith in his half-moon glasses came into her mind, making her smile. She wouldn't fancy his chances in a showdown with her stepbrother.

The enmities and alliances in Remora were complicated by this funny attachment of each Twelfth to another city, which Georgia didn't really understand. How could you live in one city but give your allegiance to another? It was like living in London but thinking of yourself as Liverpudlian. Still, you could live in London and support Liverpool football team, or Man U, or Aston Villa, come to that. She remembered first thinking that the Twelfths were like rival football clubs.

But it was even more serious than that. She had seen Cesare's fear when the Fishes were following them, and he was not a coward. And she had seen the dagger at Gaetano's belt. Luciano carried one too, although he was the least aggressive boy she had ever known. Talia was a dangerous place, in a dangerous time, and Remora seemed to be the most dangerous city in it. And the tension would presumably get higher during the Stellata. Still, she preferred the dangers of the Talian city to those of sharing a house with Russell.

The Manoush rolled out their bedding in the main courtyard of the stables of the Ram and settled themselves as comfortably as if they lay on goose-down mattresses instead of cobbles. The hospitable Teresa was perplexed and bustled out with extra pillows and blankets, which were courteously accepted but not used.

Georgia had disappeared to her hayloft just before sunset, so she missed the sight of the tall blind man and his companion stretching out their arms in farewell to the west as the red sun sank behind the city wall somewhere behind the Ram. They chanted softly in their own language. Later the whole household fell asleep to the sweet sound of notes struck gently on the harp.

Cesare was up early and saw them soon after they awoke, this time with their faces turned to the rising sun, towards the region of the Lady and the Scales, kneeling and chanting what seemed like a greeting to a wanderer returned. He didn't know the words they spoke but there was no mistaking the joy in their expressions. They never used the word 'sun', only referring to it as the goddess's companion. They were weird folk, the Zinti, as he had heard tell, but it filled him with pride that they were here in his Twelfth, in his home, or rather outside it.

But Aurelio evidently had no objections to eating breakfast indoors and Teresa was eager to demonstrate how guests were treated in her house. She was delighted to have the Manoush at her table with the visitors from Bellezza. Raffaella offered to help and was soon busy spooning semolina into babies. Cesare had three sisters much younger than himself and twin baby brothers, who crawled everywhere, including over the feet of the blind harpist, who took no more notice of them than if they had been house dogs.

Cesare rescued one of the twins from under the table and set him on his knee. This was Antonio, the more adventurous baby, and he reached his fat arms out to Cesare's face, crowing with delight. Cesare smiled back. Antonio and the others were not his full brothers and sisters. Only Cesare remained of Paolo's first marriage. Cesare's mother had died when he was very little and Paolo had married Teresa ten years ago. The other twin, Arsenio, started to wail loudly because he had got himself wedged into a corner. Teresa swooped down to pick him up but that set off one of the little girls who had already been holding out her arms to her mother. Soon all the younger members of the family were raising their lusty voices in lament. This was the sort of thing that usually drove Cesare out to the stables.

Aurelio turned his head to the source of the sound.

'Shall I play? Would it soothe the children?' he asked. Not waiting for the answer, Raffaella brought him his harp and the glorious ripple of its notes was soon filling the kitchen so that there was no room for sadness. The twins sat round eyed on Paolo's lap, with their thumbs in their mouths, and the little girls twirled their fingers in their hair and snuggled into Cesare, Luciano and Dethridge as their sobs subsided. Teresa and Raffaella finished bringing the food. All was peaceful in the stables of the Ram.

Georgia heard the harp as soon as she arrived back in the hayloft. The last sounds she had heard before drifting off to sleep in London had been Russell's favourite pounding beat and amplified guitars. It wasn't even as if she hated that kind of music, but she knew Russell got as much pleasure from disturbing her sleep with it as he did from listening to it. By contrast, just from the sound of the harp she knew that Aurelio was playing it from the sheer pleasure of making music.

When Georgia slipped quietly round the kitchen door, she found that all the little children seemed to be in a dream. Cesare smiled at her over the tousled head of little Emilia and she smiled back. This was a real family. She saw her own wistful thought reflected in Luciano's eyes, as he stroked the curls of chubby Marta. And the identical expression on the face of Doctor Dethridge, who held Stella. Again she wondered if she would ever know the full story of what had happened to them and what they had given up to live permanently in Talia.

The music came to an end and the spell was broken, but there was no more crying. Paolo saw Georgia and got up to get her a plate and cup, with a twin under each arm.

'Good morning,' said Aurelio to the air near her place. It was hard to accept that he couldn't see her, that his eyes so clear and dark blue sent no messages to his mind.

'Did you sleep well?' asked Georgia.

'Excellently well,' said Aurelio. 'I always do, with nothing to separate me from the moon and stars. Did you?'

Georgia wondered if he knew that when she climbed into the hayloft it was to stravagate back to another world. He seemed to know something about the Stravaganti, but would he have guessed about her if she hadn't revealed it yesterday? And did he know that there were three other Stravaganti in the room?

'Not very,' she answered truthfully.

The twins soon fell asleep on Paolo's knee and the little girls had been quieted with food and music. The others breakfasted companionably in silence. Georgia wondered if she would put on weight eating rolls and jam so soon after supper in her own world. Teresa was a better cook than Maura; even her simplest meal was fresh and home made. Georgia had debated long and hard about whether to stravagate again that night – she couldn't spend Monday catching up on sleep. But she was drawn to Remora. The cheerful uncomplicated family life of the Horsemaster, the stables and being able to ride whenever she wanted, her growing friendship with Cesare and the chance to see Lucien again were all too much to resist. School would just have to take its chances.

A commanding knock at the door broke up the harmony of the gathering. Paolo laid the twins in their cradle and opened it. There stood the Duke of Giglia, with Gaetano and Falco. A grand carriage with the di Chimici crest waited behind them in the yard.

'Greetings, Capitano,' said Niccolò, using the term which strictly speaking was Paolo's only during the week of the Stellata. It was a sign of favour. He seemed to be on his best behaviour. 'And to the lovely mistress of the house,' he added, kissing his hand in Teresa's direction.

'A thousand apologies for inflicting my presence upon you again so soon, but my sons told me about your visitors and I could not wait to meet them myself.'

His eyes flickered round the table. It was obvious

who the Zinti were, with their exotic clothes and brilliant colours. He ignored Georgia, taking her for another of Paolo's teeming household. But he was at a loss to place Dethridge and Luciano. Their clothes told him that they did not belong to the stables.

'May I present our guests?' Paolo was saying. 'You have doubtless been drawn by the music of the Zinti, or the Manoush as they prefer to be called – Raffaella and Aurelio Vivoide.'

The two travellers made their obeisance to the Duke, who cordially waved them to sit.

'And here are two other distinguished guests from Bellezza,' Paolo went on smoothly. 'Doctor Guglielmo Crinamorte and his son Luciano.'

Much bowing followed and the Duke then presented his two sons to the assembled company. His mind was racing, trying to work out where the two Bellezzans fitted into the stables of the Ram. Their surname was unfamiliar to him but there was something about them that tugged at his memory and, as often before, he felt there was something going on in the Ram that he ought to know about.

During the introductions, Falco leaned on his sticks and looked hungrily at the family, much as Georgia had earlier. Her heart was touched by his obvious unhappiness. His own family were the lords of Talia and yet they could not make him well and she doubted if mealtimes in the di Chimici palaces were such warm and friendly occasions.

Falco manoeuvred himself to sit on a bench next to Aurelio.

'Will you play again?' he whispered. 'We have told my father so much about you.'

Aurelio frowned and Georgia could see that he was about to demur, but Raffaella whispered something to him and he changed his mind.

'I will not come to your palace,' he said courteously to Niccolò. 'I mean no disrespect, but my people are not minstrels. We play for our own pleasure. Nevertheless, we favour music-lovers and your Grace's son is one such. If Signor Paolo permits, I shall play outside and you are welcome to listen.'

Niccolò was not pleased, but he knew it would be fruitless to argue. The di Chimici went out into the yard where Cesare and Teresa found chairs and benches for them all and a recital began, the like of which had never been heard in the Twelfth of the Ram.

While it went on, Luciano beckoned to Georgia and Cesare and they retreated into the stables.

'What do you think of the di Chimici now?' he asked.

'Those two youngsters are very different from their father, I think,' said Cesare.

'I wonder if we can trust them,' said Luciano. 'They seem all right, but that man out there, Duke Niccolò, he ordered the death of Arianna's mother – I'm sure he did. There's blood on his hands.'

'It wouldn't be for the first time,' said Cesare. 'We hear such stories in Remora all the time.'

'But it can't hurt to introduce them to your Rodolfo, can it?' asked Georgia. 'I mean, he probably won't be able to do anything for Falco, anyway.'

'I will tell you one thing,' said Luciano. 'If there is anything Rodolfo *can* do, he won't refuse to just because Falco's a di Chimici.'

Among the many passers-by who stopped to listen to the harp playing in the Twelfth of the Ram that morning, nobody paid any attention to a short stocky figure in a dirty blue cloak. Enrico had naturally followed Niccolò and his sons from the Papal palace and it was a good opportunity to get a closer look at the stables of the Ram. He slipped through the listeners in the yard and on round to the back of the stable-block, meaning to check up on the horses while everyone was occupied.

He put his eye to a knot-hole in the wood. And there were the young Rams, deep in conference – the boys that he had followed to Santa Fina and a third, that must be the one who had been with them in the square when they first met the musician. He was Senator Rodolfo's apprentice from Bellezza – that the spy knew well – but seeing him so close to brought back uncomfortable memories.

Enrico quickly made the 'Hand of Fortune', the sign made on brow and breast with the middle three fingers of the right hand. It was what Talians did to ward off ill fortune. 'Dia!' he whispered and broke out into a sweat. There was something uncanny about that boy. Even though Enrico had had him in his grasp and knew him to be made of flesh and blood, there was something inexplicable about him. He used not to have a shadow and then, just when Enrico and his master had been on the verge of exposing him as some kind of freak, his shadow had materialised. He remembered how interested his old employer, Rinaldo di Chimici, had been in that.

Enrico didn't know what it meant and that bothered him. He was a spy and it was his job to know more about his victim than anyone else – and if possible also about his employer. And Luciano had foiled him. Enrico didn't like failure and he didn't like to be reminded of it. It made him link the boy in his mind with that other disturbing mystery – what had happened to his fiancée Giuliana.

Now he moved his eye from the hole and put his ear to it instead. They were talking about Senator Rodolfo and that was interesting in itself. Why would the Senator's favoured apprentice chat about him to a couple of stable-hands? They seemed on very friendly terms.

'The Duke seems to be making a habit of visiting us,' said one of them now.

'Thank goodness Merla is safe in Santa Fina,' said another, younger, voice.

'Wouldn't he like to know about her?' said the voice that Enrico recognised as Luciano's.

'He wouldn't leave us alone for a minute if he knew what had happened in the Ram,' said the older boy.

Enrico stopped listening; he had heard enough. His instincts had told him that there was a secret up in Santa Fina and it looked as if he had been right. Time to pay his new friend Diego a visit.

Chapter 10

Luciano's Story

It was a relief when Duke Niccolò left the stables of the Ram. But he was willing for his sons to stay.

'If that is agreeable to you, Signor Paolo,' he said to his host, who of course was in no position to object.

'It likes me not to see these sonnes of oure enemy consorting with oure yonglinges,' said Dethridge to Paolo when the Duke departed. He left his carriage for Falco and strode off into the city about his business.

Paolo shook his head. 'Perhaps that is the way of the future,' he said. 'Perhaps the old enmities will come to an end. I have heard nothing against these two young men.'

'Mayhap they are doing their fathire's will nonetheless,' said Dethridge, 'and will finde oute more from the yonge folk than they sholde knowe?'

The Manoush packed up their bedding and made to move off too.

'We thank you for your kind hospitality,' Aurelio said formally to Paolo and Teresa. 'But we must now be on our way. We wish to revisit old friends in the city.'

They both bowed, touching their foreheads with clasped hands. Then they spoke in their own language, translating: 'Peace on your house and on your people – may you fare well and your enemies come to grief.'

And then they were gone, like bright birds flying south.

'Strange people,' said Teresa, 'but I liked them.'

'The Manoush are always welcome here,' said Paolo. 'They remind us of older times and better ways.'

The Duke had tried to reward Aurelio for the music but Gaetano had whispered to him and the silver had been quietly passed to Raffaella instead. Georgia was surprised that the young noble had also noticed who held the purse-strings in that couple. And then she remembered that she still didn't know whether they were a couple. The Manoush seemed open enough in their dealings with other people but now that they had gone, it was hard to pin down anything about them.

Luciano was not surprised that the two di Chimici brothers wanted to stay; he knew that Gaetano was determined to find out more about the Stravaganti. But he felt very odd about what seemed to be a sort of friendship beginning between the sons of this powerful family and the people of the Ram.

'Come for a drive with us,' Gaetano said now. 'If that's all right with your father, Cesare. We have the carriage and it's easier for my brother if he can sit in comfort.'

Paolo gave his permission and the five young people got into the di Chimici carriage, with its plumed horses and velvet upholstery. It made Luciano feel very strange indeed, to be riding out with people he had been taught to consider his enemies. And Cesare had been brought up from birth to fear and distrust them.

Georgia had no such worries. Everyone in Talia had told her that the di Chimici were bad and dangerous and she could believe that the Duke was someone you wouldn't want to meet on a dark night. But once you got over their fancy clothes and elaborate manners, Gaetano and Falco were just boys. They were much nicer than Russell and his cronies, anyway.

'Take the South road,' Gaetano now commanded, and the carriage rolled out over the cobbled streets of the Ram, skirted the Campo and turned south down the broad Street of the Stars to the Moon Gate.

Gaetano leaned forward to talk to Georgia. 'We need your help,' he said, getting straight to the point. 'If my brother cannot be cured, he will be made to enter the church.' He didn't say by whom, but it was obvious.

'And you don't want to do that?' Georgia asked Falco, playing for time.

The younger boy looked pensive. 'Not really,' he said slowly, 'not if I had a choice. I'd rather go to university like my brother and find out about philosophy and painting and music.'

Georgia tried to imagine what university might be like in sixteenth-century Talia. Falco didn't have a wheelchair, so presumably Talians didn't know about them or ramps and things. Unless he could walk properly, he'd have to be carried to lectures.

'Is there anything the Stravaganti can do that would help my brother?' Gaetano asked Georgia. 'He has had the best doctors in Talia and they can do no more. Only a superior skill, such as you natural philosophers know about, could give him a chance of recovery.'

Georgia was at a loss. She wasn't any kind of philosopher but this young noble was treating her like a learned scholar. She was prepared to believe that the mysterious Rodolfo might be a person like that, or the Elizabethan doctor, or even Paolo, who had an air of natural authority. Perhaps even Lucien, since he had inexplicably ended up here in another world, had some remarkable powers she had never suspected. But she was just a skinny Year 10 schoolgirl, whose only power was to be able to get from one world to another. How could that help the boy with the big dark eyes and the shattered leg?

Falco was watching her and he suddenly turned to his brother and said, 'I don't think that she can do anything for me.'

The atmosphere in the carriage was electric and Georgia felt the colour rising in her face.

'She?' said Gaetano. 'The Stravagante is a woman?'

Luciano came to the rescue. 'She needs to be disguised here in Talia. We Stravaganti do not draw attention to ourselves.'

He had certainly drawn attention away from Georgia. Both di Chimici turned to him, eager with questions.

'You are a Stravagante too?' said Gaetano. 'So that

is what you are learning from the Regent!'

'Please,' said Falco. 'If there is anything you know, share it with us. Can what the Stravaganti do heal bodies?'

*

When the Duke left the Ram, he was followed by a man in a blue cloak. When he reached the Campo delle Stelle, he whirled and faced his pursuer, relaxing when he saw who it was.

'I hope you are usually more discreet,' Niccolò said to Enrico. 'Otherwise your value as a spy will be limited.'

'Certainly, my Lord,' said Enrico smoothly. 'I was of course not shadowing your Grace – I would not have such presumption. I was merely following you, so that I could report to you some news.'

Duke Niccolò raised one eyebrow. He had no illusions about Enrico; his nephew had told him all he needed to know about the man.

'The Ram have a secret they are keeping from you, my Lord,' Enrico continued. He had the Duke's complete attention now; he had known there was something going on in the Ram, for all their deference.

'Something that will help them in the race?' he asked now.

'More than likely,' said Enrico. 'The secret is in Santa Fina. I am on my way there now, to try to find out more.'

'Let me know as soon as you do,' said the Duke. 'And if you need any help in Santa Fina, or somewhere to stay out of sight, use my summer palace

there.' He scribbled something on a scrap of paper.
'Give this to my major-domo. He will see to it that
you have anything you need.'

*

Luciano had made up his mind.

'If I tell you what happened to me,' he said, 'you
must both swear not to tell anyone else, particularly
your father.'

There was a short silence, while Gaetano wrestled
with his feelings about his family. The two brothers
looked at one another, one so ugly but physically
strong and vigorous, the other so beautiful and so
damaged. They nodded at the same time.

'We swear,' they both said. And to the surprise of
the others, Gaetano stopped the coach, so that they
could both kneel to Luciano and proffer him their
daggers. It was not possible for Falco to kneel
properly, but he leant forward and bent his better leg,
his face creased with pain.

Both brothers solemnly chanted together:

By the house of the City of Flowers—
May its strength never dwindle or ail—
Ever true is the word that is ours
Take our lives if our promise should fail.

They urged Luciano to take the daggers by the hilts
and make a small nick in their wrists.

They're going to become blood brothers, thought
Georgia, but it wasn't that. The two young nobles
held their wrists out to Luciano, each bright with

scarlet beads of blood, and motioned him to put his lips to each. Georgia shuddered but Luciano didn't hesitate. As soon as he had tasted the blood voluntarily shed by the di Chimici, Georgia felt Cesare relax beside her, and she realised that he had been as tense as a tight violin-string.

The whole atmosphere in the carriage had changed.

'Drive on!' ordered Gaetano, sheathing his dagger, which Luciano had handed back to him, and the coachman urged the horses on. They were now through the Gate of the Moon and heading south, but no one inside the carriage paid any attention to where they were going.

No one now had any doubt that the di Chimici would keep whatever they were told to themselves. Georgia realised that she was going to hear for the first time what had really happened to Lucien.

It was clear to her that it was an edited version of his story, but it was amazing enough.

'I was a Stravagante from another world, like Georgia,' he began. 'In that world I was very sick – not in the way that Falco is, but with a slow creeping illness that was devouring my body.'

Gaetano nodded. 'We know of such a sickness. We call it the malady of the Crab, because it grasps and pinches the organs of the body.'

'When I first stravagated here,' Luciano continued, 'or rather to Bellezza, which is my city, I felt completely well again.'

Falco's eyes lit up and Gaetano gasped. 'Does that mean if Falco went to your world, he would be healed?'

'I don't think so,' said Luciano. 'He might feel

better, but I don't think his broken bones would be mended. At most his strength would be improved. And it wouldn't last when he returned here.' He paused.

'Although I was always well in Talia, I got worse in my own world. And then I was captured in Bellezza. The thing about stravagation is that it is night-time in the other world while it is daytime in Talia. If one of us stays for a Talian night, he will be discovered in his own world during the day as a sleeping body that cannot be awakened. I was unable to return to my world while I was held captive, and during that time my body appeared to be in a coma – you know, when someone is still breathing but seems otherwise dead?'

'Yes,' said Gaetano. 'We call it "*Morte Vivenda*" – the living death. It happens sometimes after a riding accident. But such victims almost always die in truth soon afterwards.'

Luciano nodded. 'It was like that for me. Soon my otherworldly body could not even breathe for itself.'

'So you died?' asked Falco, his huge dark eyes seeming to fill his face.

Luciano hesitated. 'I come from a time far in the future,' he said, choosing his words carefully. 'The doctors can keep people alive for a while with machines. I don't know exactly what happened to me, but I think that I was kept breathing in that way for a while and that then the doctors believed that I was dead in my brain and the machines were turned off.'

There was a long silence in the carriage and Georgia found that she was holding her breath. Lucien looked terrible.

'Anyway,' he continued in a hurry. 'At a particular moment, I suddenly knew that I was alive here in Talia but dead in my own world. From that day, now nearly a year ago, I have been a citizen of Talia, under the protection of my master the Regent and living with my foster-parents Doctor Crinamorte and his wife.'

'And you can't go back?' asked Falco.

'Not permanently, no,' said Luciano. 'This is the only life I can lead now.'

'And these doctors of the future,' said Gaetano, focusing on what was for him the most important thing in the whole story. 'Could they help my brother?'

'Again, I don't really know,' said Luciano. 'What do you think, Georgia?'

'I don't know much about medicine,' she said truthfully. 'They might be able to do operations to make it easier for him to walk. And even if they couldn't do that, he could have an electric wheelchair and get about more easily.' She stopped. 'There's not much point in my telling you all this,' she said.

'Can you bring the doctors here?' asked Gaetano.

Luciano and Georgia both shook their heads.

'They wouldn't be much use by themselves,' said Luciano, 'even if we could bring them.'

'They'd need all their equipment,' explained Georgia. 'Operating theatres, electricity, anaesthetics, instruments and drugs.'

'Then there's only one thing for it,' said Falco calmly. 'I must go there. You must help me to stravagate.'

The Horsemasters of Remora were meeting to discuss the pacts that would be made between Twelfths during the Stellata. This was a meeting of allies, where Twelfths got together according to their elemental allegiances, Fire with Fire and Air with Air. So Paolo was hosting the meeting for the three Fire Twelfths in the Ram and sat in a tavern with his opposite numbers from the Archer and the Lioness.

In other taverns of Remora similar meetings were going on. Riccardo as Horsemaster for the Twins hosted the Air Twelfths – the Scales and the Water-Carrier; Emilio, Horsemaster for the Lady, entertained the Earth Twelfths – the Bull and the Goat; and Giovanni, the Scorpion's Horsemaster, bought the drinks for the other Water Twelfths – the Fishes and the Crab.

Ancient traditions of enmity prompted these annual meetings. It was the prime consideration that the Twelfths of opposing elements would block one another's jockeys in the Stellata. So all Water jockeys would block all Fire horses and all Earth riders would foul the path of all Air mounts. But within this general opposition, each rider would reserve special hostility for one particular enemy, like Ram and Fishes, or Twins and Bull.

Then there were the city allegiances that pitted Twins and Lady against the Ram; all in all there were few horses who would be viewed by their neighbouring riders as neutral once the race got under way. All riders wore their Twelfth's colours but it still required a lively mind to keep up with all the planned strategies once the dazzling kaleidoscope of a high-speed race whirled round the circular Campo.

And planning could go only so far. The order in which the horses were to take up their positions at the start was drawn by lot only just before the race. Until then, however, the allied Twelfths would mull over tactics and dig to find out any information about rivals' mounts and their riders that might prove useful.

And today the topic of most discussion in three out of the four groups was the Ram's secret weapon. Paolo trusted absolutely in his allies of the Lioness and Archer; they would be happy about an advantage to any of the three Fire Twelfths. So he told them about Merla.

'Goddess be praised!' was the response from the other two Horsemasters.

They knew of the legend of the flying horse, of course; all Remora knew that such creatures were possible, if rare. No one had ever seen one, but everyone knew someone who had, even if it was a friend's great-grandfather. And everyone believed in the power of such a good omen.

They might not have been so confident if they had known that Riccardo and Emilio were both telling the Air and Earth Twelfths that the Ram had a secret. They had just got it from Enrico, the spy who was working in the stable of the Twins, but who shared his information equally between the Pope's and the Duke's men. He didn't know yet exactly what the secret was but he knew the answer was in Santa Fina and he was sure to find it out soon.

The Water Twelfths hadn't got wind of it yet but it was only a matter of time before they did. Someone in the Twins or the Lady, because of their opposition to Bellezza, would leak the information to one of the three Twelfths of the Water signs, preferably the Fishes. So this year's race was going to be especially hard for the Ram, with three-quarters of the city plotting against them for one reason or another.

*

Cesare, who was waiting to be confirmed as this year's rider for the Ram, was blissfully unaware of the approaching dangers. He was so stunned by Falco's announcement that he had no thought for his own future.

Luciano was wrestling with his own emotions. He knew that Falco didn't understand what he was saying, that he had no idea about the dangers of stravagation. Even if the doctors of Luciano's old world could cure him, it couldn't be done on one visit; there was no way that Falco's plan would work unless he gave up his life in Talia, voluntarily. And of all the young people in the carriage, only Luciano knew what that would mean.

Everyone was looking at Luciano, to see what he would say. He cast a quick glance at Georgia; perhaps she would understand better than the others, but she was still a novice at stravagation.

But it was Falco who spoke. He turned to his brother and said, 'Gaetano, there is only one way to do this. It will be very hard, harder than death, but it is my choice. I shall go to the world of the future and make my life there.'

His older brother clasped him in his arms and the

others saw that there were tears in his eyes. 'No,' he said. 'I won't let you. You can't leave us. What would you do without the family? Without me?'

Falco's voice was muffled by his brother's embrace. 'I should rather live my whole life elsewhere, even if it has to be without you, my brother,' he said, 'than live out my days as half the man I was meant to be.'

Then he turned back to Luciano and Georgia.

'I have chosen,' he said. 'Now, what must I do?'

Chapter 11

The Sound of Drums

For Georgia most of Monday passed in a dream. She had reached a point where her ordinary daily life was beginning to seem unreal and her mind was always in Remora, with its divisions and intrigues. It didn't help that she was very short of sleep, even though she hadn't spent the whole of Sunday night in the city.

After Falco's announcement in the carriage, and Gaetano's continued opposition to the plan, Luciano had bought them all some time by saying that they needed to think more about it. Georgia had been relieved because she felt completely out of her depth and the atmosphere had become very tense. The carriage had stopped and let them out in a place called Belle Vigne. It was a grassy hill with a little village at the foot. At the top, according to Gaetano, was the remains of a Rassenan settlement. Georgia worked out eventually that this must mean 'Etruscan' and would have loved to see it but even the gentle slope up to it was too steep for Falco.

The young people had sprawled on the grass, talking of lighter matters.

'What is it like in Bellezza?' Gaetano asked Luciano. 'I have to go there soon to fetch the young Duchessa.'

'It's the most beautiful city in the world,' Luciano said simply.

'Ah, but you haven't been to Giglia, has he, brother?' said Gaetano.

Falco nodded and Cesare added, 'What about my city? There is nowhere like Remora, surely?'

'We must all love our own cities best,' said Luciano diplomatically, and Georgia tried to imagine feeling that way about London.

'Bellezza is made of silver and it floats on the water,' continued Luciano. 'Little waterways criss-cross the city – it's really a collection of over a hundred little islands. And the people enjoy living there – they have a party at any excuse. They love their Duchessa too. They were devastated when the last one died.'

He stopped. This was a sensitive subject to get on to with two di Chimici.

'What is the new Duchessa like?' asked Falco, and Georgia glimpsed Gaetano putting a finger to his lips.

'She's very young,' said Luciano, who hadn't seen the gesture. 'Still a girl – the same age as me. But she is becoming more like her mother every day. And she is very proud of her city.'

'Is she as beautiful as her mother was supposed to be?' asked Gaetano casually, and Georgia pricked up her ears.

But Luciano simply said, 'Yes,' and did not elaborate.

Soon after that, Gaetano had noticed that his brother was looking tired and they had all come back to Remora. Not much was said on the journey back, but when the three had been dropped at the stables of the Ram, Falco said, 'Don't forget what I told you. Will you come and see me tomorrow?'

And it hadn't been possible to refuse.

Paolo was out at his Horsemasters' meeting and Cesare had chores to do. It would have been a perfect opportunity for Georgia to spend time on her own with Luciano. She wanted to talk to him about his story, to find out what part his talisman had played in what happened, but he had looked at her closely and told her that she must stravagate early and not stay in Remora for the rest of the afternoon.

'I can remember what it was like,' he said, with a smile that turned her heart over. 'I know you say you are well, but even the healthiest person needs their sleep.'

And so she had come back, briefly awake in the middle of the night, listening to the small sounds of the sleeping house, before dropping into a deep dreamless state.

She was woken all too soon by her mother urging her to get ready for school. The rest of the day was a bit of a wash-out. Georgia couldn't concentrate on her lessons. Even in English, which had always been her best subject, she couldn't answer the simplest question.

Fortunately, the new girl Alice covered for her. The

two girls had lunch together and Georgia discovered to her delight that Alice was also keen on horses – had one of her own, in fact, at her father's house in Devon. By the end of the day, they were firm friends. Georgia wished she could tell Alice about Remora but it was a comfort just to talk to her about horses.

Even though Monday was Russell's football day, Georgia didn't go straight home. She decided to call on Mr Goldsmith again. He was pleased to see her and made her a much nicer cup of tea than the last one. Georgia had eaten four chocolate biscuits before she realised it.

'Sorry,' she said. 'I didn't get much sleep last night and I'm always ravenous when I'm tired.'

'I thought you were looking a bit peaky,' said Mr Goldsmith. 'I don't mean to pry, but is everything all right?'

Georgia remembered thinking that Mr Goldsmith was her ally and she decided to talk to him about Russell. But she was a bit oblique about it.

'Do you have any enemies?' she asked.

'What a strange question,' he said. 'No, not enemies as such. I would say I had rivals though. You know, the sort of people who bid against me at auctions – other dealers. It's a friendly sort of rivalry – we are quite sociable when we meet.'

That was the difference, Georgia decided, between Talia and here. The Twelfths of Remora were more like rivals even though they talked about adversaries. On the other hand, Niccolò di Chimici did seem to be an enemy of the people she thought of as being on her side. And of the Stravaganti. But what about Gaetano and his brother? They were more like friends.

Certainly more so than her supposed-to-be step-brother. She heaved a big sigh.

'Oh dear!' said Mr Goldsmith. 'You'd better have another biscuit.'

That made Georgia smile. 'I don't have many friends,' she confided. 'At least not here.'

'Nor do I,' said Mr Goldsmith. 'But you don't need many friends, you know, as long as the ones you have are good ones.'

Georgia decided to take him into her confidence a bit more.

'Do you know an Italian city where they have a special horse race every year?' she asked.

Rather to her surprise, he did.

'You mean Siena?' he asked. 'They have a race called the Palio every summer – actually twice, I think. That's a place for rivalry if ever there was one.'

'Go on,' said Georgia eagerly. 'Tell me about the Palio.'

'Well, Siena is in Tuscany, not far from where the original of your little horse must have come from. The city is divided up into lots of sections – seventeen, I think – and they race their horses round a sort of Piazza in the middle of town. It's a tradition going back hundreds of years and the city itself still looks mediaeval. Hardly any cars, narrow streets, virtually no modern buildings, at least not in the centre.'

That's it, thought Georgia. If Lucien's Bellezza is our Venice, Remora must be Siena.

'Have you seen it?' she asked.

'The Palio? No,' said Mr Goldsmith. 'But I've been to Siena, more than once. It's a lovely place. You'd like it too, if you're fond of horses.'

Soon they were chatting away about riding and Georgia told him about Jean's stables. She was in a much more cheerful mood when she left the shop, so that when he said, 'Goodbye and good luck with your enemies,' it took her a moment to remember how the conversation had started. And then, when she was almost home, she remembered that she hadn't actually said she had an enemy herself. She smiled. Mr Goldsmith was definitely a friend.

Diego was pleased to see his new friend Enrico. His duties at the moment were quite boring. Diego was used to spending all day on his feet, preferably out of doors, tending to horses, riding them, sometimes moving them down into the city or out to further pastures. But now he spent most of every day guarding the little miracle. Not her fault, of course. He was as attached to the black filly as anyone. And she was a marvel – there was no doubt about that. But he couldn't see why she had to be kept such a secret.

Diego wasn't from Remora; he was Santa Finan born and bred. He'd seen the Stellata a few times as a boy but he didn't concern himself with the politics of the city. He liked longer races, run in a straight line, where you could bet on the outcome and have some chance of winning. He had no time for the Remorans' way of doing things. Making deals and fixing results – that just made it too difficult for an ordinary punter to stand a chance of winning.

Enrico agreed. 'They're all mad down there in the city,' he said in a friendly conversational way, making himself comfortable on the bale of hay beside Diego. 'Secretive too,' he added, taking a swift glance at the groom.

'That's the Reman way,' nodded Diego. 'They'd keep their own mothers a secret if they could. In case their rivals benefited from the knowledge.'

'Are they all as bad as one another, do you think?' asked Enrico. 'Or are some worse than others? What about the Ram, for example?'

'Ah, the Ram!' said Diego mysteriously, tapping the side of his nose. 'I could tell you something about them.'

'I wish you would,' said Enrico. 'It would get my master off my back. He's sure they've got something up their sleeve for this year's Stellata.'

Diego hesitated. Then shrugged. The secret filly couldn't have anything to do with the race. Although she was growing faster than any normal foal and would be big enough to ride by then, the Ram's jockey would never be allowed up on a winged horse. So what could it hurt to tell his new friend about her?

'They've got something up their sleeve right enough,' he admitted.

*

When Georgia next got back to the stables of the Ram, there was no sign of Cesare or Luciano, but Paolo was waiting for her.

'We must talk about why you are here,' he said, leading her into the house. 'And about our brotherhood. How are you finding your way about Remora?'

'Well, thank you,' said Georgia. 'I mean, there's a lot I still don't understand. But Cesare explained it well and I've made a sort of a map at home to remind myself of all the Twelfths. It's a very complicated city, isn't it?'

'Complex, certainly,' said Paolo, 'and not just in the way it's arranged. I'm sure Cesare told you about all the rivalries between Twelfths?'

'Yes,' said Georgia. 'I'm trying to keep all that in mind too.'

'The Chimici exploit those rivalries, you know,' said Paolo.

They were sitting alone in his homely kitchen. Georgia wondered where all the family were, but Paolo said that Teresa had taken the children to visit her mother in the Lioness. It seemed unnaturally quiet without them and Georgia was too shy to ask about the visitors from Bellezza.

'You said yesterday that it might be time to drop the old enmity,' she said now. 'Do you think it's all right for us to be friends with the di Chimici princes?'

'I think so,' said Paolo. 'I don't think they are trying to exploit you.'

He looked at her intently and she realised that this broad, strong man, with his capable hands and smell of the stables, was probably as astute and clever as Duke Niccolò himself.

'I must tell you something,' said Georgia. 'Those two – Gaetano and Falco – they know about me. And they know about Luciano too. He told them. But only because I'd been stupid and given the game away earlier,' she added loyally.

Paolo looked thoughtful. 'And what do you think

they will do with this knowledge?' he asked.

'I'm sure they won't tell their father,' she said immediately. 'They took a solemn oath not to – swore by their weapons and made Luciano taste their blood.' She shuddered slightly at the memory.

'Then I'm sure you're right,' said Paolo. 'It remains to be seen what else they will do with the information though.'

Something stopped Georgia from telling him that Falco planned to use it to get to her world. And in days to come she often wondered if it would have been better if she had. But now she felt it was too soon. Nothing had been definitely decided.

But Paolo wanted to talk about something else.

'Things are coming to a head with the di Chimici,' he said. 'They have gained power in all save a few northern cities. Bellezza resists them, as you know, and that is one of the reasons the Duke has invited the young Duchessa to the Stellata. We do not know exactly what he means to do and she will be well protected by her friends, but we must all be on our guard. He must be intending to influence what he believes will be an impressionable young woman about the wisdom of joining forces with his family.'

'And she isn't an impressionable young woman?' asked Georgia. This was her chance to find out more about the girl who was her rival, while Luciano wasn't around.

'Hardly,' smiled the Horsemaster. 'I think it unlikely that any daughter of Silvia, Duchessa of Bellezza for quarter of a century, and Rodolfo, one of the greatest of our brotherhood, would be anything other than stubbornness and guile incarnate.'

'Have you met her?' asked Georgia.

'No, but I know both her parents,' said Paolo. 'And the fruit does not fall far from the tree, as we say in Talia.'

'We say it too,' said Georgia, thinking for the first time of what that expression meant. You don't get apricots from apple trees, she supposed; children were meant to be like their parents. But she didn't feel much like Maura. Maura didn't really like horses for a start. Maybe Georgia had got that from the father she had hardly known. And what about Russell? His father was a nice enough person – perhaps Russell's mother had been really awful. But perhaps it had something to do with how he had been treated too.

Georgia felt suddenly confused. Remora, with its rigid divisions and distinctions, was in some ways easier to understand.

'Why do you think I am here?' she asked now.

'I don't know,' said Paolo. 'We never know who will be found by a talisman when we take one to the other world, and we never know what they will be called on to do. Rodolfo thought that Luciano might have been brought to save the Duchessa, but he paid a heavy price for it, as I think you know.'

Georgia nodded. 'But I thought he couldn't save the Duchessa in the end. The di Chimici killed her anyway, didn't they?'

There was silence, and then Georgia heard a muffled throbbing noise from the street.

'What's that?' she asked.

'Some of your questions are easier to answer than others,' said Paolo. 'That sound is the drummers of the Ram rehearsing for the Stellata. You will hear them often now until the race is run. Come, let's go for a walk and you shall see.'

The sound of drums got louder as soon as they were out of the house. Georgia soon recognised the cobbled street leading to the square with the silver fountain. She gasped when they reached it. The Piazza del Fuoco was full of yellow and red twirling banners, bearing the image of a ram crowned with silver. Two strong young men were weaving their banners in intricate patterns in time to the insistent beat of a drummer.

Over the next few weeks the sound of those drums as the players and standard bearers of all the Twelfths rehearsed day and night would burrow its way into Georgia's brain, so that she heard it wherever she was, whether in Remora or London, in bed or at school, sleeping or waking. It was the sound of the Stellata. Every Twelfth had its company of young people who were responsible for putting on a splendid show in the procession which would wind round the Campo before the race. The drummers and ensign bearers would lead each company, Paolo explained to Georgia, and it was a great honour to be chosen to be of their number.

'Isn't Cesare one of them?' she asked, thinking that it would explain his absence from the house.

'No,' said Paolo. 'Cesare is our jockey this year, for the first time. But he marched in the parade last year.'

The flags and drums moved out of the square and wound round the narrow lanes of the Twelfth, the sound getting louder and softer as they traced a meandering pattern through the Ram. Young children ran after them, entranced by the noise and colour, but Paolo and Georgia remained sitting on the stone ledge round the fountain.

It was an idyllic scene. The strong sun, the blue sky, the sound of gently splashing water and the picturesque surrounding streets reminded Georgia of a TV travel programme. But she knew there was a lot lurking under the surface of Remora and that appearances were deceptive. It was still hard to think that she might be one of the major players in the complex contest of Talian power politics. It was a bit like being given a computer game without knowing any of the rules. Cesare was a great substitute for a manual but neither he nor she knew what weapons she possessed.

'You keep mentioning the "Brotherhood", and all the Stravaganti I've heard of, apart from me, are men,' she said now. 'You, Senator Rodolfo, Doctor Dethridge – Luciano even. Am I the only female one?'

'No,' said Paolo. 'There is a very fine Stravagante in Giglia called Giuditta Miele. She is a sculptor. And at least one in Bellona, whose name I don't know. But you are the first woman Stravagante to come from your world to ours. I admit I was surprised at first, particularly since – if you will forgive me – you look more like one of our young men. But the talisman does not choose lightly. They always bring us the person who is most needed.'

If only I knew what for, thought Georgia.

*

The Manoush were in the Twelfth of the Lioness. Not

at the stables but a house nearby, where an old woman called Grazia lived. She had, unusually for their tribe, married a Remoran and renounced her heritage. True, she still rose at dawn with her face turned to the sun and bade it farewell again at every nightfall. But she had compromised her beliefs so far as to live inside a house and give up her wandering days.

Now a white-haired widow, though still a tall and handsome figure, Grazia had, in the early years of her marriage, slept with her husband in a string-bed on the loggia of their house, to ensure that their children would be conceived under the stars. Those children – four sons and three daughters – were now all grown up, with children of their own, and all but one daughter had reverted to the Manoush way of life. Such was the star they were born under.

Aurelio and Raffaella brought news of Grazia's children to her from many places in Talia, and so were assured of a welcome in her home whenever they came to Remora. The Twelfth of the Lioness was linked with Romula, the city way down in the South of Talia, where the tentacles of the di Chimici clan had not yet reached. That was where Grazia had met her husband, as they were both visiting Romula. Love had flamed in the City of the Dragon between the beautiful young Manoush and the visitor from the Lioness's lair. A love powerful enough to keep her within the walls of her husband's house, even after his death. It was a long time since Grazia had moved back into a bedchamber under the roof of her house.

But she still observed the great festivals of her former way of life and the coming feast of the goddess was the greatest of them all. The Stellata meant almost nothing to her, though she would cheer the company of the Lioness on the day and hope for their horse to win. But by then, for her and the visiting Manoush the climax of the festival would be over. They would stay up all night to worship the goddess reigning over the starlit sky. And they would wait for the sun to rise on that morning in the Campo, where they would greet the goddess's consort as his first rays climbed the heavens and bathed it with the light of dawn.

*

'Fantastic!' said Enrico, and meant it. He was fonder of horses than almost anything else, and when Diego showed him the miraculous black filly, he thought first only of her delicate beauty and unbelievable attributes. But then his baser instincts took over and he considered the reward he would get when Duke Niccolò heard of this marvel.

And the even bigger reward that would come his way once he had captured her for the Lady. Or the Twins. Whichever offered the more silver.

Chapter 12

A Circle of Cards

Georgia found out where Cesare had been all morning. He came back to the stables in a state of exaltation: he had been riding Arcangelo on the practice track outside Remora.

'He's in great shape,' enthused Cesare, rubbing the horse down with straw. 'I really think we have a chance.'

'Goddess willing,' said Paolo quickly, making the gesture that Georgia had seen before which was like the sign of the cross but not quite.

'Why do you swear by the goddess?' she asked now. 'I mean, you have a church in each Twelfth and you celebrate saints' days, but all the people I've come across in Remora seem to believe in an older religion – it's not just the Manoush.'

'Talians are superstitious by nature,' said Paolo. 'We cling on to the past when all we people of the Middle Sea worshipped a ruling goddess. When the new religion came, with Our Lady and her Son, it was natural for us to put the two together. The Woman Encircled with Stars, that's her. She looks after our city and doesn't mind what we call her.'

Georgia did not feel much the wiser. She returned to something she understood better.

'Tell me more about the race,' she said. 'How does it work? It's not just the case that the best horse wins, is it?'

'No, nor the best jockey,' said Cesare, 'although of course every Twelfth hopes to have both.'

'You must remember,' said Paolo, 'that we've been running the Stellata in some shape or form for about three hundred years, and there's no reason to suppose we won't go on running it for as many more.'

Georgia thought about what Mr Goldsmith had told her about the Palio; if Remora really was the equivalent of Siena then the crazy horse race would still be going for more than another four centuries.

'All the Twelfths have their own stables, as you know,' continued Paolo, 'and they select the horse that is going to take part in each year's Stellata. It can be bred by themselves or bought in, but it is the very best horse that they can afford. Then the jockey is also chosen by the Twelfth.'

'It's not always a member of the Twelfth like me,' said Cesare, bursting to let Georgia know that he hadn't just been chosen because he was his father's son. 'It's the best rider they can find.'

'In a few weeks,' said Paolo, 'the dirt will go down

in the Campo and it will be turned into a race-track. Lots of horses and jockeys will ride in the moonlight and each Twelfth will finalise their decision about who is going to ride in the race. Not many are as certain as we are at this stage.' He gave his son and Arcangelo a proud glance.

'I'd love to see that,' said Georgia, then stopped, confused. Father and son were both giving her the same compassionate look. 'But I can't, can I? I mean I can't be here in Remora at night.'

'There are other heats you can see though,' said Cesare hastily. 'And you'll be here for the race itself, won't you?'

'Depends what time it is,' said Georgia. She looked at Arcangelo and remembered something else. 'Do you race bareback?' she asked.

'Yes,' said Cesare. 'We have a bridle and reins but no saddle.'

'It dates back to our ancestors, the Rassenans,' said Paolo. 'They were great horsemen and racers and always rode bareback.'

They *were* the Talian equivalent of the Etruscans, thought Georgia. Out loud, she said, 'I've never ridden bareback but I'd love to try.'

'Come with me this afternoon,' said Cesare. 'I won't be riding Arcangelo again today, but we have plenty of other horses.'

'Really?' said Georgia, her eyes sparkling. But then she remembered her promise to Falco. 'Only, Luciano and I must visit the di Chimici before I go back home.'

'There'll be time for both,' said Cesare. 'Talk to Luciano about it. He'll be here in a minute; the carriage takes longer than a horse.'

'He was at the practice track with you?' asked Georgia. 'But I thought he wasn't interested in horses.'

'He and Dottore Crinamorte were both there,' said Cesare.

The wheels of the carriage clattered over the stableyard cobbles.

'Ah, the wolf in the story,' said Paolo. 'Speak of the devil!'

Luciano sprang down from the carriage and helped his foster-father out. Georgia thought he was looking better than when she last saw him. His eyes were bright and his whole body animated and alert, as if ready for an adventure.

William Dethridge was likewise full of the races. 'Ah, bot it was a sighte!' he said, clapping Paolo on the shoulder. 'Youre sonne is a marvele – like unto a centaure!'

*

'Do you think they will come?' Falco asked his brother for the fifteenth time.

'They gave their word,' answered Gaetano, as he had all the times before. But in his heart he hoped that the young Stravaganti would think of a way of breaking their promise. He knew they were not keen to help Falco with his plan. But he himself had made no headway with his young brother; Falco was more determined than Gaetano had ever known him. And now time was running out; Gaetano would soon have to make his embassy to Bellezza and he was terrified that Falco would persuade the young Stravaganti to help him in his brother's absence.

'Even if they do come,' he said now, as gently as he could, 'you must give up this idea of yours. It is madness. Why give up the life you know and everyone who loves you to travel to another world where you will be a stranger? You don't even know that the doctors of the future will be able to help you. Even Luciano and Georgia were not certain of that.'

'Then what would you have?' asked Falco bitterly. 'That I should stay here and become like Uncle? Only I should probably need servants to carry me round the Papal palace if I grew to his size; my sticks would not support me.'

'We could find a way out of Father's plans, surely?' begged Gaetano. 'You could come and live in Bellezza with me and my Duchess.'

'I have heard they have no horses in Bellezza,' said Falco, his lip trembling.

'But I will be there,' said Gaetano, taking his brother in his arms. 'To love you and look after you. Who would be there to love you in the world of the Stravaganti?'

'Georgia will look after me,' said Falco stubbornly. 'I'm going to do this, Gaetano. Don't make me do it without your blessing.'

Gaetano held Falco for a long time, then looked into his eyes and sighed.

'Very well,' he said. 'If your mind is set on this and there is nothing I can say or do to change it, then I must accept it. But how I shall miss you, my Falconcino! More even than I have these last two years. We shall no longer grow up together but I shall always imagine you at my side, just as when we were boys in this palace, playing our sword-games.'

When Duke Niccolò entered the room, he didn't notice the two brothers' sombre mood. He himself was elated.

'Gaetano, I have heard from the Regent,' he said, his dark eyes glittering. 'They are ready to receive your suit. You must leave for Bellezza at once!'

*

Up in his room William Dethridge took a small package wrapped in black silk from his jacket pocket. He unwrapped the package and spread the black silk on a clothes chest in the corner of the room. Then he shuffled the cards in his hands and dealt a clock shape on to the silk, beginning at the nine o'clock position and moving counter-clockwise. The first card to be set down was the Princess of Birds, immediately followed by the Prince of Serpents. Dethridge paused before going on.

'Thatte will bee the stravayging mayde and one of the young nobles of the Ladye,' he muttered. The circle continued to grow.

Two of Fishes, the Magician, Two of Salamanders, Two of Birds, The Knight ('aha, thatte woll bee younge Caesar') then the Tower, Two of Serpents, the Moving Stars, and the Princess and Prince of Fishes.

Dethridge dealt the thirteenth card into the middle of the circle. It was the Goddess.

He sat back and contemplated the pattern. It was most unusual to get so many trump and court cards. And all the number cards were twos; he had no idea what that might mean. But the Princess of Fishes was the young Duchessa of Bellezza and he was glad to see her next to her own Prince. It was partly to read her fate that he had consulted the cards. The Moving Stars clearly indicated the race, but why was Cesare next to the Tower? And was it a comfort to know that the Goddess was in the centre, controlling everything?

Dethridge decided to speak to Paolo about this reading and to reach Rodolfo through the mirrors; he had no idea which of them the Magician card represented but the sooner the Stravaganti were all together, the better.

*

'What do you mean, gone?' said Luciano.

It had been hard for him and Georgia to cross the threshold of the Papal palace in Remora. It felt like entering the enemy's lair, even though it was a cool and graceful building of marble and mirrors. Luciano was no stranger to elegance after his time in Bellezza but Georgia felt awkward and out of place, acutely conscious of her coarse clothes. The Pope's footman clearly thought she was some kind of servant of Luciano's and that made her feel even worse.

Falco's eyes lit up when they were shown into a small ante-chamber where he sat at the window, and he greeted them both warmly, using the boy's form of Georgia's name while the footman was still there. But the minute the man had withdrawn and before they could even ask where Gaetano was, Falco burst out with the news that his brother had already gone.

'He left for Bellezza an hour ago,' he said excitedly. 'He's gone to meet the Duchessa.'

'Why so soon?' Luciano pressed him, suspiciously.

Falco sighed. 'You might as well know. It'll come out soon enough when they're married.'

Georgia saw the colour leave Luciano's face till he looked like the marble statue of Apollo in the niche behind him. But then it came flooding back and he was flushed with rage.

'What do you mean?' he demanded. 'Who's getting married?'

Falco was taken aback. 'Why, Gaetano and the Duchessa,' he said nervously. 'The Regent has received our suit and my brother is to speak of it to the Duchessa before bringing her back here for the Stellata.'

'Never!' said Luciano. 'Arianna would never marry a di Chimici. There must be some mistake!'

Now it was Falco's turn to colour up.

'And why shouldn't she? We are one of the oldest families in Talia and we have made alliances with Dukes and Princes all over the North. In fact my family rules by right in six cities.'

'A very good reason not to make Bellezza the seventh,' snarled Luciano. 'Come on, Georgia. It was madness to come here. There can be no dealings between us and the di Chimici. As you can see, they aren't interested in anything except feathering their own nest.'

'Wait!' cried Falco, seeing that Luciano was about to sweep Georgia away.

Georgia was as upset as the other two. Luciano's outburst left no room for doubt about his own feelings for Arianna and that was hard enough, but seeing Falco's stricken face made it difficult just to leave.

'Wait a minute,' she said, putting her hand on

Luciano's arm. It was the first time she had touched him.

'I'm sure Luciano didn't mean to insult your family,' she said to Falco. She felt Luciano's muscles tense under her hand. 'And I'm sure that if there has been a misunderstanding, it will be sorted out. But surely a Duchessa would have to listen to such a proposal?' she said to Luciano. 'I mean, this is not my world, literally, but from what I've seen of Talia, you don't just say "get lost" if one member of a noble family asks to marry another.'

She felt Luciano relax slowly. 'No-oh, I suppose not,' he said grudgingly.

'And if it's any consolation,' said Falco anxiously, 'I don't think he wants to marry her. I think he'd prefer our cousin Francesca – they always said when they were little that they'd marry each other when they grew up.'

Luciano laughed bitterly. 'Francesca di Chimici? I think you'll find she's already been married off to suit your family's plans. That's if she's the young woman Rinaldo di Chimici put up against Arianna in the Ducal election.'

'Rinaldo is my cousin too,' said Falco stiffly. 'I don't like him much, but he is a member of my family and I can't choose my relatives.'

'That's right,' said Georgia. 'None of us can. Be fair, Luciano – Falco can't help what his family does or who they are, come to that.'

'But Gaetano will do what your father tells him, won't he?' asked Luciano.

'I don't know,' said Falco, calmly. 'I'm not going to, am I?'

There was a tense silence and then Luciano seemed to regain control of himself.

'I know we agreed to consider helping you,' he said at last. 'But I am not happy about it. I don't even know whether what you want to do is possible and it is certainly dangerous. And you would have to accept that it means leaving your family for ever. I don't know if you fully understand what that means.'

'I have thought of little else,' said Falco, 'since our ride to Belle Vigne.'

'But the thinking is one thing,' said Luciano. 'The experiencing would be much worse.'

'It would be different for me from your experience,' said Falco. 'Because you got stuck here by accident. And I am choosing to go to the other world.'

'That's true,' said Georgia. 'Surely that does make a difference, Lucien?'

'Perhaps it does,' he answered slowly. 'But I want you to think this through properly. It won't be like a spell which can be reversed. If you travel to my old world – and we don't yet know if you can – you will be worse than an exile in a strange country. Remember that I knew Bellezza quite well before I ended up there permanently. You will arrive in a world so different from this that I don't think you can imagine it. A world where the speed of a galloping horse is considered slow, where you could travel the length of Talia in a few hours or speak to someone on the other side of the world by using a machine.'

'But it is just because your world has such wonders – magic I would call them – that I want to go there,' cried Falco. 'If so much can be done so quickly, then surely I could be made whole again?'

'Maybe you could,' said Luciano. 'But what then? You won't be able to come back here. You won't be with your friends and family. At least I knew some people in Bellezza. But you will have to make a completely new life among strangers. And think what it will do to your family. I know what it did to mine.' He stopped abruptly, unable to carry on.

'It would be better for my family to lose me,' said Falco. 'I know that they love me, even my father. But every time he looks at me I see the pity in his eyes, the memory of what I used to be. I have already said goodbye to Gaetano. He is the only one who knows what I intend and it was a bitter parting. But, I told you, my mind is made up. I want you two to help me stravagate to Georgia's world.'

*

'A horse with wings?' said Duke Niccolò. 'That's absurd. A child's story.'

'Would I lie to you, Master?' said Enrico. 'I've seen her with my own eyes and she's as pretty a little filly as you could wish to see in a month of Sundays.'

'And in the Ram, you say?' The Duke saw the implications immediately. If word got out that the Ram had been blessed with such a good omen, it would sway public opinion in their favour and make it harder to do deals with the jockeys of the other Twelfths in the race. Remorans were a superstitious lot. The Ram would undoubtedly keep their piece of good fortune secret until just a few days before the race.

'Born in the Ram, yes, but taken to Santa Fina with

her mother where she is now,' said Enrico.

Duke Niccolò remembered the black filly with the blanket and cursed under his breath. He had been within inches of this secret himself and yet he had to rely on a grubby little spy to tell him what had been under his nose.

'Just say the word, my Lord, and she can be yours. And all the luck that goes with her.'

'And you're sure it's not a fake?' the Duke persisted. 'Not some sort of bird's wings stuck on to a young horse?'

'I saw her fly last night,' said Enrico. 'Round and round above the stable yard when Roderigo thought there was no one there but his faithful groom Diego. But Diego is my friend and I was hiding behind some hay bales. Of course they had her on a lunge line, but suppose it got caught in some trees and broke? They wouldn't know where she had got to then, would they? Wouldn't even know she had been stolen.'

Of course the horse was real. Niccolò had known it really, even when he queried the spy's story. Everyone who had any connection with Remora knew the stories about flying horses. But it made the Duke uneasy to hear that one had been born in his time, to the Twelfth with the strongest allegiance to his toughest rival. He didn't like things to happen that were beyond his control. Well, there was something he could do to get the situation back under his control before the news leaked out.

'How much?' he asked.

*

'You will need a talisman,' said Luciano.

It was the first time he had used that word in front of a di Chimici and Georgia realised what it meant: they were really going to take Falco to their world. No, she corrected herself, to my world. Falco had been right to refer to it as that; Luciano was a Talian now. She resolved to stop thinking of him as Lucien. From now on, even to herself, she would call him Luciano. It would help.

'How can I get one?' asked Falco simply, without even questioning what the word meant.

'Georgia will have to bring one for you,' said Luciano. 'It has to be something from the other world, brought from there to here. Then when you are ready to stravagate, you must hold it in your hands and fall asleep in Talia thinking of the other place. You should wake up in Anglia, in England, I mean, in the twenty-first century. Though Goddess knows what will happen to you after that. That's Georgia's department, too, I suppose.'

Both boys looked at her as if she could solve all the problems that they were going to set her.

'Well, what sort of thing should it be?' she asked. 'Mine is a horse and Luciano said his was a book. But they were both from Talia. I won't know what I'm looking for in England.'

'May I see the horse?' asked Falco.

Reluctantly, Georgia drew the little model of the winged horse from her pocket and showed it to him.

'A *cavallo alato*!' he said excitedly. 'The Rassenans used to have them. Wouldn't it be wonderful to see one!'

Georgia and Luciano exchanged glances.

To distract him, Luciano said, 'Rodolfo's talisman comes from the other world. It is a silver ring that Doctor Dethridge brought him.'

An idea was beginning to form in Georgia's mind.

'I thought I wasn't supposed to bring anything from my world except my own talisman,' she said now.

Luciano shrugged. 'Those are the rules. But Doctor Dethridge brought Rodolfo's talisman. And Paolo's. And Giuditta Miele's. And the talismans of countless other Stravaganti from Talia to the other world. It's something we do. I am being trained so that one day I will be adept enough to take talismans to bring Stravaganti from the other world to this. It is a heavy responsibility.'

'Whoa!' said Georgia. 'You mean Doctor Dethridge, who invented the whole art of stravagation, is the only one who has ever brought talismans from my world to this and you're being trained to do it, and yet you expect me to pick up a little something and bring it for Falco just like that? Isn't that going to upset the whole space-time-continuum-thingy?'

Luciano smiled at her and she knew that she would do whatever he asked. 'I used to compare it to *Star Trek* too,' he said. He sighed. It sometimes seemed to him that hundreds of years had passed since he first stood on Rodolfo's roof garden and found he had no shadow. He missed him intensely. And Arianna too.

Quickly, he said, 'It would be used only once, if Falco is really determined to be what Doctor Dethridge calls "translated". Just the one journey – like a one-way ticket.'

'But wait,' said Georgia. 'Doesn't the talisman have to find the right person? I mean, our talismans came to us and brought us to where we were supposed to go. Can we just give something to Falco and hope it will work to help him stravagate?'

Luciano looked serious. 'We can't be sure,' he said. He turned to Falco. 'Do you understand? It's one thing for you to make up your mind that you want to go to our world. But it's another for it to work. You have to accept that even if Georgia brings you something, it might not take you away from Talia.'

Falco nodded. 'I am willing to take the risk,' he said.

'Shouldn't we ask someone?' said Georgia. She knew she had already missed an opportunity to tell Paolo about it. 'What about Doctor Dethridge? Or you could try contacting Rodolfo?'

Luciano's face set hard. He didn't really believe that Arianna was seriously considering marriage to a di Chimici, but he was hurt that neither she nor Rodolfo had sent word to him about the proposal. He had a vision of them getting on with the business of governing Bellezza and making important decisions without him. He felt left out and angry. And that was when he decided not to tell anyone about Falco.

'No,' he said. 'We'll handle this ourselves. After all, we are both Stravaganti.'

'And now I shall be one too,' said Falco, smiling his angelic smile. 'At least, for a little while. I shall make one beautiful flight and then hang up my wings. And Georgia will look after me.'

Georgia had to come home early from school on

Tuesday; she was tired and groggy. Maura was so worried about her that Georgia decided not to stravagate for a couple of nights. She was sick of feeling tired and there were only a few days till the end of term. It would be easier in the holidays and Luciano had assured her that it was perfectly possible that she might not miss any time in Talia at all because of the way that the portal worked.

But she had reckoned without Russell. All the time she was stravagating nightly, she had been super-careful about the winged horse, transferring it from day clothes to night clothes and back again and never letting it out of her possession. But on the Tuesday night she had been exhausted and she had known that she was not going to need it that night. So she had left it in the pocket of her jeans in the washing hamper in the bathroom. And on Wednesday morning it had gone.

Chapter 13

A Courtship

Georgia was paralysed with shock and fear. At first she tried to believe that Maura had taken the horse, but the jeans were still in the hamper and not in the washing-machine. And Maura had gone to work, leaving strict instructions for Georgia to ring the doctor for an emergency appointment. The house was silent and still, with that reverberating quiet that comes after chaos. Ralph had gone to work too and Russell to school. Georgia had heard the clatter and low murmur of their breakfast, through the fug of her exhausted sleep.

Now she sat on the side of the bath with her jeans crumpled in her lap and felt as if she really might be ill. It had to be Russell who'd taken it. Georgia knew it was useless, but she went and tried the handle of her stepbrother's door anyway. It was locked. Russell had demanded his own lock at the same time as Georgia got hers. Now she was sure that the winged horse was somewhere behind the locked door.

She walked down the stairs in a state of shock and poured herself a bowl of cereal, afraid that if she didn't eat something she would faint. But it was hard to get the food down. She phoned the doctor but was told she couldn't have an appointment till noon.

She showered quickly, her mind racing. What was she to do if Russell refused to give back the horse? Or, worse, if he threw it away or broke it? At the thought of Russell grinding the little winged figure under one of his size eleven Dockers, Georgia turned the water up till it nearly scalded her and vigorously shampooed her scalp.

It was one thing to decide to give Talia a miss for a few days. But the thought of never being able to go back, never to see Remora again, or Cesare or Paolo and his chaotic family – or Luciano – was an entirely different proposition. And what about Falco?

Georgia had spent a lot of time thinking about Falco recently. What he wanted her and Luciano to do for him was certainly dangerous and possibly wrong. But she had come to believe that it might have been what she was intended to do in Talia, why the talisman had found its way to her in the first place. She didn't really think she was intended to be a proper Stravagante, in the way that Luciano was. And she didn't feel specially gifted or even drawn to learn whatever mysterious arts and skills the Stravaganti had.

No, she felt she had one specific task to accomplish

in Talia and that was the rescuing of Falco. Why, she was still uncertain, only that it was the thing she was supposed to do. But without the talisman she could accomplish nothing. It was agonising. How long would it take Paolo to realise that she hadn't returned to Talia because she couldn't stravagate? And would he bring her another talisman? Georgia had no idea if this was allowed or even possible.

She decided that she would go mad if she stayed in the house any longer.

'His Highness Prince Gaetano of Giglia!' announced the Duchessa's footman.

Gaetano was shown into a large reception room, whose long windows overlooked a canal. At the far end was a wooden dais supporting an elaborate mahogany throne. To the side of it on a much less ornate chair sat a man dressed in black velvet with a lot of silver in his black hair. This was obviously the Regent, Rodolfo, father and adviser to the young Duchessa and a powerful Stravagante.

Gaetano found his heart pounding so much at the sight of one of his father's greatest enemies that he couldn't focus properly on the slight figure on the throne.

'Principe,' came a sweet musical voice, 'Bellezza welcomes you. I trust you are comfortably lodged in the Ambassador's palazzo? May I present to you my father, Senator Rodolfo Rossi, the Regent of the city?'

Rodolfo paid the young di Chimici the honour of getting up from his seat and taking a few steps towards him before bowing.

Gaetano returned the courtesy, then went forward to kneel before the Duchessa and kiss the hand she held out to him. She raised him to his feet and he found himself looking through a silver mask into amused violet eyes. Gaetano had been brought up in palaces and castles and had never met anyone without a title, except the servants, until his voice had broken. So he was no stranger to formality and courtly ways and not easily intimidated. But when he at last concentrated on the object of his journey, he found himself blushing and stammering like a stonemason in a lady's boudoir.

She was beautiful; that much he could tell in spite of the mask. Slender and tall, with an abundance of glossy chestnut-brown hair coiled in an elaborate style, revealing the perfect shape of her head, poised on her neck like a flower on its stem. Several small curls had escaped from the coiffure and strayed down on to her neck and brow, making the whole effect more natural, in spite of the formality of her dress. And those eyes! So big and lustrous and of an unusual colour that matched the dark amethysts in her hair and at her throat.

He thought fleetingly of Luciano. Lucky dog! he thought, if she returns his affections. Then Gaetano remembered what he was there for. He pulled himself together and the rest of the audience passed in pleasantries and pastries, which the servant brought in and set on a low round brass table along with a blond sparkling wine that Gaetano had never tasted before. The same servant brought a chair for the visiting prince and soon the three of them were conversing easily about Remora and the Race of the Stars.

'I met a friend of yours in the city, Your Grace,' he said to the Duchessa, 'and of yours, I believe,' turning to Rodolfo. 'A young man named Luciano.'

He was rewarded by seeing a deeper rose tinge the Duchessa's fresh complexion, just under her mask.

'Indeed,' said the Regent. 'He is my apprentice and a distant family connection. Is he well? And his foster-father, my good friend Dottore Crinamorte, did you see him too?'

'Yes, they are both well,' replied Gaetano. 'I met them in the Twelfth of the Ram, at the Horsemaster's house, along with Luciano's friend, Giorgio.'

Rodolfo betrayed no emotion at this news and talk turned to the coming journey to the city to see the Race of the Stars. No mention was made on this first occasion of the underlying purpose of the young Prince's visit. Gaetano went back to Rinaldo's old lodgings, his mind in a whirl. If he had to marry this Duchessa, it would be no unpleasant experience, he thought. But would she have him? It was clear where her preference lay. But she might have no more choice in the matter than he did.

Mr Goldsmith's smile at seeing Georgia soon turned to a concerned frown.

'How delightful! But why aren't you at school? Are you ill? You don't look very well,' he said.

All it took was one sympathetic look; Georgia burst into tears. Mr Goldsmith was horrified; he gave her his clean white handkerchief and made her sit down in his little office at the back of the shop. He even put up his 'closed' notice in the door, although business was bad and he couldn't afford to miss any customers.

He brought Georgia some tea, regretting that he hadn't got any biscuits this time. She felt better as she sipped the hot drink; she didn't go in for tears much, only when Russell had been unusually horrible.

'Now you must tell me what's the matter,' said Mr Goldsmith, who wasn't used to seeing people cry.

'It's Russell,' sniffed Georgia. 'My stepbrother. I think he's stolen the horse.'

Her expression was so tragic that Mr Goldsmith knew he mustn't make light of her loss. Though it was only a museum replica and, theoretically, not impossible to replace.

'Oh dear,' he said. 'I am sorry. What makes you think he's taken it?'

Georgia explained and the old man soon realised that she was telling him a lot more about her family than he had known before. This stepbrother was obviously a nasty piece of work. And there was clearly more.

'I need the horse,' Georgia was saying. 'I can't explain to you why – you wouldn't believe me anyway – but I have to have it in order to do something I've promised to do. And I mean that one – it can't be any other winged horse.'

Mr Goldsmith could sense her hysteria mounting; he had no idea why the winged horse had become so important to her, but he recognised obsession when he saw it.

'Then we'll just have to make sure that Russell gives it back, won't we? I don't think there's much point in your asking him nicely, given that it's something he's done to – what do you call it? – wind you up. Isn't that what you say? Good expression. I know what it does to my clocks if you over-wind them. Still, how about going straight to your parents and telling them what you think has happened? Surely he'll find it harder to lie to them?'

Georgia agreed that he was probably right, but talking about clocks reminded her of her doctor's appointment. Mr Goldsmith's clocks all showed different times, but her watch told her it was quarter to twelve and she must run.

Doctor Dethridge arranged his cards in the pattern he had made at his last reading. He had pondered long over the meaning of it and now decided to show it to Rodolfo. He used his hand-mirror to reflect the cards and peered into it himself at intervals until he found his old pupil looking back out at him.

'Gretynges, Maister Rudolphe!' the old Elizabethan said. 'Whatte thinke ye of this arraye?'

'I think it most remarkable, old friend,' said Rodolfo, looking intently at the cards, 'for the reason that I got the very same reading at the new moon.'

'The Goddesse does notte appeare at newe moon withoute goode cause,' mused Dethridge.

'Perhaps she is interesting herself in our affairs?' suggested Rodolfo.

'Thenne we moste hope hir meddlinge is for oure goode,' said Dethridge.

Luciano was not surprised that Georgia didn't turn up in Remora the next day; after all, he had advised her to take a break. But Falco was clearly disappointed when the Bellezzan Stravagante arrived at the Papal palace on his own.

'There are things we can discuss without Georgia being here,' Luciano said gently.

But Falco only nodded and Luciano thought he saw him brush away a tear. Here was a development. Was Falco's wish to be translated to the modern world being influenced by a desire to be near Georgia? It was too delicate an area to probe straightaway. Luciano decided to go ahead with the practical details and worry about this new problem later.

'There are arrangements to be made at both ends,' he said in a businesslike way. 'Georgia can sort things out about your new life and bring you a talisman. But you need to plan how you are going to leave here. You understand that if you stravagate to my old world and stay there overnight, your body will appear asleep here during the day?'

'Yes,' said Falco, 'you said. And if I stay away, it will look as if I have the *Morte Vivenda*. Until one day I shall actually die here. How long do you think that will take?'

Luciano shook his head. It amazed him how calmly this thirteen-year-old could talk about his fate.

'I really don't know. For me it was a matter of weeks, but as I told you, I was being kept alive artificially. It might be only days. The point is, there should be some sort of reason. We don't want your father to suspect what will really have happened.'

'I shall ask to go back to Santa Fina,' said Falco. 'I can say it's because Gaetano has gone to Bellezza and I want to go back to the summer palace until the race. It will be easier to escape from up there; the servants aren't as vigilant as my father.'

'But there still has to be a reason,' pressed Luciano.

'I've thought about that, too,' said Falco. 'I think the easiest thing would be if I pretended to try to kill myself.'

*

Luciano was thoughtful on his way back to the Ram. But all thoughts of Falco were driven out of his head when he saw the carriage drawn up outside the stables. William Dethridge was leaning out of the window waving to him.

'Haste ye, yonge Lucian. Word has come from Saint Fyne. The marvele has flown awaye!'

*

Gaetano went back to the Duchessa's palazzo for a grand dinner that night. He was guest of honour, seated at her right, while Rodolfo was on her other side. But the young di Chimici was astonished to find that his other neighbour was his cousin Francesca.

'Greetings, cousin,' she said, smiling at his obvious surprise. 'Didn't you know I am a Bellezzan citizen now?'

Gaetano was completely nonplussed. He had heard the rumours about Francesca but hadn't expected to meet her in the city. She was more lovely even than he remembered her, with her glossy black hair and sparkling dark eyes. He took her proffered hand and kissed it, summoning all his courtesy to ask after her health. She was dressed in red taffeta, which rustled as she spoke. Gaetano felt as if he had drunk deep of the red Bellezzan wine, even though his glass was still untouched.

'I see you are enjoying your family reunion,' said a musical, mocking voice behind him and Gaetano realised, to his horror, that he had turned his back on the Duchessa.

'Forgive me, your Grace,' he said, turning swiftly back to his host and blushing to the roots of his hair. 'I was indeed surprised to see my cousin here – so much so that my manners have deserted me. I trust I find you well?'

'Never better,' said the Duchessa and she smiled at him with genuine amusement.

At that moment Gaetano had the astonishing thought that this beautiful young girl knew all about him and his boyhood romance with Francesca and that she was deliberately throwing them together. But why would she do that? To test his resolve? To remind him that marriage was supposed to be about love? He looked past her to see Rodolfo regarding him with the same expression. These two were a dangerous pair, he decided.

For the rest of the banquet, Gaetano devoted himself to the Duchessa, although always aware of the rustling beside him and the sound of Francesca's laugh as she flirted with her other neighbour. Behind his courtly words, his mind raced. Was Francesca married? And if so, where was her husband? Gaetano was pretty sure that it wasn't the man on her other side, who appeared to be quite young. He found it very hard to concentrate on what he was here for.

Tomorrow he was to have a private audience with the Duchessa, at which he must formally make his proposal to her. They both knew the purpose of his visit and he wondered what the outcome would be. Was he expected to declare undying love? He could just imagine the quizzical look she would give him. The Duke had given him no guidance on how to woo her.

When the Duchessa rose from her seat, the rest of the company stood too. She led them into another room, where musicians were already playing and clusters of little chairs were arranged around low tables. She asked Gaetano to excuse her while she had some words with the admiral of the Bellezzan fleet and he was alone. Francesca was sitting at a little table across the room and he found himself drawn to sit beside her. There could surely be no objection to his sitting with his cousin? Especially when there was no one else there he knew.

'So what are you saying?' said Ralph. 'Russell has stolen some toy of yours? That's a bit pathetic, isn't it?'

Georgia ground her teeth. 'It's not a toy,' she explained again, trying to keep cool. 'It's an ornament which I saved up to buy from an antique shop.'

'It doesn't really matter what it is,' said Maura, using her let's-be-scrupulously-fair voice. 'Ralph, I'm sure you agree that Russell should respect other people's belongings.'

The four of them were sitting round the kitchen table that Wednesday evening. Georgia had requested a family meeting and Maura had immediately realised that something was seriously wrong. Family meetings were rare events, held only when an important decision had to be made or conveyed.

'Who says I took her stupid horse?' said Russell truculently. 'Why would I? She probably just put it somewhere and forgot it.'

Ralph immediately switched sides.

'Georgia says you took it,' he said acidly. 'And she seems to think you did it to annoy her.'

Russell shrugged. Bad move. It annoyed both parents.

'Well, did you?' asked Ralph.

There was a silence. Georgia held her breath. If Russell denied it, could she possibly ask to have his room searched? Would Ralph go along with that? He seemed to be backing her up now, but she knew how quickly adults could veer from one side to another during a dispute. What happened next could determine her whole future in Remora.

Roderigo was beside himself with guilt. The flying horse had been entrusted to his care and now she had gone. He brought Diego out to tell the story of her disappearance again to the two distinguished visitors from Bellezza. The Horsemaster's boy from the Ram was already in Santa Fina, scouring the neighbourhood for any trace of the black filly.

'The lunge snagged on a tree,' said Diego, looking haggard. He had given his account several times and did genuinely believe that he had witnessed an accident. But he had a nagging discomfort at the back of his mind, knowing that he had not kept the flying horse the secret she was meant to be.

'It was last night,' he continued. 'I had her out for exercise as usual and was flying her on the lunge. Then it caught on a tall tree at the edge of the paddock and it broke. She was away before I could do anything about it.'

'I have men out searching everywhere,' said the wretched Roderigo. 'Surely we shall soon have her back. She will fly home to where her mother is.'

'If no one else finds her first,' said Luciano.

'We moste goe to the mothire,' said Dethridge, and the two Stravaganti went into the stables to visit Starlight. She was standing very still in her stall.

'She is not eating,' said Roderigo, shaking his head.

Dethridge went over to the grey mare and fondled her ear, whispering into it. Starlight tossed her head and looked as if she understood what he was telling her.

'It was just a joke,' muttered Russell grumpily. 'I was going to give it back.'

'Go and fetch it immediately,' said Ralph sternly.

While Russell was out of the room, Ralph apologised to Georgia. He was obviously hugely relieved that his son had owned up. But not as relieved as Georgia was. At that moment she felt willing to forgive Russell anything, as long as he returned his talisman to her.

That feeling changed as soon as she saw what he was holding in his hand when he came back into the room.

'I'm sorry,' he said, feigning contrition. 'It seems to have got a bit damaged.'

The little Etruscan horse lay in the palm of his hand with both its wings snapped off beside it.

Gaetano's all-important meeting with the young Duchessa took place not in her state rooms at the Ducal palace but in her father's roof garden. The Regent's manservant, Alfredo, showed the young di Chimici up into what appeared to be a marvellous floating garden high above the city. Gaetano saw immediately that the terraces and paths stretched into a distance further away than should have been physically possible. But his awe was tempered by the fact that the Stravagante did not appear to be anywhere there. At least his audience with the Duchessa would be private.

Arianna was sitting on a stone bench scattering seed for a magnificent peacock. She was simply dressed in green silk, with a plain silk mask. There were no jewels in sight and her hair was loose on her shoulders. She looked the girl that she was, a year younger than Gaetano but already ruler of a great city-state. Gaetano suddenly felt sorry for her.

At his greeting, she rose and the peacock scuttled away; he heard it scream in the far distance.

'Good morning, Principe,' she said. 'I hope you enjoyed your dinner last night?'

'Very much,' he replied, though having no recollection of any dish that was served. It crossed his mind fleetingly that this was not like him.

'I hope also that it was a pleasure to see your cousin again,' continued the Duchessa. 'I was not sure if she would accept my invitation. You may know that she stood against me in the Ducal election?'

'So I gather,' said Gaetano, who had heard all the details from Francesca the night before. 'I am sure your Grace understands that it was not my cousin's idea.'

'Oh it was your cousin's idea all right,' said the Duchessa. 'Just not that cousin's. Your family have many plans for Bellezza, don't they?'

It was hardly diplomatic language, but Gaetano had realised that this was to be no conventional courtship or proposal. Directness was going to serve him better than any courtly pretence.

'Your Grace,' he said. 'I think you know why I am here. My father wrote to yours proposing an alliance between our two families. I am supposed to ask for your hand in marriage.'

'And is this you doing it?' asked the Duchessa, arching one eyebrow. 'Should you not kneel and profess undying love?'

'How can I?' asked Gaetano. 'I don't know you and until I know someone I cannot love her or pretend to do so. But I have been brought up to obey my father. And I shall make this marriage if you are willing. And if we were to be married, I should strive to be a good husband and devote myself to your happiness.'

The Duchessa's manner softened. 'You are honest, Principe, and I like you the better for it. But if you are to make a bargain in the marriage market, you should be able to inspect the goods.' She began to untie her mask. 'And during our courtship, if that is what it is, I think we should call each other by our given names. Mine is Arianna.'

'I am Gaetano,' said the young di Chimici, as he looked on the face of his father's enemy and liked what he saw very much indeed.

'It's broken,' said Georgia, feeling sick.

'Yeah, sorry, I said,' said Russell. 'It was an accident.'

'It was covered in bubble-wrap,' said Georgia. 'You must have unwrapped it.'

'It can be mended,' said Maura, anxious to keep the peace. 'I can stick it together for you so that you won't be able to see the join. It will be as good as new.'

'You did it deliberately,' Georgia said to Russell, 'because you knew it was important to me.'

'Why is that, George?' Russell said, almost pleasantly. 'I can't see why that horse thing matters so much. It's only an ornament and you have lots of china horses – quite childish really. Perhaps it's something to do with that creep you bought it from – that old guy you're so friendly with?'

Maura and Ralph's antennae quivered. 'What man is this, Georgia?' asked Maura.

'It's the old bloke at the antique shop,' explained

Russell. 'She's always popping in to have tea with him. I'm surprised you let her do it. My mates think he's a pervert.'

Chapter 14

Wings

The row rumbled on for ages and Russell slipped away, smiling quietly to himself. Georgia could almost hear him thinking, 'my work here is done'. He had succeeded in diverting all the flak from himself to Georgia, who was now suspected of a clandestine friendship with a dirty old man. A broken ornament was hardly a comparable offence.

But it was to Georgia. She knew that Russell had broken it on purpose. She also knew that Mr Goldsmith wasn't the sort of person Russell had made him out to be and she answered Maura and Ralph's questions distractedly, much more concerned about the talisman. Would it still work if it were mended in the way Maura had suggested?

'Look,' she said eventually, exasperated. 'Why don't

you come and meet him? He's a perfectly nice old man and we talk about stuff like the Etruscans and the horse race in Siena. There's nothing sinister about that, is there?'

Maura sighed. 'It often starts like that, Georgia. A paedophile will "groom" a prospective victim by giving her presents and seeming to be harmless.'

'Mr Goldsmith isn't a paedophile!' shouted Georgia. 'And he hasn't given me presents – only biscuits. Why don't you ever listen to me? I saved up and *bought* the horse. And now Russell has broken it and you won't even do anything to him. Mr Goldsmith is my friend. Practically the only one I've got.' At least in this world, she thought.

Niccolò took Falco back to the summer palace in his carriage. It grieved him to part with his youngest son again so soon. But if that was what would make the boy happy, he would go along with it. And Falco did seem much more cheerful, chatting happily to his father about Gaetano's trip to Bellezza and the state visit of the Duchessa for the Stellata.

'Do you think she'll like him, Papa?' he asked. 'I don't see why she wouldn't – he's so nice.'

'Liking him doesn't come into it,' said the Duke. 'It's a question of whether she likes the other terms of the offer.'

Falco knew his father too well to ask what the other terms were. 'Do you think she's looking forward to the race?' he asked instead.

'How could she not?' said Niccolò. 'It's the big

moment of the Reman year – what the whole city lives and breathes for.'

Falco had seen every Stellata from the year he was five to the year he was eleven. Since the accident, though, he hadn't had the heart to watch twelve healthy young men race round the Campo on magnificent horses.

'You will let me bring you back for the race, won't you?' said Niccolò. 'You said you'd see it this year and I'm sure it would do you good. You can sit on the stage with your brothers and me and your uncle and our honoured guests.'

'Yes, Papa, I'll come,' said Falco, but his heart was heavy knowing he might not be in Talia by the time of the race.

*

Raffaella was an unexpected guest at Paolo's house when Cesare, Luciano and Doctor Dethridge returned from Santa Fina. They had no good news to report. And the female Manoush seemed to know of their trouble already.

'Aurelio sent me,' she said simply. 'He said you might need help.'

'Has the harpist second sight?' asked Paolo.

'He sees what others do not,' said Raffaella, 'even though he can't see what others do.'

'Tell her,' said Luciano. 'We can trust the Manoush.'

'Something precious of ours has gone missing,' said Paolo. 'A horse of a special nature. She is only a week old but much bigger than an ordinary horse of that age. She has the gift of flight.'

Raffaella went quite still. 'A zhou volou?' she said reverently. 'You have one?'

'We *had* one,' said Cesare bitterly.

'It was our good omen,' said Paolo. 'Born in the Ram and destined to bring us good luck, we hope. Now, things are different. Someone may have stolen the luck.'

'Then it will turn to ill for them,' said Raffaella. 'With your permission, I shall put the word out among our people. We have family everywhere in the region; someone may have seen something.'

'How do you know about this kind of horse?' asked Luciano.

'We know about all kinds of horses,' said Raffaella. 'The zhou volou is a good omen for the Manoush too.'

Cesare hesitated. 'Forgive me for asking,' he said. 'But if your people value the flying horse, would they return her to the Ram?'

Raffaella looked at him gravely. 'We are not horse-thieves,' she said. 'Even of ordinary horses. The winged one would be a sacred creature to us and we would return it to its proper guardians.'

'I'm sorry,' said Cesare. 'I want to trust you, but I'm just so worried about Merla. I helped deliver her.'

'I understand,' said Raffaella. 'I would feel the same.'

*

It had not been easy, stealing the flying horse. Enrico had hidden in the bushes again at midnight while Diego let the filly exercise her wings high up above the stable yard. The lunge was even longer than before and it did tend to get entangled in tree branches. At one such moment, Enrico had crept from his hiding-place and cut through the leather, holding tight on to the part that was still linked to the flying horse.

This had made her tug harder against the restraint of the much shorter length of lunge, which made it more difficult to lead her away from the stable. Enrico had to guide her from many feet below, till she was flying over a field where he could gently reel her in till she stood on firm ground again. And all the time it was impossible to see her against the starless sky. She folded her strong black pinions and stood shivering, while Enrico spoke soothingly to her and draped a blanket over her tell-tale wings.

But now Enrico was well established at Santa Fina. His note from the Duke had gained him entry into the di Chimici summer palace, where he had a very comfortable room with all the food and drink he could consume. He had smuggled the black filly into a stall in the stables, where he quickly made friends with Nello, the Duke's head groom. Nello was well aware of his master's nature, so when a strange man turned up in the middle of the night with an obviously stolen horse, he didn't turn a hair. Even when he saw what kind of horse it was. The other servants were equally discreet about the new visitor; it didn't pay to ask too many questions where the Duke's affairs were concerned.

Enrico explored the palace, amazed by the sheer number of rooms and the size of the staircases.

'Dia!' he exclaimed to himself. 'I had no idea just how rich these di Chimici were.'

Today the palace was buzzing with activity. A message had come to say that the Duke was bringing his youngest son back to the palace for a few weeks. Falco was a great favourite with the household because of his sweet nature and angelic looks and the tragedy of his situation. The cook was bustling around making his favourite dishes and the maids were cleaning his bedroom and dusting all the formal rooms so that there should be nothing for the Duke to find fault with.

Enrico was watching from the loggia above the main entrance when the carriage came into view on the road from Remora. He decided to make himself scarce until the Duke had established his son in his quarters. He headed back out to the stables to check up on his prize. Actually, he was avoiding contact with young Falco; Nello had told him all about the accident and Enrico, who would slide a blade between a man's ribs without a second thought, if he was being paid enough, was squeamish about illness and physical defects, especially in children.

Georgia lay on her bed, clutching the broken horse, tears scalding her cheeks. In the last twenty-four hours her world seemed to have collapsed. She wished for the millionth time that she had stravagated on Tuesday night instead of wimping out. Now she didn't know if she would ever be in Talia again. And Russell had got away with his mean trick and was spreading vile rumours about an innocent friendship. How did he do that? He was in the wrong, no question about that, but she was the one that Ralph and Maura were arguing about downstairs. How she hated him!

She thought of Gaetano and Cesare and Luciano and how they treated her with respect and affection. Falco too. And lately she had caught him looking at her with something more in his expression. There was her new friend Alice at school too. They had started having lunch together regularly and had met a few times after school. It felt good to have a female friend again. If it weren't for Russell, her life would definitely be improving. Now she just felt trapped, unable to escape from the strain of living in the same house with someone so hateful. And she wouldn't even be able to visit Mr Goldsmith if Russell succeeded in his scare campaign.

Suddenly she wished she were a di Chimici, with the money and the power to have her enemies eliminated. She wouldn't have hesitated at that moment to send an assassin to Russell's room. Then she was horrified at her own thoughts. So that was what it was like to be someone like the Duke! The only difference between them was that he *did* have the power and money. Georgia felt ashamed.

There was a knock on her door.

'Georgia,' Maura called softly. 'Can I come in?'

'My Lord!' came a whisper from behind the Duke. By a strong effort of will, he managed not to jump but turned round slowly.

'Ah!' said Niccolò, letting the breath hiss out between his teeth when he saw who it was. 'You are getting better at this.'

'Sorry if I startled you, my Lord,' said Enrico. 'But I thought you might be about to leave. And I didn't want you to miss what I have to show you.'

He led the Duke into the stables and back to the furthest stall. Darker than the shadows in which she stood, wings drooping, was the flying horse.

'You did it!' said the Duke, eyes shining. 'The little miracle!'

He stepped forward and stroked the filly's muzzle. She huffed sadly down her nostrils.

'Nello!' called the Duke. 'Come here!'

His stableman appeared out of the shadows.

'Your Grace,' he bowed.

'What can you do for the little one?' Niccolò asked.

'She is moping a little, my Lord,' said Nello.

'Only natural,' agreed Enrico. 'Missing her mother.'

'But she will pull round,' said Nello. 'Have no fear, my Lord. I shall look after her as if she was my own baby.'

'Me too, my Lord,' said Enrico.

The Duke looked at his two men and shuddered slightly. But he did have faith in their knowledge of horses.

*

'I wish Georgia were here,' said Cesare miserably.

'Whatte coulde shee doe thatte we canne not?' asked Dethridge.

'Nothing, I suppose,' said Cesare. 'I just wish she knew about Merla.'

'But the portal has probably stabilised, hasn't it?'

said Luciano. 'I mean, ever since she started stravagating, the times in the two worlds have matched. If she's not here today, then it's likely only one night has passed in her world.'

'Not necessarily,' said Paolo. 'She could return tomorrow and we could find her four years older. But you are probably right.'

Neither Luciano nor Cesare liked the idea of Georgia coming back older than them.

The atmosphere in the stables of the Ram was bleak. They had searched Santa Fina all afternoon and returned late to Remora, planning to start again the next morning. No one really believed that Merla had gone missing by accident, or that she would be found wandering free in the countryside. Even if she were, what were the chances of someone who found her not keeping her to bring luck to his own house?

But, if someone had taken her, that meant that the Ram's secret was known.

'You are sure that neither of you let anything slip to the di Chimici?' asked Paolo.

'Certain,' said Cesare. 'We never really talked about horses, did we?'

'No,' said Luciano. 'And what's more, even if we had, I don't think they'd have told their father. Or anyone else.'

'Ye seme almoste to favoure these chimists nowe,' said Dethridge. 'Have yow forgot whatte they did to yow? And to the Dutchesse?'

'How could I?' asked Luciano. 'I live with the results of their actions every day. But those two, the young ones, are quite different from their father. And from their cousin, come to that. I don't think either of them cares about the family's plans.'

'And yette the ill-favoured one wolde make a marriage with yonge Arianne, to plese his fathire,' said Dethridge.

'Ah,' said Luciano, more calmly than he felt. 'So you know about that?'

His foster-father looked very uncomfortable.

'I am sorye, Lucian; Maister Rudolphe told mee. I meant not to speak of it, bot ye semed so certayne thatte the yonge nobile is yowre freend. Al I saye is – hee is his fathire's sonne and wol doo whatte he is bidden.'

'And what about Arianna?' said Luciano. 'What do you think she will do? Sell herself to the son and her city to his father? She would never do anything like that. She is her mother's daughter.'

'There,' said Maura. 'We'll put it in the airing-cupboard to dry and it will be as good as new.'

The wings were back on the horse and the joins could not be seen. Maura had done a good job with the glue.

'No,' said Georgia. 'It's not going out of my room.'

Her mother sighed. 'Have it your own way. But it will take longer to harden the glue if you don't put it somewhere warm.'

'It can go on the window-sill,' said Georgia. 'I'll wait. I'm not letting Russell get his hands on it again. You saw that it must have been broken deliberately.'

It was true. The wings looked as if they had been

snapped off cleanly from the horse's back. But Maura didn't want to believe that Russell had been guilty of such vandalism. She wanted the family to work and simply could not face the idea that her daughter and stepson hated one another.

'I see that you are very unhappy, Georgia,' she said now. 'Would you like to go away for a while?'

Georgia looked at her mother in amazement. Doctor Kennedy had pronounced her well enough to return to school the next day – 'Just a bit run down; it often happens towards the end of term. Too much homework,' had been her diagnosis.

'What about school?' she asked.

'Oh, you can do these next two days,' said Maura. 'You won't get any more homework anyway. But Alice's mother asked me if you'd like to go with Alice when she goes to stay with her father in Devon on Sunday. Alice asked if you could and she has a horse down there, you know.'

'I know,' said Georgia automatically, her mind whirling. It would be great to get away from the atmosphere in this house and she liked the idea of spending more time with Alice. Best of all, she liked the idea that Alice had asked for her. They had only just started to be friends, after all. But would she be able to stravagate to Remora from Devon? Still, she didn't know if she'd be able to stravagate with a broken talisman anyway.

'When did you see Alice's mum?' she said, playing for time.

'She rang me at work,' said Maura. 'Alice was anxious when you didn't come into school today. She wanted to ask you herself, but was afraid you wouldn't come back before the end of term.'

'I think I would like that,' said Georgia.

Maura sighed with relief. That would be one set of teenage hormones out of the house for a while, and perhaps she could persuade Ralph to talk to Russell while Georgia was away. And it would stop Georgia from seeing this peculiar man Russell had talked about, until Maura had a chance to check him out.

Falco limped down the great staircase of the summer palace. He had been waiting all morning for a visit from Luciano and, he hoped, Georgia. But no one had come. The palace was deserted and quiet and Falco's courage was beginning to fail. It was all very well to talk boldly of his new life in Georgia's world when he was with the young Stravaganti, but what if his plan didn't work? The talisman might not take him. Suppose he got horribly stranded between one world and the other? The half-life that he led here was better than no life at all and at least he was used to it.

And, if it did work, Falco knew how much his family would miss him, particularly Gaetano and their father. But ever since he had heard about the Duke's plan to send him into the Church without any vocation he had known that his father viewed him differently from his other sons. 'I won't be a disappointment to him,' he vowed. 'I'd rather not be here at all.'

Falco looked down the staircase at how many steps he had yet to descend, then back up behind him to see how far he had travelled. Out of the corner of his eye, he glimpsed a blue cloak whisking behind a pillar. He had seen it a few times before; there was someone else staying in the house besides himself and the servants.

But then the bell at the great door began jingling and a footman ushered in Luciano. Falco was pleased to see him, even though he entered alone.

The young Stravagante took the stairs two at a time and was in front of Falco before the boy knew it.

'I'm sorry I didn't come sooner,' he said. 'But I have been in the town all morning, on another errand. We need to talk somewhere privately.'

On Thursday Georgia lifted the winged horse gently off her window-sill and inspected it. It seemed fine. Carefully she swathed it in bubble-wrap and put it in her pocket. Today she would take it to school and tonight she would see if it would take her to Remora.

Alice was waiting for her in their classroom and her face lit up when she saw that Georgia was looking all right. In fact Georgia was feeling a lot better; she hadn't expected to sleep at all for worrying, but she had had a really good night and was feeling stronger than she had for a long time.

'You're coming to Devon?' whispered Alice during registration. 'My mum spoke to yours last night.'

Georgia nodded. 'Yeah, thanks. It'll be great. Can I ride your horse?'

''Course,' said Alice. 'We can take turns.'

'Alice,' whispered Georgia. 'Can you ride bare-back?'

There was just time for Alice to nod before Ms Yates told them off for chatting.

Luciano looked at the long ballroom in amazement. Musical instruments sat at the far end shrouded under cloths and a hundred mirrors reflected the two figures of himself and Falco standing in the middle of the room. It could not be a comforting image for the younger boy.

'Is there nowhere a bit ... smaller?' asked Luciano.

'It's all right,' said Falco. 'No one ever comes in here except when the family is entertaining.' He limped the length of the ballroom.

'It's quite snug here in the window,' he called back.

Luciano felt a surge of pity for the lonely boy, who had made this vast and dreary building his kingdom. They sat behind the ghostly shapes of harp and harpsichord and talked softly about Georgia and how Falco was to make his escape.

'I think,' said Luciano, 'that you'll have to do a trial run.'

'What's that?' asked Falco.

'Like a heat for the Stellata, a kind of a practice,' explained Luciano. 'We need to get Georgia to bring you a talisman and you can try going back with her at the end of one of her visits here. Then it will be morning in her world and you can see if you like it. I don't think you should make such a big decision without knowing what it's like. It's going to be so different from all this.' He gestured at the empty ballroom.

'Different from this is what I want,' said Falco. 'I'll do it. When do you think she'll come back?'

But Luciano realised he had no idea. And for the first time, he was worried about her.

Chapter 15

A Ghost in the Palace

Gaetano was too confused to enjoy his stay in
Bellezza. But there was no doubt that the city was
beautiful. Much as he loved his native Giglia, he had
to admit that Bellezza was spectacular. The Regent
had asked his older brothers, Egidio and Fiorentino,
to show Gaetano around and the two men spent their
days sculling the young di Chimici along the canals
and telling him all their stories from their days as
mandoliers.

They were surprisingly good company, full of
laughter and anecdotes and not at all like their
intimidating younger brother. But on the first day,
when Egidio was sculling, Fiorentino told him to pull
in at one of the traghetto jetties. 'There's a woman
there, waving us over,' he said. 'She must think we're

a ferry.'

Gaetano shaded his eyes with his hand. Even at this distance and with the sun behind her, he could tell it was his cousin Francesca. The two middle-aged mandoliers were not averse to taking on board a beautiful young woman, particularly when Gaetano explained that she was related to him.

'What are you all doing?' asked Francesca, when she had been introduced and was settled among the mandola-cushions. 'You look like a tourist, Gaetano.'

'Not really,' said Fiorentino, 'he'd have a younger mandolier to scull him if he were. My brother and I are long retired from that trade, but we still know enough to show an honoured guest our city.'

'You surely can't have been retired for long,' said Francesca. 'I've heard that mandoliers have to stop at twenty-five.'

The brothers were delighted with the compliment, which they took as a huge joke.

'I'd like to see more of the city myself,' said Francesca. 'My cousin the ambassador brought me here last year for my marriage and I have seen very little of Bellezza except the main sights like the Basilica and the market on the wooden bridge. For most of the time, I have been shut up in my husband's palazzo with just my maid for company.'

'And not your husband?' asked Egidio, who knew something of the background to this marriage.

'No,' said Francesca. 'Councillor Albani has gone south to oversee his vineyards near Cittanuova.'

She didn't add that she had insisted to Rinaldo di Chimici that he must get her marriage to old Albani dissolved and that she would not stay a minute in

Bellezza unless her husband were removed from her sight. It was true that Albani had vineyards in the south; they were doing very badly because of a blight on the vines and that was why he had accepted the di Chimici bride who came with a large dowry. It was proving more difficult than Francesca had hoped to get out of this marriage that had been forced on her, because Albani was canny enough to want to keep the dowry.

It was a delicate matter for the di Chimici family. Francesca had assumed that she would be able to return to Bellona as soon as the farce of the Ducal election was over, but a message had come from no less a person than Duke Niccolò that she must stay in the city until the dissolution of the marriage had been engineered, to save face for the family and support the illusion that she had her own reasons for coming to Bellezza.

'It would be a pleasure to show you our city with the Principe,' said Egidio.

It did not cross Gaetano's mind to wonder how Francesca knew he would be on the canal at that time and why she had been allowed out of the palazzo unaccompanied. He was just pleased to be with her. And so for the next few weeks, he spent his days with Francesca and the Rossi brothers, exploring the city by land and by water.

They visited the islands and he bought her lace and glass and a fine new dagger for himself. They ate delicious cakes on Burlesca and visited the glass museum on Merlino. Gaetano studied the glass mask and read the story of how a prince of Remora had been dancing with the Duchessa who wore its original, when she slipped and it splintered on her face. It was from that time that all unmarried women over sixteen in Bellezza had to wear a mask.

'It's the one good thing about my horrible marriage,' whispered Francesca. 'I don't have to wear a mask here. I don't know how the Duchessa can bear it. What's the point of being young and beautiful and having lovely clothes and jewels if no one can see your face? I expect she'll marry soon just to get out of it.'

This conversation made Gaetano very uncomfortable. He didn't know whether to tell Francesca why he was in Bellezza or that almost every night, when he dined privately with the Duchessa, she sat smiling at her side of table with her beauty unmasked and he called her Arianna.

'He must have been our great-uncle,' said Francesca, reading the label by the mask.

That brought Gaetano back to earth. He and Francesca were di Chimici; it was one of their ancestors who had danced with that Duchessa. He had no idea if Arianna was her descendant, but he did know that there was a family tradition that a Duchessa of Bellezza had poisoned the young Prince of Remora. He wished now that he had paid more attention to the story. No wonder there was a feud between the di Chimici and the city of Bellezza.

The question was, could a marriage between himself and Arianna bring it to an end?

*

'Nay, ladde, thou moste try to staye on!' laughed William Dethridge, hugely entertained.

He and Cesare had a secret; they were teaching Luciano to ride. At least, they were trying to. He was not a natural horseman and came off his mount quite often. But they were practising in a field full of soft hay and he suffered no more than bruises and hurt pride. He didn't want Georgia to know about this, so he had decided to have his private lessons early in the morning and late at night.

Luciano had come to this decision the morning he saw Cesare ride bareback in the preparatory races for the Stellata. He had envied the boy's easy seat and his sense of oneness with Arcangelo, the beautiful chestnut. He was also still smarting from seeing Georgia and Cesare ride off from Santa Fina with Gaetano di Chimici, while he and Falco followed in the carriage. Even Falco, three years younger than him, had apparently been a fine horseman before the accident.

'If I was still in the twenty-first century,' Luciano had told his foster-father, 'I'd be looking forward to getting my driving licence next year. You know, driving those horseless carriages I told you about? My dad had already given me a few lessons in the sports centre car park. Now all that has gone – I won't even have a bike. So I might as well learn how to get around on Talian transport.'

Dethridge had been silent. He rarely heard Luciano talk of the past, which was so far in the future, full of machines that the Elizabethan could hardly imagine. He gave the boy one of his bear-hugs. 'Thenne lerne it thou shalt,' was all he said.

And so their lessons had begun, with Cesare brought in on the secret. They started with a saddle, although Luciano was keen to progress to bareback riding and emulate Cesare's grace and skill.

'Don't try to run before you can walk,' warned Cesare.

'I'd settle for being able to trot!' gasped Luciano, bouncing up and down on the back of the gentle brown mare, Dondola, that they had chosen for him.

'Worrye notte,' said Dethridge. 'We'll make a horseman of you yet.'

Georgia didn't know what to do when she left school that afternoon. She didn't want to go home since Russell was likely to be there, but since his vile accusations she was worried about calling in at the antique shop. She had been wondering how he knew about her visits to Mr Goldsmith. But in the end she reasoned that Russell couldn't both be at home and lurking around outside the antique shop, so she went to see the old man after all.

He was in the middle of selling a pair of green vases to a tweedy woman when Georgia turned up so she waited, flicking through some old copies of *Country Life* on a round marble table in the corner. Mr Goldsmith was in a very good humour as he stashed ten-pound notes into his till. It was the first sale he had made for days.

'You're looking better, my dear,' he said.

'I'm fine,' said Georgia. 'The doctor said it was just tiredness.'

'And did you find your horse?' he asked.

'Russell had it,' said Georgia grimly. 'They made

him give it back, but he'd broken the wings off. Look.'

She took the mended horse out of her pocket and unwrapped it. Mr Goldsmith inspected the wings.

'Someone made a good job of mending that,' he said.

'My mum,' said Georgia. But she couldn't tell him that she wouldn't know if the horse was really as good as new until she'd tried stravagating with it.

'You were right about your stepbrother then?' asked Mr Goldsmith. 'What did your parents do about it?'

'Nothing!' said Georgia bitterly. 'It's me that's in trouble, not him.'

'What are you in trouble for?' he asked.

Georgia hesitated. 'It doesn't matter,' she said. 'I came in really to tell you that the horse is back and that I'm going away for a while. I think our parents want to keep Russell and me apart for a bit.'

'I shall miss your visits,' said Mr Goldsmith, 'but that sounds like a good plan.'

'Yes,' said Georgia. 'And I'm going to ride a real horse – my friend's – in Devon.'

Rodolfo had one of his mirrors trained on the Great Canal. It followed a mandola sculled by his brother and carrying the young di Chimici and his cousin. He smiled as he saw the young people's heads lean close together as Gaetano pointed out sights to Francesca.

'It's going well, isn't it?' said a voice behind him.

He turned to Arianna, the smile now for her. 'I didn't hear you. I must be getting old.'

Arianna, who had come through the secret passage,

put her hand on Rodolfo's shoulder. 'Never,' she said. 'They look happy, don't they?'

'It's a dangerous game you're playing,' said Rodolfo.

'Me?' said Arianna, wide-eyed. 'What could be more natural than for the Principe to spend time with his only family-member in Bellezza?'

Rodolfo raised one eyebrow. 'You know, you become more like your mother every day.'

And Arianna wasn't sure whether that was a compliment or not.

Georgia lay clutching the mended horse and thinking of Remora, not daring to fall asleep. She was terrified that she would not be able to stravagate. But as she felt herself beginning to drift off, she made a solemn promise – 'If I get back to Remora, I'll do what Falco wants as soon as possible, before Russell can get at the talisman again.'

When Georgia opened her eyes, she saw the sunlight shining through gaps in the roof tiles on to the golden dust of the Ram's hayloft. She heard the horses' hooves scraping on the stone floor underneath her and the chomp of their mouths in their mangers. She was back!

She looked in wonderment at the little horse in her hand. It was so tiny and vulnerable and yet Russell's attack hadn't taken away any of its power.

Georgia brushed bits of straw off her coarse Reman clothes and flung herself down the ladder and into Paolo's house, desperate to find out how much time had passed since her last visit and what had happened while she had been away.

But there seemed to be no one at home. Georgia felt disappointed and let down. She had never arrived to find the house empty before.

She sat at the scrubbed kitchen table feeling totally at a loss. Where were Luciano and Dethridge and the others? And then she heard a noise from the corner. The twins were asleep in a large wooden crib on rockers and one of them was making baby noises. Teresa at least must be somewhere near. Georgia leapt to her feet and ran out to the backyard. Teresa was placidly feeding the chickens, helped by the three little girls, who squealed in mock terror every time a hen pecked near their toes.

She looked up when Georgia came out into the yard and smiled. Again Georgia felt a tightening of her chest as she always did when she contemplated Cesare's family. No matter that she wouldn't have wanted five younger siblings; it was just something in the way they all accepted one another, took each other for granted. It produced an atmosphere that was always absent from Georgia's home.

She wondered what Teresa thought of her. Did she know that Georgia was a girl? Or that she was a Stravagante? Georgia wasn't even sure that Teresa knew her own husband was one of that brotherhood. She was always welcoming and hospitable to Georgia, treating her as another guest along with Luciano and Doctor Dethridge, even though she had not met

Georgia until after the Stravaganti had arrived from Bellezza.

'Good morning, Giorgio,' she said now, deftly keeping the rooster away from the children and making sure that all the hens got a fair share. 'Did you sleep late?'

'Good morning,' said Georgia. 'I must have lost track of time. Tell me, what day is it today?'

Teresa looked at her rather curiously. 'It is Thursday,' she said.

So two days had passed in Remora, exactly the same as in her own world. The gateway had remained stable. Georgia had realised early on that the day she had in Remora was the same day of the week as she had just experienced in her own world. She had packed eight days into four since her first stravagation; no wonder she had been exhausted! But now she couldn't wait to find out what had happened in Remora on Tuesday and Wednesday.

'Where are all the others?' she asked casually now.

'Down at the racetrack,' said Teresa, smiling. 'You won't find Cesare anywhere else much until the Stellata is over.'

Or Luciano? thought Georgia, but before she could ask, she heard horses returning.

'There they are now,' said Teresa, her eyes lighting up. 'They'll be hungry.'

Quickly she scattered the rest of the seed and began shepherding the little girls into the house. Georgia picked up Marta and held Emilia's hand. Teresa gave her a grateful smile. But once indoors, she said, 'Go to them, if you like. I can manage here.'

Georgia ran to the stable and bumped into Luciano

coming out. He was flushed and laughing. Then he saw her and delight spread across his face. 'Georgia!' he cried, catching both her arms. 'Thank goodness you're back.'

Georgia jumped as if his touch had been red hot. Then she relaxed and smiled back. 'I'm so sorry I didn't come before. The first night I was too tired and then my stepbrother broke the talisman. I didn't think I'd ever be able to get back.'

Suddenly she felt like dancing for joy in the cobbled stableyard. She was back in Remora, Russell hadn't been able to spoil the most important thing in her life, and Luciano was pleased to see her. Then she saw the happiness drain from his face. The others, coming out of the stable, had the same expression. A quick smile at the sight of her, followed by some deep sadness waiting to be revealed.

'What?' said Georgia, alarmed.

'Merla has gone,' said Luciano quietly. 'We think she's been taken.'

*

Later that day Paolo asked Georgia if she was feeling less tired.

'Yes thanks,' she said. 'But that wasn't why I didn't come sooner. My stepbrother stole the talisman and broke it.'

Paolo was shocked. 'Does he know what it is for?'

'No,' said Georgia. 'He's just destructive for the sake of it. He knew the horse was precious to me so he did it to upset me.'

'He is sick in the mind?' asked Paolo.

'You could say that,' said Georgia. 'He's a pain to live with, whatever he is.'

Paolo was thoughtful. Georgia could see he was trying to understand how a family member could behave in such a way. She knew that Cesare would never be mean to his little half-siblings like that.

'He makes you unhappy,' said Paolo. 'Perhaps that is why the talisman found you. Luciano was sick in body but you are unhappy in your mind. It makes you sensitive to our needs.'

'Perhaps,' said Georgia.

Paolo took her hand. 'Remember that nothing lasts for ever,' he said. 'The bad things as well as the good.'

*

Falco had returned to the lonely life he had been leading before Gaetano had come whirling back into it. He had nothing to do but roam the palace alone, hoping for visits from Luciano and Georgia, the fascinating alien from another world. He would read in the library until his body became too stiff and then set off on his painful travels round the great palace. Several times he sensed that he was not entirely alone. He felt watched and sometimes if he turned quickly enough, he was sure he caught a glimpse of blue. He began to feel haunted.

And yet in another way, he felt that he himself was the ghost. Now that he had decided to leave Talia for ever, he felt like a phantom in his own home, drifting from room to room, invisible. If he spent many more days like this, he began to feel that he would become gradually more and more transparent until it would be too late to stravagate – he would already be too insubstantial to cast a shadow in either world.

His reverie was interrupted by the jangling of the doorbell and he was delighted to see that both young Stravaganti had come to visit him.

'Falco!' said Georgia, as soon as they were alone and she had explained why she hadn't come sooner. 'Luciano told me his idea. Are you willing to try a test-flight?'

'Anything,' said Falco. 'I think I shall go mad if we don't do something soon.'

'Then let's do it tonight,' said Georgia. 'Come back with me when I leave here.'

'What about a talisman?' asked Luciano.

'I've thought about that,' said Georgia. 'What about my eyebrow ring?'

Both boys liked that idea. It was something from the other world but it wasn't something extra for Georgia to bring, it was made of silver and it was small enough for Falco to hold it in his hand unnoticed.

'But why tonight?' asked Luciano. 'You haven't got anything prepared at the other end.'

'I know,' said Georgia. 'But he doesn't have to stay all day – I mean all night. If I can smuggle him out of my room, he can come to school with me for a few hours and see how he likes it.'

'Go to school with you?' said Luciano, his mind boggling at the image of pale, crippled Falco in the cheerful chaos of Barnsbury Comprehensive. 'What will he wear? He won't be able to get into any classes. And what if his sticks don't travel with him? He won't be able to walk.'

Georgia frowned. It was true; this needed more planning.

'We could wait one more night. Then it would be Saturday when we get back. I'll find him something to wear. And I could find some sticks. I think we've got some in our umbrella stand. But we can't wait any longer than that for the trial. I'm going to Devon on Sunday and I can't take him there. I'd never be able to explain him to my friend Alice.'

'So when can we do the real thing?' asked Falco anxiously.

'Not till I get back,' said Georgia firmly. 'I'm not even sure if I'll be able to stravagate from Devon. What do you think, Luciano?'

'I don't know,' said Luciano. 'Rodolfo thought I wouldn't be able to stravagate from Venice to Bellezza, but I didn't try. I think it was because I was out of England. Rodolfo thinks the gateway only works from England to Talia, because of Doctor Dethridge. But I don't know if you have to be in London.'

'Is Devon in another country?' asked Falco and Georgia realised how much she was going to have to help him when he did eventually 'translate' to her world.

'A Falco is not just for Christmas but for life,' she said ruefully as she got into the carriage with Luciano to drive back to Remora.

'You're right there,' said Luciano. 'Are you sure you want to go through with this? He's going to be pretty dependent on you – maybe for years.'

'It depends what the social services do with him, doesn't it?' said Georgia. 'They'll have to put him in foster care to start with – if we're lucky, it'll be my mum who deals with that. But they'll try to get him adopted eventually. He's only thirteen. Still, yes, I think unless he goes somewhere far away from London, Falco is going to need me for a long time.'

They looked at one another, taking in just how much what they were planning was going to involve. On the journey out, they had talked obsessively about Merla and Luciano had told Georgia every detail of the fruitless search. But now the problem of Falco dominated their thoughts and their words.

For the first time since she had come to Remora, Georgia was looking forward to getting back home; she had a lot to organise.

Chapter 16

First Flight

It was a good job that on the last day of term, Barnsbury Comprehensive finished at lunchtime. Not much work was done in the morning either, as students luxuriated in the prospect of seven weeks of freedom. About half had holidays in the sun to look forward to; the others were just happy to anticipate days of idleness in an English summer, even those with long reading lists for their A-levels.

All the talk of summer plans made Georgia think about her own. She had the coming fortnight with Alice in Devon and immediately after that she had decided to help Falco 'translate'. She was supposed to be going to France with Ralph and Maura in late August – without Russell, thank goodness. In fact the great bonus of the summer for her was that Russell would be working at Tesco's for the first five weeks, then going to Greece with his mates for a fortnight.

Now she ticked off days on her fingers; the Stellata was going to be held on the fifteenth of August. That much she knew. 'It is always then,' Paolo had told her. 'The Day of the Lady, though our friends the Manoush would say the Day of the Goddess.' That was a Friday and she really wanted to see it, even though there could be problems, because it happened at about seven in the evening, as shadows began to fall.

The French holiday was due to start the weekend after the Stellata. Georgia was grateful to Ralph's work; he was re-wiring an old house and there was no chance to get away till that was finished. The holiday details had been sorted out only recently, because Maura had nagged until Ralph had agreed a date and then she had booked a cancellation – one week in the Languedoc, because he said he couldn't manage longer away. But if it had been a week earlier, Georgia wouldn't have been able to get to the race.

Georgia spent the afternoon in her room preparing for the trial stravagation they were planning for that night. She tried hard to remember Falco's size. He was slight for a thirteen-year-old, but she thought he could get away with an old T-shirt and tracksuit bottoms of hers. And his feet were small; he could fit into a pair of her trainers. He wouldn't look very smart but at least he shouldn't attract too much attention, apart from his walking, of course.

Georgia had snaffled two walking sticks from the umbrella-stand, spreading out the many umbrellas, bicycle pumps and even an old plastic sword of

Russell's to conceal their absence. But they didn't look much like anything that would be given to a young boy. Crutches would be better, but Georgia had no idea how to get hold of a pair. She hid the sticks at the back of her cupboard.

That left the difficult question of underwear. Georgia had no idea what Talians wore under their day clothes and didn't really want to ask. She always found herself wearing whatever she had on at night under her Remoran boy's clothes – in fact she had taken to wearing very light tops and pants at night so that she shouldn't be too hot in the Reman sunshine.

But she could hardly offer Falco a pair of her pants. There was nothing for it; she would have to steal a pair of Russell's boxers. This was a difficult and delicate operation since Russell was at home. Twice, when she went to the airing cupboard, he was lolling about in his doorway and she had to pretend to be getting towels or underwear of her own.

He gazed at her in open contempt. 'What are you faffing about with, now?' he asked, the second time.

'I'm packing for Devon,' said Georgia icily. 'As if it's any of your business.'

'Ah, yes,' said Russell. 'The new friend. Another horse freak. You can both have fun spreading your legs across some stallion.'

Georgia just gave him a withering look. But later she heard him go out and she raced back to the airing cupboard. She had to choose a new pair, so that the elastic would be tight, because Russell was much chunkier than the slender Falco. Her heart was thumping hard as she whisked her choice out of the cupboard and went back to hide them with the sticks.

What on earth would Russell say if he ever found her with a pair of his boxers?

Fortunately, she had no time to speculate since a glimpse of her clock told her that she was going to be late for her music lesson. She ran down the street with her violin and music case.

When she got near the Mulhollands' house, she slowed. Such a lot had happened since her last lesson a week ago. It hadn't occurred to her till now how awkward it was going to be facing Luciano's mother. Vicky Mulholland opened the door to her with her usual friendly greeting, but this time Georgia scanned her face for evidence of sadness behind her smile.

When the lesson was over, to her surprise, Vicky offered her a cup of tea. 'You're my last lesson today,' she said. 'All my other Friday regulars are off on holiday as soon as their families can manage.'

Georgia was happy to stay; surely they would talk about Luciano? She was looking at his photo when Vicky brought in a tray of mugs and some shortbread.

'You knew my son a bit, didn't you?' said Vicky.

'Yes,' said Georgia. 'From orchestra.' She sipped her tea gratefully, thinking how much older Luciano already looked than the Lucien of the photo. 'I'm sorry about what happened.'

There was silence. Georgia thought about what Luciano had told her: that he sometimes managed to stravagate back to his old world for a few moments. He said his parents had seen him and Georgia wondered what on earth Vicky must have made of her dead son's unexplained appearances; surely she must have thought she was going mad when she first saw him? Had it made it better or worse for the grieving mother? But Georgia knew she was unlikely ever to find out. It wasn't the kind of thing her violin teacher was going to mention.

'Do you think it's silly of me to keep his picture out?' Vicky suddenly asked.

'No, of course not,' said Georgia. 'I think he'd like it.'

Vicky looked at her a little oddly. 'I think so too,' she said quietly. 'I miss him so much.'

Luciano was progressing with his riding. He was learning to rise to the trot, though it left him aching and tired. Dondola was a gentle horse and Dethridge a patient teacher. But Luciano was nowhere near Cesare's standard. The young Talian was riding bareback round the racetrack on Arcangelo and Luciano wasn't the only one watching him with a mixture of admiration and misgiving. The Horsemasters of the other Twelfths were all down there watching their own likely jockeys and weighing up the opposition.

Luciano stayed down at the track watching for so long after his lesson that he was still there when Georgia came and found him.

'He's amazing, isn't he?' he said.

'Fantastic,' agreed Georgia. 'And he makes a good pairing with Arcangelo. They'll be hard to beat.'

Cesare dismounted and came over to them. He was sweating and smiling.

'You want to try now, Georgia?' he asked.

Luciano watched while Georgia took a turn on the

big chestnut. She was good, no doubt about it. She didn't go faster than a canter bareback, but her seat was secure and she got up a good speed. When she came back to Luciano, she was glowing and triumphant.

'Let's go somewhere and talk,' he said.

They sat on a grassy bank overlooking the racetrack. Beyond, they could see the fields Cesare had told them were for growing the autumn crocuses that yielded up the saffron Remora was famous for. They were already beginning to show green with the shoots of the flowers. Cesare had told them that in a few weeks the city would be surrounded by a sea of gold and purple.

'Do you want to go through with this test tonight?' Luciano asked Georgia.

'I think it's the only way to find out if Falco's "translation" is going to work,' she said. 'I've made some plans.'

'It'll be dangerous for you, won't it?' he asked. 'I mean, what if someone finds him in your room?'

'I know,' she said. 'But I can't think of any other way, can you?'

Luciano shook his head. 'I just can't see Falco adapting to life as a twenty-first-century boy,' he said.

'You seem to have managed all right, turning yourself into a sixteenth-century one,' said Georgia quietly.

Luciano thought for a bit, then said, 'Can I ask you something?'

Georgia nodded.

'Do you still go for violin lessons with, you know, my mum?'

'Yes,' said Georgia. 'I had one there today.'

'And ... does she ever talk about me?' he asked.

'Not usually,' she said. 'But she did today.'

Luciano could not say any more for a few minutes. He ran both hands through his hair. 'Can we do this to Falco's family?' he asked after a while. 'I mean, I had no choice, but he's calmly planning to leave his father, sister, brothers. What's it going to do to them? And to him? You know I've been back a few times to see my parents. And it's really hard.'

'I know,' said Georgia. 'In his place I don't think I could go through with it. But he's an extraordinary person. And it's what he wants.'

*

For Falco, the hours till nightfall crawled by. He was expecting Luciano and Georgia to arrive just before dusk. In his highly excited state, he couldn't settle to reading. He toiled out to the stables to talk to Nello, who was surprised and not a little alarmed to see the young noble.

But it calmed Falco now to be around horses. It was his dearest wish to be able to ride again, and not just as a useless passenger. He was willing to give up everything in Talia to achieve it.

He hobbled round the stalls, talking to each animal and stroking their muzzles. He still knew them all by name – Fiordiligi, Amato, Caramella – and they remembered him and whickered greetings as he passed by.

'What's that horse over there?' he asked Nello, screwing his eyes up in the dark stable to see a black shape in the shadows he didn't recognise. It had a blanket over it.

'Oh, that's just a new mare we're breaking in for your father,' said Nello nervously, trying to get Falco out of the stables. 'I wouldn't go near her. She's very nervous.'

Falco let the groom guide him back out into the sunlight, but as he left he heard the strange mare whinny – a mournful and carrying note that stayed with him the rest of the day.

*

In the Twelfth of the Lioness the blind Manoush lifted his head as if listening to something far off.

'What is it?' asked Raffaella.

'Something is not right in the city,' said Aurelio. 'It is beyond the normal dealing and conniving of the race. If someone has taken the zhou volou from the Ram, then that someone is trying to steal the luck. And the goddess is angry.'

'What will she do?' asked Raffaella.

Aurelio turned his dark and sightless eyes to her. 'We shall see,' he said. 'But it will turn out very ill for the luck stealer.'

*

It was nearing the time for Falco's experiment. He had informed the servants that his two friends would be staying the night. Rooms were prepared next to his and the three of them ate dinner in the family dining room. It was not a great hall like the one where

247

Gaetano's birthday celebrations had been held, but it was enough to overawe Georgia. What would Falco, used to palaces of endless rooms, make of her house?

She and Luciano had tried to explain twenty-first-century life to him but had given it up as a bad job. Falco simply could not grasp the concept of cars without horses. 'If they do not pull from in front, then do they push from behind?' he asked incredulously. In the end, it seemed better, on this dry run, just to show him.

Georgia ate little and all three of them were anxious to get on with the business in hand. Once it got dark in Talia they would have only a few hours to make the journey. Falco dismissed the servants and Georgia and Luciano went with him into his bedroom where Georgia took the silver ring out of her eyebrow. She handed it to the boy, who turned it wonderingly before slipping it on to his little finger.

He went to get changed behind a screen and returned looking absurdly young and small in a white nightshirt. He sat on the end of his huge bed.

'What shall I do?' he asked.

Georgia went and sat beside him. 'It's simple but hard too. You must go to sleep, thinking about my home in England, where the ring came from. I shall tell you about it so you can imagine it. Here, get into bed and I'll lie down beside you.'

The boy climbed with some difficulty into the high bed and Georgia lay beside him on top of the brocade cover.

'It'll be like a bedtime story,' she said. 'I'll describe my house and bedroom to you. Only remember what I told you about when you wake up in my world. If everything works out properly, I'll be there. If I still seem asleep, just wake me.'

She took her own talisman out of her pocket.

'Luciano,' said Falco. 'Don't leave us.'

'No,' said Luciano, settling himself into a chair beside the bed. 'I won't.' He knew he was in for a long night.

The sun streamed into Georgia's room and on to her face. She was lying on her bed, in her top and pants, spooned round the bony back of the young di Chimici. For a moment, she couldn't believe it had worked. Then, 'Falco,' she whispered. 'Are you all right?'

He turned to her, his huge eyes darting round the unfamiliar room.

'We have done it!' he said. Carefully, he took the ring off his finger and Georgia fixed it back in her eyebrow.

Then she leapt off the bed, anxious to get him dressed in his English clothes. She showed him everything, including the underwear, which puzzled him very much. Then she gave him the sticks.

'I'll go and get dressed in the bathroom,' she said, 'and while I'm away, you put these things on and hide your nightshirt in my bed. I'll lock the door after me.'

Falco just nodded and she caught up her clothes and crept out of the room.

It was early on Saturday and no one else was awake yet. Quickly she showered and dressed and went back to her room. She couldn't risk knocking so she just unlocked the door and went in, hoping that Falco was decent.

To her astonishment, she saw an ordinary boy sitting on her bed. True, he looked bemused and he had put the T-shirt on back to front. And he was unusually pretty for a modern boy. But he didn't look as if he came from another dimension.

'You look great, Falco,' she whispered.

He tried to smile.

'I'm sorry,' he said, 'but I must relieve myself.'

'Of course,' said Georgia. 'The bathroom's the first door on the right. But you must be very quiet.'

The thought of Russell bumping into Falco on the landing didn't bear thinking of. She handed Falco the sticks and he stood up, but hesitated.

'It is not a bath that I need,' he said.

Georgia cursed herself for not having explained something so basic to him the night before. Carefully and trying not to embarrass him or herself, she gave him a quick description of modern plumbing. His eyes widened.

She accompanied him to the door and kept watch while he manoeuvred himself to the bathroom and inside. She had explained the lock, but the whole time he was in there, her body was tense with fear. The enterprise was beginning to seem enormous, and this was just the trial run.

She heard the loo flush and a little while later, Falco came out and limped back to Georgia's room. They had passed the first hurdle.

Much to his surprise, Luciano managed to doze a bit in the chair. He woke to see moonlight flooding the room and he had a crick in his neck. He got up and stretched, then peered at the bed. Falco appeared to be asleep, his dark curls on the pillow. Of Georgia there was no sign.

Luciano stared at the sleeping boy. He looked perfectly normal but the Stravagante knew that he was looking at someone who was no longer there. It made him feel terribly homesick.

'What are you going to do today, Georgia?' asked Maura. 'I was wondering if you needed to do any shopping for your trip away?'

'No thanks, Mum,' she replied. 'I've got everything I need. In fact I'm practically packed. I wanted to go to the British Museum today.'

There was a snorting noise from Russell.

'What was that, Russell?' asked Ralph.

'Nothing; cereal went down the wrong way,' Russell explained.

'Is it schoolwork?' asked Maura.

'Yes,' lied Georgia. 'It's for my Classical Civilisations coursework. I wanted to get some notes done before I go away.'

'Geek,' whispered Russell under cover of the noise of breakfast being cleared away.

At least he won't offer to go with me, thought Georgia, even to torment me. There was no way that Russell would go into a museum. Still, she needed to know what he and their parents *would* be doing.

Getting Falco out of the house was going to be the hardest thing.

But she was in luck. Russell and Ralph were both in their sports gear and were going to the gym. Maura said she would shut herself up in the little room that she and Ralph used as an office and sort through all the bills.

'I've been putting it off for ages,' she said guiltily.

Georgia waited till the men had left, then made her mother a cup of coffee and took it to the office. Maura's hair was sticking up and she was biting the end of her pen as she fiddled with a calculator.

'I'm just off, Mum,' said Georgia. 'I won't be back till after lunch.'

Maura smiled gratefully. 'Thanks for the coffee, Georgia. And let me give you some money.' She took a twenty-pound note from her purse. 'This should buy you some lunch as well as your fare,' she said.

Georgia knew that Maura wouldn't be coming out of the office for a while, so she took her chance to smuggle Falco downstairs. He was surprisingly agile. After the grand sweeping staircases of Santa Fina, he was not likely to be defeated by a couple of flights in an Islington terrace.

She had told him the plan – they were going to look for an Etruscan horse like her talisman. But the subplot was to give Falco a taste of central London. And he very nearly freaked before they were even out of the front gate. A couple of perfectly ordinary cars passed and he jumped, terrified. All Georgia's attempts to explain about cars and traffic were nothing compared to the reality; it was more than he could cope with. However, he was not too disturbed by his absence of shadow when Georgia pointed it out to him.

It took ages to walk to Caledonian Road tube. Georgia had checked that it had a lift, so that Falco wouldn't have to cope with escalators, but she hadn't reckoned with the slowness of his walking and the many times he had to stop, alarmed by the traffic. In the end, Georgia took him into a café.

'You need some breakfast, anyway,' she said.

She bought them tea and fried egg sandwiches. Falco, who had never tasted either before, wolfed it all down. It seemed to do him good. The rest of the journey was easier, though Falco cowered back from the platform when the tube train came rushing in. Georgia realised how much of her ordinary daily life was remarkable now she was seeing it through sixteenth-century eyes.

The change at Leicester Square did involve an escalator, but not a big one and Falco managed it without problems. But he was already flagging when they got into the lift at Goodge Street, and it was quite a walk from there.

When they reached the corner of Gower Street and Great Russell Street, Falco heaved a sigh of relief.

'We are here – good! I don't think I could walk much further.'

Georgia realised that he must think the handsome art book shop on the corner, labelled 'British Museum', was their destination. What on earth was he going to think when he saw the real thing?

'Just a tiny bit further,' she said encouragingly, leading him along Great Russell Street past the black railings. Suddenly they were at the gates and Falco saw the museum in all its colonnaded splendour. He gasped.

'But it is a palace!' he exclaimed. 'What mighty Prince or Duke lives there?'

'None,' said Georgia, 'but I'm glad you're impressed.' She guided Falco across the forecourt, full of tourists and pigeons. He stopped by the massive bronze head at the side and paused for a long time.

'Is it a fragment?' he asked. 'The original statue must have been huge. Where is the rest of it?'

'That's all there is,' explained Georgia. 'The sculptor made it that way.'

There was still a long way for him to go, up the flight of steps to the main entrance. By the time he got to the top, Falco was exhausted. Nevertheless, when Georgia told him that what they were looking for would be on the first floor, he set off gamely for the wide marble staircase.

'Wait,' said Georgia, concerned by how tired he looked. 'There must be a lift; there always is nowadays.'

An attendant heard her and came over to them. 'The lifts are over there, Miss, just before the Great Court. But wouldn't you like a wheelchair for your friend? They're just over here.'

He led them round a corner where ranks of folded wheelchairs sat just waiting to be taken.

'How much is it?' whispered Georgia, who was getting seriously alarmed by the cost of taking Falco out and about. Thank goodness Maura had given her some money.

'It's free, Miss,' smiled the attendant. 'Just bring it back when you've finished with it.'

He took out a chair and unfolded it and showed them how to work the brakes. Falco was thrilled. He put the walking sticks carefully between his knees.

'Will it go by itself now?' he asked.

Georgia remembered telling him about electric wheelchairs.

'Not this one, son,' said the attendant. 'See, you have to push the wheels with your hands or get your friend to push you by the handles.'

'I'll push,' said Georgia firmly. 'Thanks for all your help.'

As they moved off, she heard him say quietly to another attendant, 'Poor kid. I wonder why he doesn't have one of his own? He can scarcely walk.'

Georgia moved quickly away, pushing Falco to the lift. It was very small, with not much room for anyone else once they had got inside; fortunately no one else joined them. After a couple of journeys up and down, because the ground floor was confusingly called 2 and the first floor 6, they arrived at the upper galleries. Georgia pushed Falco out of the lift and then stopped to peer in his face. He hadn't said anything while they were going up and down and Georgia had been muttering about the muddly labelling. Now she saw he was white and terrified.

'Oh, it's all right, Falco,' she said. 'It's just another one of our machines. You know, to get you from one place to another. People use them all the time. It's perfectly safe.'

What would he make of the transporters on *Star Trek*, she wondered. To distract him, she moved forward and they came to a window looking out over the internal Great Court.

'The Queen of Sheba' proclaimed a poster over the door and people were going in.

'Is that her palace?' whispered Falco, round-eyed.

'No,' said Georgia. 'It's a special exhibition about her. Look, here we are at the galleries. I'll just ask that attendant which way for the Etruscans.'

They had to go through a long gallery full of displays about money and Falco stopped several times to exclaim over the big brass scales for weighing coins. 'I have seen these in Giglia,' he said. 'My family's fortune comes from banking, you know.'

Then they were in Room 69 and were met by a terrifying marble group of a man stabbing a bull in the neck, his little dog leaping up to lick the marble blood as it streamed from the stab-wound. Falco stared at it for ages.

'Mithras,' read Georgia. 'Roman, second century AD.'

'There is one like that in our palace in Santa Fina,' said Falco in a low voice. 'It is in a courtyard – I'll show you next time we are there. We say it is Reman, of course.

Eventually they reached Room 71, Italy before the Roman Empire, and began their search for a winged horse. Falco was by now wanting to wheel himself, so the two of them went in different directions. Suddenly Falco called out 'Georgia – come and look at these!'

She hurried over to see what he had found. There were four bronzes, each about four inches high, showing boys and their horses. The label read:

'Four bronze statuettes of boys dismounting from their horses, from the rim of a Campanian urn. Etrusco-Campanian, about 500–480 BC. Probably made at Capua. The boys appear to be taking part in an ancient Greek race in which the riders dismounted and ran beside their horses in the final stretch.'

The boys were all naked, with long hair tied back in a very girly style, but they were broad-shouldered and muscular and rode bareback. They were all dismounting from the right.

'Aren't they wonderful?' said Falco. 'You know the Stellata is supposed to have come from a race like that? Our ancestors – the Rassenans we call them – used to race in a straight line and dismount for the last bit. The winners were the team whose horse and rider both crossed the line first.'

But it was elsewhere in the room that they found the flying horse. Not a model, but a picture on a black bowl. And again in a drawing under a museum notice with the chronology of the Etruscans. It was a representation of two winged terracotta horses standing side by side very close together and found at Tarquinia.

Georgia and Falco made their way slowly back to Islington after hot dogs and Pepsis from the stand outside the museum. The Talian was completely overwhelmed by all the experiences of the day and was so exhausted that he let Georgia undress him and put his Talian nightshirt back on. By tacit agreement they left Russell's boxers. Falco had no trouble at all falling asleep on Georgia's bed once she gave him back the ring. She watched him disappear, turning pale and see-through; she didn't dare go with him and had to hope he would stravagate safely on his own.

A sound from the bed woke Luciano, though it was still night. Falco sat straight up in bed staring ahead of him. He looked down at the lace on his nightshirt and began to tremble. Luciano sat beside him and put an arm round him.

'What happened?' he asked.

'It was ... beyond all describing,' said the boy. 'A world of marvels.'

He twisted the silver ring on his finger.

'And did you feel any better?' asked Luciano.

'It was as you said,' said Falco. 'My leg was not mended. But I felt strong most of the time. And I'm sure that a place like that would have the magic I need to make me better.'

'Not magic – science,' said Luciano in the dark, and remembered how he had once said the same to Rodolfo. Only now he was not so sure.

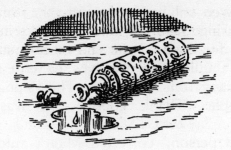

Chapter 17

Translation

It was hard for Georgia to sit and watch Falco disappear from the room. All her instincts screamed at her to grab her talisman and plunge after him. But she knew that Luciano would be waiting to receive him back in Remora and she didn't dare disappear herself for the afternoon. In fact, she could hear Maura calling her now. She would have to wait till tonight to find out what had happened at Santa Fina.

'Ah, Georgie,' said Maura, putting her head round the door. 'I thought I heard you come back. How was the British Museum?'

'Good,' said Georgia. 'I made lots of notes.' She waved her notebook vaguely in her mother's direction.

'Why have you got Nana's old walking sticks up here?' asked Maura, frowning. Georgia started guiltily.

The sticks were still propped against the bed.

'I was using them for this creative extension we have to do for English,' she said quickly, surprised at how easily the lie came. 'We have to write something in the holidays from Richard the Third's point of view as a cripple.' Thank goodness it was her set Shakespeare play for GCSE.

'Disabled person,' corrected Maura automatically. 'That's all right then, but you should have asked.'

'Sorry,' said Georgia. 'I didn't think you'd mind.'

'I don't,' said Maura. 'But aren't you overdoing it a bit? First ClassCiv coursework and now English. It is the first day of the holidays, remember.'

'And tomorrow I'm off to Devon for two weeks,' said Georgia. 'I don't want to spend my time with Alice doing schoolwork, do I?'

Maura looked at her closely. 'I suppose not.' Then, 'You're not wearing your eyebrow ring. Have you got tired of it?'

'No,' said Georgia. 'It was itching a bit, so I thought I'd leave it off for a while and put some surgical spirit on it.'

'It looks nice without,' said Maura. 'And it might be better not to wear it in Devon. Alice's dad might think you're a punk. Your hair's getting longer too. I'm surprised you didn't want to get it cut before going to Alice's.'

Georgia sighed. 'I'll put the ring back in as soon as the itching has gone. I shouldn't think Alice's dad will even notice it. And I don't care about my hair while I'm away. There'll be no one to see it but him and Alice. I'll get it cut when I come back.'

Merla's wings were drooping. She wasn't getting enough exercise and she still missed her mother. Because of her extraordinary growth rate, she was no longer in need of Starlight's milk, but she was not eating well and she was looking thin.

'You'll have to take her out at night,' Nello told Enrico, who was still living up at the palace.

Enrico had come to the same conclusion. It was a risk but there was no point in having a flying horse if it couldn't fly.

'I'll take her tonight,' he said.

Georgia finished her packing and went to bed early. At least, she tried to. But Russell had other ideas. He was lounging in his doorway in that way she so dreaded. It meant he had nothing to do and was looking for an excuse to torment her.

And it appeared he had some new ammunition.

'Where'd you pick up the boyfriend?' he asked casually.

Georgia froze. 'I don't know what you mean,' she said, as calmly as she could.

'Maz saw you,' he said. 'In the Caledonian Road with some spastic. What is it with you? Freaks and geeks, you seem to attract them. I suppose it's because you're one yourself.'

Georgia said nothing. It was a tactic that sometimes worked. Russell could get bored and leave her alone.

Or he might be infuriated by it.

'Maz said he was just a kid,' he persisted. 'A crippled kid. I wonder what Maura would say about that? Creepy old men and freaky little boys. What next?'

It had taken Falco a long time to get back to sleep after he stravagated back to Santa Fina. He wanted to hold on to Georgia's silver ring but Luciano took it from him.

'You don't want to end up back in England by mistake. Now, I'll stay with you till you're asleep and then I'll go to my room.'

Georgia had half hoped that she would find herself waking in Talia in Falco's palace, since she had left from there when she last stravagated. But her flying horse took her to their usual place of entry in the hayloft of the Ram.

She had to borrow a horse from Paolo and ride up to Santa Fina. The servant who took the horse from her and the other one who let her in both looked puzzled. As far as they were concerned, this young Remoran was sleeping late inside the palace and they couldn't understand how he was arriving for the second time, on a horse, when he had turned up the previous evening with his companion in a carriage.

But the servant let Georgia go up to her room and she opened the dividing door that led into Falco's. He was still asleep, his face pale and drawn on the large heap of pillows. The door to the room on the other side opened and Luciano came in, with dark circles under his eyes. He saw Georgia and smiled.

'You did it!' he said. 'Falco told me all about it. He thought it was all wonderful.' He gave her back the silver ring.

'Even the traffic?' asked Georgia, fixing the ring back in.

'Even the traffic,' he said.

Georgia sat down on a low chair, suddenly overwhelmed by the prospect of what she believed she must do.

'I reckon we've got two weeks,' she said, 'if I'm lucky and can get here every night from Alice's. He'd be going back to Giglia after the race anyway. And now that Russell's damaged my talisman once, I daren't leave it any longer than necessary. So we've got a fortnight to teach him everything he needs to know about living in the twenty-first century.'

'We can do it,' said Luciano. 'We'll do it together.'

The next two weeks were the busiest in Georgia's life. She left for Devon the next day, travelling down on the train with Alice. Alice's father, Paul, was waiting to meet them in his 4 × 4.

He was nice, bearded and tweedy and not a bit like Ralph, but friendly and funny. If Georgia hadn't spent time in palaces in Talia she might have been overawed by his house, but as it was she accepted it. It was a big red-brick farmhouse, with outbuildings and stables and a paddock. The stables housed Alice's horse, a tall brown mare called Truffle.

The girls went straight to see her, before unpacking.

'She's gorgeous,' said Georgia, enviously. It was all

very well having all the horses of the Ram's stable available to ride in Talia, but she would never have one of her own in real life. And here was Alice, a girl of her own age and a student at her school, with her very own horse just waiting for her all the holidays and any weekend she could get down. Whereas Georgia would have to content herself with a visit to Jean's stable once a fortnight.

There was another occupant of the stables. 'Meet Conker,' said Paul. In the stall next to Truffle was a chestnut gelding, very like the Reman Arcangelo.

'Where did he come from?' asked Alice, as surprised as Georgia.

'He's my neighbour's,' explained Paul. 'You know, Jim Gardiner down the road. He's away on holiday and was going to put Conker out to livery but I said we'd look after him if my daughter's friend could ride him. I was right, wasn't I? You would like to ride while you're here, wouldn't you, Georgia? Alice tells me you're pretty good. Do you think you could manage him?'

Georgia was speechless with joy and could only nod. This was going to be heaven.

The girls fell into a very happy routine. Georgia's room was next to Alice's and she was relieved to find that her friend was not an early riser. It meant that Georgia could usually manage to get at least a couple of hours sleep after her return from Talia.

By the time that the two girls came down in the morning, Paul had been up for hours and gone off to his work as a solicitor in the nearest town. Georgia and Alice made huge brunches of pancakes and fruit and eggs and then spent the rest of the day riding.

They took Truffle and Conker out on to the moors for hours, and when they had had enough, they let the horses graze while they lay on the springy turf picnicking on the doorstep sandwiches they had brought in their saddlebags.

It was a magical time, the days long and sunny, when the girls talked endlessly about their families. Alice explained about her parents' marriage. They had met at university. Her mother, Jane, had been a political activist, leader of the Student Union. And no one had ever expected her to get together with Paul, the only son of a local middle-class family.

'They broke up soon after I was born,' said Alice. 'And when my grandparents died, my dad moved back down to Devon. I've been coming to this house for as long as I can remember.'

'Do they get on, your mum and dad?' asked Georgia.

'Not too badly now,' said Alice. 'The last big quarrel was about my secondary school. Dad wanted me to go to a girls' boarding school near here and my mum was against it. No private schooling for her daughter – she's a Labour councillor now, you know. She insisted that the local comprehensive was good enough; Mum and I had moved to Barnsbury by then. They had a huge row and by the time I started at the boarding school they were hardly speaking. But as it happened, I wasn't happy there and Mum got her way in the end and moved me to Barnsbury Comp.'

'Do you think she was right?' asked Georgia.

'Well, it's not bad, is it?' said Alice. 'The difficult thing is that I feel I have two different lives.'

'I suppose that's true of everyone whose parents have split up.'

'Yes, but if you think of the ones in our class – Selina, Julie, Tashi, Callum, for a start – they've all got both parents in London. When they spend a weekend with their dads it's not such a performance. It takes hours for me to get here and I only have one full day on a weekend. But I love it so much. It's what keeps me from going mad when I'm in the city. I'd like to live here all the time really, but Mum would never have that. But it makes me feel different from everyone else; my dad's not like other people's in the school. I'd die if they knew what our life here is like. You're the only person from school I've ever brought here.'

Georgia felt honoured. She thought that perhaps it was easier for her, having a dad she could hardly remember. She told Alice about her family too, especially Russell. Alice knew him of course, at least by sight, but she surprised Georgia now by telling her that there were several girls in their form who quite fancied him.

'But he's hideous!' said Georgia. Then she thought about it. She only ever saw Russell's face with a sneer on it, his features distorted by his hatred of her. Perhaps if he smiled, he wouldn't be so bad looking. He was tall and well built, with thick, brown hair and brown eyes. She had to concede that he wasn't physically ugly. But he would always seem so to her because of his warped personality. He was a complete contrast to Gaetano, who was quite ugly, but had such courteous manners and such a good heart that everyone who knew him loved him.

'I'll take your word for it about Russell,' said Alice. 'He sounds horrible. I couldn't fancy someone so cruel, even if he was really fit.'

In the late afternoon, the girls rode slowly back to the farm and then practised bareback riding in the paddock. Georgia was already better at it than Alice, thanks to her regular attempts in Remora. But Alice soon improved. They were both good riders, in tune with their horses. Within a few days, Georgia knew she was going to miss Conker when she left Devon. He was quite the biggest horse she had ever ridden, but with a lovely temperament. He reminded her more and more of Arcangelo, although she had hardly ever ridden him, because Cesare was usually practising for the Stellata.

Bareback riding was a completely different experience from riding with a saddle. It was uncomfortable to start with but you felt much more in tune with the horse because of the closer contact of knees and seat. (Russell would have a field day with that, thought Georgia.) She had seen it happen with Cesare, the complete union of horse and rider, what Doctor Dethridge called being like a centaur. Georgia was always going to want that now when riding at speed. She wondered what Jean would say if she suggested it at their fortnightly lessons.

In Talia, Luciano now spent a lot of his time visiting Falco. His days fell into a pattern, like Georgia's in Devon. He spent his early mornings on his secret riding lessons, then met Georgia in the Ram. Most days they took the carriage out to Santa Fina and spent time with Falco preparing him for the great change in his life.

Their lessons would have been incomprehensible to any passing Talian.

'You'll have to go to school,' said Georgia. 'And if you live near me, that will be my school, the one that Luciano went to as well.'

'You'll be in Year 9,' said Luciano, 'and you'll have a whole year before you have to choose your options. So you'll do all the subjects.'

Georgia counted them off on her fingers: 'English literature and language – that shouldn't be too much of a problem, because you seemed to speak and understand English when you stravagated, just the way I do with Talian here, and you're always reading.'

Falco nodded. 'Go on,' he said.

'Then there's maths and science – chemistry, physics and biology.'

'I have learned some mathematics and astronomy,' said Falco. 'And a little anatomy, but mainly for drawing.'

'Ah yes,' said Luciano. 'You can do art, and music too.'

'How about languages?' asked Georgia. 'Do you speak French? Come to think of it, is there even an equivalent of France in this world?' she asked Luciano.

'She means Gallia,' explained Luciano.

'I speak Gallian,' said Falco. 'Will that do?'

'It's much the same,' said Luciano, 'as far as I can gather. The way Talian is like Italian.'

'You can do Italian in Year 11,' said Georgia. 'That could be one of your options. It's ICT I'm worried about.'

'What is that?' asked Falco.

They spent the rest of that day trying to explain to the young Talian about computers. He just couldn't come to terms with it.

Then there was television, the way cars worked, mobile phones, football, fast food, electric lights, CDs, Game Boys, microwaves, aeroplanes. Falco's eyes just grew bigger and bigger. They realised that there were going to be huge differences in his understanding of history and geography too. They had had four centuries that he hadn't and were starting on a fifth. His knowledge of the world that Talia was in centred on what he called the Middle Sea and was learned from globes that he had at his home in Giglia, which sounded to Luciano like the ones in the Ducal palace in Bellezza.

On the other hand, he was very bright and quick to learn. PE and games would be out of the question till his leg was fixed, so he could spend extra hours in the library, working from books and using the computers. And wherever he lived, there would probably be a computer and access to the Internet too. That was also something he found difficult to understand. Like Rodolfo when Luciano had tried to explain it to him, Falco saw it as a big spider's web and couldn't believe that just anyone could tap into it for information.

'Isn't it reserved for the powerful?' he asked once. Both Georgia and Luciano thought that if there were ever the Talian equivalent of the World Wide Web, Niccolò di Chimici would certainly want it under his control, but they didn't share this thought with Falco.

Another day they had to give him a lesson on twenty-first-century money.

'You remember the note I showed you in London?'

asked Georgia. 'That was twenty pounds and people of our age don't often have them. But you'll need to know pound coins and fifty pences and twenties and tens and fives at least.'

It was frustrating not having the coins there to show him. But he liked the sound of the gold and silver coins though, being from Talia where silver is valued above gold, he kept getting them the wrong way round.

On the way back to Remora one day Luciano broached the question that had been haunting him ever since Falco had asked for their help.

'You talk as if he'll be somewhere in Islington, but where on earth will he live?' he asked Georgia. 'What's going to happen to a handicapped Talian boy who turns up out of the blue?'

Georgia wondered how much of the plan she had been formulating to share with Luciano.

'You know my mum's a social worker?' she said. 'Actually she's a team leader in the section that deals with fostering and adoption. I'm going to try to work it so that she finds him a home. I think his best bet is to pretend that he's lost his memory. Then it won't matter if the authorities ask him questions he can't answer.'

*

Falco had begun to have strange dreams. He found himself over and over again in an underground tunnel with a thunderous dragon rushing towards him. He was in a tiny cell that travelled up and down with uncanny speed. He was at the top of a shining silver staircase that moved away from under his feet. His sticks clattered away from him and he fell headfirst. At this point he would wake, sweating and terrified.

Then he would sleep again and another dream would begin, this one full of new images. He would hear a high mournful cry and a rushing sound like huge wings beating. But he knew the sound was not made by a bird. Even though just before the dream ended he would catch a glimpse of black feathers.

The nights were long and troubled, particularly after one of his father's frequent visits. Then he missed Gaetano the most. The two brothers had shared their thoughts on their father many times. It was hard to be part of their family and doubly hard to be sons of a father whose deeds were well known and hard to ignore. But Falco loved his father and he knew that his father loved him. Now he never knew which visit would be the last time he saw the Duke and he had already said goodbye to his favourite brother.

*

In Bellezza, Gaetano was still leading a double life, spending most evenings with the young Duchessa he was supposed to be courting and every day with the cousin he still loved as much as when they had played together as toddlers.

But his feelings for Arianna were changing. And so were hers for him. He was a charming and witty companion, very knowledgeable and entertaining. And the longer she spent with him, the less she thought he was ugly. In fact she found herself looking forward to their evenings together. And much as she missed Luciano, it was relaxing to be with a fellow-Talian from a Ducal family, who understood her duties and her role without explanation. She had to keep reminding herself that his father was supposed to have been responsible for killing her mother.

Gaetano had to keep remembering that too. He knew the rumour that Duke Niccolò had authorised someone to blow Arianna's mother to pieces. It was that which made his father's plans for Gaetano's marriage both so outrageous and so typical.

'What do you think of this young sprig of our enemies?' asked a visitor of Rodolfo's at dinner one evening. She was dressed as Talian widows are in dark colours, with a light veil. But her cobalt dress was stylishly cut and she wore a bracelet of sapphires.

The Regent was on edge. 'You know you shouldn't visit me here, Silvia,' he said in a low voice. 'The risk is too great.'

'I've seen him on the Canal with that foolish young woman who put herself up against Arianna in the election,' said Silvia, ignoring his remark. 'But he seems attentive enough to the Duchessa now.'

'He is a fine young man,' said Rodolfo. 'Not like his father or his cousin the ambassador. But I think he is still following his orders rather than his heart.'

The widow inclined her head. 'Perhaps that is what people of his rank – and Arianna's – should do. There is more to think of here than puppy love.'

'Are you seriously suggesting she should accept him?' asked Rodolfo.

'I'm suggesting she, and you, should think carefully before turning him down,' replied Silvia. 'The di

Chimici never offered marriage to me. It might be an interesting route to explore.'

On the Friday nearly two weeks after she had gone to Devon, Georgia took the train back to Paddington with Alice. She had a riding lesson booked at the stables the next day and didn't want to miss it; she'd already had to rearrange it from the week before. It was the first day of August and only days remained before Falco's proper stravagation.

It felt weird being back at home. Maura and Ralph and Russell were all still at work and the girls had taken the tube back to Islington, hugging goodbye outside the station. They were going to meet up again on Sunday.

Georgia let herself into the empty house. It felt terribly unfamiliar – not Devon and not Remora. Georgia felt like a visitor, so she went up to her room and gazed at her posters and her picture of the black and white horses till she felt normality returning. She decided she would fix a date for Falco's stravagation with Luciano tonight.

Niccolò di Chimici went to find Enrico in the palace stables at Santa Fina. He was usually to be found gossiping with Nello during the day.

'How is the new horse?' the Duke asked them both.

'Picking up nicely,' said Nello.

'Much better since I've been flying her at night,'

said Enrico. 'She's off the lunge now. I just ride her. My, but that's an experience.'

'I've no doubt,' said the Duke. 'Perhaps I shall stay up here one night and try it myself.'

'Er,' said Enrico. 'She can't take much weight yet – she's still growing. It's all very well for a scrawny runt like me but a fine well-set-up man like your Grace might be a bit much for her yet.'

'Never mind that now,' said Niccolò. 'I came to talk to you about something else. My son has been receiving visitors here almost every day. I want you to find out what they are doing here and why he is so attached to their company.'

Enrico nodded. 'I know who they are, my Lord. They are two of the Ram but one at least is really from Bellezza. He is Luciano, the Regent's apprentice.'

'Ah yes,' said Niccolò. 'I met him when my sons took me to the Ram to hear the Zinti play. His father is an elderly Anglian. The other is some stable-boy I think.'

'Ah,' said Enrico. 'They give out that the Bellezzan is the old doctor's son now. But he wasn't when he first came to the city. He was a distant cousin of the Regent's then. And I've had him in my hands and there is something odd about him, something your Grace's nephew was very interested in.'

'You know, that girl's got a real gift,' said Jean to her business partner Angela at the stables.

They were watching Georgia ride bareback round one of the paddocks.

'Where did she learn that?' asked Angela.

'She says she's been practising in Devon for a couple of weeks,' said Jean.

'But she looks as if she's been doing it a lot longer than that,' said Angela.

'Yes,' said Jean. 'She looks as if she's flying.'

*

It was D-Day, Monday 4th August. Georgia was quite confident that it would be the same date in Talia; the gateway between the two worlds had remained steady for nearly three weeks, in spite of Luciano's frequent warnings about its instability. Falco had had a visit from his father the day before and the Duke wasn't likely to ride out to the palace two days in a row.

Georgia had got the same clothes organised as before, this time with all the labels cut out. She was also lending Falco an old duffel bag and had bought him a pack of small-sized boxers from Marks and Spencer; she knew he had kept Russell's from before, as if they were a significant relic, but they really were much too big for him.

She had planned and planned and now she couldn't plan any more; it was time to act. Besides, it was becoming a strain to spend so much of her time in Talia up at the summer palace. She was under no illusions about what it would be like once she had got Falco here but at least then she would be able to enjoy her time in Remora. Now she had to squeeze in her bareback riding practice, and all the time she had alone with Luciano was spent talking about Falco.

Georgia couldn't remember what it was like not to

feel responsible for someone else all the time. Now she decided to go and visit Mr Goldsmith at the antique shop.

He was pleased to see her but a little restrained.

'I had an unexpected visitor while you were away,' he said. 'Your mother dropped in for a chat.'

Georgia hid her face in her hands. She felt angry and embarrassed at the same time. 'I can't believe she did that!' she mumbled.

'Don't worry about it,' said Mr Goldsmith. 'I think she was just checking up on me. She must have been reassured if you're here again.'

Georgia shook her head. 'She didn't say anything about it to me. I hope she wasn't rude to you.'

'Not at all – she was very pleasant. But she did say she'd like to know when you were planning to visit me. I take it she doesn't know you're here today then?'

'No,' said Georgia. 'She can't tell me who I can and can't see – or when. It would mean I couldn't just drop in on you on the spur of the moment, without telling her first.'

'She's just looking after you, Georgia,' said Mr Goldsmith gently. 'You have to be careful these days.'

Suddenly, Georgia spotted something in the corner of the shop, behind Mr Goldsmith's desk with the till.

'Crutches!' she exclaimed. 'I knew I'd seen a pair somewhere! Are they yours?'

'They were last year,' said the old man. 'I had to use them for six weeks, after my hip operation. 'I keep meaning to take them back to the hospital. Thanks for reminding me.'

'No, don't do that,' said Georgia quickly. 'I mean,

could I borrow them for a short while? It's for a school project; I've been trying to get hold of a pair. And I could take them back to the hospital for you afterwards.'

'All right,' said Mr Goldsmith. 'It's a deal. Barts Orthopaedic Department.'

He handed them to Georgia, who now had all she needed for tonight's plan.

'Let me tell you about my visit to the British Museum,' she said.

Falco had been ready for hours. He had the mysterious undergarment on beneath his nightshirt, which he had changed into specially early. He had the bottle of poison which he had stolen from the gardener days before. He had carefully poured the contents away down a culvert but the bottle still smelled strongly and had a drop of liquid left in it.

Mentally he had said goodbye to the palace at Santa Fina, the Casa di Chimici, trailing round all his favourite rooms and up and down the avenues of the vast gardens. He stopped in the courtyard with the statue of the dying bull. 'Mithras,' he murmured, remembering the name Georgia had read out in the museum in her world. A quick death, he thought. A knife to the throat – not like the slow uncertainty he would face. Would it hurt to die in this world if he was living in the other? He could not ask Luciano that.

It seemed an age until the two Stravaganti arrived. They went through what he should do in great detail.

Georgia was looking tired, the strain of what she was trying to pull off showing on her face. Luciano's mood was sombre too. He had been thinking about the plans for so long that he no longer knew whether what they were going to do was wise.

The servants came up with fresh candles and the three friends knew it was time. Falco arranged himself in the bed with the empty bottle in one hand and Georgia's silver ring in the other. Again she curled around him and they waited for sleep to come.

But sleep was a long time coming. Luciano sat beside the bed with his eyes closed, absorbed in his own thoughts. But it was late in the night before Falco closed his eyes on his bedroom for the last time. Something changed in the atmosphere and Luciano looked up. Georgia had vanished. He went over to the bed and saw that Falco was asleep, the glass bottle fallen from his hand. That was how the servants must find him in the morning. Luciano retreated to his own room and thought he heard wings outside his window as he drifted off to sleep.

'That's it then,' said Falco, as soon as he awoke in Georgia's bedroom. She sat up and looked at him.

'Here, take the ring back,' he said, opening his hand. 'And don't give it back to me, even if I ask you for it.'

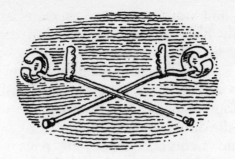

Chapter 18

Rivals

In some ways it was easier than last time. It was the holidays and Georgia wasn't really expected to come down to breakfast. When she did, everyone had gone to work and there was just a note asking her to start supper at six. She ran back upstairs and brought Falco down. He had added a baseball cap to his ensemble.

'Very fetching,' said Georgia. 'But you must wear it the other way round.'

They had a leisurely breakfast together. Falco was interested in all the machines in the kitchen and wanted Georgia to show him what they could all do. It was wonderful to be able to demonstrate microwave and kettle and toaster, rather than just explain them, though it did make for a larger breakfast than usual. Falco was fascinated by all the contents of the cupboards and wanted to taste as many as possible. He specially liked strawberry jam and orange juice and then he liked bacon and croissants.

Georgia was able to demonstrate the dishwasher too.

'Is this why you don't have servants?' asked Falco. 'Because your machines cook and make drinks and then wash the dishes for you?'

'Yes,' said Georgia. 'That's one reason we don't have servants. Also, we couldn't afford to pay them. Machines are cheaper.'

'You pay servants in your world?' asked Falco.

'You mean you don't?' asked Georgia.

They stared at one another. It seemed incredible that they could be friends; their worlds were so different. But from now on they were to be the same.

Luciano woke to the sound of scurrying footsteps and hushed voices. He struggled into his clothes and went out to find the servants who were in a great state of anxiety.

'What is the matter?' he asked, knowing perfectly well.

'We cannot wake the young master,' said the housekeeper. 'He ... he has drunk some tincture – we are not sure what.'

'Have you sent for the doctor?' asked Luciano.

'Yes,' said the housekeeper. 'And for the Duke.'

'Let me see him,' said Luciano.

He went to sit by the bed where Falco was still lying as he had left him in the night. I wonder what he has been doing in England, he thought.

When Falco had eaten his fill, Georgia showed him round the bathroom, explaining the shower, her electric toothbrush and even Ralph's razor.

'You'll have to use something like that in a few years' time, unless you grow a beard,' she said.

She gave him a quick tour of the rest of the house and showed him how the television worked and the computer. He was particularly fascinated by electric-light switches and taps, though he didn't like fitted carpets, useful though they were for getting around on crutches.

'Come on,' said Georgia. 'We must go out. You mustn't get too attached to my house. You won't be able to live here.'

'Can we go to the hospital?' asked Falco.

'Not yet,' said Georgia. 'First we have to get you noticed. Now remember what I told you about having lost your memory?'

They walked slowly through the Islington streets, this time taking plenty of time for Falco to accustom himself to the cars and the noise. Georgia was careful to explain the traffic lights and the zebra crossings to him, instead of just helping him to cross the roads.

Falco was interested in everything, especially the people who passed them in the streets. He found it hard to tell which were male and which were female. 'They all wear pantaloons!' he whispered.

By contrast, no one took any notice of him. From her own experience in Talia Georgia knew that most people paid no attention to shadows and it was even easier for a lack of one to pass unremarked on a grey English summer's day than in the bright sunlight of Remora.

As they got closer to their destination, Georgia hung back. She had thought often of this moment and now that it had come, she was very nervous.

'OK,' she said. 'Now you stay out here and I'll go in and explain.'

The Duke's horse was dark with sweat when they arrived at the summer palace. He dismounted, flinging the reins at a groom, and took the steps of the main staircase two at a time.

Luciano jumped from his chair as the distraught Duke threw open the door and swept over to the bed. He snatched his son up in his arms, but the boy's body was slack and unresisting.

'Where is the doctor?' demanded Niccolò. It was terrible to see him so frantic and Luciano tried to slip out while the servant explained that the doctor was on his way.

'Wait!' roared the Duke. 'You! Bellezzan boy! Stay where you are! What do you know about this?'

'I heard a commotion this morning,' said Luciano truthfully. 'And the servants told me what had happened. I tried to wake your Grace's son but found him as you see him. I have been watching over him since, waiting for the doctor.'

'You were here last night?' asked Niccolò.

Luciano nodded.

'And what about the other one, your servant?'

'My friend,' Luciano corrected him quietly. 'Giorgio must have gone back to the Ram. I should like to do so too and let him know what has happened.' He had arranged with Georgia that she would wait in Remora once she had stravagated back.

Niccolò shook his head like a wounded bear.

'Go for now,' he said. 'But I shall want to talk to you again. Especially if anything happens to my son.'

Luciano took the carriage back to Remora with a heavy heart.

'A boy has lost his memory?' asked Vicky Mulholland, uncomprehending.

Georgia went through it again patiently. 'Yes. I told you, he just came up to me in the street as I was passing here. I rang your doorbell because you're the only person I know round here. I don't know what to do. He seems quite out of it – doesn't know where he lives or who his parents are.'

'And you don't think it's some trick?'

'No. He seems a bit – strange. And he's very handicapped. He has a pair of crutches and a twisted leg. He won't last long on the street, the state he's in. Should we phone the police?'

'Hang on,' said Vicky, running her fingers through her curly hair. 'He's still outside?'

'I told him to wait while I asked for help.'

'Well, perhaps we'd better get him in here before we do anything,' said Vicky.

Yes! thought Georgia. She had always banked on

Falco to do the rest.

She went with Vicky to the front door and beckoned to Falco. He was standing where she had left him at the gate, leaning his weight on the crutches, looking pale and weary. Georgia heard Vicky's sharp intake of breath as she took in his black curls and his delicate, beautiful features.

'Would you like to come in?' asked Vicky, and Falco smiled at her.

The time had come for Arianna to set out from Bellezza. She was to reach Remora on the tenth of August, the day before the Campo in that city was turned into a racetrack. But a Duchessa had to travel in style, in a state carriage, at a gentle pace, with overnight stops at inns so that she should not arrive tired. She wanted to see other parts of Talia too. Rodolfo was to accompany her and Gaetano was going to ride beside her.

It was the first time that Arianna had left the lagoon and her first important state visit since becoming Duchessa. Her maid Barbara was following in a second carriage laden with trunks of clothes for her week of ritual celebrations. The trunks alone had filled three mandolas as the Ducal party left for the landing stage to take the boat to the mainland.

It was as well that Arianna was masked and hooded as she made the sea-journey to the mainland, or her face would have betrayed a most un-Ducal excitement about the trip. More new experiences awaited her on the shore. The Bellezzan state carriage was kept on the mainland and rarely used. Arianna had never seen horses before and was immediately overawed by their size and power.

It did Gaetano's suit no harm at all for her to see him mounted on the tall bay he had left in the Ducal stables on his way to Bellezza three weeks earlier. Arianna smiled up at him from her carriage window.

'You seem used to horses, Principe,' she said to him.

'Indeed I am, your Grace,' he answered her formally. 'And beautiful as your city is, it is the one thing I have missed there.'

'I'm glad to know that everything otherwise was to your satisfaction,' said Arianna, drawing her curtain.

'What is your name?' asked Vicky, settling Falco in a kitchen chair. 'Can you remember that?'

'Nicholas Duke,' said Falco, carefully reproducing the name he had agreed on with Georgia. It felt strange in his mouth, but there was no doubt that he would be able to remember it.

'Nicholas,' said Vicky. 'Can you tell us anything about yourself?'

Falco shook his head. 'No,' he said, untruthfully.

'Your parents?'

He shook his head again.

'How did you hurt your leg?' she persisted.

'I think it was a riding accident,' said Falco.

'And how did you get here?'

Falco looked pleadingly at Georgia. 'I can't explain,' he said. He could feel tears welling up.

Vicky looked distressed. She stopped asking

questions and put the kettle on. 'I think you're right, Georgia,' she said in a low voice. 'We must call the police and trace his parents as soon as possible. But let's have some coffee first – he looks worn out.'

She carried a tray through to the living room, where the piano was and her violins. But she almost dropped it when she heard Falco's gasp behind her. He was staring at a picture on the piano. It was a younger version but recognisably the Stravagante Luciano. Vicky put down the tray and helped Falco into a comfortable chair.

'I see you looking at the photo,' she said. 'It is my son, Lucien. He ... died last year.'

'He lives in another place,' said Falco. Georgia kicked his ankle.

Vicky sat down, white-faced. 'That's what that strange man said at the funeral,' she said, trembling. 'What does it mean?' She passed her hand over her eyes. 'Sometimes I fancy he's still alive in some other world. I've even imagined that I've seen him.' She looked cautiously at them to see what they thought of this.

'I think it's just a manner of speaking,' said Georgia quickly. 'Perhaps he's religious.' And she glared at Falco.

*

'We had the most extraordinary case today,' said Maura, over dinner. 'The police rang in about a boy. He's lost his memory and seems to have been abandoned by his parents.'

'Good grief,' said Ralph. 'How old is he?'

'Thirteen,' said Maura. 'At least he says he is. But

small for his age. He's very handicapped too. Has to walk with crutches. But the extraordinary thing is, he was reported by Georgia's violin teacher, Vicky Mulholland.'

Georgia felt her spaghetti Bolognese turning to ashes in her mouth. She swallowed hard. Now was the time for her to own up. But Russell was listening, not tuned out the way he usually was during meals.

'Yeah, actually, I found him wandering round outside as I was passing her house,' she said. 'I asked her if she would call the police.'

All the rest of the family turned their attention fully on Georgia.

'Why on earth didn't you say?' asked Maura.

Georgia shrugged. 'It was no big deal,' she said.

'What? You find abandoned children every day, do you?' asked Ralph.

'She finds cripples easily enough,' said Russell. 'Georgia collects them.'

'Handicapped people, Russell,' said Maura sharply. 'Well, I wish you'd said, Georgie. I might have to declare an interest at work now.'

'What interest? It's not as if I know him,' lied Georgia. 'I just found him and took him into Mrs Mulholland's. That's not a crime, is it?'

'No, but there's a complication,' said Maura. 'You see, there was no reported missing child of his description so we had to put him in temporary foster care. Well, you know how backed-up we are in Islington with children needing foster families and our children's homes are all bursting at the seams.'

'Don't tell me we have to have him here,' said Russell.

'No, Russell,' said Maura. 'But the Mulhollands volunteered and we've approved them as temporary foster-parents. He'll be living with them till we find his real parents.'

'What do you think has happened to them?' asked Ralph.

'In all likelihood, I think they're probably asylum-seekers, who have deliberately left him to be found, so that he can get proper medical care. He may even have come into the country unaccompanied. It wouldn't be the first case we've had,' said Maura.

'A bit unfeeling to abandon the kid, though,' said Ralph. 'Particularly if he's lost his memory.'

'If he has,' said Maura. 'It's more likely that they told him to pretend he'd lost it – as a cover story. I should think his family are far from unfeeling.'

Georgia felt uncomfortable; her mother's guesses were a bit too close to the truth.

'Welcome back,' said Paolo. 'We don't seem to have seen much of you lately.'

'I know,' said Georgia. 'It will be different from now on.'

'Will it?' asked the older Stravagante. 'You seem very sure. I don't know what you and Luciano have been up to. I said it was a good idea to befriend the younger generation of di Chimici, but you must be careful. The Duke is a powerful enemy.'

Georgia was let off the hook by the return of Luciano in his carriage. He had to tell Paolo and Doctor Dethridge what appeared to have happened to

Falco. The four Stravaganti were silent for a moment, each thinking separate thoughts about this event.

'And ye two knowe no thinge aboute the chylde's resouns?' asked Dethridge. 'Yt is a terrabyl thinge thatte he has done.'

'I think he was just tired of living with his physical problems,' said Luciano.

'But he didn't tell either of you what he was planning?' persisted Paolo.

It was difficult for Georgia and Luciano to withstand the two men's questioning while looking them in the eye. In the end, Paolo let them go but he looked very grave.

With great relief, the two younger Stravaganti walked into town.

'I never want to go through another night like that,' said Luciano. 'How was it at your end?'

'Fine,' said Georgia. She looked and felt quite wretched though. She now had a secret from Luciano as well as from everyone else in Talia and she didn't know how he was going to take it.

Falco lay unsleeping in Luciano's old bed in London. He did not know how to relax. So much had happened to him since this second stravagation. He hadn't had any idea that Georgia planned to bring him to Luciano's parents, but he liked them. David was nothing like Falco's real father and wasn't at all frightening. He had accepted the idea of fostering the lost boy as soon as his wife put it to him. And it was lovely to have a sort of a mother again. Falco had almost forgotten what it was like.

But he felt guilty that he was here instead of Luciano. And his heart was heavy with his imaginings about what his family would be suffering in Remora, Giglia and Bellezza, as soon as they all knew. He knew that Georgia would be with Luciano in Remora now and he felt suddenly homesick for Talia.

He was giving Luciano up as well as his family and he had grown attached to the Stravagante as an extra brother. But now, if he were to carry out his full plan, he would not see Luciano again. The choice – for now – had been removed from him though. Georgia had the talisman and she was asleep in another house. As well as awake in Remora, doubtless being quizzed about Falco right now.

He sighed and closed his eyes. At the foot of his bed a mirror reflected black curls on the pillow – not for the first time.

'You did what?' said Luciano.

He had wanted to know everything about Falco in London and Georgia, although she hadn't intended to tell him about that part of her plan yet, found his questions too pressing to parry. At least they were in a public place. They were drinking lemon sherbet bought from a stall in the Campo delle Stelle, sitting on the stone seat that surrounded the slender column in the centre.

Luciano seemed so fierce Georgia's heart misgave her. She wanted him to admire her even if there was no chance of anything deeper and now it looked as if she might have blown it.

'I can't believe it,' he said now. 'My parents! But they've never talked about fostering before.'

'Well it wasn't exactly planned,' said Georgia. 'They just offered because Social Services couldn't find any other place for him.'

'Planned is exactly what it seems to have been,' said Luciano bitterly. 'You never told me my parents were going to be involved.'

'Do you mind?' asked Georgia nervously.

'No,' said Luciano, after a pause. 'Not exactly. It's just a shock. What made you do it?'

'It was talking to your mum,' said Georgia. 'She still misses you so much. Falco needed a home and it seemed to me that she needed a boy to take care of.'

'Proper little agony aunt, aren't you?' said Luciano, but he managed a weak smile. 'I know it's selfish of me but I don't want to be replaced, even by Falco.'

Georgia squeezed his hand. 'You won't be,' she said. 'You're irreplaceable.'

They went back to the stall to return their wooden cups – nothing in Talia was disposable.

'It seems strange to think that in a week's time this will be a racetrack, doesn't it?' said Georgia, deliberately changing the subject. 'With Cesare and the others galloping round it.'

'And all the Rams out in force supporting him and Arcangelo,' said Luciano. 'The whole family will be here.'

'Will you watch it?' asked Georgia.

'Yes,' said Luciano a bit uncomfortably. 'I think Doctor Dethridge and I will have a place with Rodolfo and the Duchessa in the Pope's stand.'

'The Royal Box,' said Georgia. 'How come you get to hobnob with the aristocracy while I'm just a humble stable-boy?'

'Chance,' said Luciano. 'Or destiny. You'll just have to watch with all the other Remorans in the Campo. It will probably be more fun.'

'Look out!' said Georgia suddenly. 'Fishes!'

Luciano's hand flew to the dagger in his belt. The three young men approaching did indeed wear the blue and pink colours of the Twelfth of Fishes and they were not looking friendly. In the days before the race the enmities between Twelfths in the city became more pronounced. And Luciano and Georgia were outnumbered. Then they saw the Fishes backing off.

They turned round and saw Cesare and Paolo coming towards them. The Fishes must have thought better of taking on four Rams, particularly since one of the new arrivals was so well built.

'Well met,' said Paolo. 'But I bring news more worrying than Fishes, particularly minnows like those three. A messenger has come for you. Duke Niccolò wants to see you both up at the Papal palace. And he won't tolerate any delay.'

*

In the Papal palace Rinaldo di Chimici was having a very uncomfortable interview with his uncle. He had never told the Duke about capturing the young Bellezzan because the plan had gone so badly wrong. Rinaldo had redeemed himself by being able to send news to Giglia of a much bigger coup: the assassination of the Duchessa. But now he was being hard pressed by the Duke to tell him all he knew about Luciano.

'You had him in your hands and let him go?' Niccolò asked incredulously. 'When you knew he was a Stravagante from the other world?'

'That was the suspicion, Uncle. But if he was – and I saw him without a shadow – he is that no longer. Something must have gone wrong with whatever that old magician Rodolfo was planning. I told you, when we had the boy arraigned in court, he clearly did have a shadow.'

'And what about the book?' asked Niccolò. 'You said there was a book he valued that had something to do with his powers.'

Rinaldo shifted in his chair. 'I have it, Uncle, but we have been able to do nothing with it and make nothing of it. I suspect trickery of some kind.'

'So you let him go?' said Niccolò.

'We couldn't keep him for ever,' said Rinaldo.

'You should have slit his throat while you had him,' said Niccolò. 'If you had, my boy would not be lying unconscious upstairs.'

A footman entered. 'The young men you sent for are here, your Grace.'

'You may leave us, Rinaldo,' said Niccolò coldly.

Luciano started as he passed his old adversary the ambassador in the doorway. Georgia hadn't seen Rinaldo before and didn't know anything of his history with her friend. She saw only a rather weak and nervous young man who passed them in a cloud of scent.

For the next twenty minutes, the Duke grilled them mercilessly about Falco. Why had they visited him so often? What had they talked about? What did they know of his son's state of mind?

And he wasn't satisfied with their answers. Necessarily, since Luciano and Georgia both had to lie, in order to respect Falco's wishes. But it was very hard to lie to the Duke. They felt lucky to escape unscathed, except for his threats.

'Do not attempt to leave Remora,' he said coldly. 'I shall have the gates of the city barred against you. And if my son does not recover, you may never leave here.'

When Luciano and Georgia had left, he put his head in his hands.

*

The rider from Remora had not spared himself. He changed horses many times on the journey and pulled up at the inn outside Volana in the middle of the night. The sleepy innkeeper was most unsure about disturbing the young prince but was persuaded that the matter was urgent. Minutes later Gaetano was sitting up in bed rubbing his eyes as he tried to make sense of the message the rider had brought.

*

A smart carriage drove through the Gate of the Sun in the early hours of Wednesday morning. It was curtained so that the two occupants could not be seen, but there was a great deal of luggage stacked on the top and an elegantly-liveried servant sat beside the driver. He was tall and thin, with red hair, unusual colouration in Talia and therefore highly regarded.

The carriage rattled across the empty cobbled streets until it reached the Twelfth of the Ram. It stopped outside a tall house in the Via di Montone and the red-headed servant jumped down. The curtains were drawn back and the carriage-window lowered so that he could talk to his employer.

He then rapped at the door-knocker and went into the house to check that everything was in order. Only when the lodgings had been thoroughly inspected and passed as suitable did he hand down a passenger from the carriage. She was a handsome middle-aged woman, with a still slender figure, in a grey velvet travelling dress. She wore a veil and was followed by a maid carrying various small cases and bags, which the manservant courteously took from her. The three passed into the house unremarked except by a couple of pigeons and a grey cat as sleek as the elegant stranger.

Things moved fast for Falco in the next week. The first thing that happened was an appointment with the doctor. Dr Kennedy was a bit surprised to see him come in with Vicky Mulholland, but she had agreed with Social Services to let this boy have an emergency appointment, so that his physical condition could be assessed. Maura had come too. The two women knew each other slightly.

The doctor spent a long time examining Falco, whom she addressed as Nicholas. He had to remember that was his name now. He couldn't answer her questions about what childhood illnesses he had had.

'Well,' she said, when she had finished, filling out a form Maura gave her. 'In some ways you're in pretty good shape. You are well nourished and your heart and lungs are sound. I'd like to see you weigh about half a stone more at your age but you are a bit on the short side and could be in for a growth spurt. The real problem of course is your leg. You say you can't remember anything about the accident except that it involved a horse. But it's a bad break, badly set.'

'Can you make it better?' asked Falco. It was what his whole journey had been for.

'Not me,' said Dr Kennedy, and smiled to see his downcast face. 'But I think that the orthopaedic surgeons could.' She turned to Maura. 'I shall ask for him to be seen at Barts as soon as possible. I think it highly likely that he'll need quite extensive surgery followed by physiotherapy.'

'And do you think if he has it he'll be able to walk properly?' asked Vicky, putting the question Falco did not dare to.

'I can't make any promises, Mrs Mulholland,' said the doctor. 'I'm not the specialist here. But we'll see what the surgeons say. I'll give Mr Turnbull's secretary a ring now and find out how quickly they can get him seen. It is an unusual case and I think that will push him up the waiting list.'

'Thank goodness for that,' said Maura. 'We know what the NHS can be like.' Then bit her lip, wishing she could bite her tongue too as she saw the grimace pass over Vicky's face. Of course this intense and caring woman knew more about doctors and hospitals than Maura would ever wish to.

Falco was seen at Barts within a week. The clinic nurse looked a bit oddly at the crutches, which were the hospital's own property, but didn't say anything. She weighed and measured him, gave the crutches back and soon called him in to see Mr Turnbull. Again, Falco was accompanied by his foster-mother and his social worker. Maura was a team leader but she was handling his case personally. Falco was high profile now, his photo in all the tabloids under banner headlines like 'IS THIS YOUR SON?' and 'TRAGEDY OF ABANDONED BOY.' Social Services couldn't afford to get anything wrong about his treatment.

*

Georgia took Falco to visit Mr Goldsmith's shop. The Talian boy loved the jumble of things he saw there – snuffboxes and clocks, soup tureens and pianola rolls. The old antique dealer looked curiously at Falco's crutches and then at Georgia. But one of the things she liked about him was the way he didn't ask questions about unimportant things.

'This is my friend Nicholas,' she said. 'And this is Mr Goldsmith,' thinking, he's my friend too. Plus Alice, that's three I've got in this world.

Mr Goldsmith was a bit like Doctor Dethridge, she decided. He and Falco got on extremely well and were soon poring over the innards of a long case clock together.

In Remora the di Chimici clan were gathering. Gaetano had made his apologies to the Duchessa early on the morning after the messenger had arrived. She was a little piqued to be losing his company on the journey, which was to stop for two nights in the Prince's home city of Giglia, but softened when she saw his evident distress about his brother.

Gaetano had sent the messenger on to Bellezza and Francesca was expected to arrive within days. Other messengers had been dispatched to Giglia by the Duke and had brought the rest of Falco's family. His older brothers Fabrizio and Carlo and his sister Beatrice had all abandoned their pursuits and set out for Remora straightaway.

The boy's unconscious body had been taken from Santa Fina to the city's hospital, just across the square from the Papal palace and the cathedral, which were all in the Twelfth of the Twins. The Pope said Mass daily for him in the cathedral and the people of Remora remembered him in their prayers.

Falco was now officially suffering from the *Morte Vivenda* and there was very little hope that he would wake up. The poison bottle had been traced to the gardener at Santa Fina and he had been severely flogged. People were gathering outside the hospital, where they brought votive offerings to the goddess, on the remains of whose temple the hospital had been built.

The Duke spent almost all his time at his son's bedside, neither eating nor sleeping except when his daughter Beatrice made him take rest and refreshment. One day he sent his servants out to find the Manoush to see if the blind harpist would come and play under his son's window.

Aurelio came and played, the saddest and most plangent airs ever heard in Remora and the people outside all wept. But Raffaella took up no collection.

For Luciano and Georgia it was a tense time. They had the threat of the Duke hanging over them and they were worried about Falco too. Georgia was able to reassure Luciano that he was doing well in the other world but neither of them had thought that his body would endure so long in Talia.

Gaetano arrived back in Remora three days after his brother had been found unconscious and went straight to the hospital to visit him. It was only after a harrowing few hours that he left for the Ram. He found Luciano and Georgia and Cesare in the stable yard. At first they said nothing, just embraced.

'I didn't think he would do it so soon,' whispered Gaetano. 'To be honest, although he said goodbye, I didn't really think he'd do it at all. Were you all with him? Was it easy?'

'Not me,' said Cesare. 'I'm not a Stravagante. But I'm really sorry.'

'We were there,' said Luciano. 'Georgia took care of everything at the other end.'

'He's in good hands,' she said.

'The best,' said Luciano. 'He is with my own parents.'

Gaetano started, then hugged Luciano. 'Then we are brothers,' he said.

Luciano took a deep breath. 'How is the Duchessa?' he asked.

'Wonderful!' said Gaetano. 'She really is an amazing person. She will be here in a few days.'

And Georgia wondered whose heart was beating faster – hers or Luciano's.

Chapter 19

The Dirt Goes Down

It was late evening when the state carriage of Bellezza rumbled through the Gate of the Sun. A sizeable crowd of Remorans, mainly from the Ram, waited to greet it, waving the standards of their Twelfth, the black and white banners of the city and a few Bellezzan flags adorned with masks. Gaetano stood at the gate, with his older brothers and his uncle, representing the di Chimici family. Duke Niccolò could not be persuaded to leave the hospital, even for such an important visitor.

Heralds played a fanfare of welcome and in the background could be heard the faint throb of drums as other Twelfths kept up their perpetual practice for the parade before the race. Rodolfo alighted from the carriage and handed Arianna down so that she could accept the formal greeting of Pope Lenient VI.

The crowd sighed. She was as beautiful as her reports; though it was a pity they could not see her face properly, masked as it was in accordance with the custom of her city. But she was tall and graceful, with a riot of chestnut curls caught up only loosely on top of her head and she wore black and white satin in honour of the city colours of Remora – a touch which its citizens appreciated.

The young Duchessa curtsied to the Pope and kissed his ring, showing a proper respect for the church, of which the Remorans also approved. But the Pope drew her to her feet quickly and presented her to his three nephews. The crowd applauded the handsome young Giglian nobles bending over the Duchessa's hand in turn. But they couldn't help noticing that she spent the longest time talking to the youngest brother, who was nothing much to look at.

Luciano noticed that too as he stood among the supporters of the Ram. He hadn't seen Arianna for nearly a month and he didn't know when he would be able to be alone with her. She was being led off to the Papal palace in Twins territory, a place he was steering well clear of at the moment. And she was still talking to Gaetano. Luciano felt horrible. He really liked Gaetano – but not as much as he liked Arianna.

The stooped black figure behind Arianna turned at that moment and looked straight at Luciano. Rodolfo the Stravagante had sensed not only one of his brotherhood but his favoured apprentice. The nod and smile he gave Luciano were fleeting but enough to lift his spirits. Rodolfo was here and everything was going to be all right.

'They look well, don't they?' said a low voice in his ear and he turned to see a familiar face, even though it was lightly covered by a veil.

'Silvia!' he gasped. 'I didn't know you were coming.'

'Nor do they,' she said, smiling. 'Do you think they'll be pleased?'

'Surely it's not safe?' whispered Luciano. 'There are di Chimici everywhere, as you see, and the Duke is in a dangerous mood.'

'I heard about his boy,' said Silvia. 'Strange isn't it how someone who can order the deaths of strangers along with a new pair of boots should be such a loving family man?'

'He is my friend,' said Luciano.

'Duke Niccolò?' she asked.

'No, his youngest son, Falco,' said Luciano. 'I think Duke Niccolò would like to put me in with his next boot order.'

It had been hard for Georgia to leave Remora that night and face a new day in London, knowing that Luciano was going to be reunited with the famous Arianna. It would have been difficult enough if the old Lucien had lived and found himself a girlfriend among people Georgia knew. But this new Luciano, with his velvet clothes and his aristocratic friends, was living in a world that Georgia could only ever visit briefly, in a time that had vanished centuries ago. And now that the Duchessa had arrived, Georgia's special time alone with him was coming to an end.

The last week in Remora had been very scary – so much so that at times she had thought of giving up her night journeys there. After all, she had done what she had intended to do. 'Nicholas Duke' was safe in her world, looked after by the Mulhollands, seeing doctors and planning his new future.

But in Remora Falco was dying. No one in the city doubted it. The Duke was beside himself with grief and spent every possible hour at his son's bedside in the hospital. Still Georgia had returned every night, caught between the private drama of the di Chimici family and the public excitement that was building up towards the race.

Her two closest friends in Remora were involved in both these events. Cesare could not conceal his enthusiasm about the Stellata; he talked to Georgia about it when they went bareback riding every day, telling her about the secret pacts between jockeys of the different Twelfths, and about the many rituals and customs surrounding the great race.

Luciano was openly worried about what might happen to him and Georgia. Niccolò di Chimici had threatened both of them with serious consequences if Falco should die and that moment was getting nearer. The boy had not opened his eyes since he had been found with the empty poison bottle nearly a week ago. But the doctors of the city had been baffled. There had been none of the symptoms of a poisoning. And everyone was reluctant to think that someone so young should give up his own life. Suicide was as rare in Talia as murder was common.

Georgia and Luciano were not allowed to visit the hospital, though they had tried. The Duke kept fierce watch over his son. So instead they talked in Paolo's kitchen, Georgia telling Luciano everything she knew about how the Talian was faring in London.

And he was blooming. Georgia was a regular visitor at the Mulhollands' now, which no one found odd, since she had been the first to discover the boy. It was very difficult to remember to call him Nicholas, though. He, however, was adapting well to his new identity. The Mulhollands had bought him some clothes and he even used some old ones that Lucien had grown out of but not thrown away. It made Georgia jump the first time she saw him in the grey hooded sweatshirt that Lucien had worn the first time she set eyes on him.

She had introduced him to Alice, who was intrigued by her friendship with the younger boy.

'I suppose you feel responsible, since you found him,' said Alice.

'You're right there,' said Georgia. 'Responsible is exactly what I feel.'

Falco visited her house too and she even took him to the stables when she went riding on Saturday, since it was one of the times when Maura drove her. Fortunately, Maura didn't think there was anything wrong with the lost boy being friends with her daughter, now that the question of his fostering had been sorted out, and she also had hopes of the contact with horses being therapeutic for him.

'Perhaps it will jog his memory about his accident?' she suggested to Georgia.

Falco was ecstatic at being around horses again. This was something he could fully understand about his new life. Although he couldn't ride, Jean showed him round the stables while Georgia was out on her lesson, introducing him to all the horses who weren't in use. He was especially drawn to a black mare named Blackbird.

'Do you think I could come here and ride her when I've had my operation, Mrs O'Grady?' he asked Maura.

'Well, not straightaway,' said Maura. 'You know you'll have to be in plaster for six weeks. But when you've recovered, we'll talk to your foster-parents about riding lessons.'

'We'd love to have you,' said Jean, though privately she couldn't imagine that this damaged boy would ever be fit to ride again.

When Georgia got to Remora the morning after the Duchessa's arrival, she found a stranger in the kitchen. A very elegant middle-aged woman, with a veil, was talking to Doctor Dethridge and it was clear that they were old friends. A gangly red-haired young man, apparently the woman's servant, stood behind her chair.

'Ah, my dere,' said Dethridge. 'Let me presente yow to Signora Bellini. Silvia, this is yonge George – one of us.'

The stranger offered Georgia a cool, beautifully manicured hand and a piercing scrutiny.

'So,' she said. 'You are the new Stravagante. My ... Rodolfo said you were a girl.'

Georgia felt herself blushing. She had never felt so awkward in her coarse Talian stable-boy's clothes as she did under this woman's violet gaze.

'Ah,' said Silvia. 'I see you are in disguise. Very wise in this city. I should perhaps adopt the same stratagem. Although in a manner of speaking I already have.'

Georgia's mind was racing, trying to work out where this obviously important woman fitted into the pattern. Had she really said 'my Rodolfo'? Who would have the right to such intimacy with the great man? And why did she need a disguise?

At that moment Luciano, Paolo and Cesare came back from the racetrack. It had started to rain and the going was slippery. Cesare was anxious about it because today was the all-important laying of the earth for the racetrack round the Campo.

'It is just a shower,' his father reassured him. 'No doubt the track will be fine.'

'I see you have met Silvia,' Luciano said to Georgia, and she wondered again at his easy manner with the great people of Talia.

'When are you going to see Arianna?' asked Silvia, putting a question Georgia was interested in too.

'I don't know,' said Luciano.

There came a knock at the door and both the young Stravaganti jumped, though it was hardly likely that the Duchessa of Bellezza would be visiting in the Twelfth of the Ram.

Paolo opened the door to a figure Georgia knew must be Rodolfo. In fact she recognised him as the stranger who had come to Lucien's funeral. A slightly stooped thin man with silvered hair and a distinguished look, he stepped into the room and clasped Paolo warmly in his arms. Dethridge too was embraced and then Luciano. The visitor looked long and searchingly into his face.

'It does my heart good to see you,' Georgia heard him say quietly and saw Luciano looking at his master with open devotion.

What am I doing here? she thought, feeling small and insignificant.

But then the tall man turned to her and took her hand. She found herself held by dark and steady eyes which seemed able to fathom her deepest secrets.

'You must be Georgia,' he said courteously. 'It is an honour to meet you.'

'Five Stravaganti in one room,' said a low voice. 'We should all be honoured.'

Now it was Rodolfo's turn to be disconcerted. To her astonishment, Georgia saw his calm demeanour completely ruffled, as the mysterious Silvia stepped forwards.

And then the two embraced. But it was not a Talian formality and suddenly Georgia knew who the woman was.

She saw that Luciano was smiling indulgently at the couple, who were still in each other's arms.

'I should be so angry with you,' said Rodolfo quietly. 'But how can I when it fills me with joy to find you here?'

'I think you had better re-introduce me to the young woman,' said Silvia.

'Georgia,' Rodolfo said, still holding the woman's hand in his, 'I should like you to meet my wife, Silvia Rossi, formerly Duchessa of Bellezza and the mother of the present Duchessa.'

In the Papal palace, Rinaldo di Chimici was having another uncomfortable audience with an uncle. This one was not as formidable as Duke Niccolò, but Ferdinando was the Pope and Prince of Remora too.

'Marriage is a sacred institution,' Ferdinando was saying, in his role as head of the Talian Church. 'It is not to be unmade lightly.'

'Indeed not, your Holiness,' said Rinaldo. 'But I must take some of the blame here. This marriage was perhaps made too lightly. It was I who arranged it.'

The Pope was perfectly aware of this and that his niece Francesca had been forced into it by Rinaldo, with the threat of Duke Niccolò's displeasure hanging over her if she refused. But if the ploy had succeeded and Francesca had been elected Duchessa of Bellezza, she would have found a way to tolerate her old Bellezzan husband, so the Pope was reluctant to let her escape now that the plan had foundered. It was his duty after all to uphold the sanctity of marriage.

'On what grounds does the young woman seek an annulment?' he asked now.

Rinaldo hesitated. If their uncle was referring to Francesca as 'the young woman', there was not much hope in playing the family loyalty card.

'She ... he ... I believe the marriage is unconsummated, your Holiness,' said Rinaldo horribly aware that he was blushing.

'After how long?'

'Nearly a year, your Holiness. And she does not love him.'

'Well, perhaps if she would let him in her bed,

matters might improve,' said the Pope. 'A baby – that would give her a reason to stay with her husband.'

Rinaldo very much did not want to have to mention that Francesca had been coerced into marrying Councillor Albani. He felt it did not show him in a good light, although this was very unfair. If Francesca had become Duchessa, his own standing in the family would have been very much improved.

'If he is capable, Holiness,' he muttered now.

Ferdinando di Chimici was not a bad man. He was weak and self-indulgent but he didn't really want to see one of his nieces yoked to a man she didn't love, especially if there were to be no babies. Besides, he did not think that his brother the Duke would have any use for Albani now that the Bellezzan plot had failed. And it might be useful to have Francesca available for another dynastic union. Ferdinando would try to make sure she got a more appealing husband next time.

'Oh very well,' he said testily, gesturing for his clerk to write the necessary decree. He sank his signet ring with the symbols of the lily and the twins into the soft red wax and handed the document to Rinaldo. In that moment Francesca was a free woman.

*

In the Campo the rain had stopped, leaving the air fresh and clean. Bullock carts came in a stream, full of earth from the surrounding countryside, and teams of men spread it with rakes in a wide band encircling the Piazza. Other men were engaged in building wooden stages to house the most important spectators of the race, though the majority of Remorans would watch from inside the track.

The grandest stage was being erected in front of the Papal palace, but every house with a balcony overlooking the racetrack was already draped with banners in the colours of the Twelfth they supported. The whole Campo was ablaze with colour.

One person particularly enjoying the prospect of the race was Enrico. He was accepting bets on the outcome. The Twins and the Lady had the shortest odds of course, so members of their Twelfths did not stand to win much. Other Twelvers wanted to gamble on a win for their own horses and jockeys but sometimes had a small side bet on the two most likely Twelfths as well. Remorans were practical people.

But they did not like to be seen to be disloyal, so such bets had to be placed discreetly. Enrico became accustomed to wandering through all the Twelfths of the city. He carried a bag full of neckcloths of different colours so that he could change which one he wore according to which Twelfth of the city he was in. He regarded them merely as safe conducts, having no allegiance to any particular Twelfth.

He now spent his days in Remora, riding back up to Santa Fina every night to fly Merla. She was becoming accustomed to him and seemed not to mind letting him ride her while she flew. Enrico did not want to spend any more time than he had to up at the Casa di Chimici. What had happened to the boy up there had really unsettled him. He felt in a way as if he should have been able to stop it. Now he busied himself with his gambling venture to take his mind off the pale boy lying unconscious in the hospital. Of his patron and employer he saw nothing.

*

Arianna couldn't sleep. She stood on the balcony outside her room in the Papal palace. The Campo was filled with moonlight and shadows. All around the edge, little knots of people clustered round horses. Every now and again they would organise themselves into a start and then the horses galloped round the circular track three times sunwise. There was much laughter in the Campo and yet mystery too in seeing it so thronged with people in the middle of the night.

She was watching an odd sight when Rodolfo silently joined her on the balcony. A big powerful grey horse, most unlikely to run in the real Stellata, was carrying two people, a man and a woman. They were strangely dressed though the moonlight bleached the colours out of their clothes.

'Who are they?' asked Arianna, as the couple moved to the start-point.

'They look like Zinti,' said Rodolfo. 'The wandering people. They come here for the festival of the Goddess. It happens on the same day as the race.'

They watched as another impromptu race began. The big grey won by a neck, carrying the two riders as easily as if they were one. As they dismounted and the woman led the man out of the Campo, Arianna gasped.

'He's blind!' she said.

'Zinti have more ways of seeing than other people,' said Rodolfo. 'Isn't it time you were asleep?'

'I couldn't,' she said. 'Do you think we were right to come here?'

'I think it will be perfectly safe, if that's what you mean,' said Rodolfo. 'Whatever the situation might have been before, I think Niccolò is too distracted by his son's illness to arrange any kind of trouble.'

'What about the trouble he's already arranged?' asked Arianna.

'You mean Gaetano?' said Rodolfo. 'Is he giving you trouble?'

Arianna shrugged. 'It's been harder than I thought it would be. I really like him and now he's terribly upset about his little brother. It will be hard to refuse him.'

'You think his heart is in this courtship?'

Arianna was silent.

'I saw Luciano this morning,' said Rodolfo.

'How was he?' asked Arianna eagerly.

'Very anxious,' said Rodolfo. 'He wants to see you. But he doesn't want to come here. Duke Niccolò has got it into his head that Luciano and the new Stravagante are involved in his son's suicide attempt.'

'But that's ridiculous!' said Arianna. 'Luciano wouldn't do that.'

'I thought that you might like to meet him somewhere neutral,' said Rodolfo. 'I've suggested to Gaetano that he should take us on a visit to Belle Vigne tomorrow. Luciano will meet us there.'

Georgia was finding it hard to fill her days in London. She spent a lot of time asleep, catching up on all the hours she lost in Remora. Already she was thinking, as Luciano had the summer before, that she wouldn't be able to keep it up when she went back to school in September. And that made her very sad. Talia would be an occasional treat, to see Cesare and his family. Luciano would surely go back to Bellezza with Arianna and Rodolfo after the race and she wouldn't be able to visit him there. Her talisman would only get her to Remora and you couldn't get to Bellezza and back in a day from there. Gaetano and his family would return to Giglia once Falco had died and the same applied to that city although it was closer than the City of Masks.

She had only a week left to enjoy her time in the Talian city with all her friends and enemies still there. Now that the Stravaganti were all together, at least all the ones she knew anything about, there was a feeling that a crisis was approaching. But Georgia didn't know what it was. Would it be because of danger threatening Luciano and her?

Georgia wasn't too afraid for herself; she could always stravagate back home as long as she had her talisman. But Luciano could be killed in Talia if Duke Niccolò decided to avenge his son's death in that way. And then she would have lost him twice.

And then she would remember that Luciano had been captured before and his talisman taken from him; he had told her that story now. And if that happened to her, she would be as Falco was in Remora now, as Luciano had been when he was still Lucien and his parents had agreed to having the life support system switched off.

Such thoughts left her in a cold sweat and she became all the more impatient to get back to Remora and find out what was going on. She was dying to ask about the Duchessa. If Silvia was the person Duke Niccolò was supposed to have assassinated, what was she doing coolly turning up in Remora? And what was her daughter doing ruling Bellezza?

The Bellezzans' carriage was all ready to leave when Georgia next arrived in Remora.

'Get in,' said Luciano, waving. 'We're going to Belle Vigne.'

Dethridge was inside the carriage in a jovial mood.

'Well come, young George,' he said. 'We are going to paye a visit to the ruins of a Rassenan settlemente. And mayhap we shalle fynde othires making the same journey!'

Luciano was smiling in his corner of the carriage and Georgia felt her heart sink.

And there indeed at Belle Vigne their carriage drew up next to one with the Giglian di Chimici crest on it – the lily and the perfume bottle. As Georgia climbed up the grassy hill she had last seen with Gaetano and Falco, she made out some figures at the top. Rodolfo, Gaetano and a slim and elegant young woman who could only be the Duchessa.

Georgia hung back at the top as Dethridge went forward to embrace Arianna. Luciano was right behind them but the greeting he gave the Duchessa seemed a lot more formal and there was some constraint between them. Luciano nodded at Gaetano, then turned to draw Georgia into the group.

'And this is Giorgio,' he said.

Georgia was surprised that he used the male form of her name, then noticed that there was another member of the party. As she gave Arianna her hand, she was aware that Gaetano was introducing Dethridge and Luciano to his older brother, Fabrizio. But it was difficult to think of anything else while observed by those violet eyes. They were surrounded by a light turquoise silk mask, the first Georgia had ever seen in Talia, which perfectly matched the Duchessa's elegant dress.

She had the same effect on Georgia that her mother had, making her feel awkward and clumsy. But she was friendly enough.

'Giorgio,' she said. 'I have heard much about you.'

'So have I,' said Fabrizio, coming forward to take Georgia's hand. He was like his father, much more so than Gaetano was. Tall and broad with black hair and a strong intelligent face, he looked every inch the Duke he would one day be. 'I hear you are very close to my brother Falco.'

'I am,' said Georgia. 'He was – is – a good friend.'

'And yet my father tells me you can shed no light on this terrible act of his?'

'I can only say what I have already told the Duke – that Falco was depressed about his injuries.'

Gaetano came to her rescue. 'Leave the lad alone, Fabrizio,' he said. 'He can only tell you what you already know. Falco found his pain hard to bear – that and his inactivity.'

'But these things he had lived with for two years,' protested Fabrizio, and Georgia could see he was really distressed. 'Why give up now?'

'Because Father had plans for him that he could not

face perhaps?' said Gaetano quietly.

'What plans?'

'You must ask Father.'

Rodolfo came to show Fabrizio and Gaetano some find of his and Dethridge linked arms with Georgia. She could see what the whole outing had been arranged for – to give Luciano and Arianna some time alone together. She tried not to look in their direction but she was acutely aware of their voices behind her and found it difficult to concentrate on Doctor Dethridge's kind attempts to engage her attention. In the end he stopped and peered closely at her.

'Yt wille not doe,' he said, shaking his shaggy grey head. 'Sum thinges can not bee. Ye wol ende up lyke poore yonge Falcon if ye can not make up your minde whatte worlde ye live in.'

Georgia started. Did Dethridge know what Falco had done? Or was he just comparing her to a pale and lifeless boy because that was what her feelings for Luciano had reduced her to? You could never tell with him; he was the only person apart from Luciano who had ever made that dreadful permanent transition from one world to another so he might suspect something. Still, what he did know was bad enough.

'I know,' she said quietly. 'I know it's a hopeless case. But I can't help it.'

Dethridge patted her hand.

*

'How was your journey?' asked Luciano.

'Very interesting,' said Arianna. 'I saw Volana and Bellona and Giglia. And now Remora. What a fascinating place!'

'We don't need to make small talk now, Arianna,' said Luciano. 'The others can't hear us. I missed you. I hate it that we can't be together without all these people around.'

'Duchesse don't spend much time alone, as you are well aware,' said Arianna.

'And do Duchesse have so much company that they don't miss their friends when they are away from them?' Luciano persisted, smiling.

She smiled back. 'No,' she said. 'Not so much as that. But you haven't been exactly a hermit. You seem very friendly with the new Stravagante. Has it been pleasant for you to be with someone from your old world?'

'Not altogether,' said Luciano. 'She has brought some painful associations with her.'

Arianna froze beside him. 'She?' she said disbelievingly.

'Yes. Didn't Rodolfo tell you? Georgia goes to my old school and I used to know her.'

'So that is how girls look in your world!' said Arianna with a mixture of curiosity and scorn.

'Not all, no,' said Luciano, nettled. 'Georgia's a bit different from most girls. And because she wears her hair so short, we decided to pass her off as a boy.'

'And a good job you made of it,' said Arianna bitterly. 'You must have learned that from me.'

It brought back vivid memories of their first meeting in Bellezza, when Arianna was dressed as a boy and furiously angry with Luciano – as she seemed to be again now.

'Come,' she said. 'I must not neglect my hosts.' And

she spent the rest of her time being charming to Gaetano and Fabrizio di Chimici.

*

Georgia and Luciano were both in poor spirits when they returned to the Ram. They had not had much to say to each other in the carriage and Doctor Dethridge had appeared to sleep for most of the journey. Some time after their return there was a furious knocking on the door.

Rodolfo strode into Paolo's kitchen, not looking stooped at all now. His eyes were flashing and he appeared furious. Georgia found him quite terrifying, just as formidable as the Duke.

But at least his anger seemed to be directed mainly at Luciano.

'What have you done?' he asked. 'No, don't tell me. I *know* what you have done. Befriending a damaged boy, spending every day and some nights with him. And then he falls into a mysterious sleep after apparently taking poison.'

'This you knew before,' said Luciano quietly.

'But now I have seen him,' said Rodolfo. 'Fabrizio took me to meet his father in the hospital, since the Duke would not come to me. And I saw the boy. Did you think I would not know the body of someone who was away in the other world?'

He rounded on Georgia. 'And you, you must have brought a talisman from your world. Have you any idea how dangerous that is for an untrained Stravagante?'

He strode up and down the kitchen.

319

'You I can understand,' he said to Georgia. 'A newcomer impressed by the demands of a sick boy. I suppose you have taken him there to cure him. But Luciano – after all I have taught you. How could you be so reckless?' He turned again to Georgia.

'There is only one thing for it. You must bring him back immediately!'

Chapter 20

Flying Colours

Georgia woke up in her own world in a state of panic. She had almost expected Rodolfo to stravagate back with her, he was so furious. The idea of the black-velvet-clad figure turning up in her room and having to be explained if Russell bumped into him on the landing made her hysteria rise. But then she relaxed. Rodolfo was not here and, even if he had been, he would have been more than a match for Russell. It might almost have been worth seeing.

She hurried through the morning routine, anxious to get to Falco, but as she got near his house, she realised that she didn't know what to say to him. How could she persuade him to go back to Talia now that he was on the waiting list for his operation? And how would the Mulhollands be able to bear it if another boy was lost to them?

She respected Rodolfo but she didn't think he was right about this. Still her heart sank at the thought of defying him. Caught between him and the grief-crazed Duke, both wanting Falco back, Georgia couldn't visualise how it could possibly work out. Had she completely misunderstood her mission to Remora?

'Hi Georgia,' said Falco, letting her in. 'How's everything?'

He was already looking better than he ever had in Talia. He was eating well and enjoying being part of an ordinary family. In fact he was rapidly becoming a twenty-first-century boy.

'Not good,' said Georgia. 'Can we talk?'

'Vicky is out,' said Falco. 'She has gone to a friend's house to practise in her string quartet.'

'Rodolfo has found out what we helped you do,' said Georgia.

'And he is not pleased?'

'That's putting it mildly!'

Falco looked scared, even though he had never met Rodolfo. 'He's not coming here is he?'

'I don't think so,' said Georgia. 'Not if he didn't last night. He was so mad that I thought he might do it then.'

'What for, though?' asked Falco. 'What could he do?'

Georgia hesitated. 'He wants you to go back.'

Falco turned ashen. 'I won't do it,' he said fiercely. 'I haven't done all this just to go back.'

'Perhaps you should think about it,' said Georgia. 'No, let me finish,' she said, because Falco was already protesting. 'You don't know what effect this is having on your family. They're all there in Remora – Gaetano and everyone – and your father never leaves your bedside.'

Falco stared at her, the tears starting in his eyes. 'But I can't,' he whispered. 'It was too hard to do the first time. It will be worse for them all, especially Father, if I go back and then translate after that.'

'Rodolfo wants me to make you go back for good,' said Georgia.

'Then you must destroy the talisman,' said Falco firmly.

Georgia looked at him in astonishment.

'Take the ring and melt it down – or throw it away,' he insisted.

'You are amazing, you know,' said Georgia. 'Are you serious? I thought you might want me to hang on to it in case you changed your mind.'

'I don't want to be able to change my mind,' said Falco. 'And if you get rid of it, I won't be able to.'

In the early morning Cesare was ready down at the track with Arcangelo for the second heat. He had been nervous at the first one the night before and the Ram had come in ninth. But today was different. He felt clear-headed, energetic and ready to ride.

He was wearing the red and yellow colours of the Ram and all around him were other jockeys wearing the colours of their own Twelfths. Some of the horses had been decided on only after the moonlight races and some of the jockeys even later. So Cesare had an advantage, because he and Arcangelo had been riding at the practice-track together for weeks.

'That's the one to beat,' said Enrico to Riccardo, the Twins' Horsemaster, as Cesare manoeuvred Arcangelo between the ropes.

'You think so?' said Riccardo. 'He wasn't very fast yesterday.'

'Just feeling his way into it,' said Enrico. 'Trust me – that's the best combination in the Campo.

'Surely nothing our Silk can't beat?' said Riccardo.

All the jockeys who had ridden in a Stellata before had nicknames. The Twins' man was Silk and the Lady's was Cherubino. Paradoxically he was the oldest jockey there, having ridden in fifteen previous races. He was thirty-three, though he still had the fresh baby-face which had given him his soubriquet. Two other jockeys besides Cesare were first-timers, waiting to acquire their own nicknames; they were running for the Lioness and the Water-carrier.

Emilio, Horsemaster for the Lady, was watching with Enrico and Riccardo in the wooden stands that now encircled the Campo. He was inclined to agree that the Ram had a strong combination this year, though reasonably confident that the pacts he had made would secure a victory for Cherubino and the Lady. Unless the Twins had laid out even more money on *their* pacts, of course.

In the last twenty years, the Stellata had been won by the Lady or the Twins fourteen times. But even the most elaborate and expensive pacts couldn't be sure to secure a victory, and other Twelfths, not so supportive of the di Chimici family, had managed to win on the other six occasions. The Ram, however, hadn't had a win for a generation. And the last time it had been won by Paolo.

The omens were looking promising for the Ram. They had a good mount and a jockey who was son of their last victor. And they had a secret augury of good fortune, which only the Horsemaster's house knew about – the birth of the winged horse. Cesare held on to that thought even though Merla was now missing. He tried to forget that this was the time the Ram should have brought Merla out and vaunted their good fortune to the whole city.

The horses were lined up and ready to start. The twelfth horse, the Rincorsa, which in this heat was the horse for the Scales, entered the ropes at a gallop and the race was off to a flying start. The Scorpion was first away and led the first lap but Cesare overtook their jockey Razzo on Celeste halfway round the second lap and remained in the lead to the end.

He was beaming with joy as Paolo came up to embrace him at the finish. All the Twelvers of the Ram escorted horse and rider back to the Twelfth, singing and chanting. While Arcangelo was walked round a small paddock to cool off, Georgia arrived.

'Oh I missed it!' she said, disappointed. 'How did you get on?'

'He won,' said Paolo proudly.

'It doesn't mean anything,' said Cesare modestly. 'Everyone knows the heats don't count. It's only the race itself.' But he was still grinning from ear to ear.

*

'It's a shame that the Duke hasn't got his mind on the race,' said Enrico, who had retreated with Riccardo to a tavern.

'You can't blame him,' said Riccardo. 'He's flesh and bones like us and they say the boy's going to die.'

Enrico shivered. He didn't want to think about it. 'I think it might be up to us to do something about the opposition.'

Riccardo shrugged. 'What did you have in mind?'

Enrico tapped the side of his nose. 'Leave it to me,' he said.

*

Luciano and Dethridge were joining in the celebration breakfast at the Ram. Everyone knew it was just a heat but excitement ran through Paolo's house; the children were infected with it. The little girls had miniature red and yellow flags and were waving them enthusiastically.

'Ram, Ram, Ram!' they cried. 'I'm the best, I am!'

'I think Cesare's the best this morning,' said Teresa, smiling at him.

Cesare basked in his family's praise. Winning the heat had given him a taste of what victory in the Stellata would be like and he couldn't wait to feel it again.

The happy atmosphere generated by Cesare's win took Georgia's mind off her troubles with Rodolfo. But not for long. As soon as she and Luciano were alone together, she told him what Falco had said.

Luciano was still smarting from Rodolfo's reproaches but when he heard about Falco's resolve it made him feel better.

'He's a brave kid,' he said. 'And I think we have to

stand by him.'

Georgia nodded. 'It'll take some courage to defy Rodolfo, though,' she said. 'It means believing we're right and he's wrong.'

'He doesn't know Falco,' said Luciano. 'He doesn't understand what this means to him. I've disobeyed him before, you know. I came back to Bellezza at night-time – to see the fireworks I'd helped him make.'

'And was he angry with you then?' asked Georgia.

'No. He said it must have been Fate or something. Because I saved the Duchessa from being assassinated.'

'But everyone pretended she had been?'

'No, that was later – the second time. Another person got killed in her place and Silvia just decided she'd had enough. She thought she could do better against the di Chimici if she went underground. She's been quite active in Bellezzan politics since Arianna took over.'

'Imagine having those two for your parents!' Georgia felt almost sorry for Arianna.

'I often do,' said Luciano. 'They're both incredible when you get to know them, but it's best not to cross them. Arianna's like both of them.' He sighed.

'Do you think Rodolfo has told Doctor Dethridge and Paolo what we did?' asked Georgia.

'Hee has in dede,' said a familiar voice. William Dethridge had come out to the stables with Paolo, to find them. 'Ye are essaying to get that poore chylde translated.'

'It was not something you should have undertaken without talking to us,' said Paolo seriously. 'Not only is it a great step for the boy himself and much too advanced a manoeuvre for an inexperienced Stravagante, but have you given any thought to the consequences for both of you here? If Falco dies, as he will surely appear to do here and soon, the Duke will be looking for revenge. And his eyes will turn first to the Ram. Where he will find supporters of Bellezza and my family, not to mention several Stravaganti. Your act has put our whole brotherhood in danger.'

*

Unaware of the storms brewing for the Ram, Cesare was down at the Campo, looking at the track. There had been no rain for several days now and the conditions were looking good. Whenever there were no heats going on, bands of Remorans took the opportunity to 'walk the track', treading the earth down so that it was compacted into a good surface for racing. Cesare nodded to a group of Archers who were doing so now.

'Well ridden!' they shouted. Their horse, Alba, had come third in the morning's heat, ridden by Topolino, so they were quite pleased.

'Well ridden, indeed!' said a short man in a blue cloak. He was wearing the colours of the Ram but Cesare didn't know him. That wasn't surprising; at the time of the race, all sorts of people came back to Remora to support their Twelfth, even if they had been away from the city for years.

'Let me buy you a drink,' said the man, who seemed very friendly. 'I'd like to hear all about you and the horse – Angelo is it?'

'Arcangelo,' said Cesare proudly. 'The best horse we

have had in the Ram for years. Apart from one,' he added sadly, thinking of Merla.

But he let the stranger buy him a drink. And he didn't notice anything funny about the taste, he was so busy recounting past exploits on the chestnut gelding.

'Bit early in the day to be drunk, isn't it?' one of the other customers asked, as the man in the blue cloak led the younger man away, holding his weight up as his legs seemed to be giving way beneath him.

'Hm,' said the waiter. 'Especially since the lad only had a lemon sherbet.'

But a group of tourists came in calling for wine, so he thought no more about it.

*

A public coach brought Francesca to Remora, since Signor Albani wasn't wealthy enough to keep a carriage. But she didn't mind. She went straight to the hospital, sending her luggage to the Papal palace by porter. She was sure of her welcome with the Pope. The di Chimici stuck together, particularly in a family crisis.

Gaetano jumped up when she came in, his sorrow momentarily dispelled at the sight of her.

'How is he?' asked Francesca.

'As you see,' said Gaetano, gesturing towards the bed where the thin, almost translucent, body of his brother lay. Niccolò sat in his usual place, beside the bed, holding one of his son's hands. Francesca was shocked by Niccolò's unshaven face and bloodshot eyes.

'See who is here, Father,' said Gaetano gently. 'Francesca has come from Bellezza.'

The Duke roused himself sufficiently to greet her, running his tongue over his dry lips before speaking.

'Thank you, my dear,' he said. 'It was good of you to come. Not that you can do anything. No one can.' He passed his free hand across his face.

Beatrice bustled in. 'Oh Francesca, thank goodness for another woman!' she said. 'You'll help me with Father, won't you? Father, look, now that Francesca is here with us, you can go back to the palace for some rest. You know we will send word if there is any change.'

Gaetano began to protest that his cousin had only just arrived and must be tired from her long journey, but Francesca stopped him.

'I'd be happy to sit and watch over him with you, Beatrice,' she said. And, much to Gaetano's surprise, Niccolò stood up, relinquishing Falco's hand into Francesca's.

'I think I will take a little rest,' he said. 'You are a good girl, Francesca. And Beatrice, you swear to send Gaetano to me at once if anything changes?'

'Wouldn't you like me to come back to the palace with you, Father?' asked Gaetano.

'No,' said the Duke. 'You must be here if he opens his eyes. It is only next door. I shall go on my own.'

He walked out of the hospital, through the small knot of well-wishers, praying over rosaries or holding tokens of the goddess.

*

'What do you mean, not here?' said Paolo.

'Cesare isn't here,' said Teresa. 'He must be down at the Campo.'

'But it's nearly time for the heat,' said Paolo. 'He needs to be here so he can ride Arcangelo down to the start.'

There was no sign of Cesare anywhere about the stables. No one had seen him since breakfast. Paolo took Arcangelo down to the Campo himself, surrounded by the usual crowd of Twelvers from the Ram. Luciano and Georgia went with him, even though it was getting rather late for Georgia still to be in Talia. But Cesare was not waiting in the piazza either.

A group of the Archer's supporters waiting with Alba and her jockey came up to Paolo, perturbed to see Arcangelo riderless. In response to his whispered enquiries, they confirmed that they had seen Cesare in the Campo earlier in the day.

'He went off to have a drink with a man in a blue cloak,' said one of them. 'He was a Ram – at least he wore the Ram's colours.'

Luciano started. A man in a blue cloak meant only one thing to him – and it was bad news.

'I think Cesare may have been kidnapped,' he whispered to Georgia.

'All horses to the starting line,' called the Starter.

'Oh, no! What will Paolo do?' asked Georgia. There was a pause in the activity of horses and men milling around.

'The Ram scratches,' announced the Starter. 'The other eleven to the starting line please. Take your places for the third heat.'

And it was run without the Ram.

Cesare woke with a terrible headache. He had no idea where he was or how he had got there. He was in an unfurnished, hot and dusty room with tall barred windows. A stretch to see out of one of them showed him that he was very high up and looking out over hills and woods. Something seemed familiar but he was too befuddled to be sure what it was.

The quality of the light showed him that he had been unconscious for hours and it was the time of the evening heat. Cesare paced up and down the length of the room in an agony. Rattling the door had shown him that it must be bolted from the outside and he was caught like a rat in a trap.

'Georgia,' said Ralph the next day. 'There's a TV programme you might want to watch tonight. It's about horses.'

Georgia almost didn't look at the newspaper he was showing her. She was still paralysed by what had happened in Remora last evening, just before she had had to stravagate back. For a Twelfth to pull out of a heat was terribly shaming, but Paolo had no substitute jockey waiting. He himself was too tall and heavy now to ride in the Stellata; he had been only fifteen when he had ridden to victory for the Ram twenty-five years ago. And now it was beginning to look as if Cesare had been kidnapped.

Georgia had risked coming back so late because she knew no one would worry if she wasn't down early for breakfast the next morning. But she was surprised to find Ralph still there. He explained that he was waiting in for an important delivery of parts. And now he was waving the *Guardian* supplement with the TV listings in front of her bleary eyes.

Georgia suddenly snapped to attention. 'PALIO,' said the newspaper. 'A Documentary about the Craziest Horse Race in the World. Channel 4 8pm.'

'I thought you'd be interested,' said Ralph, pleased with her reaction.

'You bet,' said Georgia. 'Have we got a blank video I could use to record it? I think I might want to keep it.'

'Yes,' said Ralph. 'You can tape over *Four Weddings and a Funeral*. I never want to see it again.'

'Don't be daft,' said Georgia, grinning. 'Maura would kill me. She loves that film.'

'Only kidding,' said Ralph. 'You can use that tape we put the Oscars on; she won't want to watch that again.'

'I'd like to invite Fal – Nicholas over to watch,' said Georgia. 'You know he's crazy about horses too.'

'Good idea,' said Ralph. 'We can all watch it together on the big set in the living room.'

This wasn't quite what Georgia had in mind. She would have to warn Falco not to make comparisons with the Stellata; it was going to be hard for them both.

'First Merla and now Cesare,' said Paolo. 'It has to be the di Chimici.'

'I agree,' said Rodolfo, who had been summoned to the Horsemaster's house. 'Though I am surprised that the Duke has moved while his son is still in danger. I thought he was too preoccupied.'

'There are plenty of other family members in town,' said Paolo.

'What will you do?' asked Teresa. The younger children were all in bed and she was now free to worry about her stepson.

'I don't think they will hurt him, Teresa,' said Paolo. 'I think they will just keep him a prisoner till after the race.'

'But what will you do about the race?' asked Luciano.

'I think there is only one thing for it,' said Paolo. 'Georgia will have to ride for the Ram.'

Completely unaware of the plans being made for her in Remora, Georgia watched the TV documentary mesmerised. She and Falco sat on the sofa with a large bowl of popcorn between them, popcorn being one of Falco's favourite discoveries about his new life. Ralph was with them in an armchair but Maura was writing up case notes in the office and Russell had gone ostentatiously off to his room to watch a martial arts video.

'It looks pretty brutal,' said Ralph, frowning at the mad gallop round the shell-shaped Campo in Siena, the jockeys with their whips flailing.

'They ride bareback, Georgia,' whispered Falco, 'just like our jockeys.'

'It looks a lot harder than the bareback riding I do,' she said, wondering if the real Stellata was as fast and furious as the Palio. The jockeys were all much older than Cesare and were apparently professionals, almost all of them from outside Siena.

When Falco had been taken home by Ralph, Georgia decided on an early night. She wanted to be in Remora in time for the next heat; she had no idea what Paolo would do. She was making herself hot chocolate in the kitchen when Russell came down to raid the fridge.

'I don't know how you can bear to be around that kid,' he said, giving an exaggerated shudder. 'With his leg all deformed like that. He gives me the willies.'

Maura, standing in the kitchen doorway, looked scandalised.

'You don't mean that, do you, Russell?' she said.

'No, just kidding,' he said immediately.

'Well, I don't think it was at all funny,' said Maura, sounding the crossest she had ever been with her stepson.

Russell shot Georgia a poisonous look on his way out.

'Come on, my beauty,' Enrico whispered to Merla in the middle of the night. 'We're going somewhere special.'

The black mare, fully grown now, flew strongly towards Remora, urged on by the man she was now used to. It was a longer flight than she usually made and she was enjoying the use of her wings.

On and on through the starry night, flying ever south, over the walls of a great city, Merla felt memory stirring within her. She wanted to veer west but her rider held her on a true course to the heart of the city and then gently pulled her to a halt, so that she hovered in the air over an open circle. Merla had no idea what he wanted her to do; but she remembered that people who had treated her lovingly were somewhere nearby.

*

Cesare had spent a wretched night, knowing that he was still going to be holed up in this room when the early morning heat began. He had a dream that he heard a horse neighing right outside his window. It must have been a dream, because no horse could be up so high. Only Merla, he thought, drifting into another dream in which Arcangelo won the race without him. It was perfectly possible for a horse to win the Stellata 'scosso', without a rider. But not for it to start that way.

Cesare heard bolts being pulled and he ran to the door, but two burly men he had never seen before made sure he could not get out. One of them set down a basket of rolls and fruit and a beaker of milk. And then he was on his own again, free to satisfy his physical hunger but still gnawed by mental anguish.

*

'I want you to ride Arcangelo for the Ram,' said Paolo, waiting for Georgia in the hayloft, with

Cesare's jockey silks. 'You can do it, can't you? Ride bareback, I mean?'

'Well, yes,' said Georgia swallowing.

'And you've ridden a horse as big as this?' he persisted.

Georgia remembered Conker. She nodded.

'Then please put these clothes on and meet us in the yard,' said Paolo. 'We must get down to the track.'

*

Word had spread fast in Remora of a supernatural event. The Campo was full of people gazing upwards. They stood around in groups, far more of them than usually turned out for a morning heat.

In the centre of the Campo the tall slender column rising from the fountain was no longer unadorned. At the top of it, far higher than anyone could reach with a ladder, the rose and white banner of the Twins fluttered from the lioness's neck.

'It's an omen,' said the Remorans, making the Hand of Fortune. 'The Twins will win, surely?'

'No surprise about that,' said others. 'Only how the banner got there.'

'It must have been the goddess,' came a voice. And 'Dia, Dia!' echoed round the Campo.

'The goddess – or someone on a flying horse,' said someone.

And that was how the rumour began that a winged horse was living again in Remora.

Chapter 21

Go and Return a Winner

'There's no time to worry about that,' Paolo said, barely glancing at the column and the fluttering scarf. 'Now, you understand there will be no use of whips today? All you have to do is stay on for three laps of the Campo. Don't worry about where you come at the end.'

It was good advice, since Georgia in fact came last. But she did stay on and the entire heat was very close, with most of the horses bunched together. The Water-carrier won by a length, with a horse called Uccello. His young jockey was famously always hungry and, unfortunately for him, was seen munching some breakfast just before mounting up. So 'Salsiccio' he would now for ever be.

Georgia got her nickname too and it wasn't very

flattering. She had not even seen a heat before and had to be shown everything about where to wait and when to mount and what to do. 'Zonzo' she was called, the Talian equivalent of 'dozy', but it was quite an affectionate name and people were kind to her, even rival jockeys.

Word had spread fast in Remora about Cesare's disappearance and no one doubted that he had been removed from the scene because he was a threat to the di Chimici's chances in the race. Such things had happened before.

'Bad luck for the Ram,' said Riccardo to Enrico, as they watched the fourth heat.

'Terrible,' agreed Enrico. 'But it's still only a heat. Maybe their substitute will improve.'

Riccardo shook his head. 'To miss a heat is a dreadful omen,' he said. 'They won't recover from that.'

But at least the Ram now had a rider. The jockeys didn't have to give their names in to the marshals till the morning of the race itself. After that, no change was possible. If Cesare had been kidnapped then, the Ram would have had to drop out of the Stellata. But Enrico didn't want the Ram to drop out; he just didn't want them to win.

Though Georgia had been quite terrified while it was going on, once the heat was over she felt elated. It hadn't been as bad as she thought it would be. It was a lot less violent than the Palio she had seen on television. Still, it was only a heat. The real thing might be very different.

Arianna was watching the heat from her balcony with Rodolfo.

'What is going on?' she asked him. 'That's the Stravagante on the Ram's horse, not the proper rider.'

'Cesare is missing,' said Rodolfo. 'We think kidnapped. Paolo decided that Georgia must take his place.'

'Well, she doesn't seem to be doing a very good job of it,' said Arianna. 'That's just the result to make Duke Niccolò happy – Bellezza's Twelfth coming in last.'

'He wouldn't be content with that unless the Lady or the Twins won; remember this race is supposed to show the di Chimici dominance over Talia,' said Rodolfo.

Arianna sighed. 'Why didn't you tell me the Reman Stravagante was a girl?' she asked.

'I don't think I told you anything – except that the new Stravagante had arrived. Does it matter?'

'Did you know she was a friend of Luciano's?'

'Doctor Dethridge told me that she came from the same school as Luciano. Dethridge thinks that school is built on the place where his old laboratory used to be.'

'What do you think of her?' asked Arianna.

'At the moment I am very angry with her and with Luciano, because of what they did with Falco,' said Rodolfo. 'But she is brave and loyal and willing to do what is asked of her.'

'Do you think she is pretty?' asked Arianna.

Rodolfo didn't answer straightaway. He looked closely into her face but it was hard to tell what she was thinking in her elaborate mask.

'This will all be over in a few days,' he said. 'Then you and I and Luciano will all be back together in

Bellezza. This last month will soon be forgotten.'

'Then you do think she is pretty,' said Arianna dolefully.

'Not in the way that you are,' said Rodolfo. 'Young women in the future in the other world don't seem to be beautiful in that way, if Georgia is typical. But she is not unpleasant to look at.'

'I don't like looking at her,' said Arianna under her breath.

And if Rodolfo heard her, he chose not to answer.

*

Cesare was planning his escape. He was not hopeful of success but he had to think of a way to get out or go mad. The last few times that food had been brought to him, there had been only one man, but that one had been armed. Desperate though Cesare was to escape, he knew it would just be a waste of energy to hurl himself at someone bigger, stronger and carrying a dagger.

But the plan he had was hard to carry out. He had decided not to eat or drink anything they brought him. Hunger gnawed at his stomach, his throat was dry and the sheer boredom of his captivity made it virtually impossible to stop thinking about food but Cesare wanted to be in the Campo delle Stelle even more, so he gritted his teeth and kicked the dishes over on to the dusty floor, lest he be tempted.

*

Georgia was living on her nerves. Paolo took her back

to the Ram and talked her through everything that would happen in the next day and a half. There would be another heat that evening, followed by long dinners held in the streets of all the Twelfths, and most Remorans would stay awake all night drinking and talking about the race. Soon after dawn all the jockeys would attend Mass in the cathedral and then, after the last heat, their names would be formally given to the marshals as those who would ride in the evening race.

Even if Cesare miraculously should return, once Georgia's name had been entered in the lists, she would have to be the one who rode Arcangelo in the Stellata. There could be no change of jockey after that. And then there would be the last heat, run in the morning. She could rest a little around lunchtime, but the build-up to the great contest would start at about two in the afternoon, when all those taking part in the parade, including the jockeys, would be dressed in the colours of their Twelfth, and the standard-bearers and drummers would set out towards the cathedral.

'It sounds as if I'll need to be here continuously,' said Georgia, alarmed.

'It's not quite as bad as that,' said Paolo. 'But you certainly would need to be here after dark for most of the time. Can you do that?'

'Is it safe?' she asked, suddenly worried about finding herself stranded in Talia for ever like Luciano.

'I think so,' said Paolo. 'I will talk to Doctor Dethridge and to Rodolfo. But I think this is a risk we have to take. I think this may be why you found your way to us.'

A risk I have to take, thought Georgia. Out loud she said, 'Do I have time to stravagate back home now? I need to make some arrangements.'

She climbed into what she now thought of as her hayloft and took out the talisman. But sleep seemed impossible. Her mind was too busy. If Paolo was right and this was what she had been brought to Remora to do – to ride in the Stellata and make sure that Bellezza's Twelfth was not publicly disgraced – then it hadn't been her task to help Falco at all. Perhaps Rodolfo was right and she should bring him back? But was that still an option? Gaetano had told them how thin and frail his brother had become, kept hanging on to life by having warm milk and honey dribbled into his mouth from a spoon. There were no drips and feeding tubes in sixteenth-century Talia.

*

Rodolfo came to see Luciano in the Ram. Never before had they been at odds and it was uncomfortable for both of them.

'Luciano,' said Rodolfo. 'We must speak again of Falco. I know that Georgia has been distracted by this business with the race – and goodness knows that is important – but she needs to bring Falco back to his body while it is still possible. I don't think he can hang on here much longer.'

'You don't understand,' said Luciano. 'It's all got more complicated than that. Falco is living with my parents.'

Rodolfo looked at him, astounded. 'Complicated is not a big enough word,' he said. 'Whose idea was that?'

'It was Georgia's,' said Luciano. 'She organised

everything in the other world. In fact, she was sure it was what she had been brought here to do.'

Rodolfo was thoughtful. 'She is a Stravagante,' he said. 'It would be surprising if she got something like that wrong. But she hasn't had any training like you. And something like this can destabilise the gateway. Remember how time in the other world leapt forward three weeks when you were translated? We've worked so hard to keep the dates stable. We even succeeded in bringing our worlds back into alignment, so that our dates now match again those in the other world, even though they are still more than four hundred years in the future. Who knows what will happen if Falco dies here? What if he should die today? The other world could race even further ahead of us and Georgia could be an old woman before she gets here again. And we need her here tomorrow, fit to ride in the race.'

'It's such a mess,' said Luciano, running his hand through his hair. 'I don't know how it all got so difficult. It all began when we made friends with the di Chimici.'

'And how did that happen?' asked Rodolfo.

Luciano thought for a bit. 'It was the Manoush,' he said. 'We all heard their music and that's when it began.'

'The Zinti?' said Rodolfo. 'Then I cannot believe it was wrong.'

He sighed deeply. 'I must talk to Georgia again and this is not a good time to do it. But perhaps there is more going on here than I know.'

And he put his arm round Luciano's shoulder.

Georgia found herself back in her room in the middle of the night. Again she was planning – how to free up time to be in Remora, the plan she had for getting out of her house and how she was going to get Falco to agree to it. The next day was going to be Friday and, with everyone at work, she could spend the whole day away without causing any suspicion. But she had to have a plan for the evening and the next day. Her family would expect to see her then.

Quietly, she got up and switched on her desk lamp. She took a piece of paper and wrote a note to Maura. Then she crept down the stairs and left it on the kitchen table, where her mother would find it at breakfast. The next bit was going to be much harder. She would have to go to the Mulhollands' house and get Falco to let her in, in the middle of the night. And her courage quailed at the thought of walking the London streets in pitch darkness.

Preparations were afoot in Remora for one of the biggest nights of celebration of the year. Only one Twelfth would be feasting and drinking toasts the following night, but on the eve of the Stellata every Twelfth could live in hope. The streets of each were filled with wooden trestle tables and benches and, in every kitchen, pots already bubbled with sauces while women mixed and cut the dough for pasta in a hundred different shapes. Carts brought lettuces and vegetables to the markets and they disappeared almost before they could be laid out on the stalls. Barrels of ale and casks of wine were rolled along the streets to the central squares of every Twelfth in readiness for the night's carousing.

The grandest meal would be held in the cathedral square, which was also the main meeting-place of the Twins, and would be presided over by the Pope. But every member of every Twelfth would turn out to his or her own Stellata dinner with equal enjoyment.

In the Papal palace, the di Chimici were having a conference about what to do that evening. The original plan had been that Duke Niccolò and most of his children would eat at the Lady's table and then pay a formal visit to the Twins, perhaps leaving Carlo and Beatrice to represent the family in the Twelfth which owed allegiance to Giglia. But now no one knew if Niccolò could be prised out of the hospital for long enough to attend either celebration.

The visiting Duchessa and her father would of course eat with the Pope in the Twins and someone from the family must keep her company, Gaetano being the obvious candidate.

Rinaldo would eat his dinner in the Goat, joined by his brother Alfonso, now Duke of Volana. Other di Chimici family members were already arriving to see the great race. Francesca's brother Filippo was coming to represent Bellona and they would both attend the dinner in the Scales, while two young princesses, Lucia and Bianca, were coming from Fortezza to visit the Bull. Even the old Prince of Moresco, with his unmarried son and heir Ferrando, had made his way to Remora in time to join the feast in the Scorpion.

'The city is swarming with di Chimici,' said Rodolfo, as he entered Arianna's chamber in the Papal palace.

'Well, we knew it would be,' said Arianna. 'They are all supposed to witness a win for the leaders of their family and an ignominious loss for Bellezza. That's what this visit is all about.'

'Not just that, Arianna,' Rodolfo reminded her. 'The time is coming when you must give Gaetano your answer.'

'He hasn't asked me the question yet,' she said.

Georgia reached the Mulhollands' front door with relief. It had been very scary walking to Falco's in the dark. So many street-lights were out and all the houses were in darkness, except for the odd high rectangle of light in attic rooms where people studied or had rows or just couldn't sleep.

One of them was Falco and that was lucky for Georgia. She scooped some gravel from the planters outside the front door and threw it up at Falco's window, smiling as she did so. It was such a cliché of the adventure stories she had read as a child and she had never done it in real life. After a few misses – it was harder than the stories suggested – she was rewarded by the sight of a dark head at the open window.

'Falco!' she hissed, as loudly as she dared. 'Can you let me in?'

There was a long wait while the crippled boy made his way down to the front door as quickly and quietly as he could. Georgia had never been so glad to see anyone and to slip indoors out of the menacing darkness. She put her finger to her lips and motioned him to lock up again.

Silently they climbed the stairs and even when they were safely inside Falco's bedroom, they had to talk in whispers so that Vicky and David wouldn't hear them.

Georgia looked round the room, illuminated by Falco's bedside light. She had never been more acutely aware that this was Luciano's old bedroom, from which he was exiled for ever. But tonight she must be strictly practical so she looked quickly at the back of the door.

'Good,' she whispered. 'You've got a bolt. You must lock us in.'

The Twelfth of the Ram was decked out in red and yellow banners, its tables covered in red and yellow cloths and the walls of all the streets decorated with elaborate painted wooden cressets, just waiting to be lit when darkness fell. Everywhere the sign of the Ram was painted and children wore miniature helmets with ram's horns on them.

In Paolo's house the babies had gone to sleep and the little girls had allowed themselves to be put to bed only if they could take their flags with them. Georgia came down from the hayloft, still in her jockey's silks, and was embraced by Paolo and Teresa.

'Time for the heat,' said Paolo.

'Good luck,' said Luciano, and gave her a hug. At that moment, Georgia decided it was time she did more than just stay on the horse. The hopes of the Ram were all resting on her and, even more important, Luciano was willing her on.

Everyone said that the result of a heat didn't matter, but there was an atmosphere about this one that made it feel different. It was Georgia's first evening of staying in Remora intentionally and she could only hope that the arrangements she had made back in London would work. She put all that out of her mind and concentrated on the race.

This time she wasn't last. She came in tenth, ahead of the Goat and the Crab. All the Rams applauded her and she would have felt it was quite an achievement, if the Fishes hadn't won, with their jockey, Il Re, on Noè. Several Fishes booed at Georgia as she left the track and called out what she assumed were rude names in Talian.

But she was accompanied back to the Ram by a troop of enthusiastic Twelvers chanting 'Zonzo! Zonzo!' and 'Montone! Montone!' – 'The Ram! The Ram!'

Arcangelo was taken to cool down in his little grass paddock and Georgia found herself embraced by lots of strangers, who patted her on the back and told her she had done well. She had saved the Ram's honour and they loved her for it.

It was an unusual feeling for Georgia, who had never been popular, and it intoxicated her more than the red wine which was being liberally poured for her. She was led to the top table outside the Ram's huge church, the Santa Trinità, and was delighted to find that Luciano and Dethridge were to sit with her. She had feared that they might be whisked off to the Twins with the young Duchessa. Another guest at the top table was Silvia Bellini – where else would she eat that celebration meal if not in the Twelfth dear to Bellezza?

Twelvers were streaming up the main street of the Ram, the Via di Montone. Gradually all the places at the long tables were filled up, the cressets were lighted and the feasting began.

The first thing that happened was that Paolo stood up and called out loudly for silence.

'Montonaioli!' he said. 'I present to you our jockey for tomorrow – Giorgio Gredi!'

The applause was a roar.

'He has stepped in at short notice to replace my son Cesare and we are for ever in his debt.' More cheers. Then the priest of Santa Trinità stood on the steps leading up to the church and Georgia had to go and receive a special helmet from him. It was in the colours of the Ram but made of metal, unlike the soft jockey cap she had worn in the heats. Georgia gulped as she realised that the reason she was being given it was that in the real race tomorrow evening the jockeys would all have leather whips and they would use them on each other.

Paolo then stood up again and, in his role as Capitano, made a speech about the honour of the Twelfth and the importance of the Stellata in all their lives. To her horror, Georgia discovered that she was expected to reply. She had never given a speech in public in her life before. But an extraordinary thing happened. Paolo was sitting on her left and Luciano on her right and William Dethridge on the other side of him. As she stood to make her speech, already feeling a little light-headed from the wine, she saw Dethridge and Luciano clasp hands. Luciano took a piece of the edge of her silk tunic in his free hand and Paolo did the same on the other side of her.

As she opened her mouth to speak, she felt a great rush of energy running through her. Her voice seemed strangely deep to her and she found that the words came easily; she felt that she was eloquent, though she could never afterwards remember a word of what she had said. It was all about her love for Remora and for the Ram in particular and how she would do her best tomorrow to be worthy of the trust they were placing in her, but the details were a blur.

Still, the Rams seemed to like it and she sat down to thunderous applause. The Stravaganti released their hands to join in and Georgia felt a sudden diminution of her power. Silvia leaned over from her seat next to Dethridge and said in a low voice, 'You know, they could probably arrange for a small beard for you by tomorrow.' And Georgia laughed. She was among friends.

She never forgot that night. It was thrilling just to be in Remora after dark and see the streets lit by torchlight. But to be part of the singing and chanting and celebrating on the greatest night of the Reman year and even to be treated as the guest of honour, with Luciano smiling at her on her right, was sheer bliss. The idea began to grow in her mind that if this was how Remorans celebrated the very fact of running in the race, what on earth would it be like if they won? But she quietly squashed it. Arcangelo was a great horse and they were getting used to each other, but she was not Cesare. She decided to be content with what she had.

As the evening wore on, the singing became louder and more raucous. Toasts were drunk to Georgia, Paolo, Arcangelo, the Ram and anything else the

Montonaioli could think of. There was a solemn moment when Paolo called for a toast to the health of Cesare, 'wherever he may be,' and Luciano added in a whisper, 'and Merla.'

The food was plentiful – roasted vegetables pungent with garlic and herbs, seafood on beds of sharp watercress, pasta in a myriad of shapes (of which the ones like curled rams' horns were the most prevalent), sauces of wild boar or spinach and pine-nuts, grilled cutlets and chicken, bowls of beans, green and white and red, whole rounds of cheese, mild and soft or blue and tangy – the dishes kept coming.

There was a pause while wooden platters were cleared and a cloaked figure slipped in between Georgia and Luciano. A velvet hood was pulled back and Georgia found herself looking into the violet eyes of Arianna. She was unmasked. Paolo gasped and instantly stood and called for another toast. He couldn't acknowledge Arianna's presence directly – the fact that she was unmasked showed her to be there incognita – and he had no idea how she had escaped from the Twins' banquet. But he called for another toast to their patron city and the word 'Bellezza!' rang round the Via di Montone.

'Bellezza!' echoed Georgia, drinking rather unsteadily from her silver goblet.

'Thank you,' said Arianna, amused. 'And thank you for not coming last today. It seems that my Twelfth will not be disgraced tomorrow after all.'

Georgia was fascinated by her. It was not just that she was beautiful, although she was, in a dramatic, film-starry sort of way that had nothing to do with her clothes or jewels. It was her history with Luciano, a whole chunk of his life that Georgia didn't know about, and her important and dangerous role as absolute ruler of a city which had held out against the di Chimici.

'Is Rodolfo with you?' Luciano was asking.

'No,' said Arianna, without taking her eyes off Georgia. 'It was bad enough that I made my excuses – a sudden headache, you know. He had to stay to represent our city. But I couldn't let tonight pass without wishing my jockey luck, could I?'

I am not going to blush, thought Georgia, and she realised that Paolo had again put his hand on the hem of her tunic. But Luciano was looking distinctly nervous. Having the Duchessa nearby was a bit like having a wild animal in your dining-room – you didn't know what it was likely to do next. Yet in one sense anything less like a wild animal than the sleek and elegant Duchessa was hard to imagine.

Now Arianna was acknowledging the presence of her mother, very slightly – they were both playing a dangerous game. Georgia thought that the Ram was probably safe, but there could be spies – there were hundreds of people eating in the main square. For the first time Georgia forgot about being jealous of Arianna or in awe of her and instead just admired her courage.

Then she found that the young Duchessa was looking straight at her. 'We are more alike than you might think,' said Arianna quietly. 'We both wear a disguise and perhaps share a secret.'

That Friday in Islington was a long one for Falco. He was anxious all the time, worrying if Maura would ring and ask to speak to Georgia. And he had never had to go so long without knowing what was going on in Remora.

'Shall we go out somewhere?' Vicky asked. 'You seem a little down.'

Falco's first instinct was to say no, but then he thought that perhaps it would be the perfect cover to be out. He couldn't lie to Georgia's mother if he wasn't there. And, if they were out, he wouldn't be worrying about Vicky wanting to come into his room. But it was hard to leave the house knowing that Georgia's body was apparently sleeping peacefully on the floor beside his bed. And his door didn't lock from the outside.

It was a lovely hot day and Vicky drove them to the park; it wasn't far but it would have used up too much energy for Falco to walk. There was a visiting funfair and, although a twenty-first-century boy of thirteen would have found it quite tame, Falco thought it was all wonderful.

They went on the Ghost Train, the Big Wheel, the Waltzer and the Dodgems. He ate pink candy floss and drank a blue Slush Puppie but he was hungry again after the Dodgems.

'Do you think I could have one of those burning hounds?' he asked Vicky.

It took her a moment but she got him his hot dog, surprised that he knew what they were. Vicky was always unsure about Nicholas. Sometimes she thought he was only pretending to have lost his memory but at other times it seemed there were things that genuinely puzzled him about life in London. That was when she thought that Maura O'Grady's theory about asylum-seekers might be right.

Falco licked his lips and fingers and sighed with pleasure. There was so much nice food in his new world and you could get it so quickly.

The Manoush were always up before the dawn but on the Day of the Goddess they had not lain down to sleep at all. They had spent the night in the Campo delle Stelle with Grazia, their old friend from the Lioness, and when the full moon rose were standing silent, facing eastward. Other groups of brightly dressed people stood with them.

As the moon appeared, all the Manoush began to sing. Aurelio was not the only musician among them; harps and flutes and small drums all joined in the hymns of praise to the goddess which lasted throughout the night.

The one or two Remorans who were up and awake at dawn saw the Manoush raising their arms to the rising sun and heard them chanting their high wailing song about the goddess and her consort. So begins the Stellata every year, with an older, hidden ritual, known to few citizens but underlying everything that happens for the rest of the day.

*

Georgia had slept little more than the Manoush and was relieved to see the lightening sky. For this, her official night away in Remora, she had been given a room of her own in Paolo's house.

'Too dangerous to sleep in your hayloft,' said Paolo. 'We don't want another jockey kidnapped.'

After a late night at the street party and an hour or two's dozing, Georgia woke to the sounds of a home with small children and several visitors. But this day she did not join the cheerful breakfast chaos. She had to go to Mass in the Duomo with the other eleven jockeys and go fasting.

Georgia was not used to such early rising or to doing anything without breakfast. And she was not used to going to church. The imposing Duomo, with its black and white marble stripes and its clouds of incense, made her feel overwhelmed – in great contrast to her lionising of the night before. To make things worse, although there was a crowd of supporters for all the Twelfths outside the Duomo, only the dozen jockeys attended the service itself.

Georgia watched closely what the others did and followed suit. She heard Salsiccio's stomach rumble loudly and smiled to think that there was someone hungrier than her. But for the most part the short service was solemn. Georgia looked closely at the Pope, who celebrated the Mass. She had been in his palace several times, but never actually seen Falco and Gaetano's uncle. He was very different from the Duke, soft and corpulent but not unkind looking. So this was the fate that Falco had been willing to face death to avoid.

She stumbled out of the cool interior of the great church into the early morning sun. She thought she heard the faint sound of a harp in the distance. But then the bells of the Duomo started ringing and the crowd of supporters was applauding. The day of the Stellata had truly arrived.

*

In the palace at Santa Fina, the guard was worried. The boy captive was curled into a ball in the corner. He had not eaten any of the food he had been brought for nearly two days. He was obviously sick and there was no one to advise the guard what to do. Enrico had gone down into the city and would not be back till the afternoon.

Cesare tensed every muscle in his body and when the guard came over to shake him awake, he was up and out through his legs and down the first flight of stairs before he could react. Cesare ran down flight after flight, blindly, the way a wild animal will run from a trap, not knowing where he was going but using all his energy just to get away.

After several days without exercise and the last two without food, he was weak and dizzy, but he had the advantage of surprise, and his light build which made him such a good jockey gave him the edge on his stocky pursuer.

He seemed to be in a huge palace, even though the stairs he was running down were not the main ones. Cesare guessed he was in the servants' quarters. And when at last he reached the bottom and found the way out, he knew where he was. He was at the back of the Casa di Chimici in Santa Fina.

He ran through the gardens at top speed and didn't stop until he found himself in the cover of the woods.

He was scratched and panting and parched with thirst. But he was free.

*

The heat on the morning of the Stellata was the merest formality for most jockeys. But not for Georgia. It was another chance for her to ride Arcangelo round that treacherous track and she was going to give it a good shot. And as a result she came third. The Lioness won on La Primavera and their jockey got his nickname at the last minute. 'Tesoro' his Twelvers called him, 'treasure', with much kissing and hugging, because he had come first, even though this heat mattered less than all the others.

'Well done!' Luciano said to Georgia and she glowed under his approval.

And then the jockeys had to give their names into the mayor and register for the race. 'Giorgio Gredi' was enrolled along with the eleven others. There was no backing out now.

She was too nervous to eat much lunch; the afternoon's ordeals were approaching and all Georgia wanted to do was get through them without disgracing the Ram. It was a heavy responsibility.

Soon after lunch she was taken to see Arcangelo in the 'Horse's House'. He was refreshed after his morning ride and now recognised her when she entered his stall. 'OK, boy?' she whispered, into his rusty mane. 'Let's give it a good try.'

The first task of the afternoon was to go to the church of Santa Trinità for the Blessing. All the members of the Twelfth, wearing sashes of red and yellow, were crowded into the little oratory at the side but the crowd parted as the horse was led in. Georgia walked beside him along the red carpet to the altar. The carpet dulled the sound of his hooves and yet it was a strange sound to hear in a place of worship. The crowd of Rams was silent and the atmosphere tense; no one must startle the horse.

The priest intoned the ritual blessing of horse and jockey. She felt his hand rest briefly on her head. And then he turned to the horse.

'Arcangelo – go and return a winner!'

The Rams waited until the horse was safely out in the sunlight. And then the church filled with voices raised in song.

Chapter 22

Star Riders

Duke Niccolò was roused by the sound of drums outside. Like everyone in Remora, he had lived with that sound for weeks, but this was different. It was right under the hospital window and it triggered a response in the Duke's clouded brain. Falco had always loved the sbandierata – the displays of multi-coloured flags, creating elaborate patterns, being waved and tossed by the skilful ensigns of each Twelfth. It had been a treat for him to see it in Remora every year of his short life until his accident.

The Duke realised that it must be the afternoon of the Stellata, when all the Twelfths came and performed their 'sbandierata' in honour of the Pope, his brother. The day that Falco had been going to enjoy again for the first time in two years. Niccolò walked slowly to the window and looked down into the square. It was a riot of colour and noise. The numbers of Twelvers and tourists crowding round to see the flag displays had overwhelmed the well-wishers praying outside the hospital for Falco's recovery.

'Life goes on,' whispered the Duke bitterly. He of all people knew how Remorans felt about their annual race; after all, he had been plotting to exploit their credulity and superstition himself this year. It seemed to be a plan made by another person a long time ago.

He went over to the bed and lifted his son, now so light that it was no effort at all, and carried him to the open window.

'See, Falco,' he said. 'See the pretty flags?'

*

Cesare felt he had been walking for hours. He had recognised the palace at Santa Fina where he had been held prisoner and he knew how far that was from the city but he had never been in these woods before and had lost all sense of direction. The woods were silent, the ground underneath his feet already thick with dry leaves, even though it was only August. The bushes were covered in this year's withered catkins and the trees towered above him, forming a continuous green arch above the path.

But was it the right path? He couldn't see the direction of the sun clearly through the foliage but it seemed to be overhead. He hoped he was still heading south. He was tired and hungry and very thirsty; the burst of energy that had got him through his escape had all evaporated now.

Now all Cesare could think of was that this must be the day of the race and the Ram had no jockey. He plodded on determinedly, even though he knew that, whether or not he got to Remora in time, there was no way that he would be fit enough to ride.

*

Georgia had been moved by the ceremony of blessing the horse. Remorans were a funny lot, she thought. So superstitious and almost pagan in their talk of the goddess and yet the atmosphere in that Christian oratory had been electric, everyone willing the priest's final words to come true.

Paolo encouraged her to rest after the Blessing, though at first she was too wired to stay lying down. This was her only opportunity to see the great day in all its ritual splendour and she didn't want to miss a second of it. But she thought that she should try to stravagate back briefly and check on her arrangements in London and eventually managed to fall into a doze, clutching the winged horse that was her passport home.

Falco was startled when Georgia suddenly sat up and reached for his hand. Not that he had been asleep. It had been so wonderful to lie awake and gaze undisturbed at her by the light of the moon coming through his open curtains. Now it shone on her eyes as she gazed back at him.

'Is anything wrong?' he whispered. 'What is happening in Remora?'

She shook her head. 'Nothing is wrong. I'm supposed to be resting before the race. It's all so fantastic – the flags and the clothes and the horses. This morning I came third in the heat and then I went to Arcangelo's Blessing and . . .' Words failed her. 'But I had to come back and check on things here. And to check that I still can,' she added even more quietly.

'Everything's fine here,' said Falco. 'Only I wish I could be with you at the race.'

Georgia squeezed his hand. 'This is the hardest part for you, I know,' she said. 'Just hold on and I'll tell you all about it when I get back. Only I must go now.' She lay back down and concentrated her mind on her room in Paolo's house.

Soon her regular breathing told Falco that she had fallen asleep and it was all right to resume his vigil. It was many hours before he closed his eyes; in his mind he was living every moment of the big day of the race he would never see again.

Georgia stood on the steps outside the big church and watched the ensigns execute their formal flourishes, making patterns with the red and yellow flags. Like all the other Rams, she gasped when the ensigns tossed the flags with their heavy flagpoles up high above the crowd and caught each other's standard as they fell after crossing in mid-air.

'The alzata,' said a voice behind her, and she turned to see Paolo, splendidly dressed in his parade clothes.

As Capitano, he would walk with the ensigns and the drummer in the Ram's section of the parade, just like every other captain of one of the Twelfths. He was talking to a tall grey-haired man who Georgia gathered from the talk around her was head of the silversmiths' guild.

They were all lining up now, in their red and yellow velvet, with brocade cloaks and elaborate hats with rolled brims and curling feathers. Paolo had silver spurs and a sword too. Later they would be joined by the float carrying a tableau of Rams and by a Twelver leading Arcangelo. Georgia herself would have to join in the great procession, wearing her metal helmet and riding the substitute parade horse; Arcangelo mustn't waste an ounce of his energy by carrying her around the Campo before the race. But now the walking members of the party were moving off to join the other Twelfths already performing the sbandierata in the square behind the Papal palace.

Of Luciano there was no sign, though Georgia glimpsed Dethridge through the crowd with a woman dressed in red velvet with a yellow silk cloak who must have been Silvia.

*

Enrico was in the Piazza di Gemelli watching the flag displays. He thought he caught sight of the Duke's face at one of the hospital windows. He seemed to be holding something like a doll or statue. Then Enrico realised with a shock that it was the unconscious body of the young di Chimici prince.

Quite mad, he thought to himself. Was it going to

matter to the Duke who won the race now? Perhaps he should lay out a bit more of the money both Duke and Pope had given him and make a last-minute extra pact with the Twins' jockey, Silk? His sharp eyes sought him out now, locating the pink and white colours among the ever-changing palette of Twelvers wearing their sashes and scarves.

*

The Pope led the Duchessa to her place between Rodolfo and Gaetano on the Twins' stand outside the Papal palace. Fabrizio di Chimici was there already – Carlo was representing the Giglian family in the Lady – but there were several empty places, including those of the other Bellezzan visitors. But the most conspicuous gap was where the Duke should be. Whispers exchanged between his sons made it clear that no one knew if he would turn out in time for the race.

It was a hot and sunny afternoon and Barbara stood behind the Duchessa with a white lace parasol. Arianna was dressed in pure white silk with a mask trimmed with white peacock feathers. It was a tactful choice, not clashing with the rose and white colours of the Twins around her and not espousing any one Twelfth. Only Arianna and her maid knew that she wore garters of brightest red and yellow under the wide silk skirt.

The di Chimici brothers wore the purple and green of the Lady and would have been happier across the Campo in their own stand. But as with the dinners before the race they had to stand in for their father and uphold the family honour with their Bellezzan guests. The diplomatic consequences of Falco's illness had been far reaching and neither of the brothers knew what the outcome would be. They were in uncharted waters and only their upbringing kept them afloat.

The atmosphere was tense and even Rodolfo, in his usual black velvet, unadorned by any colour, seemed nervous.

'What is it?' Arianna whispered to him. 'Where is he?'

'There is something wrong,' he replied quietly. 'I wish Georgia were not riding in this race. She should be bringing the boy back. And I'm still worried about Cesare.'

'What about Luciano?' asked Arianna. 'Where is he?'

Rodolfo sighed. 'I don't know,' he said, shaking his head. 'Things are not right there either. He is unhappier than I have known him since his translation – and that is at least partly my fault.'

'Here is Doctor Dethridge now,' said Arianna, and the Elizabethan took his place in the Twins' stand with much bowing and hand-kissing. But he came alone.

*

Luciano was restless. He had hung about at the stables in the Ram while Georgia went to the Blessing. He had the strongest feeling that he was going to be in the wrong place today, wherever he was. He was reluctant to go to the Campo so early, even though he wanted to see the procession before the race. He didn't want to be in the Twins' stand though, where all the crowd would be looking at the di Chimici party, because once he was there, hemmed in by dignitaries, there would be no chance of escape.

Escape made him think about Cesare, almost certainly shut up somewhere till the race was over. The thought of his friend's confinement sent him pacing up and down the cobbled stable-yard, remembering his own capture and imprisonment a year ago. Of course Cesare wasn't in the same danger that Luciano had been. The Talian boy would be released with no worse consequence than disappointment at missing this year's race. Whereas Luciano's life had changed for ever.

And yet, every hour that Cesare spent in captivity made Luciano suffer again what he had been through at the hands of the di Chimici ambassador and his spy in the blue cloak. It seemed more than likely that Cesare was in the hands of that same spy. And then something that Falco had said before he stravagated came back to Luciano. 'I keep thinking there's someone else in the palace,' he had said. 'Someone watching me.'

Luciano suddenly knew what he had to do. He ran to see if he could put horses into the carriage but all the grooms were down in the Piazza del Fuoco and he couldn't manage it alone. Dondola was quietly munching hay in her stall and he knew how to saddle and bridle her. Clumsily he climbed up on her back from the mounting-block in the yard. They rode out northwards through the deserted streets of the Ram and only the grey cat saw them go.

*

The Ram began the procession, being the Twelfth whose astrological sign rose first in the year. The drummer started the beat of the march, which would be taken up by all the other Twelfths, and the ensigns lowered their flags and stepped through the arch under the judges' stand and into the circular Campo.

They processed slowly round to the Lady's stand, ready to perform their first ceremonial sbandierata. Georgia came to a halt on the parade horse. Because of the large float separating them she couldn't see anything of the Ram's display, apart from the alzata, when their flags leapt into the air and spiralled down to a great cheer from the crowd.

'This is freaking me out,' thought Georgia, looking at the crowd. The whole of the centre of the Campo was filled with Remorans, all wearing the colours of their Twelfths. She could see that some citizens, who must have been there since early morning to get the best view, were standing on the circular stone seat round the central fountain. The Twins' colours still fluttered from the top of the column, inexplicable except as a good omen for the di Chimici.

Georgia glanced away from the crowd inside the track and into the Lioness's stand, where her part of the Ram's procession was halted. To her surprise, among the red and black sashes, she saw the multi-coloured clothing of the Manoush. Aurelio and Raffaella were sitting with an old woman of their tribe. Georgia smiled; she would have thought that watching the race in the comfort of a wooden stand would not have been in keeping with the austere

Manoush way of life.

She caught Raffaella's eye and felt a wave of recognition pass between them. And if she hadn't had to walk her horse on at that moment, she might have realised that the recognition came as much from the blind musician as from his companion.

Arianna watched entranced from her place of honour. There was nothing like this spectacle in her water-riven city – except perhaps Carnival. Landlocked Remora and its horses seemed glamorous to her today. But Rodolfo was still restless beside her, not looking at the procession but scanning the sky and looking over his shoulder towards the hospital whose bulk lay unseen behind the Papal palace. After a while she noticed that he was holding half-hidden in his cloak a hand mirror. And she knew it was not from vanity.

*

Cesare was at the limit of his strength when he came to a fast-flowing river. Gratefully he scooped water into his cupped hands and drank till his thirst was quenched. He had nothing in which he could carry water but he splashed his face and hair and soaked his neckcloth to keep him cool on the rest of his journey. His next task was to cross the river and get back on to the path on the other side; he could see it snaking invitingly between the trees across the water.

There were several large uneven stones across the river which would serve as stepping stones, but testing the water with a branch showed Cesare that it was deep in the middle and he already knew how cold and fast it was. He stepped back out of the water and sat down to rest with his back against a tree for a while; Cesare did not know how to swim.

*

Luciano rode to Santa Fina, enjoying his sense of mastery over the horse, which grew with every yard. As long as he was on the Strada delle Stelle he trotted quite fast but as soon as he was through the Gate of the Sun and the road ran through the countryside, he urged Dondola into a canter. She was surprised and pleased at being exercised on this day when her stable had seemed so deserted and willingly carried him to Santa Fina at speed.

It was not long before the great palace loomed up before him. It was the first time he had approached it with a clear view; usually his carriage just took him in through the massive gate and into the courtyard. Now the gate was open and the palace servants seemed to be in as much disarray as when he had last been there, on the morning when Falco had been discovered with the poison bottle.

He was recognised by one of them when he jumped down from Dondola's back.

'Oh, Signore,' he said. 'I'm sorry. I'm supposed to keep this door guarded. Can you take your horse round to the stable yourself?'

'Of course,' said Luciano. 'But what's the problem?'

The man mumbled something, clearly not wanting to say. Luciano shrugged and led Dondola round to the stable block. It was quite deserted. He put her in a stall and gave her hay and water.

'I'll be back soon,' he said to her. 'I just want to search the palace. I'm sure that Cesare is here somewhere.'

And Merla, recognising his voice, or perhaps the name of the boy who had been with her the night she had entered the world, gave a long whinny from the back of the stable block.

*

Arianna felt Rodolfo suddenly tense beside her.

'What is it?' she hissed.

The procession had now twined the entire circumference of the circle. Georgia was opposite the Twins' stand and the Twins' own parade had reached the Ram's stand, with a pair of boy twins playing on the float under a huge papier mâché lioness standing on a bed of pink and white paper roses. Teresa looked on appreciatively, thinking of her own twin boys back in the Twelfth.

Rodolfo exchanged glances with Dethridge and they both signalled silently to Paolo, proudly walking alongside the stand. The triangle made by the thought-lines among them was almost visible.

The Fishes' parade had just entered the Campo, followed by the last float carrying the Stellata itself, the banner covered with stars. On it was the figure of a woman in blue, but whether Christian Queen of Heaven or pagan goddess was not clear.

The crowd erupted at the sight of the banner, pulling off their coloured sashes and neckcloths and waving them at the painted silk standard. Under the cover of the renewed noise, Rodolfo showed Arianna what he could see in his mirror. A young man with long black curly hair, and wearing the red and yellow of the Ram, was clinging on to the back of a black horse. He looked like someone unused to riding. But as the image dwindled, Arianna saw that he sat the horse bareback – between a huge pair of black wings – and that the horse was soaring above tree-tops.

*

Cesare woke with a start. He could tell by the light that it was now late in the afternoon; shafts of green sunlight were slanting down between the trees. Hunger gnawed at his belly but he willed himself into the water and on to the precarious stepping-stones.

A third of the way across the river his courage gave way. The stones were slippery and even the bigger ones tilted as he moved his weight on to them. With every step he took he was in danger of tipping into the rushing water and being swept off his feet. There was a choice of stones and he didn't know which ones were stable and which treacherous.

Cesare halted, unable to move forwards or back, unsure now which stones had been safe on his way across and feeling giddy. A black dragonfly came and hovered just in front of his face. Its two pairs of wings were glossy and caught the light. It reminded him of Merla. Concentrating on the shiny insect made him feel less faint. Then it flew ahead of him and settled on one of the honey-coloured stones.

Keeping his eye carefully on the dragonfly, Cesare moved one foot forward and set it on the stone. It held. The dragonfly flitted ahead and landed on another stone; it rested for a second, then flew back to Cesare before returning to the stone that lay ahead of him.

'That's the one is it, my beauty?' said Cesare, and stepped forward. Stone by stone and step by painfully slow step, the dragonfly led him across the river. When he got to the other side and at last found that both feet were on dry ground, the insect flashed its jetty wings three times, then flew up into the trees.

'Thank you!' cried Cesare, looking up. And then he saw Merla herself flying slowly above the woods, with a rider on her back.

*

Luciano looked down through the treetops that rushed past sickeningly fast underneath him. He understood that Merla could go much faster, but she seemed to be looking for something and he was grateful for that. When he had decided to learn to ride, he had had nothing like this in mind. Even getting on to the winged horse had been an operation; Luciano had never ridden bareback and had always had someone to help him mount. Sitting precariously between Merla's wings and clutching her mane, he had pressed his knees into her flanks and clicked his tongue.

The black horse had flowed into a canter, a gallop and then lifted smoothly up and mounted diagonally into the sky with just a few slow flaps of her strong wings. While Luciano closed his eyes and hoped for the best, she had brought them across these woods.

The woods appeared to stretch south of Santa Fina

towards Remora and Merla seemed determined to head for the city.

They both heard the cry beneath them at the same time. Merla stopped beating her wings and hovered in the sky, treading air. Luciano peered fearfully over her shoulder through her thick black mane. There was a gap in the treetops like a parting through a thick head of hair. Luciano could see a thread of blue running through it and a figure beside it jumping up and down waving something red and yellow.

As the figure grew larger, he realised that Merla was looking for somewhere to land. Luciano closed his eyes and prayed to the goddess. The trees rushed past his head and he heard Merla's wings swish as she folded them neatly over her back, wrapping him in a dark cloud of soft feathers. She lowered her neck so that he could slide down it.

Luciano could hardly stand, his legs were so wobbly. But then he heard a crashing noise and Cesare came running through the trees into the clearing that Merla had found.

The two boys clasped each other in an affectionate hug.

'Cesare! I'm so glad I've found you!'

'You found Merla!'

'Only because I was looking for you!'

Cesare ran to the winged horse who was cropping the grass in an absurdly ordinary horsey way. He threw his arms round her neck and laid his face against her cheek. For a moment horse and boy just stood quietly breathing in each other's scent.

Then Cesare turned to Luciano. 'We must get to the Campo. It's nearly time for the race.'

'It's OK,' said Luciano. 'Georgia's going to ride Arcangelo.'

Cesare wrestled with conflicting emotions. He knew that the Ram would have had to scratch or hire another jockey. And he knew that another jockey would have been signed up by now and not be changeable. Georgia was at least used to riding bareback, and enough time had elapsed since his capture for her to forge a relationship with Arcangelo. But he was bitterly disappointed. The Stellata was run only once a year and he had been preparing for this one for a long time. Maybe he would be too tall or too heavy to be a jockey next year?

Cesare sighed. 'Will she carry us both?' he asked, still hanging on to Merla's mane.

Luciano shook his head. 'Perhaps for a short distance,' he said. 'But not all the way to the city. Still, I have a horse at the palace and it's only a mile or two north of here.'

'I'm not going back there,' said Cesare. 'That's where I was held captive. It's taken me days to escape.'

'What about Roderigo's place?' said Luciano.

'Brilliant!' said Cesare. 'That should be just west of here and Starlight is still there. Merla would love to go to her and one of us could ride her to Remora.'

'That would be me,' said Luciano, already feeling nervous about the short flight to the Santa Fina stables and quite ready to return to riding on solid ground.

Merla let them both climb up, Cesare giving Luciano a heave and then leaping lightly up in front of him. He leaned forward and whispered in Merla's ear. She spread her great wings and moved forward in the clearing, getting up enough speed to lift off. It seemed touch and go whether she would be airborne before reaching the trees on the other side of the clearing, but slowly her powerful muscles and huge wingspan raised her from the ground. And then she was off, up and away, flying towards her mother.

*

There was a tight knot in Georgia's stomach. The procession had wound its way round the Campo three times and the Stellata had been hung over the Judges' stand. The ensigns of each Twelfth had executed a final spectacular alzata simultaneously in front of the Twins' stand and had seen with satisfaction that the beautiful Duchessa of Bellezza had jumped to her feet and applauded them.

The jockeys had all changed horses in the Cortile of the Papal palace and were now seated on their proper mounts for the race. The Archer's jockey, Topolino, touched his helmet in greeting to Georgia and she returned his salute. She didn't like the look of the Fishes' jockey, known as Il Re – the king. He was giving her some very unkingly looks and she remembered what he had been like in the heats.

The great bell of the palace suddenly stopped and only then did Georgia realise that it had been tolling all afternoon, ever since the Blessing ceremony. A hush fell in the Cortile.

Then a tall, dishevelled figure shambled in front of the horses. He barely looked at his own jockey, Cherubino, who leaned down to get some sort of blessing from the man.

'Your Grace,' whispered Cherubino, and the Duke stopped and stared at him.

He raised an exhausted hand. 'Victory and rejoicing,' he said woodenly, remembering the formula, and continued his way out into the Campo.

*

Arianna's heart was pounding. She knew that the race was a sham, rigged so that a di Chimici Twelfth would win. And she knew that the purpose of bringing her here to see it had been to put on a show of di Chimici power and if possible engineer a humiliating defeat for Bellezza's Twelfth, the Ram.

But in a few minutes she would be escorted to the Judges' stand to choose the order in which the horses would take their places. That could not be rigged; she would put her hand into a velvet bag and draw out wooden balls painted in the colours of each Twelfth. The order in which they came out was the order in which the horses would start, beginning from the inside of the track.

Arianna prayed now for a good placing for Georgia, somewhere near the beginning. The Duke was supposed to take her to the Judges' stand but he hadn't shown up and there was much whispering among his sons, which Arianna was trying to ignore. Then there was a sort of ripple in the stand and Niccolò di Chimici was there, looking like a phantom. He gave her a ghastly smile.

'Time for the draw, your Grace,' he said, and offered her his arm.

Georgia was handed a whip as she entered the Campo on Arcangelo; the jockeys came in through an arch under the Twins' stand. The start-line was in the neutral zone that ran down from the Strada delle Stelle in the north; it was matched by another neutral area in the south, where all the people who had taken part in the procession were sitting in a stand reserved for them.

Georgia moved to the start-line, opposite the Judges' stand, in a kind of dream. She could see the Starter with something that looked like a very big trumpet but was probably a sort of megaphone. The Duchessa of Bellezza stood at his side, looking like a long glass of iced water in the hot stuffy Campo. And beside her Georgia made out the Duke, looking in need of one. She hadn't seen him for days and was shocked by his appearance.

Arianna was putting an elegantly gloved hand into a black velvet bag. She drew out a red and purple ball – 'Archer,' she said in a clear voice, but the Starter repeated it through his trumpet and 'A-a-rr-cherrrr!' echoed round the enclosed Campo. Topolino moved Alba towards the first place.

The Archer's ball was put in number one position in something that looked like a cross between a branched menorah and a row of glass eggcups. The Duchessa selected the next ball and 'Rrramm!' was resounding while Georgia was still trying to believe that the red and yellow had been chosen next. She was second from the inner barrier – an excellent position! And she had her ally on her inside.

But the blue and pink colours of the Fishes came next and Georgia found herself wedged between her greatest ally and her greatest foe. Worst still was to come as the pink and white ball was placed in the fourth holder; the Twins would be right next to the Fishes, waiting to gang up on her and give her a bad start.

Some of the crowd began to groan as the lower positions were used up and they realised that their Twelfth would be near the outside barrier. The Lady was drawn last – number twelve, the Rincorsa. This last horse would be the one to start the race, entering the ropes at a gallop and setting all the others off, if the Starter thought it was a valid start and no-one had been out of place. They had all had the same rules for the heats but no one cared too much about keeping to them. The real race was much more serious.

The glass cups were all full now and the spectral Duke was leading the Duchessa back to the dignitaries' stand outside the Papal palace. Horses were all milling around at the start; there were no starting boxes and several mounts were facing the wrong way, including Arcangelo. Georgia watched the two Ducal figures, so different, walk the few yards back to the Twins and scanned the VIP stand. She couldn't see Luciano there.

But there was no time to worry about it. After two false starts the race was suddenly under way and Georgia had no time to worry about anything except the rain of blows on her helmet from Il Re. Topolino put on a spurt to get out of her way so that she could ride on the inner rail behind him, but Silk pushed Benvenuto into her path and blocked her.

She had had a disastrous start but at least the Fishes and the Twins were now leaving her alone. They thought they had done a good enough job of keeping her out of the race and were now concentrating on their own runs. Georgia was furious but she was still riding and Arcangelo was a fast horse.

She pulled up on the others and as they finished the first lap, she was lying sixth, with a knot of other horses and jockeys. Somewhere in her brain she knew that she had passed Paolo and the others in the southernmost stand. She had completed one whole sunwise circuit of the Campo, racing past every sign of the zodiac. Dukes and Princes, butchers and bakers were all one blur to her. Georgia was unaware of everything and everyone except her horse and her fellow-riders.

They were galloping flat out on the second circuit when one single voice pierced through the shouting of the crowd. 'The zhou volou!' it cried. 'The Ram's luck returns!'

Georgia knew the voice was Aurelio's at the same moment that she heard wings. Jockeys wavered and slowed just fractionally and Arcangelo was lying third, behind the Water-carrier and the Twins, as they all swept past the start line again and started on the last circuit.

'Don't look up,' Georgia muttered, gritting her teeth as she heard the crowd cry out with a single voice.

Something pink and white fluttered past her eyes and still she didn't slacken or waver. She drew abreast of Salsiccio on Uccello and felt him falter beside her; she caught a glimpse of his huge frightened eyes, cast up to the heavens.

'Don't ... Look ... Up,' she panted, nearly level with Silk on Benvenuto. The Twins' jockey raised his whip again but it fell uselessly to the ground as Georgia just had time to see him make the hand of fortune and turn white.

She raced past him, keeping her eyes firmly fixed on the goal of the little black and white flag that marked the finishing line.

She passed it and, as she slowed the big chestnut, could not believe what she had done. She had won. Won for the Ram. But all was eerily silent. It was like being inside a freeze frame on a video. Everyone was looking up at the central column in the Campo. The Twins' colours had been cast down and Cesare was waving to her from the back of Merla, who hovered patiently while he untied a very grubby-looking red and yellow scarf from his neck and fixed it to the pinnacle.

He leaned perilously over the side of the flying horse and yelled down to her, 'Victory! Victory and rejoicing!'

And the whole Campo burst into life and the cheering began.

Chapter 23

The Ram on Fire

Luciano arrived panting in the Campo, having ridden Starlight all the way from Santa Fina. He got there long after Cesare on Merla to find all the stands empty and the remnants of the crowd still pouring out under the Twins' stand to reach the cathedral. He tied Starlight to one of the iron rings in a road leading into the Piazza and hurried towards the Duomo himself.

'Who won?' he asked a passing Remoran, but the answer was lost in the noise coming from the black and white cathedral. Luciano fought his way in, and the sight that met his eyes told him all he needed to know. The interior was a blaze of red and yellow as Twelvers from the Ram waved flags and banners high in the air.

Up by the altar in the distance he could see the blue and silver of the Stellata standard and two figures both in the Ram's colours, being carried on the shoulders of deliriously happy Montonaioli. The great nave of the cathedral echoed with cheers and chants; there was no chance of getting to Georgia and Paolo.

Smiling, Luciano left the cathedral and took Starlight back to her home in the Ram.

*

Arianna was back inside the Papal palace and at a loss what to do. There should have been a splendid banquet served at least nominally in her honour, but the palace was eerily quiet. Everything had gone wrong for the di Chimici; they had been expecting to celebrate a victory for the Twins or the Lady.

It was traditional after the Stellata that the winning Twelfth would hold another massive street party, dining under the stars and feasting the night away. But the other eleven Twelfths would be in darkness, all torches and candles extinguished as if in deep mourning.

Now the trestle tables in the square outside the Duomo with their pink and white tablecloths, which had already been set out in anticipation of a night's feasting, were empty.

But the Pope was not going to give up on a feast; even if the Twelvers of the Twins had been cheated of their party, that was no reason to cancel the banquet inside the palace. Ferdinando di Chimici suddenly assumed responsibility as the second most senior member of the family. The Duke was virtually useless and, although Ferdinando could not replace him as a statesman or strategist, he knew what was owed to visiting nobles and it was up to him to save face for all the di Chimici and throw as magnificent a celebration as possible, even if there was nothing to celebrate.

*

The Duke had gone back to the hospital as soon as the race was over. He seemed scarcely to understand that Bellezza had won. But when Gaetano went to find his father, it seemed that the lagoon-city was still on his mind.

'Father,' said Gaetano gently. 'Won't you come back to the palace for the banquet? You need refreshment and I can stay with Falco.'

'No,' said Niccolò. 'You must be there. The Duchessa likes you, I can tell. You must take advantage of her good mood to make your proposal tonight.'

Gaetano was horrified. He had been glad to set the courtship aside while Falco was so ill. Now it seemed that his hand would be forced.

'But Father,' he said. 'It cannot be right to talk of marriage while Falco lingers here in this state.'

'It will not be much longer,' said Niccolò. 'The physicians say he can't last the night.'

A new grief gripped Gaetano. He would have to mourn his brother without sharing with any of his family the knowledge that would comfort him, the certainty that Falco would live and thrive in another world. And the doctors did seem right; Falco was little more than a shadow of his former self.

Back in the Ram the torches blazed and the drums pounded. All the children were allowed to stay up late, though the Montalbani twins had fallen asleep under one of the tables. Teresa found them and scooped them up into their wooden crib and sat rocking it with her foot while the little girls ran round between tables waving their flags and crying 'Wictry! Wejoything!' to anyone who would listen.

Georgia was carried back to the Twelfth in triumph on the shoulders of two muscular men. Paolo was carried beside her. Arcangelo was accompanied by a crowd of excited Twelvers all desperate to pat and stroke him. Cesare led Merla, docile because she was happy to be going back home to the Ram and her mother. A small empty space surrounded her as Twelvers, overawed by her, thronged round but didn't dare get near enough to touch. William Dethridge escorted Silvia, and the chief standard-bearer had relinquished his flag to his companion in order to carry the Stellata banner.

While the horses stood outside, the Rams took the banner and their victorious jockeys into the church, carrying both Georgia and Cesare up the stairs to the front door.

Whichever Twelfth won the race, their first thought was to give thanks to the Virgin, first in the great cathedral and then in their own special church.

Santa Trinità was full of waving flags and jubilant Twelvers. The priest who had given Georgia her helmet, and had blessed Arcangelo only a few hours ago, sprinkled holy water liberally over her now and over any Ram within reach. There was a carnival atmosphere in the building, normally so quiet and solemn. For a Twelfth who had won the Stellata after a drought of twenty-five years, all rules were suspended.

Georgia's feet literally had not touched the ground since she had mounted Arcangelo in the Cortile of the Papal palace an hour ago. After the race she had been practically pulled off her horse by the enthusiastic embraces of her fellow Rams and had to struggle not to let them tear her jockey's tunic off. Now her supporters let her down on the church steps and she fell into Cesare's arms.

'What a night!' he said. 'What a victory!'

'Only because of your diversion,' she said. 'I wouldn't have won without you and Merla. I'm sorry it wasn't you on Arcangelo.'

'Really?'

'No, not really!' said Georgia, smiling broadly.

Another horse came into the square and Merla whinnied a greeting to it. Luciano was leading Starlight up to the others at the foot of the steps. He leapt off her back and threw the reins to a willing Twelver. Rumour had soon got around that this grey was the mother of the miraculous flying horse.

'Luciano!' gasped Georgia. 'You can ride!'

'He's a real horseman now,' laughed Cesare. 'Rode all the way to Santa Fina on one horse and all the way back on another. He even had a couple of flights on Merla!'

'Lucky devil!' said Georgia, looking longingly at the winged horse.

And then Luciano had reached them and grabbed her in his arms and she forgot all about flying.

'Georgia, you did it!' he said and planted a kiss on her lips.

She felt herself turning hot and cold. Never before tonight had she been so embraced and caressed, but this was different. This was Luciano. She kissed him right back and felt him react in surprise. So she tore herself away and kissed Cesare too, so that Luciano wouldn't feel singled out. Out of the corner of her eye, she saw him relax, even as she registered Cesare's warm response.

*

Rodolfo had his mirrors trained on many different places: one on Bellezza in the Duchessa's palazzo; one on the hospital where Falco lay still and silent; and one on the Ram, because he knew Silvia was there. He could make her out in the crowd outside the big church, even though all the figures were so tiny. And then he saw Luciano kissing the Ram's jockey, for just a fraction longer than was consistent with congratulations on the victory.

He sighed; another complication.

*

Georgia could see she wasn't going to get away from the Ram again that night. Even more than yesterday, she was the star of the show. Twelvers of both sexes kept coming up to congratulate and kiss her; some of the young female Rams, who really were remarkably pretty, looked as if they would like to stay and get to know the winning jockey better, but Paolo and Cesare protected Georgia from them.

What on earth were Maura and Ralph going to think if she didn't get back that night? Her note had said that she was going to spend all day with Falco and the night too at the Mulhollands'. That had taken care of last night and today in Remora. But the sky was dark here now, which meant that it was day in the other world and, since it would be a Saturday, everyone would be home and wondering where Georgia had got to.

It was only a matter of time before Maura rang Vicky and then she would discover that the Mulhollands had no idea where she was. The fact that she actually *was* at their house was no help. If they found her in Falco's room in her apparently comatose state, they would rush her off to hospital like Luciano a year ago. And she dreaded to think what that would do to Vicky and David.

But after a few goblets of wine, Georgia decided she was just not going to worry about it; Falco would have to cover up for her somehow. And she was not going to miss a second of her night of celebration. She couldn't have forced herself to sleep even if she had been able to sneak away from the party.

*

Gaetano sat beside his uncle at dinner. For once he was not next to Arianna, although she filled his thoughts. The Duchessa was on the Pope's other side, next to her father. Fabrizio and Carlo were next to them, arguing under their breath about who should make the speech after the banquet – Fabrizio as son and heir to the Dukedom of Giglia, or Carlo as next Prince of Remora.

Beatrice came and sat opposite Gaetano.

'How is everything at the hospital?' he asked anxiously.

She shook her head in answer.

'You haven't left Father on his own have you?' he asked.

'No,' she said wearily. 'Francesca has relieved me there. She said I needed a break.'

The Pope caught the name. 'Ah, Francesca,' he said. 'She's a good girl, isn't she? Always so concerned for the family. I'm glad I granted her that annulment. She deserves a better fate than an impotent old husband.'

Gaetano choked on his pheasant. Francesca was free to re-marry! And within hours he must ask Arianna to be his wife.

Back in London, Falco was on tenterhooks. He was missing Talia and his father and Gaetano so badly and it was agonising not to know what was happening to Georgia in the Stellata. And he had to cover up for her too. She was still sleeping in his room and he wanted to be with her all the time, in case she suddenly returned to her body, as she had last night. But Vicky would have been alerted to something strange going on if he stayed closeted in his room. Every time the phone rang he hurried to be first to answer it but his leg made him slow and Vicky sometimes beat him to it.

Another thing was bothering him. He had stravagated twelve days ago and was still without a shadow. That meant he was still alive in Remora and as long as he was, there would be a temptation to ask Georgia for her ring and see if he could return to his Talian body. He didn't know if she had destroyed the talisman or not. Falco longed for it to be over so that he could concentrate on his new life and on getting better.

The phone rang. Vicky was only yards from it.

'Georgia? No, she's not here, I'm afraid. Last night? No, she wasn't here last night. Wait a minute – I'll ask Nicholas.'

'Yt was juste as mye readinge sayed it wolde bee,' a rather inebriated Doctor Dethridge was trying to explain to Georgia. 'Al the numbire cardes were twos – the numbire assigned to ye in the race. Aye, ye were there – Princesse of the Birdes.'

'Princess of Birds?' asked Georgia, puzzled.

'Yonge mayde,' said Dethridge patiently. 'Princesse. And of birdes by cause thatte this place is of the aire – home to the flying horse and Citie of the Starres.'

'OK, if you say so,' said Georgia. 'What else did your cards tell you?'

'That the Dutchesse – Arianne is Princesse of Fishes – was wel protected by Lucian when shee came to the celebratioune of the Moving Starres.'

'I don't see what he did to protect her,' said Georgia.

'And that the Knyghte – yonge Caesar – was to be shutte up in a towre,' Dethridge continued unconcerned. 'And on the other side of ye the Prince of Serpentes – thatte is one of the yonge lordes of the Ladye, but whether it bee poore Falcon or Prince Cayton, I doe notte knowe.'

'How do you work that one out?' asked Georgia, uncomfortable at the thought that the Elizabethan had already predicted her intervention in Falco's life.

'The Ladye is an Erthe sygne,' said Dethridge. 'Juste as the Ram bilonges to Fyre and the Twins to Aire,' as if that explained it all.

Perhaps you should do another reading, thought Georgia. She had no idea how the tangle of herself and Luciano, Arianna and Gaetano and even Falco and Cesare, might be unravelled and made to lie smooth.

A fanfare of silver trumpets announced the arrival of a visitor. Unlike the night before, the Duchessa of Bellezza could now travel openly to visit and congratulate her city's Twelfth. Arianna swept into the Ram holding her head high. She wore a scarlet cloak over a yellow silk dress and a mask made of red and yellow feathers. Followed by Rodolfo and Gaetano, she walked the length of the steep Via di Montone to a standing ovation and made her way to the high table.

Paolo fetched chairs for the new visitors but Arianna did not sit down until she had been to stroke the horses. It was traditional for the winning horse to be guest of honour at the victory banquet, but the

Ram had gone further and Merla was there alongside Arcangelo. And where Merla was, Starlight had to be too. The three horses had their own hastily fenced off space in front of the church, with the silk Stellata lashed to a tall pole behind it, and throughout the evening Twelvers and visitors went to marvel at the 'Sorte di Montone', luck of the Ram.

The Duchessa patted Arcangelo a bit nervously and stroked Starlight's nose. But she stood for a long time admiring Merla.

'I would not have believed it,' she said to Gaetano. 'Until a week or so ago horses were something I had seen only in paintings and engravings. And now here is a creature of myth, such as are found only on fragments of ancient pottery or in old mosaics.'

'And here it is in reality,' said Gaetano. 'This too my family stole from the Ram as well as their jockey.'

Arianna placed her hand affectionately on his arm – a gesture not lost on several guests at the top table.

'I have never held you accountable for the deeds of your family,' she said.

'You have others to congratulate besides the horses,' said Rodolfo, leading her back to the feast.

'Indeed,' said Arianna, suddenly vivacious again. She came over to Georgia and held both her hands. Projecting her clear musical voice across the square she said firmly, 'I congratulate the Ram and its fine jockey, Giorgio Gredi,' not stumbling over the name. 'You have upheld the honour of my city tonight and Bellezza thanks you. As a small token of my gratitude I give Giorgio a bag of silver and this kiss.'

Startled, Georgia felt her lips brushed by the Duchessa's and saw the violet eyes fixed briefly on her before Arianna handed her a velvet bag heavy with coins. She stammered her thanks as the Rams all hollered with appreciation, banging the tables and stamping their feet. This was their idea of good entertainment.

Georgia sat down confused as the Duchessa calmly accepted a goblet of wine poured for her by Paolo. Arianna must know she couldn't take the silver back when she stravagated home. She decided to give it to Cesare, just as soon as he could stop eating; he was making up for lost time.

Luciano was eaten up with jealousy. Arianna had not given him one glance or smile and yet he felt that everything she did was directed at him. And what she was doing now was flirting with Gaetano. And yet what had Luciano done to make her angry with him? He remembered Georgia's kiss but surely that had meant nothing? She had kissed Cesare too and half the population of the Ram; it was what Remorans did after a great victory. In fact Luciano himself had received a number of embraces from girls of the Twelfth whom he had never seen before.

There was an air of recklessness and abandon in the Twelfth of the Ram that night. The Stellata had been wrested from the di Chimici and returned to the Ram after a quarter of a century. Who knew when they might win it again? Many babies were born in the Twelfth the following May as a result of the licence of that night of celebrations and many of the boys were called Giorgio or Cesare, the girls Stella or Merla.

Gaetano was not immune to the atmosphere or to the attention Arianna was giving him. He drank more wine than he should have done to give himself courage for what he had to do. He had almost talked himself into it, thinking tonight, as he had often thought before, that it would be no hardship to be husband to the beautiful ruler of Bellezza.

His musings were interrupted by a sudden shout.

'Look!' cried Cesare. 'The Manoush have come!'

Aurelio and Raffaella had entered the square quietly and were standing talking to Merla; she appeared to listen to them and understand. Slowly the square filled with other colourfully dressed members of their tribe and, when Paolo went to speak to them and offer the Ram's hospitality, they set up their instruments and gave an impromptu concert. The Ram's drummer joined in, soon picking up the intricate rhythms and even the heralds tried to play along on their trumpets.

Most Twelvers were so pleasantly befuddled with wine, lack of sleep and happiness that they were not about to judge the music harshly. But after a pause, Aurelio played something on his own. It was sweet and sad and it made Gaetano think of his brother and then of his cousin, the girl he must soon give up for ever.

'It is an air to break your heart, is it not, Principe?' said a woman he had not noticed before. Now he saw that she was very handsome, dressed in the colours of the Ram. For a moment, she reminded him of the Duchessa, but then he realised that she was much older. Still, she had a look of Arianna; perhaps she was a visiting aunt? He seemed to remember that an aunt of the Duchessa's was married to Doctor Dethridge.

'It is very moving, ma'am,' he said politely.

'It seems to tell of love lost and duty triumphant,' she continued. 'Of wrong choices made and a life of sacrifice, lived with the consequences of those choices.'

Gaetano was seriously startled; was this woman a clairvoyant, or perhaps another Stravagante?

'You can read so much into a simple air?' he asked.

'There is nothing simple about the music of the Manoush,' she said.

He turned to look at the harpist and when the melody ended and he looked back, the woman had gone. There was a pause, while the notes of the lament faded into the night. And then another, merrier tune began and the tables were pushed back for dancing.

Gaetano danced with Arianna and saw out of the corner of his eye that her father was dancing with the mysterious woman.

'Who is that with the Regent?' he asked her. 'She has just said some extraordinary things to me. I think she is some kind of enchantress.'

Arianna laughed. 'You are not the first to say that,' she said. But she didn't answer his question.

Luciano and Cesare were in a dilemma. They both wanted to dance with Georgia, but as far as the Rams were concerned, their jockey was a boy. Remorans were indiscriminately affectionate and no one thought it odd for young men to embrace or even kiss one another, particularly during a great feast. But they did not dance as couples.

The three friends found themselves all caught up with pretty and willing female Twelvers. Arianna looked daggers at Luciano, whose current partner was a lively black-haired girl, and Georgia cast desperate glances at Paolo. But he was dancing happily with Teresa.

It was William Dethridge who rescued her. When the music changed he got all the young men, including Georgia, to dance in a circle, while the women clapped and beat time. Georgia found herself just where she wanted to be, between Luciano and Cesare, with everyone singing the hymn of the Twelfth lustily at the tops of their voices.

Gaetano was on Luciano's other side and both young men wished that the dancing would go on for ever and the next day never come. They both knew that by the morning something would be resolved about their future. But for now all they wanted to do was dance and drink and sing.

*

Enrico was the only person in Remora, apart from loyal Rams, who had made any money on the race. He still had a healthy proportion of the silver that the Duke and the Pope had given him to lay out on pacts with other Twelfths, and the betting had brought him more. Now he was wondering whether to leave the city. He wasn't at all sure where he would go; he liked Remora and being around horses but he didn't think it would be wise to stay on. He had committed horse-theft, kidnapping and imprisonment and, once this was known in the Ram, he would be in danger.

And it had all been for nothing; the di Chimici had lost the race and Bellezza's stock was higher than ever. News of the victory would soon spread throughout

Talia, encouraging other cities to resist alliances and usurpations. The Duke was crazy with grief now but one day he would come to his senses and then he might remember that his spy had failed him.

On the other hand, the Duke was the most important person Enrico had ever worked for and he was loath to give him up; perhaps he could persuade his employer that he could be useful to him in some other way?

For now, he had to face the Rams, because he owed them money. Enrico was a scoundrel, but he was also deeply superstitious; he had stolen their luck but he would not try to rob them of their winnings.

*

The party in the Ram began to break up as the Manoush gathered to salute the dawn in their usual way. Georgia sat on the steps outside the church, yawning, suddenly dog-tired. She saw Rodolfo and Gaetano escorting Arianna from the square. They stopped by the fountain and Rodolfo turned back to talk to Silvia. Georgia watched the young couple leave together and saw Luciano looking after them with an expression of sheer despair.

Paolo came over to Georgia. 'You look exhausted,' he said. 'Do you want to come back to the stables?'

All over the square, overturned chairs and tattered flags lay among spilt wine and fragments of food. Dogs scavenged among the leftovers and men with long-handled snuffers extinguished the last of the torches. Suddenly a scuffle broke out and Georgia saw that Cesare was hanging on to a man in a blue cloak.

She and Paolo and a few other young Rams rushed over to help him.

'This is the man who kidnapped me!' said Cesare. 'And he probably stole Merla too, yet he dares to set foot in the Ram!'

Enrico looked scared but he stood his ground. 'Only acting on orders,' he said. 'Don't tell me worse things haven't happened in the Stellata before. And I've come to pay the Twelvers who bet on the Ram.'

A few of the young men who were holding on to him relaxed their grip. This was the first time they had thought about their winnings but now it seemed like a good idea. But they weren't going to let Enrico get off lightly. They turned out all his pockets and emptied his bag. The spy took it all without protest; his main stash of silver was safe up at Santa Fina. Cesare was disgusted at all the different coloured scarves in Enrico's bag and confiscated the whole thing.

So in the end, Enrico left the square unscathed.

*

'It's a beautiful night,' said Gaetano, guiding the Duchessa back to the Papal palace through the narrow streets.

'Morning, you mean,' said Arianna, picking her way over the cobbles in her red silk slippers.

All of a sudden, he decided he had to get it over with.

'Your Grace,' he said, stopping her underneath one of the smoking torches. 'Arianna, this might not be the right time or place, but you will be going back to Bellezza soon and I can't wait any longer. We have spent nearly a month together and we know each other quite well now. I want to know what you think of our offer. Will you marry me?'

'There,' said Arianna. 'That wasn't so hard, was it? Not elegant, not romantic, but it did the job.'

*

Georgia made her way back to the stables hanging on to Cesare and Paolo. The Montalbani didn't think it right that their triumphant jockey should sleep in the hayloft, but that was what Georgia wanted. Cesare hung Enrico's bag of neckcloths on a post in the stables and gave her a final hug before stumbling into the house to sleep. Paolo embraced her too.

'Thank you,' he said. 'You have the courage of a warrior. You will prevail over your stepbrother.'

And then he was gone. Luciano and Dethridge had disappeared off somewhere together and Georgia had no idea where Rodolfo and Silvia were sleeping, except that it was probably in the same place. She lay down in the straw, hearing Arcangelo and Merla and Starlight and the other horses of the Ram moving beneath her. Even Dondola was back, ridden down to Remora by Roderigo, who had collected her from the Casa di Chimici and ridden her down in time to join in the Ram's celebrations.

Georgia's mind was a kaleidoscope of swirling colours and shapes – the procession, the flags, the horses, the noises, the sight of Merla hovering above the Campo, the bright ribbons of the Manoush, the kisses, the music, the wine, the . . .

Gaetano burst into the hospital. The Duke had fallen into a deep sleep in his chair by Falco's bed, but Francesca was still awake. The room smelled of burnt-out candles. Gaetano paused to see that Falco's chest still rose and fell, even though very lightly. Then he took Francesca's hands in his and led her from the room.

Out in the corridor where the morning light streamed on to the pictures painted on the walls of patients being bled or leeched or springing up miraculously cured, he fell on his knees on the cold tiles and asked her to marry him.

And Francesca said yes.

Georgia woke to find herself in Falco's room with the door closed but not bolted. There was no sign of him but there was a scrap of paper on the pillow beside her, containing the single word: 'Discovered!' It was evening and the house seemed deserted. She peeled herself off the floor and went downstairs and let herself out. She had to go home and face the music. She was consoled by the thought that, whatever she had to go through now, it had been worth it.

Chapter 24

Nets of Gold

When Georgia entered the living room of her own house, it took her a few seconds to adjust. She was deadly tired and the people she had just left behind in the Ram were more real to her than her own family. She focused on Falco, who was in some ways the most familiar person there.

While the others all stared at her, she mouthed at him, 'I won!' and had time to register his surprise and delight before the storm broke. Maura and Ralph were there and Russell and the Mulhollands and a man and a woman who Georgia gradually realised were police officers. These last two didn't stay; as far as they were concerned, a missing person inquiry had just ended happily and they had crimes to investigate.

As soon as they left, Ralph went to the kitchen to

make coffee, dragging a protesting Russell with him. He wanted to stay and see the fireworks but his father was firm.

The row raged on for what seemed like hours. The same questions were asked over and over again: Where had Georgia been? Who had she been with? What had she been doing? What did Nicholas know about it?

But they made no headway. What could she say? That she had been riding a horse race in another world and had won and feasted and danced the night away, kissed by nobles and commoners? That she had seen a winged horse? That she had foiled a political coup? That she had been with the Mulhollands' son? That 'Nicholas' was an aristocrat, hundreds of years old, from another dimension? That she was a hero called Giorgio?

Whatever Maura and Ralph had thought before, they would have been sure she was on drugs now if she had given any of these answers. She clung doggedly to a few simple ideas.

'I can't tell you. It was nothing wrong. I was keeping a promise. Nicholas knows nothing.' (For this last she had to keep her fingers crossed but it was Falco who knew where she had been, not Nicholas.)

'I bet that old perve in the junk shop knows something about it,' said Russell helpfully, and the inquisition intensified.

Fortunately David Mulholland turned out to know Mortimer Goldsmith and he scotched the idea that there was anything sinister about the old man.

'It has nothing to do with Mr Goldsmith,' said Georgia dully. 'Can I go to bed now? I'm very tired.'

'But you can't stay out all night and most of the next day and expect us just to let you get away with it!' fumed Maura. 'I have been worried sick about you. I never want to live through another day like today.' And she burst into tears.

Georgia felt terrible. It shouldn't all end like this, the glory and the triumph. She couldn't bear to see her mother cry and the anxious faces of the others, apart from Russell who was gloating and Falco, who had known where she was in both worlds.

'I'm so sorry, Mum,' she said. 'It was just something I had to do. Not illegal, or dangerous (she crossed her fingers again) or stupid. But I can't tell you about it, ever. You'll just have to trust me. I told you I would be at the Mulhollands' so that you wouldn't be worried. But what I had to do took longer than I thought – that's all. It will never happen again, I promise. Now you can ground me or punish me in whatever way you want, but I must go to bed – I haven't slept since I can't remember when.'

'Leave it now, Maura,' said Ralph. 'Let her rest. We'll talk about it again tomorrow.'

'What do you mean, engaged?' said the Duke blearily, when Gaetano and Francesca came back into the room holding hands and told him their news. 'What about the Duchessa?'

'I asked her, Father,' said Gaetano, who had explained everything to his cousin. 'I did what you told me, but she refused. She said that she would always be my friend but that her heart belonged to another. Then she told me to go and find Francesca.'

'And I am free to accept him, Uncle,' said Francesca. 'The marriage with the Bellezzan has been annulled.'

Duke Niccolò stared at them. Everything had gone wrong with his plans. But he saw that the two young people were in love and already his brain was clicking with new schemes. Gaetano would not have Bellezza but he could inherit the title of Fortezza when old cousin Jacopo died, since Jacopo only had daughters. And those daughters could be married off to Niccolò's other sons or nephews, to keep them happy and make sure they didn't have title-less husbands to threaten Gaetano's claim.

'Very well,' he said. 'You have my blessing. Now go and tell your news at the palace. I shall stay here with Falco.'

*

Arianna had a visitor at the Papal palace; she had not been able to sleep and was already changed into her day dress when a servant showed her mother into her apartment.

'Signora Bellini,' he announced and withdrew.

'Silvia,' said Arianna when he had gone. She never called her Mother, because that name was reserved for the aunt who had brought her up in obscurity on a lagoon island while Silvia Bellini had ruled Bellezza and kept the di Chimici at bay.

'Good morning, my dear,' said Silvia, removing her veil.

'I suppose I don't have to tell you how dangerous it

is, coming here?' said Arianna.

'Not at all,' said Silvia. 'No one here has ever seen my face except you and your father.'

'You didn't stay here last night did you?' asked Arianna, appalled by the thought of the risk.

'What night was there, after all that feasting? No, I stayed in the Ram,' said Silvia. 'Where I spoke to your young man.'

'Which one?' said Arianna, wryly.

'The one who is going to ask you to marry him – the one who wants Bellezza.'

'You mean Gaetano,' said Arianna. 'What did you say to him?'

'I suggested he should think very hard before throwing away his old love and taking a new.'

'Well, you don't seem to have had very much effect,' said Arianna. 'He proposed on the way back to the palace, as dawn was breaking.'

Silvia looked at her in silence. Then said, 'That was much too early in the day to say anything serious. What was your answer?'

'I refused him,' said Arianna.

'On what grounds?'

'On the grounds that I didn't love him and I thought he loved someone else – quite good reasons, I thought.'

'Yes, for a simple island girl, maybe,' said Silvia. 'But you are that no longer. You know that your choice must be influenced by considerations other than feelings.'

Arianna's eyes opened wide. 'You surely don't mean I should have accepted him? A di Chimici? He would become Duke of Bellezza and his family would never rest until he wore me down to join their Republic. And then he would become Duke indeed, not as consort, but as ruler. Bellezza would lose its independence and its traditions – all the things you fought for, for so long.'

'Are you sure you didn't turn him down for less high-minded reasons?' asked Silvia. 'Because you preferred to stay free for someone else?'

'And what if I did?' said Arianna, stung by her mother's question. 'You talk about duty and responsibility, but you married for love. You can't tell me not to do the same.'

'I am not telling you to do or not do anything,' said Silvia. 'Only to be clear about your reasons.'

There was a knock on the door and a servant ushered Gaetano in. He was grinning broadly and leading Francesca by the hand.

'Excuse me, your Grace,' he said formally. 'I did not know that you were engaged.' He glanced curiously at his interlocutor from the night before.

'I think perhaps it is you who are engaged,' said Arianna, smiling. She held out her hands to Francesca. 'And I think we shall get on much better now you are not a Bellezzan!'

'Father has given us his blessing,' said Gaetano. 'I hope you will, too.'

'Of course,' said Arianna. 'And I shall expect an invitation to the wedding.'

Georgia slept for six hours, from half-past eight in the evening to half-past two in the morning, when the alarm-clock she had stuffed under her pillow woke her with its muffled ring. She sat up, yawning, and stared at her unfamiliar room. She had dragged her chest of drawers across the door, to make up for the dangling lock, which had been smashed when Ralph broke the door down.

She took the winged horse from her pocket and settled back against the pillows; it was no trouble to fall back to sleep.

No one got up very early in the Ram the day after the race. Cesare felt he could sleep for a week after his imprisonment and escape and the wild finish to the Stellata, not to mention all the food and drink he had consumed at the celebrations. But the horses still needed to be seen to and the idea of breakfast was very appealing, even though it was long past his usual lunchtime.

He stumbled downstairs and found Teresa in the kitchen setting out bread and cheese and olives and fruit.

'Where is everyone?' he asked, taking a heavy jug of ale from her and placing it on the table.

'Your father is out in the stables,' she said, 'with Luciano and Doctor Dethridge. The twins are playing in the yard. The Bellezzans have devised an ingenious sort of cage for them and your sisters are playing in it too – though I suspect the novelty will soon wear off in their case.'

Cesare took a slice of bread and went out into the yard. There were his half-brothers and -sisters, sitting or standing in a large wooden pen with bars too close together to allow their escape. Dethridge and Luciano were feeding them sweetmeats through the bars. As Cesare looked on, Georgia came out of the stable. She had set aside the red and yellow silks of the Ram's jockey and gone back to her ordinary Remoran boys' clothes.

'Oh, you've made a playpen,' she said to no one in particular.

'Yonge Lucian tolde mee aboute them and I builded yt with him and Signor Paul,' said Dethridge, highly pleased with the result.

'They kept trying to get in the stables to see Merla,' explained Luciano. 'And Teresa was afraid they might get trampled.'

Teresa came to the back door and called them for lunch, but the children insisted on having theirs as a picnic in their pen.

'Yt is al ryghte,' said Dethridge. 'I wol watch over them.'

But in the end Teresa took a tray of food and drink out for him and herself with enough for the little ones and only Georgia and Luciano ate indoors with Cesare and Paolo.

The young people were a bit shy with one another after some of the freedoms of the night before.

'He seems to love children, the old doctor,' said Cesare.

'He never talks about his own,' said Luciano, 'but I think it was very hard for him to leave them.'

'How did you fare at home, Georgia?' asked Paolo.

Her deep sigh made them all look up.

'It wasn't too bad,' she said. 'I don't really know the

worst yet, though. I must stravagate promptly tonight and be ready to talk to my parents first thing in the morning – they let me go to bed because I was so tired but they haven't said yet what my punishment is going to be.'

'I am sorry that you are going to be punished for us,' said Paolo. 'But you said "my parents". That is the first time I have heard you refer to them both in that way.'

Georgia was surprised herself. That's true, she thought. Although Ralph had kept out of the way as much as possible when Maura was laying into her, he had been concerned and understanding. Perhaps one day she would think of him as something like a father?

There was a knock at the door and the tall figure of Rodolfo entered.

'I come with news,' he said, when he had joined them at the table. 'There is to be a wedding in the di Chimici family.'

Georgia saw that Luciano had turned white and she felt little better herself.

'Gaetano is to marry his cousin Francesca,' Rodolfo continued. 'You may remember her, Luciano. She was the candidate that the ambassador set up against Arianna at the election. Her marriage to Councillor Albani has been annulled.'

'Yes,' said Luciano, more calmly than he felt. 'She is daughter of the Prince of Bellona, isn't she?'

'Indeed,' said Rodolfo. 'The two young people have been sweethearts since they were babies. I left them telling the Duchessa all about it.'

'Arianna knows?' asked Luciano. 'And she doesn't mind?'

Rodolfo raised one eyebrow. 'You must ask her,' he said. 'We shall all be travelling back to Bellezza together in a few days.'

Luciano smiled with relief and delight. 'What are we waiting for?'

'I am sorry to say that I think we are waiting for Falco di Chimici to die,' said Rodolfo. 'Or recover.' He looked seriously at Georgia. 'This had to wait until the race was over,' he said. 'But I must ask you again to bring the boy back.'

*

Rinaldo di Chimici was visiting his brother in the Twelfth of the Goat. Alfonso, the young Duke of Volana, had been disappointed in the race. The Goat's jockey, Papavero, had got nowhere on Brunello and there hadn't even been a good fight afterwards. Alfonso had dined at the Papal palace but the air of gloom in the Twins had not made for an enjoyable occasion and the Duke was thinking of returning to his own city. Still, he, like everyone else, did not think it proper to leave Remora while Niccolò's youngest son was still in such danger.

Alfonso sighed. 'I suppose I'd better visit Uncle Niccolò at the hospital and see how the land lies,' he said. 'It's a wretched business.'

'I'll come with you,' said Rinaldo. 'I need to know what his plans are for me now that the latest attempts on Bellezza have failed. You heard that Gaetano's suit was refused? He's going to marry cousin Francesca instead.'

'Really?' said Alfonso. 'It seems only months ago

that we were all children, playing up at Santa Fina in the long summers. She was always sweet on him, even then. And Fabrizio always paired up with Caterina.'

'Perhaps they too will make a union?' said Rinaldo, pleased at the possibility of his younger sister being married to the heir to the di Chimici title and money.

Alfonso looked thoughtful too. 'That may not be such a bad idea, while Niccolò is in such an accommodating mood. Let's go and suggest it.'

*

Georgia was in as tight a corner in Talia as she had been back at home. Rodolfo had asked to speak to her alone and they were sitting in Dethridge's room. Luciano was not there to help her; she was going to have to stand up to the Bellezzan Stravagante on her own.

'Falco's going to have an operation that will help him walk again,' she said. 'He likes living with the Mulhollands too – I think they might even adopt him.'

'So everyone will be happy again?' asked Rodolfo. 'That is not the way things work, Georgia. Luciano cannot be replaced.'

'Do you think I don't know that?' asked Georgia, furiously blinking back tears. 'But people can be comforted. They've lost their son and Falco has lost his family. It feels right.'

'I do not question your feelings,' said Rodolfo, gently. 'Only your knowledge and perhaps your wisdom. Falco has not lost his family – he has abandoned them. When he dies, as he will very soon in Talia if you don't save him, you have no idea what repercussions there may be. For Talia, for the gateway, for all of us who travel between worlds. If you want me to, I will go with you.' He stopped. 'You are no longer wearing the ring he used as a talisman – where is it?'

'In the waste-disposal unit of my kitchen,' said Georgia. She was more afraid than when Duke Niccolò had questioned her or when the Fishes' jockey had rained blows on her head. Mentally she braced herself for Rodolfo's reaction. But he merely stood up and walked to the window.

He turned and faced her. He looked very tired and Georgia had a sense that he was bowed down by responsibilities.

'I take it that means you have destroyed it,' he said. 'You have defied me. But I think I understand why. You believe that the comfort given and received in one world can be balanced against the grief and loss in the other. And I hope you are right. Because you and Luciano are now both in terrible danger.'

*

Duke Niccolò seemed hardly to recognise his nephews. He was sitting as he had for nearly two weeks now, holding his son's skeletal hand.

'The physicians were wrong,' he said. 'Falco is still alive.'

'Uncle, I am so sorry,' said Alfonso, and meant it. Like all the di Chimici he had been fond of the little prince. They had all grieved two years ago at the time of the accident and now their hearts were even heavier. 'But it is good news about Gaetano,' he said.

'Good that my cousins can find happiness in our time of sorrow. And they are young and healthy and will give you grandchildren.'

The Duke was so startled that Alfonso wondered if he had been tactless. But it seemed he had started a positive train of thought in the head of the family.

'You are right,' the Duke said, 'and kind to say it. It is something to look forward to. But why should Gaetano marry so young when he has two older brothers unwed? And a sister too? They must all marry – you too, Alfonso – and Rinaldo, if you want. The di Chimici need more family members. You have a sister, do you not? My niece, what is her name – Caterina? A pretty little thing as I recall. Would you be willing for her to marry one of my sons? The Volanas are a successful branch of the family – not like the Morescos, who are going to die out.'

The Duke was rambling, his mind scheming, visualising a string of descendants and an ever-branching family tree, filled with the fruit of di Chimici loins. Alfonso was a bit taken aback but pleased to find his uncle in such a compliant mood.

'I believe that Caterina used to be rather attached to my cousin Fabrizio,' he began.

'Splendid, splendid,' said the Duke. 'I'll talk to him about her tonight. No time to waste. Do you have any matrimonial plans of your own?'

'I wondered if you had any ideas for me on that subject, Uncle,' said Alfonso. 'I should not want to make a marriage without your approval.'

'Quite right, quite right,' said the Duke, his mind clearly getting to work on the problem. 'What about old Jacopo's younger daughter Bianca? I thought the older one – what's her name – Lucia? I thought perhaps she would make a match with Carlo. I want Gaetano to have the Fortezza princedom when Jacopo dies, and those girls need good husbands.'

Alfonso nodded. He had no idea what Bianca, whom he had seen with her sister at dinner yesterday, would say to such a sudden proposal, but it seemed that there would be a rash of marriages among the di Chimici cousins this year and he was twenty-six and ready for a bride. And Bianca was certainly an attractive girl. All the female di Chimici were; only the occasional male like Gaetano or Rinaldo was less than handsome. And even Gaetano had drawn the beautiful Francesca in this sudden marriage lottery.

'What about you, Rinaldo?' said the Duke, pleased with the reception of his new plans.

'I – I have no wish to marry, Uncle,' said Rinaldo, embarrassed. 'I beg you will excuse me from these plans. I will do anything else to serve you, of course.'

'Mmm,' mused the Duke. 'Are you religious at all?'

*

After her interview with Rodolfo, Georgia felt wretched. Who was she to set her will against the best Stravagante in Talia? Small consolation that Luciano was on her side, when she knew that Paolo and Dethridge were both uncertain. She wandered out to the stable-yard, at a loose end now that the race was run and her tasks in Remora seemed to be over.

Cesare waved to her from the stable door; he had the grey cat in his arms.

'You look in need of a diversion,' he said. 'How

about a ride on Merla?'

Georgia couldn't believe her ears; ride on a winged horse? It would make any punishment she had to come in her own world endurable.

'Is it OK?' she asked. 'I mean with Paolo?'

'He suggested it,' said Cesare. 'He's gone out now to settle all his Stellata debts but he said you'd need something to lift your spirits after talking to Rodolfo.'

Georgia didn't need to be told twice. Cesare led the black horse out of the stable and the two of them groomed her out in the yard. As well as the usual combing of mane and tail and brushing of her glossy coat, they had to pay attention to her feathers. Obligingly, Merla spread each great wing in turn, letting them smooth each feather into place and gently brush off any speck of dust.

There was no question of putting a saddle on Merla and Georgia decided to ride her without even a bridle. After all, Luciano had managed without one. Georgia led her out of the stable and away from the streets until they found a big enough open space for Merla to make her take-off. Cesare went with them and gave Georgia a leg-up. She looked down on his open, cheerful face from the back of the winged horse and realised how fond she felt of him. He was a real friend, like Alice. Someone she could rely on absolutely.

'Thanks, Cesare,' she said.

'My pleasure,' he replied. 'She's hard to climb up on with her wings in the way.'

'I mean thanks for being so nice about everything, the race and all.'

Cesare shrugged. 'There'll be other races,' he said.

'And you gave me the Duchessa's silver. Now, fly!' He slapped Merla lightly on the rump.

The black mare raised her head and neighed, then stretched her neck and started her run. She gathered pace and Georgia clutched on to her mane. It was like lifting off in an aeroplane, except that you were much more intimately in contact with the process. After one last thrust off from the ground, the legs stopped moving and Merla's wings took over the work of carrying horse and rider. The ascent was rapid and once Merla had straightened out at a comfortable height for her, the wing beats were slow – just enough to carry her forwards through the blue sky above Remora.

They were flying north, away from the city, but once Georgia had adjusted her seat, she nudged Merla with her right knee and gently tugged on her mane to let her know that she wanted to change direction. The flying horse was willing; she did not want to return to the place of her imprisonment. She was enjoying flying by day, exercising her wings with the warm sun full on them.

Below them lay Remora, its many divisions and factions blurred by distance into one bustling city. Tiny citizens stood in its squares and piazzas, shading their eyes and looking up. Merla was no longer a secret; she was the city's pride and joy, although most of her glory went to the Ram. Yet even Twins' and Fishes' hearts swelled at the sight of her; they were Remorans, after all, and no city but theirs in all Talia could boast a flying horse.

They flew out towards Belle Vigne, where Georgia had ridden in the di Chimici carriage the day that the young princes had become their friends. That had been little more than a month ago and now Falco lived in another world and Gaetano was about to be married. Georgia, Cesare and Luciano had all ridden the flying horse and the Ram had won the Stellata. But what would happen to them all next?

Georgia felt that her own adventures in Remora were coming to an end. She would be leaving for France in a week, if her parents still wanted to take her. And the Bellezzans would probably be gone before then. It was too hard to think about.

For now all she wanted to do was to fly for ever, her face on Merla's warm neck and the sound of her black wings beating slowly, regularly, through the clear air.

Falco lay awake in Luciano's old room. The scene at Georgia's house had been terrible, but at least she was safely back in her body. Still, he missed her presence in his room and he couldn't sleep for wondering what had happened to her in Talia. She said she had won the Stellata, but that seemed impossible. Falco knew all about the sums of money that his father and uncle were willing to spend on securing a victory for the Twins or the Lady.

He wondered if Georgia had stravagated back there now and felt very cut off from his old life. How was Gaetano's courtship of the Duchessa going? What was his father doing? He would have no answer to these questions until he could speak to Georgia again. And until he had answers he would be unable to sleep.

Georgia wheeled back over the city as the light was beginning to fail. As Merla flew slowly home, a line of poetry that Maura was fond of came into Georgia's mind: 'You cannot cage the minute within its nets of gold'. It's true, she thought, and yet if she had had a gold net, this was the moment she would want to keep for ever.

Slowly, Merla began to descend and the glorious flight was over. But ever afterwards, whenever life was difficult for Georgia, she had only to close her eyes and she was back aloft on the flying horse again, wheeling over the City of Stars, surrounded by its saffron meadows of purple and gold.

After Georgia had dismounted, Merla shook her wings and a black feather drifted on to the paving stones. Georgia picked it up and put it in her pocket, with the Etruscan horse. It was probably wrong, but she wasn't going to leave it in Remora.

Luciano was waiting for her as she led Merla back to the stables. He waited until the winged horse had been rubbed down and fed and then asked Georgia to come for a walk with him.

'OK,' she said, 'but I can't be long. I have to be back on time today.'

They went, as often before, to the Campo. Cesare's red and yellow neck-cloth still fluttered from the central column, but Remorans and tourists now strolled where the race had been held less than a day before. Many of them recognised Georgia and saluted her with shouts and applause.

'You're a local hero,' said Luciano, smiling at her.

'It could go to my head,' she said. 'I'll expect the same treatment when I walk through the school gates next term.'

'And I'll be back in Bellezza, learning to be a better Stravagante,' said Luciano.

'Beats GCSE,' said Georgia.

'I'll miss you,' said Luciano, unexpectedly.

'Really?' said Georgia, thinking, please God, let me not blush or cry.

'It's helped meeting someone from my old world again,' he said. 'At first it was quite painful, but now I want to know everything that's going on, with Falco and my parents.'

'You said you'd been back a few times,' she said. 'Can't you go and see for yourself?'

'Yes, but it's very hard,' said Luciano quietly. 'I don't feel really substantial there now. And it's so weird, being able to see my parents but not being able to live with them. Knowing they can see me but not being able to explain to them what really happened to me.'

'Perhaps it will become easier the more often you do it,' said Georgia. 'And perhaps I could see you there too?'

'I'd like that,' said Luciano, taking her hand. 'I can't explain what I mean very well, but I feel you're special to me, a link with my other life that no one else here can ever be, even Doctor Dethridge. The world he left to come here is nothing like the one I was taken from.'

It's good to be special for something, thought Georgia, even though it's not the right thing.

'I must be going back,' she said. 'I have to stravagate.'

'Then I'll say goodbye here,' said Luciano, 'if you don't mind. I think I'll call at the palace and see Arianna.'

'Is it safe?' asked Georgia anxiously. 'What if the Duke is there?'

'I can't live my life in fear of the Duke,' said Luciano and he leaned forward to hug her, brushing her cheek lightly with a kiss.

And then he was gone, walking lightly across the Campo.

Chapter 25

The Shadow Falls

Niccolò sat in the armchair, with Falco on his lap, a mere husk of his old self. They were alone; all the other family members were back at the palace talking to the Pope about weddings. The last light of evening streamed through the window, sending motes of dust dancing in its shafts.

'It is time,' said the Duke. And, very gently, he put a fold of his cloak over the boy's face and pressed.

Falco felt a sudden jolt through his body. It was like a bolt of lightning and it brought him to his feet. His body felt heavy, solid in a new way. He had never felt particularly light in Georgia's world, but now he knew he had not been fully present in it until this moment.

'It has happened,' he said, marvelling. 'My old body has died.'

He limped over to the window and pulled back the curtain. The sun was rising over Islington and its first rays shone into the room. Falco stood with his back to it and saw his shadow stretching black across the bed.

'I'm here now for good,' he said, and felt more lonely than he ever had in his life.

*

Georgia was up early, ready to take whatever the day would bring. And what it brought first was Russell. He pushed his way into her room, shouldering the chest of drawers aside as if it had been from a doll's house.

'Oh, whoops,' he said. 'Was that supposed to keep me out?'

'What do you want, Russell?' Georgia asked wearily.

'I want to know where you were last night,' he said conversationally, sitting on her bed. 'And don't give me all that guff about promises. I bet you were somewhere with that little cripple.'

'I wasn't,' said Georgia truthfully. She felt strangely calm even though her old tormentor had invaded her private space.

Russell was provoked by her cool manner. He would have to try harder for a response.

'Well you were with some bloke, I bet. And I bet it was a creep of some kind.'

'Yes,' said Georgia. 'I expect you'd think so. I was

with two "blokes", as a matter of fact, both considered rather good-looking if the number of other girls around them was anything to go by.'

Russell's eyes bulged out of his head.

'And I drank a lot of red wine and danced a lot too,' she continued, thinking of her last night in Remora. 'And everyone drank toasts to me and I was given a king's ransom in silver.'

'Oh, I get it,' said Russell. 'It's another of your fantasies, like being popular at school or having a boyfriend.' He raised his voice, seriously annoyed by her casual tone. 'But that's only ever going to be a fantasy, isn't it? You're pathetic and ugly. No one likes you and no one ever will, except for no-hopers like Alice and creepy little spastics like Nickel-arse!'

'Russell!' cried Maura and Ralph in unison from the doorway.

Georgia didn't have to say a thing. Russell's voice had risen so much in the course of what was in fact quite a routine display of Georgia-bashing, provoked by her lack of reaction, that their parents had overheard his last speech. They looked so shocked, peering into the room over the chest of drawers that Georgia felt almost sorry for them. She had tried and tried to tell them what Russell was like to her, but now that they had heard it for themselves, she really didn't care.

She shrugged, turning her hands up. Russell turned to her, his face red with fury. 'I'll get you for this,' he whispered.

'Get me for what?' said Georgia, distinctly. 'You're the one who dropped yourself right in it. I was just here, the way I always have been.'

Niccolò removed the cloak from Falco's face. The long, agonising wait for Falco's death was over. His son was at peace now and the Duke could bury him in splendour. He would take the body back to Giglia and inter it in the di Chimici family vault and get that woman, what was her name – Miele? – to sculpt a memorial for him. Or perhaps he'd have a new chapel specially built. Such thoughts were easier to bear than Falco's slow descent into death.

He looked down at his precious boy, then threw back his head and howled. His cries brought Beatrice running. She had been on her way back to relieve her father at his long vigil. The terrible sounds of his keening told her what had happened.

But when she entered the room, she gasped with shock. Niccolò's hair was the first thing she noticed. Only the day before it had still been mainly black, touched here and there with grey. Now it was pure white. He had aged ten years in a day. And after that shock, she saw something that made her cross herself repeatedly.

The shadow of the Duke's bulky form was cast on the tiled floor by the evening light. Falco's body was lying across his lap like the dead Christ in the cathedral in Giglia ... but of its shadow there was no sign.

When the Duke saw what she was looking at, he fell silent. He stood, holding the little weight of Falco's corpse in his arms. He walked slowly over to the bed and rested it there. But the shadow-duke had empty arms and laid down a burden of nothing.

Niccolò's eyes met Beatrice's and now she made the Hand of Fortune, as well as the sign of the cross.

*

Luciano was in Rodolfo's room at the palace with his master and Arianna. All three of them were jumpy. Rodolfo and his apprentice had felt a wrenching of the ground beneath them, as if the city had been torn by an earthquake.

'What is it?' asked Arianna, who had felt nothing.

Rodolfo had gone over to his mirrors and re-focused them on different places. Luciano came to sit next to Arianna. Tentatively, he put his arm round her. 'It will be all right,' he said, offering her a reassurance he didn't feel. She leaned against him, suddenly weary.

'I want to go home,' she said quietly. 'Let's go back to Bellezza.'

'I think that would be a good idea,' said Rodolfo.

And then a wild stranger broke into the room unannounced. It took a little while for them to realise it was the Duke. His hair had gone completely white and his eyes were red with lack of sleep.

'They told me I would find you here,' he said to Luciano. 'You who once had no shadow! Now tell me what you did to my boy!'

'Is he worse, your Grace?' asked Arianna, startled.

'He is dead,' said the Duke. 'Dead, and yet his dead body casts no shadow. Who is going to explain it to me? This old sorcerer or his follower in evil?'

Niccolò suddenly caught sight of something in one of Rodolfo's mirrors. To his horror, Luciano saw his old bedroom, with Falco sitting on the bed, his head in his hands. The early morning sun painted a clear shadow on the bedspread behind him.

The sight was too much for the Duke. His reason and his health were too precarious to bear it. He fell down on the floor in a swoon. Rodolfo went to him and pressed his fingers on Niccolò's eyes, murmuring something under his breath.

'He will sleep for hours now and will not remember this,' he said. 'Still, we should leave before he awakes.'

Hastily Rodolfo dismantled the arrangement of mirrors and stowed it in his valise while Arianna called for servants. She explained that the Duke had been overcome by grief while telling them of his son's death and had fainted. The servants carried him to his room and took the news to the Pope.

Within minutes the bell of the palazzo's campanile started to toll and the city went into mourning.

As soon as Falco arrived in Georgia's house, she knew what had happened. The Mulhollands had brought him, so they couldn't talk about it straightaway, but she saw the shadow at his feet and the light in his eyes.

'How are you?' was all she could say, in conventional greeting, but she put as much meaning into it as she could.

'All right,' he said. And meant it.

The grown-ups were having huddled, whispered conversations. Russell had gone out to see his friends; he was supposed to leave for Greece the next day and both Ralph and Maura wanted him out of the house. The atmosphere had changed completely since the evening before when the same people had gathered to grill Georgia. Now it was Russell who was the subject of their concern and Georgia's transgressions took a back seat.

'Georgia,' said Ralph suddenly. 'Would you mind making coffee for everyone?' She knew they wanted to talk on their own.

'Nicholas can keep you company,' said Vicky.

So the two of them got what they wanted – time alone together. No cup of coffee had ever taken so long to make. Georgia had to tell Falco all about the race, Cesare and Merla and about the banquet in the Ram. And then about Gaetano and Francesca. And then Falco wanted to tell her about the moment when he had felt his shadow return.

'What does that mean for Luciano, I wonder,' said Georgia. 'Your father threatened him and me if anything happened to you.'

'I can't ever go back now, can I?' asked Falco.

'Not without a talisman from Talia,' said Georgia.

He looked so woebegone that she drew the black feather from her pocket and gave it to him.

'Here,' she said. 'I'm a Stravagante and I give you this talisman. I'm sure it will take you back one day.'

Several carriages were drawn up in the Ram while their occupants said their goodbyes. Rodolfo was going to travel back to Bellezza with Silvia, giving his place in Arianna's carriage up to Luciano. But

Dethridge was not to be alone in his. Francesca was coming back to Bellezza with him, to collect her belongings from old Albani's house. Gaetano had come down to the stables to bid her farewell.

And he was charged with messages for his father about the Bellezzans' hasty departure. He would do what he could to soften Niccolò's suspicion and rage towards the Stravaganti but it was a dark cloud on all their horizons.

Paolo and Teresa were saying goodbye to their guests. Luciano and Cesare and Gaetano clasped arms, the last left there of the five who had made their pact on the way to Belle Vigne. They could still hear Falco's passing bell tolling; Luciano wondered if he would ever be able to get the sound out of his ears.

'Say goodbye to my substitute jockey for me when he next comes back,' said the young Duchessa to Cesare. 'But I trust I'll see you riding for the Ram next year.'

'Indeed, your Grace,' said Cesare, who had never got over his awe of this beautiful lady.

'And be sure to tell him to look after my brother,' added Gaetano in a whisper. Then, out loud, to the Bellezzan party, 'And look after Francesca for me in your city of masks. I shall be counting the hours until she joins me in Giglia.'

'There,' said Arianna. 'You see, you can be romantic when you try. Of course I shall look after her.'

The three Stravaganti who were leaving embraced Paolo. Each took strength from the others and gave it back in equal measure. And then the carriages rolled out towards the Gate of the Sun. And on their way they overtook a party of brightly clad and be-ribboned people carrying musical instruments.

'Stop!' Arianna cried to her coachman. 'Won't you ride with us?' she asked Raffaella. 'There is room on top and in the fourth carriage if you don't mind travelling with my trunks.'

'Thank you, your Grace,' said Aurelio, answering for them both, 'but for us the walking is part of a long journey. I'm sure we shall meet again, in the City of Flowers if not in your own dukedom.'

'I hope so,' said Arianna. 'I should like to hear the music of the Manoush again.'

Georgia's punishment was to be banned from her riding lessons for a term. It was hard but she felt she could cope. She had ridden so much that summer and she was unlikely to forget all she had learned in Remora. And, in a way, any horse would have been such a come-down after Merla, that she didn't mind deferring the time when she would have to make that comparison.

And there were compensations. She was still to go to France and Russell would be leaving for Greece in the morning as planned. Ralph and Maura had at last taken her problems with Russell seriously.

'I see now why you wanted the lock on your door,' said Maura sadly as Ralph fixed a new one on for Georgia. 'And I'm sorry I didn't listen when you tried to tell me about Russell before.'

'I'm so gutted that any son of mine should behave like that,' said Ralph.

'He's always resented me,' said Georgia. 'I think he was just taking it out on me because he was so jealous when you married Mum.'

'Well, it's going to stop now,' said Ralph. 'Maura and I think he needs counselling.'

'Has he agreed to that?' asked Georgia.

Ralph and Maura exchanged looks.

'Not exactly,' said Ralph. 'But he's only allowed on this holiday on condition that he sees someone when he gets back.'

It was such a relief to be able to talk about it but Georgia knew that Russell had already lost his power over her. She recalled Paolo's words. 'He will not always be there. Remember that nothing lasts for ever, the bad things as well as the good.'

She didn't speak to Russell again before he left. She had decided not to stravagate that night. Perhaps I am being cowardly, she thought, but I don't want to face the Duke until I've caught up on lost sleep.

And by the next night, it was too late. Russell had gone and so had the Etruscan horse. And this time she thought it was probably for good.

One of the first to pay his respects at the Papal palace, after the family, was Enrico the spy. He was wearing a black armband.

He was told that the Duke was sleeping but the Pope would see him. Enrico smoothed his hair and went in to see the prelate.

'Holiness,' he said, prostrating himself in front of Ferdinando di Chimici and kissing his ring.

'Ah,' said the Pope, motioning him to rise. 'You have heard of our great sorrow?'

'Indeed, indeed,' said Enrico. 'Terrible, terrible.' And he meant it.

'It is a small loss to set beside the death of our youngest prince,' said the Pope, 'but I was disappointed that no champion of our family won the Stellata. It was very embarrassing for my brother and myself.'

'I regret that, Holiness,' said Enrico. 'But what can one man do against the force of destiny? You must agree that the goddess was against us.'

'I shall agree no such impious thing, you insolent man!' said the Pope, flushed. 'As leader of the church, I do not believe in any goddess!'

'A figure of speech, merely, Holiness,' Enrico recovered himself smoothly, making the Hand of Fortune and disguising it as a scratch and a cough. The Pope flinched.

'What I meant to say,' continued the spy, 'is that some things are just not meant to be – like the survival of the young prince. I did everything I could to fix the race, but Remorans are superstitious and once they saw the winged beauty, all the jockeys went to pieces – except that one from the Ram.'

'I know who won,' said the Pope peevishly. 'But I agree the odds were stacked against us from the moment that horse was born in Remora. But the question arises of what to do with you now that the race is over. I suggest that you accompany my brother the Duke back to Giglia, as soon as he is fit enough to travel with the body of his son. I'm sure he'll find something for you to do.'

Falco had an appointment for his operation and he couldn't wait to tell Georgia. He phoned but found her distraught.

'What do you mean, gone?' he asked.

'Russell's gone to Greece till the end of the holidays and I think he's taken the talisman with him – or broken it beyond repair. He said he'd get me and this is how he's done it.'

'I'm really sorry,' said Falco. 'Do you think you could use my feather? I'll give it to you if you want.'

There was a long silence at the other end of the phone.

'No, I don't think so,' said Georgia at last. 'It wasn't brought for me. It probably wouldn't work.'

Duke Niccolò slept for twelve hours and awoke with renewed energy. He sent for his body-servant to shave him and trim his newly white hair and then ate a solid breakfast, to the relief of his remaining children. The Duke wanted to put grief behind him and get back to his normal machinations. Of the day before, his recollections were vague. Deep in his mind somewhere he knew that the story of Falco's death was not quite as he gave it out, but he buried that thought as deep as he would his child.

But he could not entirely forget what had happened afterwards. There was something uncanny about Falco's leaving the world and it was connected with the Stravaganti, even though Niccolò could no longer remember what he had seen in Rodolfo's mirrors. He was determined to redouble his efforts against them and to find out exactly what it was that they could do.

To this end, he sent for all his remaining sons, to have a family council. Gaetano was first to arrive and the news he brought his father was unwelcome.

'Gone? The Bellezzans have gone?' said Niccolò uncomprehendingly. 'Without even the pretence of politeness or waiting for my son's funeral?'

'The Duchessa was most insistent that I should make her deepest apologies, Father,' said Gaetano. 'And we didn't want to wake you when you were sleeping properly for the first time in days. But yesterday was always the appointed time for her departure and she was anxious at having left the affairs of her city for so long. It has been without her and the Regent for two weeks and you know how vulnerable a dukedom can be when its ruler is away.'

'I myself have been away from Giglia for more than twice that long,' said the Duke contemptuously.

'But no one would dare move against you, Father,' said Gaetano. 'The Duchessa has borne her title for only a year; she is bound to feel at risk.'

'It is time we were all back in our own cities,' said Niccolò. 'We have important matters to plan – a funeral, weddings and all out war on the Stravaganti.'

'Why?' said Gaetano bravely. 'Because we have lost Falco? That was hardly their fault.'

Niccolò looked at him uncomprehendingly.

'Please, Father,' he said gently. 'Falco is at rest now. Can't we forget about vendettas and mourn him in peace?'

'You don't understand,' said Niccolò. 'The Stravaganti are behind it, at least Rodolfo is. I saw something ... something unnatural. There is witchcraft at work here and I intend to get to the bottom of it.'

Mr Goldsmith was taking a little holiday. He had put the CLOSED sign up in his shop and gone to visit Georgia at her house. Maura was there too and was surprised to see him at the door. But she made tea for them all and sat to drink it with them.

'I'm going away for a few weeks,' he said. 'I just wanted to drop by and tell you. My nephew rang last night and offered to have me for a holiday with him and his family in the Norfolk Broads.'

Georgia was glad. Mr Goldsmith had never talked about his family before and she had thought he might be rather lonely.

'I shouldn't want you, or Nicholas, to come to the shop and find me closed,' he continued. 'I don't often leave it in the summer, but this was too good an opportunity to give up.'

'Does your nephew live in Norfolk?' asked Maura.

'No, he lives in Cambridge,' said Mr Goldsmith. 'That's where my family was from. My wife too.'

'I didn't know you were married,' said Georgia.

'I lost her years ago,' said Mr Goldsmith. 'Before we had children. But I have three great-nephews and I shall enjoy sailing with them.'

After he had gone, Maura apologised to Georgia.

'I was wrong about Mr Goldsmith,' she said. 'He seems a nice old chap. It was Russell who was warped.'

Georgia gave her a hug.

'It doesn't matter now,' she said.

Enrico was up at the palace in Santa Fina collecting his money, when he saw the Duke. Niccolò di Chimici was wandering through the rooms of the great house as if searching for something.

'My Lord,' said Enrico, hesitantly.

The Duke wheeled, startled, then relaxed.

'Ah, the spy,' he said. 'There is nothing to spy on here – only an empty palace and an old man.'

'Is there anything I can do for you, your Grace?' Enrico asked. 'I was sorry to hear about the prince.'

Duke Niccolò thought for a few moments.

'Tell me,' he said. 'If you were burying your favourite child, what would you put in his coffin with him?'

Enrico had no children and no prospect of any now that his Giuliana had disappeared. But he had a good imagination.

'Some childhood remembrance, my Lord? A favourite plaything? Some ornament or picture?'

'A picture? Yes, you are right.'

The Duke took from inside his shirt a miniature. 'I have carried this with me since my wife, Benedetta, died. She should go and watch over our child in his grave. All that is finished for me now.'

Georgia was at the Mulhollands', saying goodbye

before she went to France.

'Do you think you'll ever go back to Remora?' Falco asked.

'I hope so,' said Georgia, with a deep sigh. 'It's such a fantastic place and I'll miss Cesare and his family.'

'Yet I think that the person you will miss most is not to be found in that city,' said Falco quietly.

Georgia said nothing; it seemed as if she had been less good at disguising her feelings in Talia than she was in her own world.

'Were you surprised that the Duchessa refused my brother?' he persisted.

'Not really,' said Georgia. 'He was a di Chimici, after all, even if a very nice one.'

'What about me?' asked Falco. 'Am I a nice one?'

'You aren't a di Chimici at all any more, remember?' said Georgia. 'You're a Duke, now, and maybe one day a Mulholland.'

'But you do think I'm nice?'

'Don't be daft!' said Georgia. What was the matter with everyone all of a sudden? It seemed as if, ever since she had won the Stellata, she was irresistible in both worlds. 'Of course I do,' she added, seeing that Falco looked downcast.

'I can't explain exactly what I mean,' she said, suddenly remembering. 'But you'll always be special to me because you're a link with my life in another world that no one else knows about.'

Then she leaned forward to give him a hug and brush his cheek with a kiss.

Epilogue: *The Thirteenth Rider*

Remora, September 1578

The Campo delle Stelle was being turned into a racetrack for the second time that summer. It happened occasionally that there was an extra race – a Stellata Straordinaria – to commemorate some important public occasion. The last one had been twenty years ago, when Ferdinando di Chimici became Pope and was given the revived title of Prince of Remora.

Now the Pope's brother Niccolò had decided that there should be a Straordinaria to celebrate the short life of the youngest di Chimici prince. There was much bustle in the city, to prepare for another race so soon after the last one. A new track had to be laid, officials appointed, parade clothes cleaned and more flag manoeuvres practised. The drums of the last race celebrations had scarcely ceased before they started again and Remora once again lived its life against the background of their perpetual beat.

It was even more important that the Lady, or at

least the Twins, should win this race – the Stellata di Falco – and a larger than usual prize was to be awarded to the winning jockey.

Cesare couldn't believe his luck – he was going to get another chance to ride Arcangelo in the race without having to wait a year. And this time he had no intention of getting kidnapped. Life had been a bit flat in the month since the Bellezzans had left and the di Chimici returned to Giglia. He had felt sad about the death of Falco because, although Cesare knew the boy was alive in another world, it was one he didn't expect ever to visit, so he was unlikely to see him again. And Cesare had become fond of the young prince. As for Georgia: she had not been back to see them since the day after the race.

Cesare wondered if she would be there for the Straordinaria; she must have come back from her holiday by now.

London, September 2004

Georgia had in fact been back for a year. A lot had happened in that time, but there had been no more trips to Talia because the talisman had gone. When Russell had returned from Greece, he had been asked about it, but this time he didn't budge. He denied that he had ever taken the winged horse.

He had gone to his counselling sessions, much to Georgia's surprise, and her life at home had greatly improved, even though it wasn't perfect. Ralph and Maura, who went with Russell to some of the family therapy sessions, were clearly shocked by the extent of his problems.

He was never going to like Georgia, nor she him, but he stopped persecuting her. They maintained a kind of cold war and Ralph and Maura were now so vigilant that it never escalated further.

It was ironic really. Now that Russell had completely lost the power to hurt or scare her there was no more bullying for her to handle. And her own life was terribly busy. It was her GCSE exam year and she had masses of homework and coursework to do.

Her friendship with Alice grew; she went down to Devon with her on several weekends, which was especially welcome in that first term, when she was missing Remora and banned from Jean's stable.

In the spring term, Georgia had her first boyfriend, Dan, from the year above. It lasted eight weeks, fizzling out conveniently in time for Georgia to concentrate on her exams. The results had come three weeks ago and she had done well enough to be taken out to dinner by Ralph and Maura and bought a digital camera.

But the best present was hearing that Russell was moving out. His A-level results had been good enough to secure his place in Computer Sciences at Sussex. He didn't want to celebrate with family but got spectacularly drunk with his best friends and had a hangover that lasted two days. His reward was the deposit on a rented house in Brighton and he was going to move out of the Islington house before the beginning of term. 'Nothing lasts for ever,' thought Georgia delightedly.

Georgia had spent most of the summer in Devon

with Alice, riding and meeting some new local friends. One of them was a boy called Adam, with dark eyes and hair, and she was hopeful that future weekends might lead to getting to know him better.

Georgia was making more friends at school now too. Winning the Stellata had changed her more than she ever supposed it would. She had a new confidence that came from a deep inner satisfaction at having been good at something, which altered her attitude and even her looks. She stopped pushing people away when they made friendly overtures and found that more of them than she would have guessed seemed willing to like her. And once Russell stopped undermining her at home, she felt her personality expand into the space he left around her.

Georgia hadn't replaced her eyebrow ring but she now had a tattoo of a flying horse on her shoulder and she had let her hair grow and dyed it dark red with white and black streaks in front. And she had acquired breasts – not spectacular Page Three ones, but they were pleasingly noticeable and she took to wearing tight, short T-shirts instead of baggy sweaters. No one would mistake her for a boy now in either world.

But, if Georgia's life had changed since her last visit to Remora, Falco's had been transformed. He had leapt up the waiting list for surgery because of his age and the severity of his condition and had been given a total hip replacement before the first Christmas in his new world.

There followed months of treatment, physiotherapy and learning to walk without crutches. By February he could walk unaided but still had a limp. By May, after months of work in the gym and learning to swim, the limp had gone and he was two inches taller than when he had stravagated nine months earlier.

Falco was now a Year 9 pupil at Barnsbury Comprehensive and surprisingly popular. Girls admired his exotic good looks and boys approved of his strenuous training regimen. And it didn't do his image any harm that his best friend was a girl in Year 11 widely regarded as a bit of a hard nut.

It was the night before the Stellata di Falco and again the Twelfths of Remora were ablaze with light. The city had always been good at recovering from one race and preparing for the next – there was a local saying 'The Stellata is run all year round' – but this year they were enjoying the bonus of a second chance to win. A Stellata banner had been commissioned in Giglia and hastily executed, with a small portrait of Falco on horseback in the bottom right-hand corner.

Cesare didn't expect for a moment that the Ram would be allowed to win but he enjoyed being guest of honour at the banquet in his Twelfth the night before, being given the helmet by the priest and getting up to make his first speech.

'Rams!' he said, addressing the diners in a sea of red and yellow tablecloths and banners. 'I am honoured to be your chosen jockey. I was unavoidably prevented from taking part in the last Stellata, but we all remember what happened then, don't we?'

A roar of approval from the Twelvers.

'So, although he cannot be with us tonight, I ask

you to drink the health of the Ram's last champion –
Giorgio Gredi!'

And 'Giorgio Gredi!' rang round the square.

Georgia had been feeling peculiar all day. She hadn't
yet properly settled in to her new routine as a member
of the Lower Sixth. She had a new form teacher and
the luxury of only five subjects; she could use the
Sixth Form Common Room – a space with armchairs
usually bagged by the Upper Sixth and a kitchen in
which to make instant coffee – and she had free
periods when she could sit and study in the Resources
room or even, when the weather was fine, on the grass
outside.

And it was fine today, just like high summer, though
it would be cold in the evening. Georgia had a free
period just before lunch and sat outside with Alice,
reading *The Handmaid's Tale*, which was one of their
set books for English literature.

'Imagine a world where ordinary people couldn't
have children,' said Alice.

'Good thing, if they turned out like Russell,' said
Georgia.

'Oh yeah, he's moving out today, isn't he?' said
Alice. 'Have you said your fond farewells?'

Georgia snorted. 'Good riddance!' she said and
wondered if that was why she had been feeling odd.
'Happiest day of my life.'

But it wasn't. The happiest day of her life had been
when she had won the Stellata and been kissed by
Luciano, but she could never tell Alice or anyone else

about that and it made her sad. And she was restless. When the fifteenth of August had come round again this year, it had been agonising imagining what was going on in Remora. She and Falco, Nicholas as she had to call him now, had spent the day together talking about the race and wondering what horses and jockeys would be taking part and whether the di Chimici would win this year.

Then there had been the anniversary of Nicholas's 'translation' and he had been depressed and homesick. They often talked about his trying to use the feather talisman to see if he could stravagate back to Talia on a visit, as Luciano had in the other direction, but Falco didn't want to go without Georgia and her talisman had vanished.

Georgia sighed. She had hoped that maybe during the course of a whole year she might have seen Luciano again, that he might have made one of his difficult stravagations to London, to see his family. She had kept up her violin lessons – was going to take Grade Seven in fact – and of course she was often at the Mulhollands' house visiting Nicholas. But of Luciano there had been no sign.

Dan had been all very well and Adam was nice, but still she longed for a glimpse of Luciano.

'A penny for them,' said Alice. 'That was a deep sigh.'

'Did you ever hear about that boy who died in the year above us two years ago?' Georgia suddenly asked. She had never talked about him to Alice before.

'You mean the one with the black curls who was supposed to be such a dish? Most of our year had a crush on him, didn't they? What about him?'

'Nothing,' said Georgia. 'I used to see him at orchestra. I really liked him.'

'Oh,' said Alice surprised. 'You never said.'

'Not much point was there?' said Georgia. 'Nothing to be done about it. I'm never going to see him again.' And she realised it was true. She was going to have to mourn Lucien all over again.

Alice looked really concerned. But at that moment the bell rang for lunch and their chance to talk was over. Students from all years streamed out into the sunshine, glad to catch a last fragment of summer.

'Does your friend Nicholas look anything like him?' asked Alice unexpectedly. A group of Year 9s was spilling out into the yard. A willowy figure, with curly hair, detached himself from the group and strolled over to where they were sitting on the grassy bank.

Georgia shielded her eyes against the sun and looked up at Nicholas; it was good to see his shadow stretched out behind him on the asphalt.

Luciano was working with Rodolfo and Dethridge in his master's laboratory in Bellezza. Ever since their return from Remora, the Stravaganti had been worried about the consequences of Falco's death. First because of fear of reprisals against them by the Duke. But also because Rodolfo had been convinced that there had been a shift in the gateway that allowed them access to the other world.

After William Dethridge's translation, the world that Luciano had come from had moved much further on in time than sixteenth-century Talia, but the difference had slowed by the time of Luciano's first visit. The gateway had stayed stable for months and then time slewed again when Luciano became stranded in Talia. It was only by a few weeks and the efforts of all three Stravaganti working together had stabilised it again, clawing back those weeks a day at a time, until the dates in the two worlds matched again even though still separated by over four centuries.

But now, with the death of Falco, there had been another lurch in time in the other world. And they were still trying to work out by how much it was ahead of them. Rodolfo kept a mirror trained on Luciano's old bedroom as he had done on the day of Falco's death, when the Duke had seemed to lose his mind. But he discouraged Luciano from looking in it.

The two older Stravaganti had watched while the Talian boy lived a life in sudden changing pictures. If they had ever seen a film in which time was supposed to pass or watched a video on fast forward, they might have compared what they saw to that. As it was they noted Falco's absence and his return with his leg heavily plastered. They saw him gradually grow stronger and do exercises and then one day the plaster was gone and he walked with only one crutch.

They tried to judge the passing seasons by the quality of the light through his window, but sometimes they needed Luciano to interpret what they saw.

'Whatte is thatte scarlet hose with packages sticking oute of yt?' Dethridge asked him one day.

'A Christmas stocking,' said Luciano, feeling homesick. They didn't have them in Bellezza and it was still the end of August in Talia.

They tracked Falco through the months of his convalescence and recuperation, the boy unaware that he was watched by old friends. They saw him grow stronger and taller and sometimes they saw Georgia sitting on the bed beside him. They always called Luciano when that happened and he was glad to see her. There was no sound to be heard through the mirror that linked Talia to the other world but he liked to think that sometimes Georgia and Falco were speaking about him.

By the time that Rodolfo heard of the Stellata Straordinaria, through the mirror he had trained on Remora, the other world seemed to have slowed again. He estimated that a year had passed, going by the physical changes in both Georgia and Falco.

'Shall we go back to Remora for Falco's race?' asked Luciano.

'No,' said Rodolfo. 'It's not necessary; Arianna won't be going and there's no need to expose you to meeting the Duke. The di Chimici will all be there, without doubt.'

*

The di Chimici clan were all mustered in the square outside the cathedral, taking their pre-race dinner in the Twins. Their own cities' Twelfths were being neglected in favour of family unity. Duke Niccolò sitting next to his brother the Pope looked out over all his remaining sons and his daughter and his many nieces and nephews.

His plans for their inter-marriage had been well received and he looked forward to a new generation of di Chimici, to a future when his descendants ruled every city-state in Talia, as Prince or Duke. He closed his mind to the thought of the troublesome young Duchessa of Bellezza. He would find a way of dealing with her; it was just a matter of time.

'Can I come round and see you after school?' asked Nicholas. 'I want to talk to you about something.'

'OK,' said Georgia. 'See you then.'

She remained jumpy all day and it was a relief to get home. The house was empty with a new emptiness that shouted ABSENCE OF RUSSELL! Georgia went up to her room and saw that Russell's door was standing open. She had never seen it like that unless he had been standing in the doorway taunting her.

She pushed the door wider and went in. His bed, chest of drawers and desk were all still there. But his stereo, computer and TV had all gone to Sussex with him and the bed was stripped. And there, in the middle of the bare, ticked mattress, was the winged horse.

No message, no note, just the horse and it was undamaged. Russell must have known she would go into his room to revel in his absence and he must have gone back in to place the talisman there after Ralph and Maura had been in and out with boxes and cases for the last time.

Gingerly, Georgia picked it up. It felt just as it always had, smooth and warm, its wings vulnerable, the fine lines of the last mend just visible at their base. The doorbell rang.

Nicholas stood on the doorstep and Georgia realised with a shock that he was now as tall as her.

'How are you?' he said. 'I've been feeling so peculiar all day. I think it's something to do with Remora so I wondered if you felt it too.'

And then he saw what she held in her hand.

The morning of the Stellata di Falco dawned fine and clear. Cesare went through all the rituals he had missed a month before: the jockeys' Mass in the cathedral, the last morning heat, the registering, and then went back to the Ram for a light lunch before the afternoon's demands.

He went out to the stables to calm his nerves and jumped out of his skin. There, in the shadows, stood a slender, tiger-haired girl, wearing a skimpy top and baggy pantaloons that struck a chord of memory.

'Georgia?' he asked wonderingly.

'Cesare!' she cried, giving him a big hug. She smelled lovely. 'You'd better find me something to wear – my old boy's clothes aren't here any more.'

'I don't think boy's clothes would suit you now,' said Cesare, admiring her new figure. Georgia blushed a bit but punched him on the arm.

'Wait till you see who's come with me,' she said, grinning. It felt wonderful to be back in Remora. 'It took us ages to get to sleep – we were so excited about coming back.'

Behind her, a slender boy with black curly hair, wearing the loose outlandish clothes of the other world, stepped forward into the light. Cesare didn't recognise him until Falco greeted him by name.

And then the Remoran made the Hand of Fortune. For this was Falco, an older, taller Falco, walking normally without sticks. The other world must be magical indeed.

'I'm back,' he said. 'Tell me what's been going on this last year.'

'Year?' said Cesare. 'It's only a month since you left. I can't believe how you've changed! And that you came back today of all days.'

'Why?' asked Georgia. 'What's special about today?'

'There's going to be a special Stellata,' explained Cesare. 'And I'm riding Arcangelo for the Ram. It's in Falco's honour.'

'Brilliant!' said Falco.

'We'll come and watch you,' said Georgia. 'Only we need clothes.'

Cesare raced into the house to tell Paolo and Teresa the news.

*

In honour of the dead Falco, the Lady's float was draped in black along with the purple and green of the Twelfth. It was pulled by black horses with silver harness and sable plumes. It carried an empty casket with the crest of the Giglian di Chimici – the lily and the perfume bottle – and a portrait painted by a Giglian master. A small orchestra of musicians on the float played a dirge.

The ensigns had black ribbons tied at the top of their flags and all the parade members of the Lady wore black under their green and purple sashes. As the Lady's part of the procession passed each stand, the spectators removed their hats and made the sign of the cross. Weeping was heard, even in the Scales; it was a sad story even if it happened to your enemy.

The great bell of the Papal palace, which always rang its single note throughout the afternoon of the Stellata, now recalled the day it had tolled for Falco a month ago. But however sombre the parade, there was still the excitement of the race to come.

Georgia sat in the Ram's stand with Teresa and the children. She was wearing a red dress of Teresa's and a red and yellow sash of their Twelfth. The dress and her hair attracted admiring glances around her and she felt quite different from the jockey who had won the Stellata over a year ago.

Only it wasn't a year ago here. It was hard to wrench her mind round the thought that she had been away hardly long enough to be missed. For one of those weeks the Montalbani had assumed her to be away in France and, though they had wondered a little about her absence since, they had not really begun to be concerned.

Little had changed in Remora since she had last been here. It seemed as if the city was in perpetual festival mode. And yet this Stellata was hardly a celebration. She scanned the crowds, looking for Falco. He had stayed longer than her in the Ram. They had both been to see all the horses and spent a long time with Merla but Falco was loath to leave her.

Georgia trusted he wasn't going to risk sitting in the Lady's stand or trying to gatecrash the Twins. He might be a year older and stronger and fit in body but he was still recognisably Falco. She hoped he was all right; it was an impressive first stravagation back to his old world. Georgia remembered Luciano saying how difficult it was for him but Falco seemed bright-eyed and full of energy.

The parade came to an end and the bell stopped, without any sign of Falco. Georgia decided to give up worrying about him and just enjoy the race. The twelve horses started to enter the Campo and she soon picked out Cesare on the tall chestnut. He looked stylish and confident. There was always an aura of respect around the horse of the Twelfth to win the most recent Stellata and it didn't matter that it carried a different jockey.

The whips were handed out and the horses moved to the start. Duke Niccolò himself drew the Twelfth balls out of the bag and the order was determined. There was the usual shuffling and blocking and the crowd's attention was fixed on the start-line.

Then, just as the Rincorsa (this time the Water-carrier) was making its run, down through the air sailed the winged horse. There was no warning cry from a Manoush this time. Just a folding of black wings and an elegant landing at full gallop, as the thirteenth horse joined the race.

The crowd went wild; who was this jockey, in his strange costume? He wore no single set of colours but had the scarves of all the Twelfths tied on to his ordinary stable boy's clothes. He wore no helmet and his black locks streamed out behind him. He was a handsome boy and the Remoran girls began to cheer for 'Bellerofonte! Bellerofonte!' instantly naming the stranger after a flying horseman of old legends.

Merla and her rider flowed round the first circuit well ahead of the twelve other horses and then the first rumour began in the Twins' stand and rippled through the Campo faster than any steed. The cry changed to 'Falco! Falco!' and soon the spectators in the centre began to fall to their knees and cross themselves.

'A phantom!' went the rumour. 'Prince Falco has returned to his own commemoration!' Gaetano sat like one made of stone, barely able to breathe and clutching Francesca's hand. No one heard him whisper, 'It worked!'

The Duke was the only one on his feet, his face a white mask of terror – or perhaps fury.

Fear filled all the jockeys except Cesare, but Falco would have won easily anyway. He didn't fly Merla but she was still faster than any normal horse. He was racing towards the finish line, yards ahead of the Ram and the Lady.

As soon as he reached it, he whispered in Merla's ear and urged her up into flight. As the flying horse took off into the setting sun, her mighty winged shadow fell over the upturned faces of the crowd beneath. And then came the intake of breath and the cries of 'Dia!' The shadow-horse had no shadow-rider.

As it passed over the Lady's stand, a purple and green scarf came fluttering down to be caught by the Duke's mailed fist.

It took a moment or two for people to realise that the race was over. Cesare had pulled back at the last moment and the Lady's jockey had taken his chance. Cherubino had urged Zarina across the finish point and waved his whip aloft, victorious. The Lady's supporters invaded the track to embrace the jockey and pat the horse. Georgia left the Ram's stand and pushed her way towards Cesare, against the swelling rush of the Lady's Twelvers wanting to wrest the Stellata banner from the Judges' stand.

'Why did you do it?' she whispered to Cesare, who stood sweating beside Arcangelo.

'Look at the Duke,' said Cesare. 'It doesn't do to keep crossing the Lady.'

'But Falco would have been disqualified and you would have won easily for the Ram,' protested Georgia. 'Imagine, two Stellata banners in one year! Arianna would have been delighted.'

'Rules or not,' said Cesare, 'Falco was the real winner.'

They looked at the Duke, who was being guided down from the stand to congratulate Cherubino. He was glassy-eyed and clutching the green and purple scarf, still warm from his son's body. In spite of the clamour of the spectators, he did not believe he had seen a ghost. As he descended into the Campo, he caught sight of the flame-coloured girl and the chestnut horse and remembered the mysterious jockey of the Ram's who had robbed his family of victory a month ago.

Duke Niccolò knew exactly what he had seen, even if he didn't understand it: his son, transformed, whole and well again, had returned to show him and his family that he still lived, in another world. And the Stravaganti had the secret. From now on, he would move heaven and earth to find out what it was.

A Note on the Stellata and the Palio

As Georgia discovers, the annual horse race in Remora is not quite the same as that of Siena. Some of the differences arise from the differences between the actual and imagined cities. Remora is divided into twelve wards – called Twelfths, naturally – while Siena is divided into seventeen *contrade*.

The Twelfths are named after the Talian version of the Zodiac, whereas the *contrade* take their names from a range of animals, even slow ones like *Bruco* (caterpillar) and *Chiocciola* (snail), and a few objects – *Nicchio* (shell), *Torre* (tower), *Onda* (wave) and *Selva* (forest).

There is only one ward which is the same in both cities – the Ram in Remora and Valdimontone in Siena. The colours of Valdimontone are also red and yellow and their symbol of the crowned Ram can be seen everywhere in the south-west of the city of Siena, in the Third of San Martino.

The Palio is run twice every summer – on 2nd July and 16th August – whereas the Stellata happens only once, on 15th August. Both can have extra races to commemorate special occasions. Only ten *contrade* run in any single Palio – seven by right, because they won't have had a horse and jockey in the equivalent one the year before, and three drawn by lot. It is therefore possible for a *contrada* to win twice in a year, though this is rare.

The great Campo in Siena is not circular, but shell-shaped; nevertheless, it is still the case that the Palio, preceded by a two-hour procession, the *Corteo Storico*, takes only about a minute and a half to run.

(It may take an hour or more, though, to get an approved start!)

The Palio used to be run on the straight, from as far back as the fourteenth century, but transferred to the Campo in 1650. In Remora, the Stellata has already been run in the circular Campo for at least a century in 1578.

There are three aspects of the Stellata which I thought I had invented, only to discover that they had actually happened in the Sienese Palio. Hundreds of years ago, the jockeys in Siena were likely to be young teenage boys, and there was even a girl racing in a special Palio of 1581. She was called Virginia and rode for Drago (the dragon), but did not win.

And I discovered that there was an ancient tradition of *contrade* having special allegiances with other cities, long after I had decided on the Reman custom that linked the Ram to Bellezza, the Lady to Giglia and so on. As Alan Dundes and Alessandro Falassi say in their book *La Terra in Piazza* (University of California Press, 1975), 'We must not forget that every *contrada* considers itself a little republic or state ... Many *contrade* have established twinning arrangements with other Italian cities, as if they were political entities completely separate from the city of Siena.'

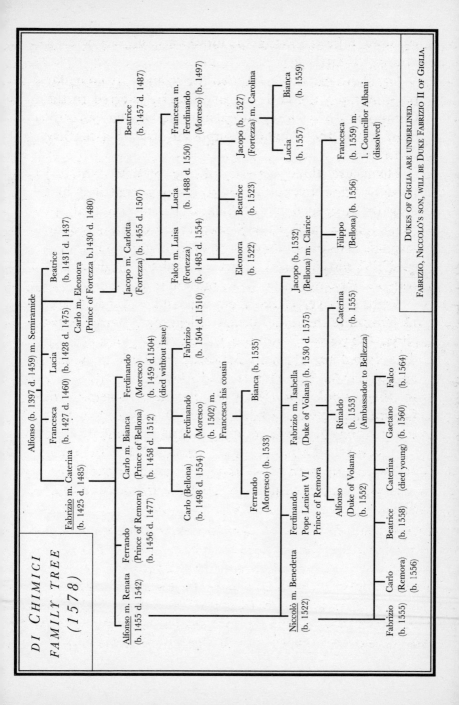

DI CHIMICI
FAMILY TREE
(1578)

Alfonso (b. 1397 d. 1459) m. Semiramide

Francesca (b. 1427 d. 1460)

Lucia (b. 1428 d. 1475)

Beatrice (b. 1431 d. 1437)

Carlo m. Eleonora (Prince of Fortezza b.1430 d. 1480)

Beatrice (b. 1457 d. 1487)

Francesca m. Ferdinando (Moresco) (b. 1497)

Jacopo m. Carlotta (Fortezza) (b. 1455 d. 1507)

Lucia (b. 1488 d. 1554)

Jacopo (b. 1527) (Fortezza) m. Carolina

Falco m. Luisa (Fortezza) (b. 1485 d. 1554)

Lucia (b. 1557)

Bianca (b. 1559)

Eleonora (b. 1522)

Beatrice (b. 1523)

Francesca (b. 1559) m. 1. Councillor Albani (dissolved)

Filippo (Bellona) (b. 1556)

Fabrizio m. Caterina (b. 1425 d. 1485)

Alfonso m. Renata (b. 1455 d. 1542)

Ferrando (Prince of Remora) (b. 1456 d. 1477)

Carlo m. Bianca (Prince of Bellona) (b. 1458 d. 1512)

Ferdinando (Moresco) (b. 1459 d.1504) (died without issue)

Fabrizio (b. 1504 d. 1510)

Ferdinando (Moresco) (b. 1502 m. Francesca his cousin

Carlo (Bellona) (b. 1498 d. 1554))

Bianca (b. 1535)

Ferrando (Moresco) (b. 1533)

Fabrizio m. Isabella (Duke of Volana) (b. 1530 d. 1575)

Caterina (b. 1555)

Rinaldo (b. 1553) (Ambassador to Bellezza)

Jacopo (b. 1532) (Bellona) m. Clarice

Niccolò m. Benedetta (b. 1522)

Ferdinando Pope Lenient VI Prince of Remora

Alfonso (Duke of Volana) (b. 1552)

Caterina (died young)

Gaetano (b. 1560)

Falco (b. 1564)

Carlo (Remora) (b. 1556)

Beatrice (b. 1558)

Fabrizio (b. 1555)

DUKES OF GIGLIA ARE UNDERLINED.

FABRIZIO, NICCOLÒ'S SON, WILL BE DUKE FABRIZIO II OF GIGLIA.